DISASTER PLAN

DISASTER PLAN

Ed Plaisted

Copyright © 2001 by Ed Plaisted.

Library of Congress Number: 2001117658
ISBN #: Hardcover 1-4010-2010-0
Softcover 1-4010-2011-9

All rights reserved. No part of this book may be reproduced or transmitted in any form or by any means, electronic or mechanical, including photocopying, recording, or by any information storage and retrieval system, without permission in writing from the copyright owner.

This is a work of fiction. Names, characters, places and incidents either are the product of the author's imagination or are used fictitiously, and any resemblance to any actual persons, living or dead, events, or locales is entirely coincidental.

This book was printed in the United States of America.

To order additional copies of this book, contact:
Xlibris Corporation
1-888-795-4274
www.Xlibris.com
Orders@Xlibris.com

CHAPTER 1

"The worst is not
So long as we can say 'This is the worst.'"
William Shakespeare
King Lear

To THE CREW of Sun Airlines Flight 469 waiting for passengers at Dallas/Fort Worth International Airport, it was just another ordinary evening. There was no whisper of warning from anyone's sixth sense, with the exception of Captain Richard Norton's.

Norton checked his Rolex. It was 9:15 p.m. Dallas time, and 10:15 p.m. back in Miami. The pilot finished his walk-around inspection, paying extra attention to his checks because this was a different DC-10 than the one that had brought the Miami Sharks pro football team here Wednesday for their Thanksgiving afternoon game with the Dallas Texans. This was a DC-10, Series 10, boasting a 345-seat capacity. With a passenger list of 142 and a crew of eight, Dick felt sure that everyone should be comfortable for the three-hour flight back to MIA.

The ground personnel were mostly strangers to Dick because they were replacement workers, non-union Sun Airlines management. As chief pilot, Dick was management, and he didn't honor picket lines anymore. Why should any pilot make sacrifices to help a bunch of grease monkeys that were already overpaid?

"How come a new plane, Captain?" asked Flight Engineer Vince Lombard, who despite his strong union convictions had decided this week to cross the picket line.

"Our original bird has a minor problem," Dick explained. "Seems our replacement workers forgot to secure the nose landing gear locking device and, whoops!"

"No shit, Captain! So where did they find another 10?"

"The station manager scrubbed our Dallas-Bogotá flight and transferred this equipment to us," the pilot replied.

Lombard shook his head in disbelief. "Our fruitcake of a station manager scrubbed a full load to Colombia so this loss-leader football charter can return to MIA?"

"That's affirmative, Vince. He was under orders from corporate. I guess Westinghouse considers this a good publicity flight." He was referring to Sun Airlines CEO Bruce "Bud" Westinghouse.

"Right. I hope those stranded Colombia full-fares never learn the truth."

The circumstances, while not unusual, were nevertheless troublesome to the veteran captain. *Damn! I had the same feeling seven years ago in Detroit. Got to put it out of my mind. Think positive. This is going to be a routine flight.*

While it was always SOP to load the Miami Sharks charters away from the passenger terminal after road games, Dick was especially pleased this Thanksgiving night to be away from the surly union pickets in front of the Sun Airlines station. As for the strike, the captain believed Westinghouse was winning the war. Regardless of his politics, he knew he would feel safer when the regular mechanics returned.

"Here they come," Lombard announced.

With emergency red lights flashing and shrill sirens blaring, a pair of police motorcycles led the Sharks' caravan from the stadium to the airport. Team owner Sol Rubin's Lincoln limo was followed by three chartered buses and a rented equipment truck. The caravan was led onto a remote part of DFW's landing field by the police escort. It was dark, and a light, cold rain started to fall as the vehicles approached the parked jet.

The passengers boarded by a portable stairs platform, but not until a catering service pair passed everyone a two-pack of Coors and a sub sandwich. This was to sustain them until the in-flight meal of a holiday turkey dinner could be served.

Flight purser Mary Rich was at S.R.'s seat in first class and was serving his first martini before Coach Don Sherman and his staff arrived. She realized the team owner was already drunk but, hey, he was paying for this flight. Mary noted the empty seats assigned to Veronica "Bunny" Rubin, the Sharks' owner's wife, and team general manager Jack Cabot.

"Is Mrs. Rubin flying home with us?" she asked.

"No, that whore isn't coming home with us," S.R. snarled. The noise of the boarding passengers and S.R.'s slurred speech scrambled his remark—not that the purser really cared what the old drunk was saying.

At 47, Mary was the oldest flight attendant, and she was senior flight attendant with a rank of purser. Her tired skin showed the ravages of chain smoking and boozing during layovers. Her dull blonde hair hung limp from a cheap dye job.

She made her way from first class to the coach section. "I think we'll have three extra dinners," she informed flight attendant Ann Parker, who was headed for the lower galley.

"You mean Mr. Rubin?" Ann asked.

Mary nodded. "Yeah."

"He appears to be stuffed already. I hope he doesn't throw up and spoil everyone else's turkey dinner. Who else are we missing?"

"Mrs. Rubin and Mr. Cabot," Mary answered. "Oh! You and I will work coach. Put Nancy Hill up front with Chris Gaylord."

#

The unexplained absence of Mrs. Rubin and Cabot opened two seats in the first-class section, and Sherman invited defensive end George Carver and quarterback Johnny Longo to join tackle Norm Amundsen up front. The selection was made by seniority.

The quarterback really wanted to be alone, but he appreciated the comfort of the dentist-chair-style reclining seats in first class. He took the window seat before Carver could make a move.

"Hey, man," said the defensive end, "if you want to talk about Casey's column, I'm here for you."

Johnny wanted to think, not talk about it. He also didn't want to alienate any of his teammates, because he needed their support.

"Thanks, George," he replied while popping open a can of Coors. "I appreciate your concern. But I'm very tired, and I hurt. Old age is taking its toll."

Carver drained the beer can in three rapid swigs. Then he crushed the can in his right hand. It was more of an automatic reflex than a show of his strength. "I knows about old age, my man. Ten years in this league ages you. I'm tired, and I hurt, too. You knows, I just. . .well, Johnny, my man, I'm here for you. If you wants to talk, I'll be in my office here for the next three hours."

"Okay, thanks, Dr. Carver," replied the quarterback.

Carver nodded his head and dropped the matter. Johnny, however, had more than concern for his health on his mind since the Dallas game. His marriage was in jeopardy, and he had big-time money woes. He thought about his wife and kids.

Martha just couldn't understand the rush he got from gambling. *That goddamned Casey! How the hell could he write such shit that I'm a murderer? I'll bury that SOB in court.* He knew, however, that a gambling investigation would bury his career if the hits in the Dallas game had not already doomed him.

Johnny found it hard to concentrate on anything except the money he owed in sports gambling debts. *It's only a few million. Hell, I can make that up with one good score. They can't cut me off. They have to give me more credit.*

#

In the cockpit, Mary asked, "Captain, do you want coffee as soon as we're airborne?"

"Thanks, honey," Dick replied. "That will be three coffees. You know our sugar and cream needs. Oh, Mary, you don't have to lock the cockpit door. This is a charter. The passengers are welcome to visit."

"I know, Captain," she replied in an irritated tone. "Who do you think I am? Some silver-winger?"

"Sorry, Mary," Dick said quickly, sounding sincere. "You look so young, I often forget you aren't a rookie."

"Thanks, but save the bull for the passengers," the purser retorted.

"Oh, and Mary, we. . .I appreciate your volunteering to work this charter. I know it took guts to cross the picket line."

"We don't have a strike fund," she said a bit sadly. "My rent, car payment. . .You know, I'm a working girl." Mary wasn't proud of herself for accepting a promotion to management as a purser from flight attendant, but it was more money and it freed her from union obligations.

The captain, First Officer Ralph Buckmaster, and Engineer Lombard went over the preflight checklist. They tested oxygen masks, brakes, fuel, flaps, cargo and cabin doors.

"Okay, let's see if all the lights are on and everything is a go," Dick said. "Ralph, set the radio altimeter to 2992. Now set the flap selector at 10 degrees. Oh, and make sure the stewardesses check all the doors while I call the bag boys to see if they're through loading the luggage and equipment."

Dick smiled slightly when he overheard Buckmaster whisper to Lombard, "The captain is showing his age when he still calls flight attendants stewardesses."

The luggage and equipment loaded, Buckmaster prepared for takeoff. He started the engines, the middle engine on the tail section first. Immediately, it started to rotate as a light came on to indicate it was working. Within 15 seconds, the fuel flow had started.

"The engine is running, Captain," the first officer said.

The process was repeated on engines three and one, the sequence creating less air pressure after push-back.

"All engines are running now, Captain."

"The wipers?" asked Dick.

"Wipers on, Captain. Body gear disarmed, landing lights on. Checklist completed."

"We don't have ATC clearance," Dick said in a monotone voice.

Upon closing the throttles, Buckmaster replied, "I know that. Go ahead and ask, Captain."

Dick pressed the mike button and requested both takeoff and the air traffic clearances in the same transmission. "Sun Air 469 is now ready for takeoff, and we await our ATC clearance."

The DFW tower responded: "Sun Air 469, you are cleared to Runway One Zero Left. Climb to and maintain flight level nine zero."

"We're cleared, Ralph," Dick announced. "The thrust computer is set. Set the trim here for 3.5. We have 330,000 pounds. Flap retractors at 150. Annunciator's lights are out.

"Gentlemen, here we go."

Normally, Dick wouldn't let a junior first officer do the takeoff. But this was Buckmaster's first flight since qualifying for the DC-10 at the Sun Airlines Academy in Miami. He was a replacement for pilots who were honoring the mechanics' strike.

On this flight, Dick Norton was also functioning as a check rider. While the huge plane taxied smoothly out onto 10L,

Buckmaster put his feet on the rudder. The three CF6 jet engines suddenly began producing about 150,000 horsepower as they pushed the DC-10 down the runway and lunged upward, off the ground.

"V1, V2. Gear up," the captain said. "Good. We're doing about 180 knots. We're at 1,500 feet and climbing to 28,000. . .now at 250 knots."

Dick watched the young first officer in the right seat at the controls. With less than two years remaining until mandatory retirement at age 60, he realized how fast the years had gone and how little time might be left. Flying was Dick's life. He didn't like the thought of having to leave his career in the cockpit.

Buckmaster reminded the captain of his own first year as a commercial pilot. He, too, had traded uniforms from Air Force blue to Sun Airlines black. He, too, had brought with him to civilian life the military crew cut, the spit-shined shoes, and the respect for rank.

"Nice takeoff, Ralph," Dick said. "Can't beat that Air Force training."

The captain was still lean and trim. Seen from the rear, his six-foot-one frame and 185 pounds fit nicely into a tailored uniform. From the front, wrinkles marred a gaunt face and disarming smile. He wore aviator-style prescription glasses, and behind the clear glass was a pair of brown eyes. He looked better with his uniform hat because he was nearly bald, with the exception of the temples and the back of his head.

"What about the rear cargo door, Vince?" the captain asked.

"It took about five minutes to close it," replied the engineer. "I needed one of those scab ramp workers with a strong knee to close the damned thing."

"I know I was happy when the 'door light' went out," Dick said. Then he felt a sudden chill crawl down his spine. That was what had happened in Detroit. It was the damned cargo door. But that problem had been fixed. Vince Lombard had been on that flight. *He doesn't see any connection. Got to get my mind off negative thoughts.*

His mind wandered back seven years to his DC-10 flight from Detroit to New York's La Guardia. What turned out to be a defect in the rear cargo door resulted in the door being blown open after takeoff, causing explosive decompression of the aircraft. The door had been torn off by the airflow, damaging the left tail plane in the process. *God was on our side that night. We were damn lucky to get back safely to DTW.*

Dick decided to make small talk. He wanted to forget Detroit. He turned to Buckmaster. "You graduated from the Air Force Academy, didn't you?"

"Yes, sir."

About the only thing the cockpit trio had in common were their uniforms. Buckmaster sported a fresh crew cut. He was exceptionally lean and trim, and his muscles showed under the white, short-sleeved pilot's shirt.

"Why did you leave the Air Force, Ralph?" Dick asked. "You were Regular Air Force, weren't you?"

"Yes. I graduated from the Academy. I was up for major, too."

"If you were a major today, you'd be making a lot more than a starting first officer," Dick observed.

"True. But I was unhappy with the heavier work schedules, thanks to the downsizing of the service. I wasn't alone. More than a hundred in my graduating class quit."

As former Air Force reservists, Norton and Lombard were civilians at heart. Vince Lombard was a career flight engineer. Short, portly, and bald, he was a chain smoker and often smelled of garlic. His white uniform shirts were all so tight that he had to leave the size 17 collars unbuttoned.

The cockpit conversation went from airline gossip to the weather, and finally to sports. That was a given, because Lombard was a sports fanatic, especially when it came to the Miami Sharks and the International Football League.

"You a football fan, Ralph?" the captain asked.

Before the first officer could answer, Lombard asserted, "He was a jock at Air Force. Our first officer was a quarterback."

"That so, Ralph?"

"Yes, I played at the Academy."

"He was an All-America. Even drafted by Buffalo," Lombard continued. "He cost me money. I bet on Air Force in the Tangerine Bowl."

"We won," Buckmaster replied, obviously on the defensive. "We beat Michigan State 24-21."

"I remember that score because I had Air Force and 3 ½ points," the engineer said with a laugh. "That one point cost me a hundred bucks."

"That'll teach you to bet on football," the captain said.

The three men grew quiet, momentarily preoccupied with their own separate thoughts. Dick loved flying the DC-10. Sun Airlines operated only four types of aircraft in its fleet of 153: DC-10s, Boeing 777s, 767s, and 734-500s.

"I wonder why I'm qualifying for the 10s," Buckmaster said. "They'll be replaced soon by the 777s."

"Probably, but I hope to be drawing my pension when that happens," the captain responded. "Until then, guys, the DC-10 is the flagship of this airline. Even our boss, Captain Westinghouse, is qualified to fly a 10."

Dick took time to remind the first officer that the DC-10 was originally envisioned as a twin-engine Airbus, but McDonnell Douglas convinced Sun Airlines that the tri-motor version would be better for over-water routes.

Unlike the 727, which handled like a truck, the DC-10 was an automated preview of the two-man cockpits of the future, and was a near-twin of the Lockheed L-1011. The most notable difference was the mounting of the third engine. The L-1011 had its third engine mounted on the rear of the fuselage, while the DC-10's middle engine was placed on the tail, eliminating the need for the "S"-duct air intake, thus adding to the usable cabin space. The two aircraft also differed in their choice of engines—the DC-10 employed General Electric's CF6.

Flight 469 was running about an hour behind because of a number of delays, the most notable being the late arrival of the Sharks from the stadium. And, of course, there were the usual air traffic control problems.

Dick was aware that these factors served to increase Buckmaster's nervous tension on his first commercial flight. The banter about his football days, as well as the lecture about the DC-10, had helped the first officer. But it hadn't calmed Dick, and he continued to have an uncanny feeling about the flight.

Heading east, Buckmaster increased the speed to 260 knots. The DC-10 broke through cloud cover into a clear evening and a setting sun. A Lufthansa 747 could be seen through the cockpit windshield above, still climbing toward 36,000 feet.

"Hey, that's what you could be flying if you worked for Lufthansa," Lombard said.

"That must be Hun Air's Dallas-Frankfurt flight," Dick noted. He told Buckmaster to engage the autopilot, then watched the other jet for a few minutes. "But I'll tell you something, guys. I never wanted to be a German whale driver. I'm glad I'm not flying that thing."

"Whale driver?" Buckmaster asked, puzzled.

Dick and Lombard chuckled. "'Whale' refers to the shape of a 747," the captain explained. He turned toward the engineer. "How did you and Mary make out last night at the crew motel, Vince?"

"She got smashed, and I couldn't even have one drink because of today's flight," Lombard said. "Terrible layover."

"Better than a hangover," Dick observed. He liked the veteran engineer. Lombard was the last of a breed of flight engineers that were mechanics, not pilots filling the third seat of a three-man cockpit. *Vince is the kind of guy I want in that engineer's seat. I'll take him in a jam over any young kid pilot who only has making the left seat on his mind. I was damn lucky to have him with me that time out of Detroit.*

#

Mary had never married. She remained a gung-ho flight attendant who could recite every Sun Air, FAA, and union contract rule and regulation that had ever been written. Dick and other captains marveled at how this woman could booze all night on a layover and get up the next morning, raring to go to work. She preferred slacks to the short skirts because, as she often put it, "I don't want all the old farts trying to look up my skirt."

"I have a rotten headache, Ann," she said. "I think Lombard was trying to get me drunk on cheap Italian wine last night. I told him up front that I don't put out for an old, bald, fat guy, especially if he's only an engineer. Speaking of which, let's offer our celebrities some drinks."

#

Jim Moses, the Sharks' offensive coordinator, occupied the window seat next to Sherman in first class. He and the head coach had been together for all but one and a half of 30 seasons. Moses was the only assistant Sherman treated as a confidant.

"What are your thoughts about Longo?"

Moses pondered Sherman's question. "On the field or off?"

"Both."

"Another couple of hard sacks, and he's history. You know it's the age thing. He's no longer fast enough to avoid sacks. I'm not defending our blocking performance today. It was weak. Amundsen had a bad day. Let's face it, Longo has been getting by with his experience the last year or so. His arm strength is fading fast."

Sherman said nothing. He nodded a few times while toying with his bifocals.

"As for that shit in the morning garbage wrapper, I don't know. The gambling part, I can believe. If he's not betting on IFL games, he's in the clear. He wouldn't be that stupid, would he? I don't believe he could kill anyone. That, I find, is strictly sensational yellow journalism crap."

Sherman handed Moses a cold can of Coors while opening one for himself. "Right. We have enough problems after today's loss to Dallas without losing our starting quarterback and having a scandal, too. Not to change the subject, but I've decided to activate Johnson on Monday. I think he's clean of drugs. We can use another wide out, although that kid Doe looked pretty good out there today. Why don't you take a walk back there and tell Johnson."

Moses started to get up, but Sherman waved him down.

"Wait until after we eat, Jim. It's turkey, you know, and it is Thanksgiving."

#

The Rev. Francis J. O'Malley wanted to be alone, too, and think about a parishioner's confession.

In his 31 years as a Roman Catholic priest, he'd had his share of confessions from criminals—but never one for murder, and certainly not from a prominent parishioner.

Some of the Catholic players, however, wanted to chat with him. Some chats were of minor personal problems, and others just social.

"Do you mind if I sit next to you, Father?"

It was wide receiver Muhammad Johnson. Surprised, O'Malley gestured for Johnson to be seated.

"I guess I'm trying to hang out now with the right kind of people," the five-foot-eleven, 165-pound African-American said in a nervous voice. He toyed with his uniform number 85 in 18-karat gold on a rope necklace.

O'Malley sensed that Johnson was trying to say he had cleaned up his drug problem, but he didn't quite know how to put it in words. O'Malley was impressed by Johnson. *A bright young man. Wonder how he let himself get hooked on cocaine?*

"Muhammad, my son, some of your Muslim brothers will think you are considering defecting to the Catholic Church," the priest said in a warm and jovial manner. "Or perhaps you simply are trying to convert me to your faith. Whatever. Let's talk."

Mary interrupted the conversation, passing the priest a tall glass of what appeared to be water, but was in fact 100 proof Russian vodka. "Here's your holy water, Father. Muhammad, here's a two-pack of Coors. I'll be back later, guys, with your Thanksgiving dinners."

"You don't mind me drinking, do you, Father?" Johnson asked.

"Of course not, Muhammad. But tell me. . .isn't it against your religion to drink?"

Muhammad gave him a sheepish look. "I've a confession, Father. I'm not really a Muslim. I just adopted a Muslim first name for. . .er, publicity purposes. I was brought up a Methodist, and I wasn't a very good one."

"Why was that, my son?"

"Being religious wasn't cool, Father. Making big bucks at age 22 put me in the fast lane. It almost destroyed my football career, my life. I wasn't cool. I was a jerk. So thanks to the help of God and the drug rehab program, I have a new respect for religion—any man's religion."

O'Malley nodded and provided an understanding smile.

"More important, I learned that all white folks aren't racist. Mr. Cabot taught me that. I owe a lot to that man."

"What did Mr. Cabot do that impressed you so, my son?" O'Malley asked.

Meanwhile, the 163-ton metal bird glided majestically through the cold night sky. The flight plan took the DC-10 over New Orleans and the Gulf of Mexico before reaching the Florida peninsula at Tampa.

Mary's flight attendants had served a special turkey dinner. The players had wolfed down the food, and most tried to nap the rest of the way home. The cabin lights were dimmed with the exception of the rear of the coach section, where six players were engaged in a game of poker, and two sports writers were composing stories on laptop computers.

Jorge Cunill, the Sharks' beat writer for the *Miami P.M.*, was checking quotes on his tape recorder from the Dallas victory over Miami that afternoon. He had most of the game story finished on his tangerine iBook. The wild-colored laptop was a birthday gift from his friend and colleague, sports columnist Bob Casey.

He was holding off finishing a sidebar about a post-game locker room brawl involving the Sharks' quarterback and Casey. *What an asshole! Longo is in enough shit, and he was dumb enough to attack a columnist of Casey's stature. But it makes for a helluva story. That's the joy of working for a metro tabloid.*

Jorge was tired, but he was looking forward to a couple of glasses of wine with his wife and making love later.

#

Dick was beginning to feel better. *Just another 30 minutes, and we'll be safely on the ground in Miami. Still, I have that damn premonition of disaster.* He would have liked to share his feelings with Lombard, but he didn't want anyone to think he had lost his nerve as a pilot.

The DC-10 stayed at a 390, or 39,000 feet, until it reached the Florida coast, where Buckmaster brought the ship down to 26,000 feet. Although it would require only about 15 minutes after that for the final descent into MIA, the Miami Approach Center asked him to climb to 29,000 feet before starting his descent.

Buckmaster began the climb.

#

B-O-O-M!

It sounded like a bomb! The rear section of the cabin floor

collapsed completely with the force of explosive decompression. The last two rows of double seat units above the door were ejected, along with parts of the aircraft. The cabin fogged instantly, and dust swirled in the rush of air.

Shock slammed Dick, Buckmaster, and Lombard. Dick jolted forward in his seat. Buckmaster's face paled. Vince Lombard's mouth dropped open. The throttles snapped closed, and almost immediately the DC-10 banked to the left and then pitched down rapidly.

Whoop! Whoop! Whoop!

A flashing red light blared across the console.

"Pull up! Pull Up!" The computerized voice of the Ground Proximity Warning System added to the seriousness of the situation.

Buckmaster froze. Dick grabbed the controls, disengaging the autopilot as the aircraft dove toward the ground and the cabin pressurization warning horn sounded.

Dick believed history was repeating that flight out of Detroit seven years ago. Still, he asked, "What happened?"

"The fuselage burst, Captain," Vince Lombard replied. "I think it was a bomb."

"Are you sure, Vince? It feels like our old Detroit adventure."

The control cables and hydraulic lines running rearward below the floor were damaged, as were the elevator stabilizer controls. The crew fought to control the plunging aircraft as Buckmaster recovered and joined the battle by grabbing the wheel.

"Bring it up, Ralph, pull her nose up," Dick said calmly.

"I can't bring it up, Captain. Shit! She doesn't respond."

There were frightened screams and voices from the cabin as the plane continued its rapid plunge through the night Florida sky.

Outwardly, Dick was cool and in command. Inside, though, he felt his heart thudding sickeningly. Sweat darkened his shirt, and he was beginning to feel that he had betrayed the trust of his passengers.

"It's twelve thousand feet, Captain. Damn it, we're losing it!"

Buckmaster realized he no longer controlled his destiny. He felt warm urine fill his pants. He thought of his wife and three kids. "Dear God, help us!" the first officer cried. "Don't let us die."

Dick grabbed the controls. *A crash landing can save some lives. I just have to slow this sucker down. Please, Lord, give me the chance to save some of these people.*

By good fortune, he had remembered the lesson from that Detroit incident, and had routinely practiced it in the Sun Airlines' simulator by flying the DC-10 on engine power only. Thus, he was able to stop the dive and maintain 7,000 feet.

"Alert MIA," he said, his voice surprisingly steady. "I don't know if we can make it or even land it."

Ashamed by his panic, Buckmaster struggled to regain his composure and to radio a "Mayday. Mayday."

"Sun Air 469. This is Miami Tower. You have declared a Mayday?"

"That is affirmative, Miami Tower."

"Ooops! We are going down, gentlemen," Dick asserted. There was now fear in his voice.

The engineer wished he had his rosary beads. "Hail Mary, full of grace," he mumbled, his words full of stress and fear.

The captain knew the flight was doomed. Survival depended upon slowing the angle of descent and cutting the speed.

The Everglades loomed below in the darkness. Landing a jumbo jet in the swamp wouldn't be easy, but it would be better than slamming into the side of a mountain. Dick remembered that an Eastern L-1011 crash in the Everglades back in the '70s had a large number of survivors. The key was executing a belly flop at as slow a speed as possible, and skimming the water as if skipping a rock across a pond.

#

The explosion reminded Mary Rich and Ann Parker about the Detroit incident. They strapped themselves into jump seats and held hands while reciting the Lord's Prayer. Flight attendants Nancy Hill and Chris Gaylord did the same in first class.

Bedlam broke loose. Most of the Sharks' players and staff had been sleeping or dozing. Things happened so fast that most could not react. Some, who had failed to fasten their seat belts, were thrown into the aisles. There were loud voices, some laced with profanity. Most of those roused from sleep were too confused to grasp what was happening.

"Maybe next time these fuckers will pay attention to our safety briefing at the start of the flight," Mary muttered to Ann Parker. The purser couldn't help her thoughts at a time like this: *It was like Detroit all over. What the hell could four flight attendants do in such a situation, but pray?*

Ann Parker prayed: "Our Father who art in Heaven. . ."

Down and down. Nothing would stop the falling aircraft.

Ann was shaking with fear. She felt cold, and yet sweat was soaking her uniform blouse. She nodded to Mary, too full of panic to try to talk, but she managed to mumble the Rosary. "Hail Mary, full of grace, pray for us sinners. . ."

"Say one for me, darlin'," the purser said softly.

It calmed Ann Parker down as she watched Mary. *That Mary is magnificent under pressure. I can't prove to be a coward.*

Ann took a deep breath and squeezed the older woman's hand hard. "Hail Mary. . ."

#

Dick watched the air speed indicator as he fought to slow the falling craft. He understood true fear for the first time in his life. The last figure he saw on the air speed indicator was 135 knots. The cabin lights flickered. Shouts came from scared and confused passengers.

The captain gripped the steering yoke so hard his nails were clawing at it. *I've got to make this baby bounce like skipping a rock across a pond. Just like I did as a kid.*

It was black outside the cockpit windshield. Dick wasn't sure when he would hit the ground, but he kept fighting, trying to belly flop, hoping for the skipping result. He held his breath and prayed.

The big jet smashed into the swamp, the impact tearing off the right wing, along with an engine. The tail section pulled apart. The doomed aircraft struck several trees, one of which tore open the right side of the cockpit. Dick heard a series of impacts envelop the plane's occupants in a cacophony of breaking, tearing noises while they were violently shaken inside the cabin like dice being rolled to their fates. Screams and moans laced with profanity ceased as if they were from a radio that had been turned off.

The captain lost consciousness.

The aircraft broke into three pieces. A deafening explosion transformed the first-class cabin into a fireball. Bits of debris burned slowly, feeding off the kerosene floating on the water. This was followed by a stillness in the darkness except for a half-dozen scattered fires. Eerie quiet was all that remained as the inside of the aircraft became pitch black and settled into the muck with a gurgling sound.

#

In the MIA control center, the controllers watched helplessly as the echo that was Sun Air Flight 469 disappeared from the screen.

"My God, that's the plane carrying our football team!" a controller screamed. "The Sharks are down in the Glades!"

Thus the alarm was sounded in both Dade and Broward Counties. Rescue operations were activated to unleash an army of police, fire, and medical units. The trick, however, would be to find the downed aircraft at night—in a snake-and alligator-infested swamp.

A Dade County Public Safety helicopter cut off a mission to

aid police ground units in the hunt for two burglars in Hialeah. The pilot turned for the swamp and the hunt for any survivors.

News of the disaster was on television screens within 60 minutes of the 1:13 a.m. estimated time of the Friday crash. In their passion to be first at all costs, the TV news teams just went with the initial report of the crash and assumed the rest. So viewers across America watched the following message flash across the bottom of their TV sets:

MIAMI SHARKS TEAM PLANE CRASHES;
NO SURVIVORS

At the same time, International News Service issued a terse bulletin that was received on newspaper computers throughout the land at 2:00 a.m. Eastern Standard Time.

BULLETIN

MIAMI (INS)—A Sun Airlines DC-10, chartered to carry the Miami Sharks back to Miami after a Thanksgiving Day IFL game in Dallas, reportedly crashed in the Everglades early Friday morning. There is no report of survivors.

CHAPTER 2

*"Death lines on her, like an untimely frost
Upon the sweetest flower of all the field."*

William Shakespeare
Romeo and Juliet

AT THE DALLAS/Fort Worth Marriott, Bob Casey wasn't paying attention to the 27-inch TV set over the bar. The bartender had turned the sound way down at the request of the other two patrons, leaving only the picture.

As it was Thanksgiving night, the bar was nearly deserted. Bob stretched his six-foot-one, 240-pound frame and scratched his face where five o'clock shadow had set in. After passing his fortieth birthday last June 1, he disliked looking into any mirror. He still had a full head of dark brown hair, but gray was showing at the sideburns. Travel, booze, bad eating habits, and the pressures of a metro daily newspaper sports columnist had given him quite a few extra pounds. He carried his weight well, though, because tennis kept his legs firm and strong. He had that Marlboro Man look. The Florida sun had given his face a tanned, leathery appearance that combined with his hair, which he dyed, to make him appear several years younger.

Despite himself, he stole a glance at the mirror behind the bar. *What does Suzy see in this old fart?* he asked himself.

Bob was on his second Chivas and soda, and he was thinking about the new love in his life, Suzy Mary Peters. At the bar, he really felt lonely.

I've never felt this way about any woman. I'm hyper. I can't think of anything except Suzy.

"Is the ace sports columnist for *Miami P.M.* all alone?"

It was Roberto Castro, the Sharks' beat writer for the rival *Miami Morning Journal.*

Bob laughed. "Pull up a stool, Roberto. I'll buy you a drink, but I'm giving no quotes about the Longo bout."

Castro grinned. "Cool it. I'm off duty, Bob. But I was impressed. For an old guy, you held your own in that wrestling match on the locker room floor with Longo. Hey, where is your Man Friday, Cunill?"

"Jorge went back with the team," said Bob. "He felt bad about missing Thanksgiving with his family. Frankly, I think he was just horny and wanted to sleep with his wife tonight rather than wait until tomorrow night."

Castro laughed, and then ordered a rum and Coke. "You know, amigo, you and Cunill are surely the odd couple of sports journalism," the young *Morning Journal* sports writer said.

"I guess you could say opposites attract," Bob answered dryly.

"And, how!" replied Castro. "You can't even speak Spanish."

"Jorge speaks excellent English," replied the columnist, with no trace of emotion to the provocative statement.

"And Cunill is handsome and an immaculate dresser," continued Castro.

"Hey, Roberto, who's buying the drinks?"

Castro laughed heartily as he had succeeded in getting a reaction from Casey. "Sorry, Bob. I'm only pulling your leg."

Bob knew Castro was right. Cunill was a dashing fashion plate. He was a stereotype of a Latin lover, with black, wavy hair and a macho mustache. He was a proud Cuban with a wife and two kids.

After taking a long sip of his drink, Castro extended his right hand. "Congratulations on your engagement, Bob. That Suzy is a real fox. Does this mean you can now fly free on Sun Air?"

Bob was slightly irritated by the remark, since Suzy was a flight attendant. But he rationalized that it was envy from a guy like Castro. So he found it more effective to go along with the flow.

"Ah, those buddy passes," he said, beaming. "London, Paris, Rome. In truth, I think Suzy is more excited about the 50% employee discount for home delivery of *Miami P.M.* She's much too bright to want a rag like the *Morning Journal*."

Castro laughed good-naturedly. "Okay, amigo, you made your point. Let me show you my sincere wishes for a happy marriage by buying the next round."

"Good deal," Bob said.

"To Suzy and Bob," Castro said, and the two men clinked their glasses. "Happiness and long life."

#

It was a Continental flight crew, just arriving at the hotel for a layover, that brought the crash to the attention of the newspapermen. A gray-haired man in a captain's uniform stormed into the bar. "What's the latest on that crash in Miami? Have you got Headline News on?"

Castro and Casey were startled by the outburst, but joined in a chorus with the Continental crew to turn on Headline News. The bartender stopped washing glasses and turned his attention to the TV set.

On the screen was a female network reporter with an MIA backdrop. ". . .crashed shortly after midnight, Miami time. We do know that it was a Sun Airlines DC-10 that was transporting the Miami Sharks. It reportedly crashed in the Everglades. A massive rescue operation is under way. As soon as we learn about survivors, we will be back with you."

Bob felt as if he had been flattened by a linebacker. "My God, Suzy is on that flight!" The columnist panicked. He felt fear. Worse, he felt totally helpless.

Castro was stunned by the news, too. "My God. . .my God," he kept saying over and over.

"My fiancée is on that flight," said Bob, his voice choking with emotion. "So is Jorge. . .I've got to get to Miami at once. You know, I have to go now."

Castro restrained Casey. "Easy, Bob. I share your concern. But, man, there's no way we can get to Miami any faster than the nine a.m. flight on Continental."

"I can get a rental car. . ."

"Bob, Bob. I understand your feelings, but even driving straight through would take you almost two days. We'll be in Miami before noon on that Continental flight."

Bob kicked a barstool hard. He didn't even feel the pain from the blow to his right foot. "I have to get to Miami now! Damn it! Jorge and Suzy are aboard that fucking flight! Don't you understand that? They may be. . .hurt or. . .or worse." Tears welled in Bob's eyes as he imagined the worst. "I'm not sitting here and doing nothing."

Bob stormed into the hotel lobby, grabbed a telephone directory, and turned to the yellow pages. He asked a pursuing Castro to get a fistful of quarters from the front desk while he manned a pay phone to begin calling air charter services.

"Bob, it's still a holiday," Castro said. "We could do this from your room. Anyhow, there won't be anyone on duty at this time of the morning—"

"Get the fucking quarters!"

Castro didn't argue. He understood Casey's state of mind. *Maybe it is better to do this and keep him occupied.*

Bob knew Castro was right. Yet he kept dialing and getting recorded messages. He was down to three numbers when a human but sleepy voice answered, "Trans Texas Air Taxi."

Later, in the airborne Lear jet, pilot J.R. Gardner told Bob, "You all know I wouldn't have normally been at my hangar except

I had a spat with my wife. I stormed out of our Fort Worth home, and decided to cool off for the night on a cot in my office. I only answered the phone 'cause I thought it was Dolly."

Maybe it was the urgency and emotion in Bob's voice that had resulted in Gardner not hanging up. When he learned why the caller wanted to charter his Lear jet, he quoted him a $5,000 fee. That was the one-way fare, and Gardner knew he would deadhead back empty.

He understood the emotional wringer the columnist faced, knowing his lover and friend were aboard that downed flight. Gardner accepted Casey's Gold American Express card without even running an authorization check.

#

Meanwhile, in a smoke-filled, blue-collar bar outside DFW Airport, three men in jeans and long-sleeved sports shirts, who had been drinking long necks of Budweiser, stopped when the news of the crash came over the bar TV.

At first, Alvin "Bubba" Youngblood, T.J. Lewis, and Jose Cortez appeared to exchange knowing grins. Then, acting confused, they looked back and forth at each other.

The bartender thought this was an unusual trio, with Youngblood a real redneck type, Lewis an African-American, and Cortez a probable Cuban. *This is their third night in my joint. I don't like having a nigger in here, but he and his pals have behaved themselves.*

"Did they say the plane was carrying pro football players?" Cortez excitedly asked the bartender.

"I think so," replied the bartender, who had been opening two bottles of beer. "I wasn't paying much attention—"

"It was carrying the Miami Sharks," a man said loudly from the end of the bar.

All eyes were on the TV. The bartender had to step on a stool to turn up the volume. "Don't you guys work for Sun Air?" he asked the trio.

"Yeah, we work for Sun," Youngblood answered. "But, you knows, we is on strike."

"Then that wasn't the Bogotá flight?" asked Cortez. His face was pale, and he fumbled for a fresh Marlboro from a full pack.

"Why? Do you have kin on that Bogotá flight?" the bartender asked, reacting to Cortez' Spanish accent.

Before Cortez could reply that he was a Cuban, he got his answer.

"Yep, it was the plane carrying the football team," volunteered a man in work clothes with an American Airlines emblem on his blue cotton shirt. "TV says everyone on it died."

"What did you say happened?" asked Lewis. "We're mechanics with Sun. Did you say everyone is dead?"

The bar patrons huddled near the TV set and spoke excitedly about the news.

"The DC-10 scheduled for the football team had a mechanical," said the AA man. "They swapped equipment, you know, leaving a full load of Bogotá revenue in the terminal."

"How did you all know?" asked Youngblood.

"My buddy works for the non-union ground service handling Sun Air at DFW," said the AA man. "I know we all feel bad about the crash. But Sun Air management shouldn't have compromised safety by letting scabs service their equipment."

The 20 bar patrons, many of them off-duty airline workers, saluted the AA man with a round of "The union! The union!"

Cortez, however, wasn't thinking about the union. *The wrong suckers died tonight. We still have problems big-time. Fuck fate! Fuck fate!*

#

It was quiet as the private jet made its way southeast toward the Florida peninsula. The two passengers were in no mood for small talk, so the pilot concentrated on flying while figuring out an apology for his wife.

Bob had invited Castro to make the trip. He wasn't thinking of Castro as a competitor at this time; he just wanted the company and support of a guy he knew.

"The TV bulletin said 'No survivors,'" Bob kept saying.

And Castro kept answering, "Since when do we trust the assholes in TV news? They aren't even on the crash scene."

Castro eventually fell sound asleep, but Bob couldn't even close his eyes. He was too hyper. The thought of losing Suzy was devastating. He didn't want to believe this was happening to him. Finally, he dozed off.

Bob was jolted awake by the new day's rising sun. The three men said nothing as below them, on the approach to MIA, they saw a sea of red, blue, and white flashing lights belonging to rescue vehicles spread across Alligator Alley. The sky was filled with emergency and TV news helicopters.

The small jet had barely touched down before Bob was on his Nokia cell phone. He dialed Larry Bloom's private line at the *Miami P.M.*

#

The managing editor was organizing coverage of what could be the biggest story in his newspaper career. This explained his brusque manner in answering his phone.

"Yeah. What do you want?" His mood changed instantly when he realized it was Casey. "Bob! Where the hell are you? In Miami? Here? How the hell did you do that?"

"Larry, please." Bob was pleading, "I need to get to the crash scene. Suzy was on that plane. . .and so was Jorge."

Bloom calmly replied, "Stay where you are. I'll dispatch Miami P.M. Air One to fetch you. Bob, you know. . .well, get going. The chopper will be there shortly. Talk to you later."

#

Dick Norton, seated in the left cockpit seat, pulled himself out of his shock and daze. His head throbbed. Blood had been splattered all over his uniform. He slowly removed the seat belt and tried but failed to stand up.

I think my right leg is broken. It sure hurts like hell.

"Buckmaster is dead," Lombard said solemnly in the darkness as he got his flashlight and pointed it at the first officer, still strapped into the right seat. The light passed over Buckmaster's white uniform shirt, which was soaked in blood from the piece of metal that had struck his heart.

Lombard tried to free the captain. Dick screamed in pain.

"Leave me for now, Vince," the captain said, biting back the pain. "Let's see what kind of damage we have."

The engineer pulled a number of switches, but he knew nothing worked. He turned to the cockpit door. It was jammed shut. "I'll have to climb out the emergency window." He stopped and gasped.

"What's wrong, Vince?" Dick asked.

"We. . .we're all by ourselves," the engineer said. "The flight deck must have broken away on impact."

Vince, who was surprised that he had no broken bones or injuries, knew the only way to find the rest of the aircraft was out the door. So he pushed, pushed harder, and finally forced open the door.

Vince's flashlight cut into the darkness. He appreciated the captain's skill as he surveyed the scene.

A nosedive would have smashed the aircraft into bits, as had happened with a discount carrier's DC-9 in 1996.

The engineer knew the action by Norton could be compared to skipping a rock across a pond. Except this was a 163-ton rock traveling at 130 knots. The impact on hitting the water had torn off the right wing, along with an engine. The tail section had pulled apart.

The quiet caused Vince more terror than the fear of the crash. No one spoke or shouted for help. Not a sound stirred, except the splashing of swamp water as the aircraft settled in the muck.

For Dick, all he felt was the physical pain of his injuries and the mental anguish for the fate of his passengers and crew.

Was it an accident like at Detroit? Or was it a bomb? If it was a bomb, he knew there could be no punishment except slow torture to the death to fit this crime. *And why would anyone want to bomb a commercial jet? Maybe some crazy foreign terrorists?*

His anger only triggered pain from his leg and his stomach. He closed his eyes briefly and prayed for his passengers' and crew's deliverance.

The fires on the water had faded and posed no threat, because the remaining wing and its engine were under water. This had reduced the risk of any of the remaining kerosene fuel igniting.

Standing at the gaping hole of the coach section were flight attendants Mary Rich and Ann Parker. They were captured in the rays of Lombard's flashlight.

The engineer knew the first-class section with 22 passengers had become a funeral pyre for them, including flight attendants Nancy Hill and Chris Gaylord. The engine had sprayed the section with kerosene, and it had ignited into a fireball. Vince shivered with the thought of being burned to death. He knew that if the cockpit had not broken off and slid another 100 yards, he would be dead. He couldn't understand how he and the captain had survived. He really didn't want to understand. His only concern now was to save the living.

By instinct, he made the sign of the cross and closed his eyes for a brief prayer for those lost souls whom he figured included Rubin, Sherman, the coaching staff, and at least two flight attendants. He was glad to see Rich and Parker, and to know that they had survived.

Fortunately for most of the cockpit and coach occupants, the sections had torn and the murky water had prevented a spread of the fire. A thick cloud of black smoke was all that marked the first-class section. If the crash had been on dry land, speed of evacuation would have been required. The water, however, had smothered the chances of further explosions.

#

Mary had lost her shoes. She stood in her stocking feet, but was happy that she had sustained no noticeable injuries. She knew that in this dark hellhole, there was no place to flee that was safe of alligators and water mocs. *We will have to wait for rescue.*

Mary and Parker had obtained hand-held fire extinguishers and a first-aid kit. Parker had the only light, a small flashlight. With it, she helped Mary locate another flashlight.

#

Muhammad Johnson had suffered what proved to be fatal internal injuries. In barely a whisper, the wide receiver had provided some chilling information to the priest.

"They. . .they said they'd get me if I ever talked. . ."

"Who are they, my son?" the priest asked, understanding that Muhammad had to get something off his chest.

"The drug dealers. . .oh, God, I'm hurting. . .they thought I was going to the cops. . .I wasn't going to snitch. . .I. . .I. . .I'm dying. I'm afraid, Father."

"Hang on, Muhammad," the priest encouraged in a soft voice as he cradled the man in his arms. "Help is almost here."

It wasn't.

Could it be possible that this disaster was drug related?

O'Malley held Johnson in his arms and recited the Rosary and prayed for help to arrive quickly.

It didn't make sense to O'Malley that drug dealers would go to such extremes. The old priest regretted that he wasn't a medical doctor at this time. He knew he could do nothing to save this man who had been turning his life around from drug addiction.

Why did God choose this young man?

"Who did this to you, to us, Muhammad?"

The priest put his ear almost to the lips of the man to catch his last fleeting words. Johnson went limp, and O'Malley knew he was dead.

Father O'Malley, wandering about in a bewildered state, found a flashlight in his bag and joined the flight attendants in searching the wide cabin. There were moans and calls for help in the mangled coach section. Damaged wires dangled from the roof. The priest stopped and stooped to bless the dead, not knowing their religion.

#

Mary spotted the light from the cockpit. Lombard put the light to his face and yelled, "It's me! It's Vince! The captain is alive, but he's hurting. How is everyone back there?"

"Not too good, Vince," yelled Mary. "We need help, and we need it quick!"

Despite the distance, Lombard's voice sliced through the darkness, and it made both flight attendants feel better to know that at least one of the officers was healthy. They waved and shouted, but stopped abruptly when the coach section settled into the muck.

"Do you think we'll sink before help comes?" Parker asked.

"I don't know, Ann, I don't know." Mary was scared, but she wasn't about to panic. She was alive, and in that moment, that was all the emotion she could handle. She wanted to reassure Parker, so she said, "I think we must be in shallow water, because DC-10s don't float. We should stay with the cabin and wait for help."

Siegfried von Katzen, the kicker, suffered only the loss of his shoes and little more than a bloody nose. He managed to struggle out of one of the coach lavatories.

Running back Richard Baldwin felt himself trapped in a window seat and was beginning to panic in the dark. He had a deep fear of snakes, and he could imagine all those water mocs out to get him. Then he remembered to unfasten his seat belt.

Meanwhile, Vince wanted to assist the injured captain. He tried not to look at the body of the first officer. A second attempt to free Dick proved unsuccessful, and it became obvious that rescue equipment would be needed.

"It was a helluva landing, Captain."

"Oh my God, those poor bastards in first class," Dick replied, tears welling in his eyes. "What an awful way to die. Sol Rubin. Coach Sherman, Johnny Longo, and those flight attendants. Why? Why?"

#

Tommy Flowers and his son Billy, who operated an airboat rental store, had been the first on the scene at about 4:00 a.m. The older man bathed the scene in a floodlight while Billy used his cell phone to call 9-1-1.

"We've found the downed airplane. It's only about 1,000 yards off Alligator Alley, about 15 miles west of the Broward County toll booth."

The police helicopter had spotted the floodlight. Soon rescue units were en route down Alligator Alley. Their flashing blue, red, and yellow lights became a blur of color from the air as they raced along the highway. In hot pursuit were the media, coming by air and land.

It was nearly dawn when the vanguard of rescue crews reached sections of the aircraft. Two firemen in an airboat spotted Lombard outside the cabin. The firemen initially were turned away by Dick, who insisted they attend to those in the coach section before bothering with him. He was assured that there were plenty of rescue workers already on the scene. Firemen used power saws to cut through the DC-10 cockpit's roof and managed to free the injured captain from the tangled metal and wires.

The sun was rising when rescue workers combed the coach section, ignoring the dead and concentrating on the seriously injured. The rescue floodlights exposed a cabin in shambles. Clothing, hand carried luggage, pillows, blankets, and dining ware were mixed with muck and debris.

Father O'Malley knew that Johnson had saved his life. *That young black man threw his body over mine when all the debris was flying through the cabin. He was impaled by a spear-like metal rod. It was intended for me. Oh, God, why did you choose to spare me, and not this young man?*

The priest believed God had decided who would live and who would die that night. Dr. Dan Barker lived because he had left his first-class seat to give a painkiller to running back Baldwin. Moses survived because he had gone back to tell Johnson he was being reinstated.

The six players who were seated in the tail section playing poker were killed by the initial explosion. Pieces of their bodies were mixed with muck, cards, and cash.

"This is supposedly the safest place in a commercial jet, but not when a cargo door is blown open," Mary explained to O'Malley. "But there really isn't a safest place."

Rescue crews later that Friday found a middle row of five seats, with two passengers strapped in, about a mile from the crash site. The bench of three coach seats was upright but embedded in muck. The two men looked alive. They weren't, of course, having fallen from an estimated 10,000 feet after the initial explosion. Both would be identified as sports writers for South Florida dailies, one of which was still clutching his tangerine iBook computer.

O'Malley met firefighters helping fullback Larry Wargo and linebacker Brutus Neswiacheny, who had escaped with only cuts and bruises. Backup quarterback Eddie Malloy fractured his wrist.

Fortunately, it was his left one, not the passing one. Paul Dungan, the team security agent, was carried out with both legs smashed. And so it went as the tropical sun started to bathe the crash scene with golden light.

O'Malley heard a faint pounding from inside a coach lavatory. The door was jammed. He summoned firefighters, who used a power saw to cut through the door. Inside, they found Longo. The quarterback was alive because the first-class lavatories were full, and he had gone to the coach section a minute or two before the explosion.

#

Robin Martin, the Sun Airlines corporate relations vice president, huddled with police and fire public information officers at a command post: a fire department van with a green flashing light on the roof. It was agreed that Martin should handle the release of the names of the survivors and the dead.

"This should be done back at Sun Airlines headquarters, not in the swamp," Martin argued.

The police and firemen selected a Public information officer to act as spokesman for the rescue workers. Martin knew that the FBI and NTSB agents would arrive soon, and they would designate their own spokesmen.

The *Miami P.M.* helicopter landed on Alligator Alley despite the efforts of a Florida Highway Patrol trooper to wave away the craft. The trooper was angry, but his lieutenant pointed out that it was a "law enforcement friendly" aircraft.

"If you spot The *Morning Journal's* chopper, you are free to shoot the fucker out of the sky."

Bob Casey climbed out of the chopper and hunched his way under the rotating blades toward the two troopers.

FHP Lt. Bill Sanders recognized the sports columnist. "Mr. Casey. Can I be of any assistance?"

"Lieutenant, my fiancée, Suzy Peters, was on that flight. Who has a list of the survivors?"

"The airline PR guy, Robin Martin, is over at the command post," Sanders said. "Maybe he can help you, Mr. Casey. That's the van with the green flashing light on top. We're supposed to keep you guys from there. Since this is a personal matter, I'll make an exception."

Bob swallowed hard. "Thank you, Lieutenant. Thank you."

Martin recognized Casey from his column mug. "I'm scheduling a three p.m. press conference back at corporate—"

"I don't care about any goddamned press conference, Robin! Do you have. . .does anyone have a list of survivors? My fiancée, Suzy Peters, was on that flight. She's one of your flight attendants."

Martin remembered Peters. She had just become management. *So this is her boyfriend?* The PR man studied a computer printout of the passenger list he had attached to a yellow legal pad of notes. He followed each line with his index finger, and to Bob the process was both slow and painful.

"She's not on either list, Mr. Casey."

"What the hell does that mean?"

"It means simply," Martin said slowly, trying to appear compassionate, "that Ms. Peters is not on the confirmed dead list or on the survivor list. I don't even know yet where they are taking the survivors. They are going to hospitals as far as Fort Lauderdale and Naples. So there is still reason for hope, but. . ."

"But? But what? Talk to me, Robin, talk to me!" Bob was losing control. He was angry, and he was scared of losing the only person who truly mattered in his life.

"Mr. Casey, you made the flight to DFW with the team. Where was Ms. Peters working? I mean first class, coach. . ."

"First class," Bob said.

There was a brief but telling silence. Bob feared the worst by Martin's expression.

"There are only two known survivors in first class. And they survived because they happened to be in the coach section. That first-class section. . .it exploded on impact. . .Maybe she was in another part of the. . ."

Martin's words were like a sword thrust into Bob's stomach. He felt his life being sucked out by the blow. *She's dead! Oh my God, she's dead.*

Bob walked slowly away from the command post. He felt the tears, the pain in his gut. He knew Suzy was dead. He was trembling, and he felt so very, very helpless. He looked toward the heavens, squinted his eyes against the morning sun, and shouted, "I love you, Suzy! I will always love you! Please, dear God, be kind to this wonderful woman."

The FHP officer realized the columnist had received bad news. "Mr. Casey, would you like someone to talk to? I'd be pleased to get you a cup of coffee at the Salvation Army canteen."

Fatigue and grief was reflected in Bob's demeanor. He managed to mutter a "Thanks" for the coffee Sanders handed him. After a couple of sips, Bob tried to trace the events that had led to this fateful event.

It had started in Berlin last July. Or was it earlier in Miami?

CHAPTER 3

"Everything ponderous, vicious, and solemnly clumsy, all long-winded and boring types of style, are developed in profuse harmony among Germans."

Friedrich Nietzsche
Beyond Good and Evil

Berlin, Germany, four months earlier

It was unusually warm for the first Monday morning in August in the German capital. The Adlon Hotel's automated guestroom wakeup call message reported 68 degrees at 7:00 a.m. Bob Casey, adjusting to the realization that it was only 1:00 a.m. back in Miami, didn't want to sleep away his first day. He was excited about returning here for the first time since the infamous Berlin Wall came tumbling down.

Unlike commercial flights, which left the United States in the evening so as to arrive in Europe early the next morning, the Sun Airlines DC-10 chartered by the Miami Sharks had departed MIA Sunday afternoon and had touched down at Schonefield Airport the same night.

Bob was as fascinated by the historic grand hotel at 8 Unter den Linden as he was by the changes in the city. From its opening in 1907 to its destruction on May 3, 1945, by a fire caused by drunken Russian soldiers in its fabulous wine cellar, the Adlon was the most famous hotel in Europe. It had been the embodiment of Berlin's most glorious pre-World War II era.

During his U.S. Army service in Berlin, the site of the Adlon had been a vacant lot just inside the Berlin Wall on the East German side. Bob tried to imagine what this neighborhood had been like in the late 1930s. He concluded that it would have been ultimately exciting to be a foreign correspondent assigned to Berlin before the start of World War II.

During a quick morning walk outside the hotel, he was impressed by the countless construction sites, especially in the Potsdamer Platz, once the "Times Square" of prewar Berlin. Under the regime of Communist East Germany, it had been a no-man's land, watched over by snipers positioned along the Wall. Nearby, a new government plaza was being developed. The sounds of banging hammers, screaming skill saws, and whining crane motors assaulted his eardrums. Clouds of dust wafted across the walkways.

Bob had spent a restless night, and he wanted some fresh air to help him think. His problem, however, was back in Miami, not here in Berlin. Still, even the distraction of a new Berlin and the Adlon couldn't stop him from thinking about it.

Returning to the hotel, he strolled through the lobby of the Adlon. Built in 1997 at a cost of $266 million on its original site facing the Brandenburg Gate, he felt as though he was an art patron visiting a gallery. There were 276 rooms and 51 suites, and he was delighted that his room provided a view of the Brandenburg Gate.

He removed his reporter's slim notebook and jotted some thoughts. The hotel would be his travel article. He knew he could get help from the hotel public relations staff. That would help justify the cost of the trip to his boss, Larry Bloom.

He noted the details of the Carrera marble, the inlaid wood

paneling, the stained-glass cupolas, the mosaics, the coffered high ceilings, the extravagant use of gold leaf, and the rich textiles used in the upholstered furniture and draperies. Then there was the grand staircase that recalled the glories of the previous Grand Hotel Adlon. The decor was awesomely impressive and executed in the best of taste.

Bob thought to himself, *A grand hotel is like a rich, beautiful woman, but the difference is I can spend the night with the Adlon for $420, without any complications.*

The travel article was to help justify the expense of sending both a reporter and columnist to Berlin to cover a Sharks preseason exhibition.

#

"Guten morgen, Herr Kapitan!"

Seated alone at a table in the hotel coffee shop, Dick Norton looked up from his second cup of black coffee and smiled. "Your German is pretty good for an Irish refugee," said the Sun Airlines chief pilot, motioning his friend to be seated. Even out of uniform, Dick's attire of black patent leather shoes, dark trousers, and a white pilot's shirt open at the collar betrayed a military look. "You having breakfast so early? I figured you were recovering from our flight in coach."

"Those steerage seats were designed for jockeys, not football players," said Bob Casey.

"Your fault, Scoop. If you sucked up to Sol Rubin instead of ripping him every chance you get in your scandal sheet, he'd let you sit in first class."

Bob laughed. "Hell, if they let the millionaire players sit in coach for nine hours, who am I to complain?"

The DC-10 charter carrying the Sharks' players, staff, camp followers, and the media had taken its toll in jet lag. The passengers were recovering. Coach Don Sherman had given the team the day off to adjust to the circus atmosphere of the coming exhibition game between the two International Football League teams Saturday in Berlin Stadium.

Bob usually flew first class. That was in his contract with *Miami P.M.* This, however, was a Sharks charter. Even though the newspaper paid the team for its writers, Rubin decided the seating. It had been a struggle for the columnist to squeeze his six-foot-one, 240-pound frame into a coach seat. It made it impossible to sleep.

"Herr Ober, bitte." Bob summoned the waiter. "Ich möchte frühstücke, bitte. Drie gekochtes Ei weich. Und, Bröchten und tasse Kaffee mit zükar und shawn."

The waiter, who was a second generation Turk, was impressed that the American's German was better than his own.

"Three soft-boiled eggs?" Dick was sorry he asked, because he expected—and received—a lecture about the German custom of eating soft-boiled eggs in a holder with a tiny spoon.

He was truly happy the columnist had made the trip, because this gave him a chance to play tennis during the week.

Although it was hot by German standards, Bob reacted like a true Floridian: that anything under 90 degrees was cold. He was glad that he wore a white tennis sweater over a red polo shirt. He was anxious to see the city again. But there was that problem which kept interrupting Bob's focus on enjoying the visit.

Managing Editor Bloom had reluctantly agreed to send him and Cunill, the Sharks' beat writer, to Berlin for a week. Bob had failed, however, to convince the ME to send a staff photographer. Bloom had screamed, "This is nothing but a fucking practice game!" He had made Bob responsible for writing a travel piece for the Sunday section.

The Adlon should take care of that obligation earlier than I anticipated, Bob told himself.

What should have been the most important consideration, however, was a lead on what could be a blockbuster story. That could have been worked better in Miami. He, however, had rationalized his response: *I need a vacation, and this is a free trip to Germany. I can work on the story here.*

Dick was in a talkative mood.

"You know, Bob, I started flying at age 16," he said as he sipped a fresh cup of coffee. "I was just a farm kid back. . ."

Oh, no! Here it comes. I've heard Dick's history so often, I know it by heart. What the hell! One day, I'll be 58 and facing early retirement at 60 from a job I love, too. Still, I must spend some time checking out my sources.

Bob pulled out a Canones' cigar from a black leather case, looked approvingly at the eight-inch Churchill with a 52-inch ring, clipped the tip with a cutter, and lit the other end with a wooden match. He watched the blue smoke swirl into the air, settled back, and became a good listener.

Dick interrupted his story when he saw the cigar. "You aren't going to smoke a stogie before breakfast, are you? You won't even have it burning before your food arrives."

Bob smiled. He knew the captain was right, but he was dying for a smoke after being cooped up on that long flight.

Six puffs later, the waiter arrived with breakfast. Bob placed the cigar in an ashtray and welcomed the food. He ignored the smoke that mingled with the aroma of the freshly cooked food.

He savored cutting off the top of the egg with a table knife and anticipating it. As he'd expected, the soft-boiled eggs at the Adlon were soft and hot.

"Ah. . .strong German coffee and these wonderful rolls," he said, briefly interrupting the captain's life story.

Bob was no stranger to German food. He had spent almost two years in Berlin as a military police lieutenant following graduation from Fairfield (Connecticut) University, where the good Jesuits had prepared him for life. His ROTC commission gained him an assignment to the Berlin Command, where he was assigned to 287th Military Police Company.

Later, as a newspaperman in Boston, he had won a United Press writing contest for a series of columns on DDR Olympic athletes in training.

Good grief! The Berlin Wall, the DDR, and the Commies are all history. My, how time flies when you're having fun. Am I having fun? Hell, I'm 20 years from reaching 60!

The cigar was down to its last inch when Dick finished his lengthy tale. "Well, enough about me. Are the Sharks going to win Saturday?"

"Dick, for crying out loud! You know this is just a practice game. We are in the Fatherland for one reason: Sol Rubin's revenge on the natives for the Holocaust. Pro football exhibitions are about as honest as pro wrestling. American fans are too smart to pay good money to see an exhibition that includes most of the stiffs who won't survive the August cuts. So the league started moving such practices overseas."

"Now, Bob," the captain said, enjoying the baiting of his friend, "you write stuff like that, and you'll get your Miami Beach readers upset. Why do you always pick on Sol Rubin?"

Bob ground out the butt of the cigar in the empty coffee cup. He was mildly upset. "Rubin is a shmuck. His being Jewish has nothing to do with the matter. My managing editor is Jewish, and he thinks Rubin is a shmuck. My next door neighbor, Federal Judge Hugh Glickstein, thinks Rubin is a shmuck. His rabbi probably thinks Rubin is a shmuck."

"Okay, okay. Sorry I bothered to ask," Dick said as the waiter discreetly removed the coffee cup with the cigar butt and replaced it with a clean cup.

"Since you asked," Bob continued as he pulled out a fresh cigar, "Rubin is a drunk, a womanizer, a gambler, and a cheapskate owner in everything but in paying his star players. He treats his employees like shit. In short, he is the typical IFL franchise owner."

Now Dick was really sorry he'd asked. Bob continued his tirade. He related seeing Rubin throw up over Norm Amundsen on a return flight from last year's Pittsburgh game.

The stories about the Sharks' owner momentarily removed Bob's thoughts from the issue that really troubled him: the tip on Johnny Longo.

"Rubin's policy permits the most senior players to fly in first class on the team charter," the columnist continued. "The six-foot-five, 295-pound offensive tackle doesn't drink. Amundsen, you know, is president of the Sharks' chapter of the Fellowship of Christian Athletes. He was in the window seat, with Rubin on the aisle. Rubin heaved right into Amundsen's lap, then buried his head in the vomit. Rubin was out cold. Poor Amundsen didn't know what to do. Finally, Mary Rich, the purser, got two assistant coaches to pull up Rubin. Amundsen fled back to coach section before the coaches dropped Rubin back in the two seats to sleep it off."

The captain laughed. "That Mary is a pistol. I always love to have her in charge of my cabin. Tell me, why don't you write some of this good stuff?"

"Because my publisher Jack Patterson and Rubin are social buddies. Rubin gives Patterson a discount on the paper's skybox at Rubin Stadium. We do have sacred cows in the newspaper business, you know, and I care enough about having my contract renewed next year not to take on the publisher—even if he is a jerk."

Dick mentioned that Rubin had a new, younger, and more beautiful wife.

"That Irish slut? She sold her soul to the Devil to break up Rubin's marriage of 35 years. I have a great deal of respect for Sadie Rubin. I hope she took that SOB of a husband to the cleaners in the divorce courts."

Dick raised his hands in mock surrender. "Okay, okay." He realized it was time to change the subject. "We having dinner tonight?"

"Damn right, Dick. This is your reward for making chief pilot, so to speak. I noted a fine restaurant down on the Kurfurstendamm. It's Das McDonalds."

Dick shook his head. "No way. You're on an expense account, and I've had the Adlon desk make reservations at the Hardtke. Oh, and wear a tie and jacket. The Hardtke takes the American Express card, but it doesn't accept Americans dressed like sports writers."

#

Bob realized the Adlon's lobby would be bedlam for the rest of the week as players and coaches were forced to endure the stalking of American tourists and Germans alike. Hotel security did its best, he knew, to maintain the decorum of a five-star establishment, but it was almost impossible. Security was heavy, not heavy-handed. In a grand hotel, you could no longer judge the guests by the way they dressed. Anyhow, the management liked the free international publicity resulting from being the headquarters for the Sharks.

The New England Minutemen were in the old DDR section at the Berlin Hotel, a rather modest facility in the Spartan manner of the former Communist regime.

Bob had to admit he appreciated Rubin's passion for posh hotels. Sherman would rather keep the players at a modest motel in the country for road trips, but the owner wanted to flaunt his $750 million toy.

I'm glad that I mentioned that in last Sunday's column, how Rubin played hardball with the league about the Berlin exhibition, demanding his team get the Adlon or he wouldn't agree to the trip. The new IFL commissioner, Peter J. Wilson, not wanting to get in a row with an owner so early in his tenure, gave in quickly to S.R.'s demands.

Knocking out a column a day on an Apple PowerBook G4 laptop wasn't a challenge, Bob reflected, as it took him no more than two hours of pounding on the keyboard. The only hassle was transmitting over the hotel phone. He solved that by sending e-mail over America Online. He enjoyed writing in his third-floor room overlooking the Unter den Linden and Brandenburg Gate, where he could watch the sidewalk and street traffic.

At times, he would daydream about guests who had stayed here in the old Adlon. He wondered if there were ghosts roaming through the halls at night.

Bob found most of his column subjects in the Adlon lobby.

The challenge was always getting a free AOL line from the phone in his room. *I should have been in this business during the days of hot metal type and typewriters. Technology has made me more of a technician than a columnist.*

While trying not to let it consume his thoughts, he was living with a gnawing internal conflict. Should he enjoy the game week in Berlin and the following week on vacation in Munich, or concentrate on being an investigative reporter? Ten years ago, there would have been no conflict. He would have been gung-ho, and nothing would have mattered except the scoop, the big story. He tried to excuse his lack of urgency, because it was only an unsupported tip about a possible gambling problem.

Well, if I can get hold of Father O'Malley, maybe he can. . .Hell, I can be in this city for a week and not get laid. Wouldn't that be a bummer!

Bob hoped to get lucky. He was upset that sex, at this time in his career, was more important to him than a big story. But he couldn't help it.

He felt that his age now made it harder to find a dream girl. Dick had offered to fix him up with one of the senior flight attendants, but on the flight over, he hadn't seen one under the age of 60.

It was a fun dinner with Norton on Wednesday. There was also a really important one with Father O'Malley on Thursday.

Bob was nervous about his proposed dinner with the priest. Now he felt as if he were seeking a payback. It wasn't easy being a newspaperman. He had made many friends, but he had also lost some by doing his job. He didn't want to lose the priest's friendship. Yet the part that made him think like a newspaperman knew he would risk it.

#

The Rev. Francis Joseph O'Malley was the Sharks' chaplain, and pastor of St. Vincent's Catholic Church, the one the Sherman family attended in Miami Shores. Only 56 years old, he could pass for 66. Even without the JC Penney black suit and Roman collar, O'Malley had the look of a priest in a Bing Crosby movie. His thin head of hair was white, and his face always seemed flushed.

He was, however, very bright, a charmer, but most of all, a man of character. He combined his Jesuit training with a sense of humor tailor-made for his New York and Irish accents. His father had been a New York City police captain, and his mother went to Mass every day. They were good Catholics, and he owed them for helping him financially through the early years of the seminary and later the priesthood.

O'Malley was both honest and compassionate. He had been a bright student and a hard worker, but he had been too honest and outspoken in the politics of the church to move beyond a local parish. St. Vincent's had been a reward from Cardinal Murphy for the priest's service in the slums of major southern cities.

The old priest liked Casey because of the columnist's sense of humor, his talent as a writer, his honesty. . . *And the lad knows how to hold his liquor.*

Bob enjoyed Father O'Malley because the priest loved martinis, good food, and expensive cigars, and he was a great conversationalist. Bob always picked up the tab on these occasional road game evenings, but believed it sacrilegious to put it on his expense account.

He spotted O'Malley at the newsstand in the lobby. "You can't buy any Miami papers here, Father."

"Bob! Tell me, my son, will you be attending team Mass Saturday morning?"

Bob said nothing.

"After reading that last column of yours on the plane coming over," O'Malley continued, "I think you should be visiting the confession booth, too."

Bob grinned respectfully while trying to get off the subject of his church attendance. "We still on for dinner, Father?"

"I'm looking forward to it, Bob."

"Great. I want to confess, you know, I. . .I sinned with a young lady." He was only kidding, of course, but he loved to see the priest's reaction. O'Malley's expression was similar to that of his parochial school nuns when he had misbehaved. The only thing missing was that Father wasn't armed with a ruler.

"Do you think a meal will gain you forgiveness, my son?"

"I hope so, Father. You see, the girl was a Baptist."

The priest realized Bob was pulling his leg. "Oh my, oh dear. Bob, this had better be dinner at a good restaurant."

The two exchanged grins and agreed where to meet Thursday night for dinner.

#

Bob selected the Borchardt. Since the fall of the Wall, it was one of the most fashionable meeting places in the old East Berlin. The high ceilings, columns, red plush benches, and art nouveau mosaic helped create the impression of a 1920s café.

He waited at the bar with a vodka martini. He checked his watch. O'Malley was a bit late. Bob had selected the Borchardt to set a relaxed atmosphere in order to coax information—possibly privileged information—from the priest.

Bob took a sip of the martini, hating the position he found himself in.

O'Malley finally arrived, and they were directed to a corner booth by a tuxedo-clad captain.

"You like it here, Father?"

The priest nodded. "It is wonderful, Bob. You know, the food is more French than German. Plus, they mix a great vodka martini!"

The priest sensed that the dinner was more than a social event. Bob, however, waited until after the strawberry parfait with the rhubarb foam. Then both men went through the cigar ritual as the captain served the cognac and coffee.

"Hennessy's XO," said O'Malley. "This is indeed a special evening. You should sin more often with those Baptist women."

"Father," the columnist began slowly, nervously feeling his way. "I'm working on a story about addiction. . ."

"Drugs?"

"No, Father, gambling."

There was a pause and a silence as the waiter refilled their coffee cups.

"Perhaps you are concerned about some of the ladies who play bingo at St. Vincent's?" O'Malley asked.

"No, not bingo. I, well, I. . .would you like another after-dinner drink?"

"Later. Go on. You were talking about gambling." O'Malley was trying to feel the columnist out. He sensed Bob's discomfort, and he was concerned about the conversation's direction. So he tried to buy time. "Okay, Bob, I'd like another cognac. I hope your expense account can cover the Hennessy's XO."

There were a couple of awkward minutes between the drinks being ordered and served. Both savored the cognac, sipping it from the heavy crystal snifters.

Finally, Bob looked straight into the eyes of the man seated across the table. "I've had a tip. Reliable source, I believe. I hope it isn't true, but. . .I need your help because. . .because it concerns a player on the Sharks. And he is one of your parishioners." The columnist had finally said it. He took another sip of cognac and waited.

The priest appeared relaxed and displayed no emotion. "Bob, if I knew anything about such a problem, I couldn't reveal such information about a parishioner. That's privileged information. As a good Catholic, you know that."

Bob wondered if that would be the end. The priest's reply was as encouraging as going in for an audit with the IRS.

"Who are we talking about?" O'Malley asked.

"Johnny Longo," Bob replied quickly, almost excitedly.

There was another telling silence, but O'Malley's face did not betray anything.

"Look, Father, I don't want to hurt anybody. I have a job to do."

O'Malley believed him.

"I do know he is very religious, and he trusts you," Bob continued. "If he has a problem—and I say *if*—he needs help. Like now. That's because my source tells me he is deeply, very deeply, in debt for gambling. And the folks he owes money to don't honor a Chapter 7 filing."

The priest pondered the accusation. "How big a debt?"

"My sources say it's about $2.5 million," a breathless Bob said. "As for the shylock's interest. . .well, it's probably more than he makes in a year."

"Jesus, Mary, and Joseph!" O'Malley recovered slowly after taking a gulp of liquor. "Who told you such a story?"

"Look, Father, I'm not a muckraker. This story is going to break sooner or later. If it was a case that he was cheating on his wife, something simple, I could forget it. I'm not asking you to confirm or deny it. I just want you to realize this is a major scandal. My source claims he's not only betting on pro football, but on Sharks games, too."

There was a brief silence as both men pondered the gravity of the situation.

"We both have ethical problems, my son," the priest said at last. "I need some time. You know, Johnny has a wonderful wife and three wonderful children. Would you mind bowing your head a moment? I'd like to say a silent prayer and ask for divine guidance."

Bob bowed his head, but he didn't hear the prayer. He was shocked. His tipster was right about Longo. He had a story, a helluva story. Yet how could he jeopardize the priest's position?

I'm a Catholic! If O'Malley and Longo keep mum, and I go public, he will believe O'Malley gave it to me.

"Bob, could you tell me where you got this information?" O'Malley asked again.

"I. . .I can't, Father," the newspaperman replied. "I can't reveal the name of a source. It isn't ethical. And if I did, I'd never have any informants."

The priest nodded knowingly.

Bob knew now that both he and the priest faced moral and ethical dilemmas. He thought about his informant as they prepared to leave the restaurant, and O'Malley excused himself to use the men's room.

The tipster had been Dominic Conte. A former Miami police lieutenant, he had left the force under questionable circumstances five years before retirement. He was a licensed private investigator. He did odd jobs for cheap law firms, and he also sold information to the Miami media. Some of his tips had paid off.

In Miami, Conte had approached Bob in the newspaper parking lot next to Biscayne Bay. It had been dusk, and Bob had been opening the door to his yellow Corvette. It had been a short conversation, not more than five minutes.

"I'm gonna make you a star," Conte promised. "I got something big, and it should be worth big bucks. It's simple. Johnny Longo owes his ass in gambling debts. Big time. Like $2.5 million. Plus interest. Lots of interest."

Bob had been in a hurry to go home and pack for Berlin. "You're shitting me, Conte," he had replied. "Where did you come up with a tale like that?"

Conte had grinned like the proverbial cat that swallowed the canary. Bob remembered that he'd wanted to knock the grin off Conte's face. He hadn't. He had been in too much of a hurry.

"Look, newsboy, you've got the scoop," Conte continued. "Don't believe me. Just ask his priest. Just ask O'Malley. I'm giving you 30 days to prove what a hotshot you are. If you don't use it, then I'll sell it to the morning paper."

"Why are you being so nice to me?" Bob asked suspiciously.

"I like the *Miami P.M.*"

"Bullshit!" Bob quickly overcame his dislike for Conte because he realized, *What if his tip is true?* Changing his tone, Bob asked, "How much do you want if this wild tale proves true?"

"Tell Larry it's a bargain at five Gs."

"You've got to be kidding! Five grand?"

"Listen, Casey, I could get 20 times that from one of the supermarket tabloids. I know Bloom has that kind of money to cover correspondents like me."

Bob knew now that he should have talked to Bloom about Conte's tip, but he really didn't believe it.

He couldn't understand how Conte knew that O'Malley knew—and Bob was convinced that the priest knew. *My God, how could you gamble away $2.5 million?*

CHAPTER 4

"Love sought is good, but given unsought is better."
William Shakespeare
Twelfth Night

At practice in Berlin Stadium Friday morning, Casey and Cunill watched Longo run the first team offense. If he had a $2.5 million gambling problem, Longo didn't show any evidence of such at practice, the two newspapermen agreed. In fact, when Muhammad Johnson dropped a 15-yard sideline pass, the quarterback playfully ran downfield, picked up the dropped ball, and placed it in front of the wide receiver's face.

"This is a football, Herr Johnson. You are paid to catch it. Ve do not tolerate failures in the Fatherland! You will be on the next freight train to the Eastern Front."

The players hooted. Johnson grinned when he realized Johnny was clowning and just trying to relax everyone.

"What the fuck! Is this the comedy hour?" Sherman wasn't amused. He slammed his Sharks baseball cap onto the turf and blew his whistle several times. "We can stay here all day until we run this play right. I've got a roster of 80 today, and in two weeks it will be down to 50. Get my drift?"

On the next play, Johnny threw a strike, and Johnson grabbed it with both hands.

"Now that's the way that play is designed!" Sherman screamed.

Bob knew that the need for four preseason exhibition games in pro football was a joke. He had often shared this view with his readers. Few personnel changes were decided by play in exhibitions. For most veterans, it was part of the boring boot camp mentality of summer training that made them compete against a bunch of low draft picks and free agents. The top couple of draftees would survive, because the club had invested a lot of money in their signing.

Bob often pointed out that the starters saw limited action in the first three exhibitions, but spectators paid regular season prices. Clubs routinely included one or two home exhibitions with the season ticket package. This had resulted in angering many season ticket customers. Then the International Football League discovered foreign cities for exhibition games.

He knew that everyone except the coaching staff loved the exotic week's vacation in foreign locales, because the team permitted each player to bring a buddy along. Rubin liked the foreign trips because the league paid for the expenses and guaranteed each team a profit.

Bob was aware that Sherman didn't like the foreign trips because the coach didn't like to fly, and they created too much of a circus atmosphere. *Sherman probably has a blackboard in his bedroom and calls out formations when they make love.*

#

Sherman wasn't pleased about playing an exhibition in Berlin, but S.R. loved it. Mrs. Sol Rubin was well aware of that.

"Think of it, Bunny," S.R. had told his wife on their arrival Tuesday at their Adlon suite, "a Jew being welcomed back to Germany."

Veronica "Bunny" Rubin had laughed. "Yeah, probably by some of the same Hun bastards who 60 years ago would have tossed your ass in the gas chamber."

S.R. let his wife's cynical remarks go without comment.

Bunny knew that her husband and his coach survived a love-hate relationship. As long as the Sharks won, and Sol provided the money for the talent, they co-existed. In public, they played the role of equal partners in the success of the franchise, but in private they took digs at each other.

Bunny had been a witness to two telling incidents.

On the Sun Air charter flight back to Miami following a win in Indianapolis, S.R. had been drunk as usual. He was seated in the first-class cabin, and the flight attendants knew enough to keep his martini glass full. Bunny was still in the lavatory when the plane landed. When she returned to help her husband, he had already left his seat and staggered onto the jet-way as Sherman and assistant coach Jim Moses watched.

"I hope S.R. isn't driving himself home tonight," Moses said.

"Why?" Sherman snapped.

Unaware that Mrs. Rubin was behind them, the two coaches had laughed heartily as they followed the staggering drunk into the airport lobby. Bunny admitted she had to put her hand to her mouth to repress joining in the laughter—and maybe the hope?

Then there was the owners' meeting in Chicago. The league had forgotten that the American Legion convention took place the same week. Hotel space was scarce. She was in the lobby with her husband just when the Sharks' public relations director T. George Cockerill III had reached the owner.

"S.R., we have a problem," reported Cockerill. "You have your suite, but there isn't even a room available for Coach Sherman."

"Now that's a shame," S.R. had replied. "I guess when it comes to finding a room in this city, we'll see if Sherman can really walk on water."

Therefore, Bunny wasn't surprised by Sherman's reaction during an interview after practice Friday afternoon in Berlin Stadium.

Bunny liked to see the young studs in action at practice. *I wish I were sleeping with some of them. They are so lean and athletic. Me? I have this old fat slob who can hardly get it hard.*

The owner's wife mingled with the reporters at the edge of the practice field.

When Cunill asked the coach what he liked about the Berlin trip, he exploded.

"Nothing but a goddamn waste of time. It's only the league and the owners that love these international games."

Bunny shook her head in disbelief as the coach rambled on.

"They make a lot of money because the dumb foreigners don't know anything about American football. Meanwhile, it's a bitch to keep 80 players focused on football with all those Nazi whores bothering them. I'm already tired of this Kraut food. Give me a good ol' American T-bone any time."

What a public relations disaster that asshole is, Bunny thought.

Sherman's life was football. Bunny figured the coach didn't know yet that World War II had ended in 1945, and that it was doubtful that any Sharks player would be seduced by a "Nazi whore" old enough to be his great-grandmother. Sherman probably was also unaware that the team hotel—the Adlon—was once on the German Democratic Republic side of the wall. *What a shmuck!*

After practice, Bob spotted a Sharks player at the Adlon bar, enjoying a draft beer. "All alone tonight?" Bob asked as he pulled up a stool and ordered a draft.

"You aren't so dumb for a sports writer," said Siegfried von Katzen, the Sharks Berlin-born place kicker. "God, even you sports writers know about German beer."

The columnist laughed. "Guess you think Sherman is dumber? He had the airline stock his suite with Coors."

Bob understood that kicking specialists suffered a lonely life. Unlike the straight leg kickers of the earlier days of the game, who had been football players, the specialists had soccer backgrounds. He knew that the coaches and players treated von Katzen as a non-player until his foot could decide the outcome of a game. The kicker had become friendly with Bob because the columnist could speak German.

"You enjoying your homecoming, Ziggy?"

"Yes and no," the kicker replied. "The German media, you know, has featured me on TV and in the papers and magazines. Hey, I was born in Berlin, but my mother divorced my father when I was only five. Then we moved to America. I was actually brought up an American. I got a soccer scholarship to Indiana University. Hell, my wife Cindy doesn't even speak German."

#

It was strange Saturday in a press box dominated by the German media. Only a handful of the South Florida media made the trip, because their bosses knew that the trip amounted to a free week's vacation in Berlin. The *Miami P.M.* had sent Casey and the beat writer, Cunill, while the rival *Miami Morning Journal* assigned only its beat writer, Roberto Castro.

Bob knew that Cunill and Castro had family ties to Cuba, and both spoke fluent Spanish and English. Despite their similar backgrounds, the two sports writers were only cordial to each other, not friends.

"If it is true that opposites attract, then this would explain the friendship between Jorge and me," Bob had once explained to Bloom. Bob considered Jorge a stereotypical Latin lover with his black, wavy hair and macho mustache. Bob admitted he was envious of Cunill. Perhaps even a bit jealous.

Jorge was an immaculate dresser, and clothes fit well on his sleek six-foot, 180-pound frame. He was a proud family man with a wife and two children. He had a master's degree in journalism from Columbia University, and he could be working for any major newspaper in the United States. Miami was his home, and the *Miami P.M.* was his kind of rag.

Cunill and Casey had that special friendship. They didn't suffocate each other, but would always be there for one another.

Jorge called Bob a "gringo," and Bob nicknamed Jorge "Wetback." Both had a sense of humor, and frequently played harmless practical jokes on each other.

Well. . .*almost* harmless.

When Bob had a flight attendant write a love letter to Jorge and mail it to the sports writer's home, his wife tossed him out of his house for almost a week until Bob confessed. Jorge got even by picking up a $534 hotel bar tab on a trip to New York and charging it to Bob's room.

On this trip, however, Jorge brought his wife, and they did the tourist things when he wasn't at practice. Bob missed having dinner, smoking a cigar, and hearing Cunill talk about his Cuban background and how his grandparents had fled Havana when Castro took over the little island nation in 1959.

Bob regretted that Jorge couldn't spend the next week with him doing the beer halls of Munich.

Bob had been hesitant in sharing the Longo gambling rap with Jorge. He was hesitant in sharing the accusation with anyone but Bloom back in Miami. But he had shared it with Jorge. What he needed now was more evidence that Longo was a bad guy.

#

The Germans in the Berlin Stadium press box were eager to learn the mystery of American football.

"Americans want offense, lots of offense," Bob explained to Kurt Vogel, a reporter for the *Berliner Morgenpost*. "They think soccer is a bore with all those 1-0 games."

"Ja, Herr Casey, but I think our football is more exciting," Vogel said. "In American football, you run one play, and then the players rest for 40 seconds."

The Miami Sharks were running out the clock Saturday. They were in front of the Boston Minutemen 35-17. As it was the first exhibition of the preseason, both coaches cleared their benches early in the second half to play the free agents and other marginal talent on the 80-man rosters.

Bob had lost interest early in what he considered a meaningless practice. His Sunday column was done and in the laptop, waiting to be sent over the phone lines to *Miami P.M.* Jorge was banging out his game story on a battered IBM laptop, slowing only to check his notes on the play-by-play sheets.

"Damn! What a piece of junk," moaned Jorge. "I wish Bloom would let me have a new laptop."

Bob smiled. *I know what I'm going to get Jorge for his birthday. A new Apple iBook. He'd go bonkers over a tangerine one.*

Using his Zeiss field glasses to scan Berlin Stadium, Bob noted that most of the 68,000 spectators were still in their seats, as if the game meant something. The stadium seated 110,000, but the turnout was a tribute to the growing worldwide popularity of American pro football. This was the site of the 1936 Olympics.

Bob closed his eyes to imagine that there was a time warp that would send him back to yesteryear. There was Hitler in the Führer's box with a horde of Nazis in black and brown uniforms surrounding him. There was the band playing *Deutschland Uber Alles* and the *Horst Wessel Leid*. There was Jesse Owens, the humble, black track star from Ohio State, embarrassing Hitler's Master Race by winning four gold medals for the United States.

Bob tried to envision being a sports reporter there in 1936. He would have reached Germany by ship and rail. He would not have had the aid of a tape recorder for interviews. He would have used a portable typewriter, and his copy would have been entrusted to the German telegraph version of the old Western Union. He wondered if the Dr. Josef Goebbels' propaganda staff would have censored his column? Probably.

Americans beat up on foreign tyrants for censoring the press, but there was still censorship in the U.S.A. Censors ranged from publishers, editors, and advertisers to political groups. Bob believed the biggest censor of all was the end of newspaper competition that resulted in cities with one daily and chain ownership.

The bottom line of the bean counters discouraged enterprise reporting. That was why working for Andy Lyon's Kangaroo News Ltd., the parent company of *Miami P.M.*, was a throwback to the good old days of newspapering.

A German Federal Republic Army band in the stands broke Bob's daydream with a rendition of the Notre Dame fight song. Now his mind was back on gambling and Longo. And time was running out.

Sherman had seen all he needed of Longo in one series. The quarterback had unloaded a 15-yard touchdown pass to wide receiver Johnson with two minutes gone in the first quarter.

The exhibition came mercifully to an end. The lucky gladiators would soon be at the airport for their nine-hour charter flights back to Boston and Miami.

Jorge and his wife would fly back with the Sharks. He had to return to the boredom of another month of summer camp and exhibitions.

"You flying home tonight?" asked Vogel, the *Morgenpost* sports reporter, interrupting the American's thoughts.

"No, I'm staying over for another week. I have vacation. I'm going to Munich to spend every day and night in the Haufbrauhaus."

The German laughed. "Ja, ve know how you Amerikanisher journalists love to drink."

"Especially one with an Irish name," joined in Holger Obermann, a German TV sports director.

"I'm not a journalist," snapped Bob in a good-natured manner. "I'm a goddamned newspaperman! A journalist has a master's degree from an Ivy League school, carries a Gucci handbag, and marries a National Organization for Women member. I'm a Zeitungman!"

"Ja, you definitely are not a journalist," Obermann agreed. Others seated nearby laughed.

Bob wanted to explain how his mother—a German born in this city—had married his father, a GI who was part of the U.S.

occupation forces here following World War II. He didn't even bother to try. Everyone had work to do in filing stories and getting interviews in the locker rooms.

Bob skipped the locker room ritual and transmitted his column by connecting his laptop to a phone line. It was 10:00 p.m. in Berlin, but only 4:00 p.m. back in Miami.

What's my next move on the Longo matter? I'm fucking off, I know, with this week in Munich. Am I suffering job burnout?

#

The Adlon bar was nearly deserted. It was August in Berlin, and most of the upscale residents were on vacation. The departure of the Sharks had returned the hotel's public places to a degree of quiet and sophistication. Still, a piano player banged out Big Band American music while the bartender looked a bit bored.

"Eine gross bier?" the bartender asked.

"Nien, Herr Ober," Bob said. "Bitte. . .oh, give me a double Hennessy XO straight up."

"Ah, an Amerikanisher," the bartender said as he poured the cognac into a Waterford crystal snifter. "You here to write about the Amerikanisher football game?"

"How'd you guess?"

"Mein Herr, on your belt there is a ticket saying Press."

Bob laughed.

"Anyhow," continued the bartender, "I am a fan of the Green Bay Holsteins. We watch your football on AFN-TV (U.S. Armed Forces Network), you know. The Holsteins are, you say, super. Like our dairy cows, a goot Deutscher namen, ja?"

The bartender complimented the American on his German. The two men laughed because the bartender still recognized him as an American. Bob removed a cigar from his case and clipped off the end of a Canones' Churchill. The bartender was quick to offer a match.

"Havana?" the bartender asked.

"Ja. Can't buy 'em in the States. I bought a box of 20. Cost me almost five hundred Eurodollars."

"You could buy a Porsche sportwagon for that many dollars," the bartender said in a bit of an overstatement as he admired the cigar.

Bob offered a Cuban to the bartender.

"That is most kind of you, mein Herr." His grin showed his pleasure. "I will save to enjoy on my day off tomorrow."

Bob returned to his thoughts, cigar, and cognac, but not for long.

"My goodness, that's a mighty big cigar."

It was a young woman's voice. Her English lacked any trace of a German accent. Bob looked across the bar to the other side to make eye contact with a blonde. She was sipping a black Russian and opening a fresh pack of German cigarettes.

Probably a hooker, he thought. *No one that young and beautiful would be sitting here alone, starting a conversation with me.*

It was hard for the columnist to judge her age. *Probably about 30. What a fox! Wonder what her husband or boyfriend is like? God, could you imagine making love to her? Wow! The only reason she's paying attention to me is that I'm a potential trick.*

Bob tried to ignore her, as the bartender became preoccupied restocking and cleaning the bar.

The woman stood up. She appeared to be a size eight. The two-piece forest green knit suit was conservative, but still did her body justice. He thought she was calling it a night.

Instead, she brought her drink and her cigarettes over to his side of the bar. "You like Big Band music?" she asked.

The German piano player was belting out a rendition of *Don't Sit Under the Apple Tree*, a 1940s American hit song.

Before he could answer, Suzy Mary Peters had joined him on an adjoining stool.

"Look, fräulein, I'm just a poor old American tourist."

The woman smiled slightly. "No, you're not," she said softly, in a warm and almost sexy voice. "You're Bob Casey, the Miami sports columnist."

He was momentarily confused. "The press pass gave me away, huh?" he said while ripping it off his belt.

"No, Mr. Casey. I read your column every day in Miami. I must say, your column photo doesn't do you justice."

Now Bob was embarrassed, and on the defensive. He had come here to get slightly drunk and prepare for Munich. He realized painfully now that his khaki slacks were wrinkled, his running shoes were covered with mud from the stadium turf, and his red polo shirt had mustard stains from the press box lunch of bratwurst.

"It's always nice to meet a reader," he mumbled while trying to concentrate on his cigar and hoping the woman would leave.

Suzy, however, introduced herself. "I fly for Sun Air. I'm on vacation. I hitched a ride on the Sharks charter, because I was too junior to bid for it. I saw you back in coach. You didn't act like a happy camper."

"I wasn't," he said as he began to relax. "So what are you doing here? The team is flying home after the game. In fact, they should be in the air by now." He was sorry as soon as the words escaped, because he sounded like a cop quizzing a suspect.

The piano player changed to ragtime with a rendition of *Alexander's Ragtime Band.*

"I know," she said while gently removing the cigar from Bob's hand. She took a long drag. "Strong tobacco. Cuban?"

Bob nodded as she handed him back the cigar.

"I got bumped," she continued. "The Sharks' owner added some extra passengers who filled the plane."

Bob took a swig of cognac. "So?"

"So, Mr. Casey, I can't catch a pass ride back for a week. And then I have to catch it from Munich, because we normally don't fly to Berlin. So what's a poor working girl to do?"

He shook his head in disbelief. "You mean Rubin packed that cattle car with more passengers? The players must be enjoying the flight home, packed in like sardines."

"Now that you mention it, Coach Sherman was a bit upset," she said. "It was some Miami fan group. Mr. Rubin met them at a party."

"That figures. Rubin was probably drunk as a skunk."

Suzy laughed. "You remind me of my dad. He'd say something like 'drunk as a skunk.'"

"That old, huh?"

"No, silly," Suzy replied with a pleasant smile and briefly brushed his arm with her hand. Bob downed his cognac.

"How interesting. Herr Ober, bitte. What's that you're drinking, Suzy?"

The bartender made a fresh black Russian and poured a Hennessy's XO. He smiled as he realized that the two Americans were fast becoming a romantic number.

#

Suzy wasn't a hustler. She had gone to the hotel bar simply to have a couple of drinks, people-watch, and then get a good night's sleep before going to Munich.

Romance had been the last thing on her mind this late Saturday night. Spotting a familiar person, who appeared to be alone, too, she made her bold move simply for companionship.

There's something special about this guy. Hopefully, he doesn't have a wife and three kids.

Bob's initial rejection added to his appeal, because Suzy was not a swinger.

He's even nervous, she thought. *I like that in a man. No pickup lines, either. It is obvious from the way he is dressed that he didn't come here to pick up women. I enjoy his writing style. He's bright. More importantly, he has a sense of humor.*

The liquor, the tobacco, and the music soothed the pair. They talked easily, mostly about flying and sports. Bob scored more points, because he wanted to talk about Suzy more than himself.

Man, that's a new one. Most guys I date want to impress me. This guy's different.

Suzy did impress Bob. It was more than a sex thing. She laughed easily. Plus, she smoked and drank booze. He liked that in a woman. It was obvious that she was no bimbo. She didn't try to impress him with her knowledge.

What next? Sex? Hell, I just met her. She doesn't appear that desperate. I couldn't be that lucky. She really is a fox.

The bartender smiled as he turned down the lights for closing. The American couple was a bit tipsy, but very friendly as they left.

Bob felt the warmth of his companion's breath against his ear as they swayed toward the bank of elevators. Almost by instinct, he pushed the button for the third floor and his room, 327.

"Where we going, Bobby?"

Suzy's question wasn't demanding. It was sobering enough to make him realize that she might not be in the mood to be seduced.

But Bob was horny, and that made him bold. "My room. And don't call me Bobby. It's Bob."

There was a pause of silence. He was afraid of her reply about their destination. When he looked in her face, she smiled, and asked, "Bobby, do you snore?"

She giggled slightly and affectionately slapped Bob on his butt as he fumbled with his key card. The booze buzz made it seem a bit unreal to be in his room with Suzy.

God, she's just a kid. What the hell does she see in an old fart like me?

#

Suzy wouldn't blame the black Russians for her behavior. True, she was horny, too, and she felt interested in more than a quick romp in the hay with this man. She was excited, but the booze was making her mind cloudy with confusion. At this moment, she wasn't thinking of consequences; she was just glad that she was on the pill. She thought about asking if he had a condom, but that seemed a turnoff to her.

Maybe I'm just a one-night stand, but my instincts tell me this guy is going to be something special. Hell, I'm almost 30. Maybe it's time I took a chance on romance before it passes me and I become another Mary Rich.

The room door swung open. Bob struggled to find the light switch, but failed. Suzy stood on her toes to embrace him. He could feel her firm, young body under the two-piece knit as she rubbed her breasts against his chest. Her first soft kiss tasted of a mixture of cigarette smoke and booze. It didn't matter to Bob. It was delicious.

Suzy made the first move. Her boldness surprised her. She zipped down his fly with her left hand while holding onto his neck with her right. The tingle of her hand on his organ excited him. He reacted by nibbling on her lips while reaching inside the knit top to release her bra. His mouth hungrily devoured her nipples that swelled in passion. He had to bend over to pull down her short skirt, black half-slip, and black panties. Suzy staggered, kicking the garments off her ankles. All the while, they French kissed, passionately building toward a climax that both wanted to delay as long as possible.

"Can we make it to the bed?" she moaned, rubbing his hard penis against her thighs.

"I can't wait," he replied breathlessly.

Suzy didn't want him to come too quickly. But she couldn't gamble. So she slowly pulled him inside her. He staggered as his khakis lay tangled around his ankles. The two became one as he pulled her tighter with one hand around her thighs while the other groped for the bed.

They eventually landed on the bed, where she wrapped her firm legs around him. Even in the dark hotel room, they made eye contact that instantly confirmed both shared the same hunger, the same passion.

Her Catholic upbringing briefly made her feel ashamed for making love to a man who wasn't her husband. *Having a man inside me may be sin, but it is heaven to me at this very moment.*

She could no longer control herself. "Give it to me, Bobbie, fuck me!"

Suzy, who rarely uttered profanity, found herself completely uninhibited in her excitement. She heard Bob moan, and she started moving. As one, the couple rolled over.

"Let me be on top," she pleaded.

He was too excited to respond verbally. His reply was a struggle to roll over again and exchange missionary positions.

The passion and the booze put them to sleep wrapped in an embrace.

#

She awoke first. It was hard to tell the time of day, because of the blackout curtains. She had a mild headache, and her mouth felt like a sewer.

She leaned over and looked at her lover. She brushed his cheek and smiled as she felt the growth of whiskers. Her instant concern was that he might want her to leave, now that they both were sober.

"What kind of razor do you use?" she asked softly.

Bob opened his eyes slowly. His head was pounding from the hangover. At first he wasn't sure if the woman's voice was real or if he was dreaming. It was too dark to see Suzy. The touch of her hand confirmed that this wasn't a dream.

"Razor? Ah, I use a Gillette. Why? You want to slit my throat? You want to shave your legs?"

"No, silly. Just curious. My father uses the same kind of razor."

Bob was now wide awake, and he reached out for the naked woman. They embraced gently. She realized he was a gentle and caring man. This could be the end of all the one-night stands with guys who said they weren't married but were.

A sudden terror struck her in her stomach. "Bobby, are you married?"

"Why, Suzy? Would that make a difference?"

She jumped out of the bed and turned to face him. "You bastard! You *are* married. You. . ."

Bob realized his smart-alec answer had triggered the wrong reaction. "Am not. I've been divorced for almost eight years."

"You. . .you're not married?"

Bob nodded reassuringly. "Honest, Suzy, honest."

Relieved, she climbed back into bed. "Why did you and your wife split?" she asked as her body relaxed, and she enjoyed the strength of a man's arms around her.

"She wanted me in a normal job, like public relations," he explained. "You know, a respectable job with good pay and normal working hours. She couldn't accept that I'm a newspaperman. The hours suck, and so does the pay. I'm away on most weekends covering some game or event. Betty couldn't cope with that. Frankly, I can't blame any woman for not wanting to be married to a newspaperman. The newspaper is kind of like a mistress. . ."

Since the airline life was hardly a normal routine, Suzy shook her head in disbelief that some woman would dump a guy like Bobby.

"She moved out one weekend when I was covering the Sharks in Kansas City," he continued. "Great homecoming. She married a lawyer. Now she's driving a Jaguar convertible and living on Fort Lauderdale Beach."

"Did you love her?" Suzy asked.

Bob pondered the question. "Oh, I don't know now. I thought I did when we married. I was hurt, of course, when she dumped me. I guess I'm not the best catch. You ever been married?"

"No, silly," she said with a cute smile he was growing attached to. "I've had offers. Most were from boys or old men. Most guys your age are married or divorced with several kids. Most guys, you know, are interested in one-night stands. Passengers mostly. They have a thing about getting it on with a flight attendant."

He asked her why she had chosen to be a flight attendant.

"I graduated from Trenton State College," she explained. "I was a 4.0 student. My parents were hoping I'd become a teacher and find a husband. I didn't want to teach, and at 21 I wasn't ready for marriage. Oh, I guess I wanted travel and adventure. So I answered a classified in *The Trentonian* for Sun Airlines, because the base would be Miami. That sure beat living in New Jersey.

"Course, dummy me didn't know then that Sun Air has crew bases in New York, Houston, and Los Angeles, too. I spent my first five years based in New York, sharing a down-scale apartment, at $2,000 a month, a mile from La Guardia Airport with three other flight attendants."

They had been together less than 24 hours, and both were running motor-mouthed. Suzy wondered how two total strangers could suddenly be talking like long-time lovers.

Suzy felt good, warm, and most importantly, comfortable with him. *Never in my life have I paraded around naked in front of a man.*

Her experiences were few and not very fulfilling. It was probably because she was a romantic, and most guys just wanted to get into her panties, and they had treated her like a bimbo. She felt God had given her two crosses to bear, because a beauty with brains scared most men.

She wanted desperately to believe that Bob was different. His willingness to let her dominate their initial lovemaking was remarkable. She felt she knew something about the man after reading his column for nearly five years. She didn't. *He's almost the complete opposite of the way he writes. This is the man I want; no, this is the man I could marry.*

#

Bob understood her shock of New York City living for wage and hour folks. Not that life was cheap in South Florida, but there was no comparison to living in Gotham.

"I'm from Upstate New York," he said. "I'm not a big city guy either. I started as a sports reporter with the *Albany Knickerbocker News*, moved on to New York, then Boston, and then I was seduced by the sun and sand of Florida—" He stopped in mid-sentence.

Looking into her eyes, he struggled to say what was most on his mind. "I know this is premature. I mean, you know. . .well, I think I'm very fond of you, and. . ."

She stopped him short, gently placing her trigger finger to his lips. "I kinda feel the same way, Bobby. Let's not rush this. If we are meant to be, we will be married in six months."

Bob was stunned. "Married? Not living together? Married? Did you say. . .married?"

Suzy nodded. "None of that shack-up stuff, thank you. If you want Suzy, you will have to make her an honest woman."

He was overwhelmed by the turn of events in his life. A few hours ago, he was wondering if he would ever get laid again. Now he had a dream girl talking marriage.

Was it a dream? Good grief, what did he know of this woman? Would they be compatible? He had to know quickly.

"I used to get my ex-wife pissed because I would leave the toilet seat up," he said to break the mood. "So I'm hardly a candidate for NOW's Male of the Year award. . ."

Suzy didn't hesitate to reply. "I promise you I can pull the seat down, and I won't fall in. Look, you have bad habits, I have bad habits. So what? Life is a series of compromises, and so is marriage. As for the women's liberation thing, don't get paranoid because the NOW president is a former Pan Am flight attendant. She's also a lesbian. My father wears the pants in our family, and I expect the same from my husband!"

Suddenly they were bombarded by the blare of Wagnerian music.

"My God, Suzy, I don't hear fireworks, but I'm engulfed by the music of love."

"You silly, the clock radio just went off. We've been awakened by the *Ride of the Valkayres*."

"Are you my mein Brünnhilde?"

"Ja, mein Siegfried," she replied, impressed with his knowledge of classical music. *So he knows Wagner and Der Ring des Nibelungen. He sure isn't the stereotype of a sports writer.*

The two lovers sat up naked in the bed. They started to laugh uncontrollably. Then they noted that the clock said it was 1500 Uhrs.

"Good Lord, we've slept until three p.m.," she said.

"Looks like we'll have to take the night train, after all," Bob said.

"Coffee, Munich, or me, Mein Herr Siegfried?" she offered.

"I'm greedy, Fräulein Brünnhilde," he replied. "I want all three."

"You've got them, Herr Siegfried. We could fly on Lufthansa to Munich. I can get us passes."

"Nien, Fräulein Brünnhilde," he replied. "Ve vill ride the night train and enjoy the sleeping compartment. Ja?"

"Well, I've always wanted to make love on a train," she replied with enthusiasm as she leaped from the bed. "For now, I've got the bathroom all to myself."

He expressed mock anger by hurling a pillow at the naked young woman skipping playfully to the bathroom. The pillow missed.

"You're no Johnny Longo," she said, blowing him a kiss.

The Longo remark brought him back to reality. He realized he had to make a decision soon.

As soon as I get back to Miami, I'll lay the problem on Larry. For the next six days, the only important thing is Suzy. I can't believe I'm putting a woman before a major exclusive story, but I am.

CHAPTER 5

"[Gambling] is the child of avarice, the brother of iniquity, and the father of mischief."

George Washington

THE DC-10 WAS on autopilot as the Sharks charter left Europe's sky in the early Sunday morning hours. Its three engines cruised at 475 knots at 32,000 feet.

"Crossing the Big Pond now," First Officer Eddie Hickox said.

"Roger, set 247 as our outbound course. When ATC advises, tune in and identify Newfoundland Center," the captain said.

"Autopilot on. Cruise check, please."

"Cruise power set, Captain. Oxygen set at 100 percent."

"Roger. See if we can get a bit higher, Eddie."

"You want to go to manual, Captain?"

"Keep it on autopilot, Eddie."

As chief pilot, Dick took the football charter because his pal Casey would be a passenger. Plus, it had been a week's layover with pay and per diem.

Vince Lombard was a Sharks fan, and he regularly bid for the charters. Hickox was a senior first officer waiting for the next opening to move into the left seat. The conversation switched to the Sharks' coming exhibition with the Green Bay Holsteins.

"What's the morning line?" Eddie asked.

"Green Bay by seven," the engineer quickly replied.

"I'll put a couple of bucks on the Sharks with seven points," the captain said. "Miami will kill Green Bay by a couple of touchdowns." He made his point by reaching into his trouser pocket and pulling out two crumpled dollar bills.

"You'd be right in the regular season, Captain," Vince said. "But this is the funny season, or exhibition season. There is no pressure on Sherman to win, and Longo will see only a quarter of the action."

Dick and Hickox glanced at each other but said nothing. They would listen to the gambling expert and learn.

"On the other hand," continued the engineer, "Green Bay has a rookie coach in Danny Ryan, and a helluva quarterback war between Jake Scott and Tommy Jankovich."

Dick was impressed with the football betting know-how of the engineer. It was obvious that he was aware of the guidelines that professional handicappers used to determine point-spreads.

"Look, guys, there is no secret to betting on football," Vince explained. "When preparing for this IFL season, forget about last year. Think about the off-season. What teams made big moves in free agency? What teams drafted well?"

Unlike commercial flights, the cockpit door remained open, and players, coaches, and camp followers would occasionally step in and look in awe at the instrument panel.

Dick knew that the crew, especially the flight attendants, loved this association with a pro football team. The young faces of the gladiators were in stark contrast to the senior and matronly attendants working this flight. S.R.'s rules for the German trip had permitted each coach and player to bring a guest.

Heck, even a senior stew like Mary Rich didn't have enough seniority to gain a bid on this trip. Since they kept the aircraft in Berlin, it was a week's layover for the crew.

Dick knew that the old mamma flight attendants probably convinced mothers, wives, and gal pals that their sons and/or mates were safe from being seduced on the eight regular season road trips. It was fortunate for all concerned that Suzy Peters didn't work the flight over. She wore civilian attire, and no one noticed that she used a jump seat on the Miami-Berlin leg of the trip.

#

The players were not happy when they learned that their drunken owner had invited a group of fans to make the return trip with them. The fans' no-frills charter service had suffered a mechanical breakdown, and it had appeared that they could be stranded for a week or more in Berlin until S.R. came to their rescue. The players, who were exhausted and battered by the jet lag and the football exhibition, were forced to give up space in the coach section.

"Airline coach seats are not designed for football players. Maybe for kicking specialists, but not real athletes," Johnny Longo asserted. Only exhaustion prevented a mutiny among the gladiators, who struggled to survive the nine-hour return flight.

Johnny was accompanied by his wife Martha. The Sun Airlines' seat configuration of a DC-10 coach section was 2-5-2. This meant there were two seats, an aisle, five seats, another aisle, and two more seats.

Thus, the players and their guests had been assigned to the two-seaters on both sides of the cabin, while the camp followers were given seats in the middle. On commercial flights, Sun Air could pack 24 passengers in first class and 350 more in coach. But on this charter, Rubin had limited the passengers to 250. Then came the fan group.

#

Martha Longo had wanted to talk to her husband since the jet left Berlin. She was a dedicated housewife and mother of their three kids. They had been married 16 years, and her family was her life. The trip to Berlin was a treat, but she worried about the kids back in the Miami suburb of Miami Shores.

She hated to remind her husband of the need for money to pay for Johnny Jr.'s braces while the old washer-dryer needed to be replaced. Martha knew her husband made mega-bucks, but she couldn't understand why she had to struggle with the family budget. Johnny blamed it on taxes.

For the most part, Martha had enjoyed the trip. It had been escapism. But as the flight headed back to Miami, she started thinking about her money woes.

"Johnny, we have to talk," she said after a sip of Coke from a plastic cup.

"Later. I'm bushed."

"Johnny, please," she persisted. "I have bills to pay, and my checking account is nearly empty. Plus, I was embarrassed in Berlin when my American Express card was rejected for a purchase."

"Martha!" he exploded. "For Christ's sake, knock it off. You're sounding like an old hag."

Martha was stunned by her husband's reply.

"You can fool others about what you're doing with your money," she said. "But I'm your wife. I know."

"You don't know shit! Just shut your mouth."

Martha started to cry.

"I need another beer," he said as he climbed out of his aisle seat and headed for the serving station. He helped himself to a can of Coors, and when he returned, his wife had turned toward the window and appeared to be sleeping.

He drained the can before he sat down, and returned for another before finally settling down.

The quarterback was relieved that Martha was finished asking questions. He really didn't feel like chitchat, and he especially didn't want to talk about her need for more money. His mind was engulfed in his gambling problem that had become a monster. His visit with Father O'Malley was helpful in that it gave him someone to talk to about it. But Johnny knew he had to get rid of some of his debt.

Augie "Lucky" Syracusa, one of the big guys in the syndicate, personally handled the taking of Longo's football bets. Johnny remembered how, at first, Syracusa had been charming and accommodating. Now he was acting like a real mobster in demanding payment while cutting off his credit line.

The interest alone was killing him. *My God, and people complain about that 22 percent on credit cards. They ought to try dealing with the syndicate boys.*

Other than gambling, Johnny had few vices. He never cheated on his wife. She was good in bed, and she was the mother of their kids. He didn't smoke or do drugs. Only on occasion did he drink, and then it was only a beer or two with the players.

He beckoned to a flight attendant for a fourth can of beer.

This gambling thing had him scared. An injury could suddenly end his career. Both his knees were barely able to support his 36-year-old body. He had been more of a scrambler at Notre Dame, a school that did not play the Pro Set offense. However, he had learned quickly after being drafted by the Sharks 14 seasons ago that leaving the pocket in the IFL could be a career-ender for any quarterback.

Both knees throbbed, and he wished he had asked Doc Barker to give him a couple shots of painkiller after the game.

Obtaining a fresh beer, the quarterback pulled the tab and took a long swig.

Johnny wished he could stretch out his legs, but after a couple swigs of the beer, his mind went back to paying off the gambling debts.

I can't do it in the preseason. I won't play very much. Maybe in the second game in Boston. That should produce a sizable point spread that I could trim down. I have to convince Syracusa to give me some more credit.

He knew that non-gamblers couldn't understand why people got hooked. Yes, gambling was an addiction, but unlike booze and drugs, it was not done for escapism. For him, it was the thrill of the unexpected. It was the challenge of protecting a risky outcome, but more simply—action! *Playing sports is a gamble*, he reasoned. *You gamble that a blitz is coming. If it is, you win with the screen pass. Hell, every play is a gamble. Winning is like a high, and losing is depressing. Sure there is luck involved in gambling, but as a pro football insider, I should be able to make money, not lose it.*

#

In the first-class section, Sol Rubin had passed out, a victim of martinitis. The owner's wife ignored his loud snoring, and was pleased that he was in such a condition.

Bunny glanced at General Manager John "Jack" Cabot III, who was chatting with Father O'Malley. Sherman and the coaches were poring over notebooks and getting ready to watch films that would soon be ready that morning at the Sharks' training camp.

Seated next to Sherman in the first-class section was Jim Moses, the offensive coordinator.

"What about Longo?" Sherman asked. "Is he going to make it through the whole season? Are there any telltale signs of his age or his bum knees?"

Moses shook his head. "No, Don, I haven't seen any evidence in the practice films or in yesterday's game. But. . . " Moses was the only coach who addressed Sherman by his first name. The rest called him "Coach."

"But?" prompted Sherman.

There was a brief silence while Moses pondered a reply. "I'm hearing some disturbing things about his off-field activities," Moses finally said.

"Such as broads, booze, drugs?"

"No, Don. Gambling."

"Oh, gambling." Sherman took a swig from a can of Coors. "You had me worried there for a while, Jim. I'm not a gambler, not even on fourth-and-short. But, hell, most Americans gamble. Even the good Father O'Malley has bingo every Tuesday night. Our wives even go to bingo, for heaven's sake."

"I think, Don, that Longo is into more serious stuff. Like betting on sports. Maybe even football."

"Jim, Jim. I hear you. It doesn't make any sense. Guys like Longo make too much money these days to risk it all on fixing games or shaving points. Yeah, when we played for peanuts, I could understand why some guys might get involved. Not Johnny. He's a good Catholic. I see him at Mass every morning at our chapel at training camp."

Don Sherman was not a man of the world. His world was pro football 24 hours a day, 365 days a year. His only non-football activity was attending Mass every morning. He read only the sports sections in the Miami newspapers and watched football on TV.

His workday was from dawn to late in the evening, but he managed a 15-minute phone call home at exactly 6:00 p.m. daily. Sherman did bring his wife Gloria on the Berlin trip. She sat in the coach section with the other coaches' wives, including Noreen Moses.

Moses knew Sherman well enough not to push a subject once the head coach had considered it. So he dropped the matter. *Don is probably right. Why would Longo risk his career for some nickel and dime bets?*

"I've got some good news, Don," he said changing the subject.

"What's that?"

"Casey isn't on this flight. He's staying in Germany—"

"Forever?" Sherman interrupted.

"No, Don, just for another week. Cunill told me Casey is on vacation. That means we won't have to read any of his shit for at least another week."

"I hope he gets VD from some German hooker."

"We couldn't be that lucky, Don."

#

On road games, Bunny Rubin made mental notes about the coaches, staff, and players. She was already looking ahead to the day when she would be operating the Sharks. It was important to her to know the strengths and weaknesses of the employees. She was confident of Cabot's expertise about playing personnel. It was the rest of the business operation she was learning by watching, listening, and asking questions.

What a life it must be to be married to a pro football coach! Those guys are never home. They're always watching film. I wonder how often they have sex? I can't imagine Sherman ever having sex.

Thinking about sex always got Bunny aroused. Her breasts were getting hard, and she had a burning desire. She finally left her snoring husband and squeezed into the first-class lavatory. Seated on the toilet, she pulled down her panties and hiked up her knee-length skirt. She closed her eyes, and slowly, ever so slowly, started to rub her clitoris.

She envisioned being on top of Jack Cabot and moving up and down, up and down. She started to moan as her fingers worked faster, faster, and even faster. But before her passion could explode, she let out a shrill scream of ecstasy.

She was saved embarrassment, because at her moment of climax, the captain's voice came over the PA.

"Ladies and gentlemen, this is your captain speaking. In a few minutes, we will be serving a meal. I don't know if this is dinner or breakfast, but anyway we're glad you all are aboard. The sky is clear, and we should even be back in Miami a bit ahead of schedule. In Miami, the temperature is 92 degrees with possible showers."

#

It was warm in Munich. Munich was the third largest city in Germany, and capital of the Free State of Bavaria. The temperature soared to the high 70s by day, and they could see the towering Alps looming to the south. Bob and Suzy were glad they had checked in at the Munich Marriott, which was fully air-conditioned.

Under such conditions, it was almost easy for Bob to forget Longo and gambling. Suzy sure was proving to be a major distraction to work.

Downtown was jammed with tourists. *Every summer day in Munich is like a festival,* Suzy thought. *A carefree spirit infects this city.*

"It is a definite non-Teutonic joie de vivre that most Bavarians refer to as *gemültichkeit*," Bob told her. "Loosely translated, this means eat, drink, and be merry."

Munich was one of Bob's favorite cities. This was Suzy's first visit. She enjoyed it with her lover, sharing his passion and interest in this city of 1.3 million that was like a time warp. Munich boasted of being a cosmopolitan city, yet to her, it seemed more like a fairy-tale city.

"You should be here for Fasching, which I like better than Oktoberfest," Bob said as they strolled through the Marienplatz holding hands. "Beer and sausage is what this city is all about. Some day we'll catch Oktoberfest and go on a 16-day beer-drinking binge."

Suzy laughed. She liked it when Bob said *we*. "Why do they call it Oktoberfest when it takes place the last couple of weeks in September?" she asked.

"Right," he replied. "But the Germans are sure it ends on October first."

They both took long gulps of beer out of their liter glass steins.

"Did you cover the Summer Olympics in Munich?" she asked.

The columnist stopped and turned to her. "Sky Princess, how old do you think I am? The Munich Olympics were in 1972. And I didn't cover the 1936 Berlin Olympics, either!"

#

The age difference didn't bother Suzy. Her dad was 13 years senior to her mom. Ten years was fine. She appreciated Casey's maturity, and she didn't concentrate on his imperfections. He had a great sense of humor, and he made her laugh. She felt very comfortable with him.

Both lovers were dealing with the reality that such a chance meeting had resulted in what both had been searching for: love at first sight.

Not really, Suzy knew. Both had been looking for what each other offered. *Beauty for a woman is like wealth for an old man,* she reasoned. *How do you find someone who really is interested in you as a person?*

Her beauty had been a handicap since high school. She had no trouble attracting men, but not her knight. Leo Peters was her knight as well as her father. He was a career New Jersey government administrator from the old school. He adored her mother Helen, who was a librarian back in their native Princeton, New Jersey, and her parents set the example of what she wanted in the future. They were strict but loving. Her father had a terrific sense of humor. She still regretted the pain she had caused her parents when she had been arrested her senior year in high school on a drug charge.

On prom night, her date had introduced her to pot while parked at a rest stop on the New Jersey Turnpike. She had only taken the first couple of puffs on the joint her date had offered when her act was spotted by the headlights and flashing red lights of a state police cruiser.

She remembered the trip in handcuffs to the state police station and the humiliation of her father bailing her out. Her date's father was a prominent lawyer, and the two kids beat the rap. She had never again come close to drugs.

Bobby was the kind of man she could bring home to her parents. *It is said that you know more about a person the day after the wedding than ever before. I don't buy that theory. If I can share a hotel room and the bathroom with a man for a week, this must be true love. I dig his Irish sense of humor and gift of gab.* Just as important, he was a Catholic. Like her, he was basically a loner.

The days in Munich whizzed by, but Suzy realized she was

becoming more comfortable living with the newspaperman as each day dawned. Was this really true love? *God, I pray it is.*

#

Bob started to relax when it appeared this would not be a one-week stand. He was pleased by his lover's physical beauty, but the bottom line was that she was intelligent. *She not only laughs at my jokes and puns, but she gets the point! We can talk about more than newspapers, sports, and flying.*

He knew he was on the way to his second—but it would be his last—trip to the altar.

"I should take Judge Glickstein's advice, you know," he said as they enjoyed the late afternoon sun and nursed a liter stein of beer at a table in front of the Café Spiegel in the Marienplatz.

"What's that, Bobby? Get a prenuptial agreement?"

He even enjoyed her calling him Bobby. "No, Sky Princess. Hugh's motto is: 'Rent, lease, but never own.'"

Suzy smiled and looked lovingly at the man seated across from her while she poured the remainder of a liter stein of beer into his lap.

"Hey! What the hell. . ."

"Either I keep that via a marriage license, or this will cool off that monster in your trousers."

He squirmed in mock discomfort as the beer slowly soaked his lap. "Only kidding, Suzy, only kidding." He was, of course. He wanted her to be Mrs. Suzy Casey in the worst way. He would have married her in Munich if it weren't for the red tape and the fact that she wanted a small church wedding that her parents could attend.

#

It was on their last night in Munich that a chance encounter would someday prove important to their future.

Hand in hand, they entered the famed beer hall, the

Haufbrauhaus. The cavernous hall was filled with the deafening echo of a brass oomph band and rows of swaying Bavarians and tourists being served by frumpy women in flaring dirndl dresses.

Suzy marveled at the waitresses toting six liter mugs of beer with the six-to eight-inch heads of foam. Bob had taught her that Germans demanded a good head on their beer.

Finding a seat at one of the picnic tables was a challenge. The hall was packed, and most of the tables were filled.

The band, in Bavarian costumes, belted out drinking songs, and the patrons stood with their beer mugs to participate. Bob spotted space at a table near the pretzel stand, and asked, "Ist das frei?"

"Sit down, mister, if that's what you want," came the English reply from an elderly man seated with a woman and two teenagers. The man's accent had a trace of Italian and New York.

"We're Americans, too," Suzy volunteered. "My fiancé speaks pretty good German."

The older Americans nodded.

Bob ordered two liter steins of draft beer and asked if his table companions would mind if he smoked a cigar.

"Enjoy yourself, mister," said the elderly man's female companion. "I even let Sal smoke his cigars at home."

Bob offered the man one of his Havanas.

"I haven't seen one of these since my last visit to Cuba," he said. His smile showed his appreciation for the gift. "You look familiar. Where are you folks from?"

"Miami," Suzy replied without hesitation.

"Say, you aren't the sports columnist, are you?" the man said as he lit the cigar.

"I'm Bob Casey," Bob said, extending his hand. "This is Suzy Peters. I guess she is my fiancée."

"What do you mean, you guess?"

"She is!"

Everyone chuckled.

"I am Sal Gattino, this is my wife Maria, and our grandkids,

Danny and Connie. We live in Hollywood. That's Florida, you know. The kids are our son's. They live on Long Island. They're getting their combined birthday presents with a trip to Germany."

The couple did not appear prosperous. Only the 18-karat gold Rolex on the woman's right wrist and a quality diamond ring on her ring finger would dispute that, Bob noted, but he drew no conclusions. Both had gray hair, and they dressed like blue-collar retirees. So what? They were nice people, he decided.

"They probably wouldn't have come with their old grandparents," continued Maria, "but Sal enticed them with the trip to Berlin to see the Sharks play football. Me? I wanted to go to Rome. Ah, well, when you have grandkids, you make compromises."

Gattino looked lovingly at his wife. "Ah, Mamma, we'll go back to Roma, and you can see the Pope give the Mass." Looking back to Bob and Suzy, he said, "My wife, she is very religious. Good Catholic, you know. Goes to Mass every day at St. Vincent's. I think if she hadn't married me 52 years ago, she'd have been a nun."

Mrs. Gattino blushed and tried to hide her embarrassment by taking a long sip from the liter beer mug.

"Men!" Suzy said to the older woman. "They're all alike."

"No, my Sal is a good man," came the shy but firm reply. "I hope the Blessed Virgin blesses you with a good husband, too. And good children. You know, there is so much divorce today. Even Catholics do it."

"So you're one of Father O'Malley's flock?" Bob said, trying to make small talk.

"You know the father?" Mrs. Gattino asked.

"He's a friend. We had dinner in Berlin. Good man."

"Oh yes, Father O'Malley is a good Irish priest," the old woman said with a trace of disappointment. "I do pray some day we'll have an Italian priest so we can have a Mass in Italian. That's what we had back in Brooklyn. Now they don't even do the Mass in Latin, only English."

The teenagers had beer steins in front of them. They were very happy to escape their grandparents' supervision for a while. They joined with the masses to raise their steins as the band delivered a Bavarian drinking song.

Bob was momentarily lost in the circus atmosphere of the ancient beer hall. But then thoughts of Longo hit him, so he tried to concentrate on German history.

"It was here in the 1920s that Hitler was a frequent speaker," Bob said. "It was hard to imagine that Hitler could cast his evil spell over these beer-drinking, singing, and outwardly happy Bavarians, but the founder of the Nazi Party had obviously found the way."

The Gattinos nodded.

"You covered the Sharks' game in Berlin, Mr. Casey?" Gattino asked.

The question ended Bob's thoughts about the history of the beer hall. "I did the column. Our beat writer, Jorge Cunill, wrote the game story. It was just a meaningless exhibition, you know."

Gattino nodded. "Longo looked pretty good. Looks like Miami will be a title contender again. Of course, from where we were seated in that old stadium, it was hard to see."

"His legs are bad," said Bob. "This could be his last year. I don't know how he's hung in there this long. He must have a lot of guts to play hurting like that."

"That so? I'm not a student of the game like you. I'm just an old fan."

But as the conversation continued, Gattino's questions called for more insider information about the Sharks. Bob should have questioned why this old guy wanted information that only a future opponent or a gambler would want. *Probably he's just a rabid fan.*

The beer and the music were appealing to the young couple. But they had an early flight back to Miami in the morning. The lovers excused themselves and headed back to the Marriott to pack.

"The Gattinos are a nice couple," Suzy said during the short cab ride back to the hotel. "Maybe we will be like that some day. You know, visiting the Haufbrauhaus with our grandkids."

Bob nodded, but his thoughts were now back in Miami and on the Longo matter.

CHAPTER 6

"O judgment! Thou art fled to brutish beasts,
And men have lost their reason!"

William Shakespeare
Julius Caesar

Bob Casey's Working Press:
Football gambling harmless?
Don't you bet on those odds!
MIAMI—It isn't even autumn, but the IFL's practice season continues Sunday in Chicago's Stock Yards Stadium, and already the morning line favors the Miami Sharks by 10 ½ points.

This newspaper, like most others, prints the gambling line on major sporting events.

Why? Because while betting on sports games is against the law in 49 states, many Americans think of it as socially acceptable.

Or haven't you noted the friendly football pools in your work place?

In fact, many politicians see legalizing sports gambling as a cash cow for government. These, of course, are the same politicians who sold us that bill-of-goods on the Florida lottery that would cure all our state's educational financial problems.

The truth about sports gambling is that there is a real need for bookmakers. Guess who controls the bookies? The Mafia. Sorry about that, all you Italian-Americans. I know how you hate it when I mention the Mafia, because you say there really isn't any Mafia.

So before you call, write, fax, or E-mail me, I hear you. There is no Mafia.

According to the FBI, however, illegal sports gambling is a multi-billion dollar racket. And, according to the FBI, this racket is operated by—the FBI said it, not me—the Mafia.

Turn on your radio or your TV. You'll hear or see gambling gurus analyzing pro football games, dissecting point spreads, and giving their "guaranteed lock of the week." They'll list every meaningless statistic in the world, such as, "The Sharks are a tropics team and don't like to play in the cold." See them smirk as they mockingly state the disclaimer that their picks are "for amusement only."

Walk into any local newsstand, and you will find several fat magazines dealing with sports gambling. Read any newspaper's sports section. You'll see the point spreads listed prominently as well as weekly predictions from staff writers as to who will beat those spreads.

"All of this makes you forget that this is legal only in Nevada," says Miami crime fighter, Maj. Leroy Hess. "Even if you place a bet with a legal bookie in Vegas but you make it from Florida, you have violated the law."

Even the IFL recognizes that sports gambling carries the potential to undermine the integrity of its games. That is kind of a joke, however, as long the league permits owners such as Sol Rubin to go unchallenged with his love of casino gambling.

This is a wake-up call, America!

> There is a time bomb set and ticking somewhere in the IFL. When it explodes, it will blow open one helluva scandal involving point-shaving and game-fixing.
>
> I have reason to believe that there are IFL players who could be induced to shave points, and even to throw games. Please don't buy that line from the league that "Our players are too well paid to jeopardize their careers."
>
> There are IFL team owners, such as Miami's Sol Rubin, who are notorious gamblers. Many justify such conduct by explaining that they can afford it. The Mafia—oh my, there I go again—has a way of getting its Black Hand around even the highest-paid stars.
>
> As Major Hess points out, "When there is enough profit to be made from a fix, the mob can find a way. In fact, there probably have been points shaved and games thrown that may always remain unknown. In football, all you need is a crooked quarterback."
>
> Are you listening, Pete Wilson, or are you going to be another toothless IFL commissioner and the toady to owners such as Rubin?

\#

Casey's column that Friday afternoon was greeted with mixed emotions.

"That fucking cocksucker! I'll sue him and that fucking scandal sheet."—Sol Rubin.

"No you won't, honey. He'd like that. My father used to say, 'Don't get into a pissing contest with someone who buys ink by the barrel.'"—Bunny Rubin.

"Why would anyone print such shit about pro football? Pro football is our national pastime. I always knew he was a goddamn fucking queer!"—Coach Don Sherman.

"No one on this football team would be involved in illegal gambling. Drugs, yes, but gambling, no."—Sharks security agent Paul Dungan.

"All gambling is a sin. No Christian should be involved."—Sharks Fellowship of Christian Athletes leader Norm Amundsen.

"For a white boy, that Casey is pretty smart."—Sharks wide receiver Muhammad Johnson.

"Does that Casey know something, or is he just a loose cannon? Oh, shit! He does know Father O'Malley."—Johnny Longo.

"Merciful Father, I pray that our son Robert is not about to betray his Catholic faith."—Rev. Francis J. O'Malley.

"I will not comment on any story that is printed in that Miami tabloid. We have no gambling problem in the International Football League."—Commissioner Pete Wilson.

"Did some fucking rat tip off Casey? How the hell could he know about Longo? He doesn't. It's just some fiction, like most of the shit in that rag."—Augie "Lucky" Syracusa.

"Sal, did you read Mr. Casey's column today? He seemed like such a nice boy when we met him in Munich. Why does he tell bad stories about the Mafia?"—Maria Gattino.

"Yes, Maria, I did read it. He is a nice Irish boy. But you know that newspaper is kinda like a supermarket tabloid. It's fit only to wrap fish in. So what are we eating tonight?"—Salvatore Gattino.

"He really didn't write this! Bloom, you have to keep Casey in chains. He'll get our ass sued!"—*Miami P.M.* publisher Jack Patterson.

"Helluva column. No, Jack, I don't think Rubin will eject you from your season luxury box."—*Miami P.M.* managing editor Larry Bloom.

"Great piece. That lad's got balls. He should have married my daughter."—Kangaroo News Ltd. CEO Andy Lyon.

"Our paper would never print a column like that."—*Miami Morning Journal* sports writer Roberto Castro.

"Yes, Chief, I am aware that we have a public information officer. I just gave Casey some background stuff. No, sir, I didn't think he'd quote me. But, Chief, you know how those liberal newspaper bastards are. You can't trust any of them."—Maj. Leroy Hess.

#

The phone rang in Bloom's third-floor office at the *Miami P.M.* Building. He dropped the newspaper to answer it, knocking over his cup of coffee. "Shit!" He tossed part of the paper on the desk to act as a blotter.

It was Jack Patterson, the publisher, calling from his fifth-floor executive suite. "Larry, have you read Casey's column?"

"Yeah, Jack. What about it?"

"Oh, God! Larry, my phone is ringing off the hook. I've got Italian-American groups, politicians, and plenty of others screaming at me. How could you let him write such stuff? They're threatening to sue us, cancel their home delivery, and force advertisers to drop us. . ."

Larry lit up another Camel while listening to the hysterical voice on the other end of the line. "Jack, I guarantee our blue-collar audience will eat it up, and so will our advertisers who cater to our blue-collar readers."

"But, but. . .Larry, he even knocked this newspaper for carrying gambling news."

"Geez, Jack, I thought it was nice of him not to nail us for running those massage parlor and escort service ads on the sports pages." Bloom enjoyed it when the publisher was bent out of shape. The veteran managing editor didn't have any respect for Patterson. And why should he? Larry understood that *Miami P.M.* was a big-city tabloid, not some suburban daily that covered sewer board meetings. Patterson didn't know the difference, and never would. The only reason he was in the publisher's office was because he married the boss's daughter.

Larry understood, too, that Australian native Andy Lyon, the CEO of Kangaroo News Ltd., had needed a job for his worthless son-in-law. *So he dumped him in this tropical paradise because he knew I could manage Patterson.*

So he sent Patterson to Miami, but he gave the real editorial power to Larry, a Jewish kid who had started as a clerk and worked his way up on the tabloid *New York Examiner*. It was Larry who had hired Casey from the *Boston Record*. Larry knew Lyon respected him and loved the muck-racking style of the sports columnist.

"Okay, Jack, I'll tell Casey your thoughts," he said after a respectful couple of minutes. "Right now I have a second edition to put out, and we're holding for a new lead on the serial rapist."

Mentally having gone to the rapist story, he could not remember if he'd bothered to say goodbye to the publisher before hanging up and calling City Editor Millie Locastro.

"Millie, love, this is a daily newspaper. I want a fresh lead and angle on our serial rapist."

"Boss, I don't have a fresh lead yet. I've got three reporters working on it. What do you want, fiction or fact?"

"Millie, put Tom Edwards on it. He'll give us a street sale rewrite, and in time to make the second edition."

"But, but. . .I can't give Edwards anything fresh," she protested. Locastro knew, however, that Edwards could write breathtaking fiction, even without new facts. That was why he was *P.M.'s* ace rewrite man. "Okay, boss, Edwards has the ball in his court."

Larry's office was glass-enclosed and to the left of a bank of five elevators on the third floor. From this front corner office, he enjoyed a commanding view of the newsroom. His door was rarely closed, and the blinds were hardly ever drawn. He left the door open when chewing out a reporter, because he wanted to send a message. He was a chain-smoker in a building that was smoke-free by state law, but no one would dare challenge the M.E. in his own office.

He returned to Casey's column while taking a bite of bagel and a sip of fresh, hot, black coffee.

The middle elevator door opened, and out stepped Bob.

"Good afternoon, Bob," Bloom's secretary, Mary Jane Williams, said with a wide smile. "Thank you for your postcard from Berlin. I know the cost is probably buried in your expense account, but I appreciate the thought."

Bob laughed.

"Hey, welcome back, you male Prussian pig!" That greeting came from the city editor. "That column today is going to cost us a lot of Italian-American readers," she called from her workstation in the midst of bedlam, where reporters and desk editors hustled to make the second edition. "As an Italian-American, I don't believe there is a Mafia." Locastro was only kidding, and a smile gave her away.

"Since when did you nice Italian-Americans start reading our scandal sheet?" Bob asked. "They read the upscale daily, *The Miami Morning Journal*. No serial rapists will be found there."

"You're wrong, sports guy. This afternoon, they'll be reading fiction by our resident novelist."

Bob bopped into the M.E.'s office. "Miss me, boss?"

"Why? Did you go someplace?"

"Wait till you see my expense account, an' you'll know I've been out of the country."

The two men grinned as Bob pulled up a chair in front of Bloom's desk. He removed a cigar from his case, clipped the tip, and lit it. It was the only other place outside his cubbyhole of an office in the sports department that he could smoke a cigar.

"Larry, I'm in love. You, my friend, may be the first to congratulate me on my good fortune. I am engaged."

The M.E. pondered the news for a moment. "Come again? You couldn't even get laid two weeks ago by a hooker, and now you're telling me you're going for wife number two?" Larry was careful not to dump his coffee this time. He was so shocked that he just sat in silence and listened to Bob's exhilarated account of his romance. "You mean I spent all that money to send you to Berlin, and you took advantage of me by getting engaged? I better not see any of those expenses on your cheat sheet."

Bob laughed.

Larry couldn't keep up his tyrant act. "This calls for a celebration. Hey, Mary Jane, bring us two fresh coffees," he called out to his secretary. "You got any more bagels and cream cheese left?"

After sharing his Germany tour with the M.E., Bob stood up and closed the office door. "I've got something important to discuss."

"Shit, Bob," you're not going to quit before your contract expires and go to work for the money in TV or something?"

"No, boss. I know when the minimum raise is passed by Congress, I'll automatically get more money."

"Fuck you, you ingrate!" Larry snapped. "What is it, then? You want me for the best man at your wedding? I won't wear one of those monkey suits, even for you."

The columnist hushed his boss and poured out his Longo revelations as the M.E. listened intently, while mulling over in his mind what a helluva story this could be if Casey could pull it off.

"That prick Conte wants five Gs of my money for his tip? That part concerns me, Bob, not spending Patterson's money. But why would Conte give such a story to us for a piddling five Gs?"

Bob shook his head. "My concern, boss, is compromising Father O'Malley. As a Catholic, I really have a problem with that."

"But not as a newspaperman, Bob?" Larry understood Casey's dilemma. He didn't want to push it by saying, *Damn it, Bob, you have a blockbuster scoop!* Instead, he said, "I agree we need more evidence before we print anything. I'm sure you can get it. That way the priest will be off the hook. We don't have to implicate him at all."

"I think I'll have lunch with Leroy Hess today and see what, if anything, he might have or be working on," Bob said. "I'll leave the five-grand matter to you. The Sharks are on the road this Saturday night, so I won't be leaving town, because it's only a meaningless exhibition."

"That's good news. That will save my budget for another week," Larry replied. "But we can't delay. This story is too hot. It could eventually leak. I'd hate to see those bastards at the Brand X Journal get the story first."

As Bob left, reporter Buffy Zei almost ran him over in her excitement to see Bloom. "Mr. Bloom! Mr. Bloom!"

"Cool it, girl," he replied. "What's so important? The mayor get caught in bed with a hooker?"

"No, sir," she said breathlessly. "I've just come back from union headquarters, and Mike Kelly says they're going to strike over at Sun Air."

The news of the airline strike concerned Bob. He wanted to call Suzy and assure her that she didn't have to worry if she was out of work for a while. *Damn! Who will fly the Sharks this season if Sun Air isn't operating?*

#

El Rick's was a blue-collar restaurant with a Spanish name, because the Greek owner wanted the Cuban-American trade. It featured Cuban sandwiches, black bean with rice soup, chicken wings, and beer. It was a favorite hangout of Hess, the commander of Miami Police Criminal Investigations Section, or CIS. CIS was located on the top of the five-story Miami Police Headquarters, which was a two-block walk from El Rick's.

Hess, a strapping six-foot-four, 260-pound career cop, had climbed up the civil service ranks of the 1,200-person department. This was an impressive feat, considering that in an area of affirmative action, he was a white male of German ancestry. However, Bob knew that he was popular with street cops of all races, nationality, and gender because he was a hard-nosed, fearless leader in the field. When an officer on patrol called on the car radio for CIS 701, Leroy never hesitated in speeding to the scene.

Bob understood that the geography of the city of Miami created a jurisdictional nightmare for police agencies in Hialeah, as well as in Metro Dade County. Plus, Miami was always tottering on the brink of bankruptcy, and there remained a demand by some for the city police to merge with the county police agency. The Miami police had recovered from the bad-cops scandals of the early 1980s, but the *Miami Morning Journal's* editorial policy wouldn't let those old scandals fade away. This was in contrast to *Miami P.M.*, which considered every cop a hero.

Leroy was already on his first draft beer when Bob sat down in a corner booth.

"You always drink on duty?" Bob asked.

"Screw you, you dumb Mick," Leroy replied. "Who's buying lunch today?"

"Me."

"Shit! That means Bobby-boy needs something. You get another speeding ticket? If the Florida Highway Patrol tagged you, I can't fix it. That yellow ass-catcher of a Corvette can be spotted by a cop a mile away."

Bob and Leroy made lunch an almost weekly occasion. Bob loved the Cuban sandwiches and the black bean soup. While the major was a great source of news, the columnist enjoyed the hard-nosed street cop who either loved you or hated you. With Leroy Hess, Bob had found, there were no shades of gray. If he loved you, Leroy would go to hell and back for you.

Bob trusted the major. After all, Larry had risked getting in trouble with the top brass for feeding him information.

"That damn column today must have pissed off a lot of wop dirtbags," the major observed. "Do you have a concealed weapon permit, Bobby? If you don't, I'd get one."

Bob laughed, and then turned serious. "Leroy, I'm sorry you got your ass chewed out by the chief. Now I need some more help."

The major showed no emotion. "You campaigning for my early retirement? Okay, you're buying lunch."

Bob smiled and nodded.

"Okay, Bobby, what can I do for you?"

The columnist poured out all he knew about Longo's gambling problem.

"No one ever listens to us cops when we talk about the evil of sports gambling," Leroy said while he continued eating. "The $2.5

million gambling debt didn't surprise him, either. "We have guys in this city who make fellows using the $10,000 window in Vegas look like pikers when it comes to betting with bookies on sports."

"The IFL claims that guys like Longo make too much money to risk their career on such addictions," Bob said.

"You don't really believe those IFL cocksuckers, do you?" said Leroy, with a bit of a sneer in his voice. "Pro jocks are no different than any other people. They get caught with their pants down, do drugs, and get hooked on gambling.

"Some of these players were snared in college by the Mafia. The fucking college organizations raid the ghettos and make these kids play for free. At least the fucking IFL is honest in that it shares the wealth. How do you think those poor kids survive at our state's football factories? Alumni and other supporters take care of them, that's how. A car, clothes, spending money, broads, and even drugs. Later, if they make it to the pros, there will be a payback. But you know the saddest part, Bob? No one really gives a shit."

The columnist had no argument with the major about the mob's in-roads into college athletics. The Mafia worked like the CIA in recruiting coaches, players, and officials to work for them. Greed, blackmail—you name it, and the mob had the way to shave points and throw games.

"Bob, do you think dirtbags like Augie 'Lucky' Syracusa, Tony 'The Snake' Costa, Salvatore 'The Saw' Gattino. . ."

"Hold it, Leroy. Did you say Salvatore Gattino? He's not the same nice, old grandfather who lives in Hollywood, is he?" Bob had dropped his Cuban sandwich into his half full bowl of soup, and his expression concerned the major.

"Yeah, Salvatore 'The Saw' Gattino," Leroy asserted. "He's a fucking don. He's connected with the Lorenzo family in New York and lives in Hollywood, Florida."

"A don living in Hollywood?" Bob asked in disbelief.

"He's in charge of gambling in the Southeast," the major continued, after a pause for a swig of draft beer. "He started as a hit man. Likes to use a chain saw and send the remains home to the victim's family in the trunk of a car."

"Can't be," Bob protested. "Gattino is an old man with a wife and grandkids."

"Right," snapped Leroy. "And Hitler had a mother, married his mistress, and loved dogs."

Bob shook his head and told his companion of the meeting in the Haufbrauhaus.

"If I was porking some hot stewardess, I wouldn't have paid any attention to learning the identity of some old wop either," Leroy said with a knowing grin. "Are you serious about this broad, or just looking to fly free on Sun Air?"

This was one time Bob wasn't amused by Leroy's' earthy commentary. "Do you think Longo owes Gattino?" he asked.

The major sensed the serious tone of the question. "I may be wrong, but I don't think so." The major had served 11 years in the Special Investigations Section, or SIS. Bob used to rib him about being a poor imitation of the once-popular TV series *Miami Vice*.

Hess had worked with Dade and Broward vice units to keep track of Gattino, who lived in Broward County.

"The Mafia has learned that they don't benefit from negative publicity," the major said. "Gattino isn't a dumb wop. He's old-time mob, but he's sharp, very sharp. Our intelligence indicates there may be a territorial dispute brewing between the New York and Detroit families."

"You mean an old-fashioned gang war right here in South Florida?"

"Just like *Miami Vice*," Leroy said. "And if you're a betting man, put your money on Gattino. This underboss avoided the limelight and was one of the most elusive dons in the United States. He seldom has seen the inside of a prison cell, despite the considerable efforts of state and federal agents.

"He started his crime career as a lowly gunman for the Lorenzo family in New York. He quickly became more valuable after he helped the family get into New York boxing. However, boxing popularity faded from the Friday night cards to an occasional pay-per-view TV production."

Bob gave the major his full attention.

"Gattino got Mafia-controlled managers listed with the New York State Athletic Commission, and soon they were maneuvering fighters through mismatches and fixed fights, and then ripping off more than the standard one-third fee from the fighter's purse," Leroy said.

Bob pulled out a reporter's notebook and started taking notes as Leroy continued.

"He rose quickly to become a top *caporegine*, or lieutenant, for Santo 'Cigar' Lorenzo, who sent him first to Havana where he gained experience in gambling. After the fall of Batista, Gattino moved over to the east coast of Florida, where he organized widespread gambling and opened several posh hotels.

"By the early 1990s, Gattino was managing a multi-million dollar gambling empire in east Florida. The Lorenzo family owed Gattino, because it was he who had personally gunned down 'Little Tony' Galante outside the Fort Lauderdale-Hollywood Airport. Galante was trying to oust the older Lorenzo from power."

"Okay, Leroy, but what is a New York family doing in South Florida?" Bob asked.

"Florida had always been an open territory," Leroy explained. "Several families had interests here, but for many, it was the land of recreation as well as retirement, especially in Hallandale, Hollywood, and Fort Lauderdale.

"Gattino has survived by keeping a low profile. No fancy $3,000 suits, no expensive cars, no imposing home. No long felony rap sheet. Many dapper dons are doing time."

Taking a break to order another round of draft beers, Bob asked Leroy for more. "Tell me, Leroy, how does this fucker survive?"

"He never cheated on the Lorenzo family, and his operations rarely resulted in problems, only profit," Leroy continued. "He never cheated on his wife or treated her poorly. Her love and loyalty ensured his safety."

Bob wondered: *How many other dons have been done in by ex-lovers and bitches for wives?* But his real concern was finding proof that Longo was indeed in hock for gambling debts.

"Look, Leroy, I need a small favor. . ."

The major smiled. "Like?"

"Some proof that Longo is betting on pro football. And maybe. . ."

"Yeah, Bob, maybe I can dig up some dirt for your scandal sheet," interrupted Leroy. "Don't bother to quote me. I'll check with some of the boys and see if we have any ongoing investigations."

"Thanks, Leroy. Oh, also could I get you to check other law enforcement agencies?"

The major gave him a dirty look, but Bob knew he'd do it when Leroy said, "Scoop, pick up the check. And leave a healthy tip, too."

#

A week later at the Fort Lauderdale/Hollywood Airport, Gattino waited to board a Sun Airlines flight to New York. He had a problem, and he had plenty of time to think about it in the airport.

He realized that the problem was Syracusa, a young and overly ambitious *sagarrista*, or foot soldier, from the Detroit family who was threatening to screw up not only Gattino's sports betting operation, but the worldwide gambling operation of all the families. Sal knew he had to take action, but not without permission.

Syracusa has Longo in his clutches, and my worst nightmare is that Syracusa might get the quarterback to shave points. Or worse yet, throw a game or two.

Gattino understood that at five-foot-six, Syracusa was a loud-mouthed, hotheaded goon, but he had managed to capture the attention of Detroit's number two mob boss, Vincent Perrone.

Syracusa had been involved in eliminating some problems in Chicagoland, and Perrone had rewarded him with a posting in South Florida, where he was expected to become involved in the construction business by controlling the unions.

Informants had told Gattino that Syracusa, once a small-time gambler, had been doing some freelance sports betting out of his Fort Lauderdale apartment, which was how he met Longo.

Gattino remembered when the Chicago and Detroit families controlled most of the Mafia enterprises in Florida, but the New York family gained control of sports betting following a late 1980s mob war in the Northeast.

The nerve of that cocksucker Syracusa! This requires a decision by the godfather.

Al Capone started the Chicago connection in the 1920s, and the Detroit family moved much of its operation south after some major crime crackdowns in Michigan during the 1950s. So Gattino knew this was a delicate matter. A miscalculation by him could lead to another war, and the New York family wasn't strong enough in Florida to win a bloodletting. This required a visit to the godfather.

As it was his custom to keep a low profile, Gattino was booked inconspicuously in coach on Sun Airlines Flight 401 to La Guardia. He recognized Peters as a member of that flight's cabin crew. Most flight attendants avoided him. His wife Maria said it was because he used too much garlic, and he dressed in old-fashioned suits. Old men flying coach were of no interest to young stewardesses.

"Why Mr. Gattino, what a nice surprise," Suzy said with a warm smile. "You going to visit the grandkids in New York?"

He smiled. "You remember?"

"And how is Mrs. Gattino?"

"She's fine, but she doesn't like to fly," he said. "It was a great accomplishment to get her to fly to Germany."

He was flattered that Peters recognized him from their brief Munich visit. He had asked for a glass of milk to go with his pills, and had been ignored by the other flight attendants. Suzy, who was working in first class, had spotted him and had come back to coach to visit.

Nice girl. She shows me respect. And she doesn't even know me. Some day maybe I can do her a kindness.

But that boyfriend of hers was a real cocksucker. Why would a nice girl get involved with a fuckin' yellow journalist?

At New York's La Guardia Airport, Suzy bid goodbye to the passengers. "Enjoy your visit, Mr. Gattino," she said, handing him a small brown paper bag. "It's a pint carton of milk. Just in case you need to take some pills before reaching your final destination."

The godfather, or boss of bosses—*capo di tutti capi*—Angelo "Seville Row" Lorenzo, however, did not live a Spartan life. He dispatched a black Mercedes sedan with a uniformed chauffeur to meet Gattino at La Guardia and drive him to the Greenwich, Connecticut, estate.

"Mr. Gattino?" The chauffeur had been looking for well-dressed gentlemen at the jetway exit inside the airport. But when the only remaining passenger was the old man in the rather tired brown JC Penney suit, the driver figured it must be his passenger. "I'm Carmine, your driver. You have a nice flight?"

The don quickly sized up the driver. He was armed. He could see the bulge under the driver's black coat. *Probably a nine mm, 15-shot automatic.* Chauffeurs, the don knew, were plausible Mafia "rags to riches" stories. That was because the chauffeur was in a unique position, often knowing more about mob activities than even a consigliere. Chauffeurs such as Carmine were privy to top secrets, and they often became the boss's confidant, even the appointment secretary and, of course, the bodyguard. Not all chauffeurs made it up the organizational ladder. Some went down with their bosses.

As the black Mercedes 600 sedan hurried toward the Connecticut border, Gattino remembered his assassination of a chauffeur back in the late 1950s.

God, what year was it now? I was only a young man. Let's see . . . Eisenhower was president, and the fucking Yankees beat the Dodgers in the Series again . . .

Dick O'Brien had been a New York P.D. vice cop who had infiltrated the mob, but was so overcome by the lifestyle that he became a rogue cop. He eventually became the driver for Carlo Gambino, who aspired to be the "boss of bosses," and Gambino had taken a liking to him.

Gambino had pissed off too many families, and I got the contract. I got 15 Gs for the doubleheader whack. It was at Mary's Italian Restaurant in Brooklyn. Gambino and O'Brien had just finished eating when, wearing a ski mask, I burst out of the kitchen. Gambino had just put a cigar in his mouth when I unloaded both barrels of a shotgun. Gambino died with the cigar still in his mouth.

"Good shooting!" the ex-cop turned mob chauffeur had asserted. It had been the Irishman who had sold out his boss. Earlier that evening, he had phoned their dining location. I calmly reloaded the sawed-off shotgun, turned on the chauffeur, and said, "Fuck you, you Irish rat." Both barrels cut down O'Brien.

The memory of that whacking brought a slight smile to the old don's face as the Mercedes left the Connecticut Turnpike at the first Greenwich exit. His thoughts now turned to the godfather.

Lorenzo's father had been training him to take over the New York family when a team of hit men gunned him down outside a Manhattan restaurant on Christmas Eve, 1991. Shortly thereafter, the son made peace with the Detroit and Chicago families. Young Lorenzo had been arrested for the first time in his life in 1993, and indicted for "giving false and misleading testimony" during four appearances before a Manhattan grand jury. The rap was about labor racketeering. He beat the charge.

It was a modest estate by Greenwich standards. The main house did have eight bedrooms, and there was a servants' house, he noted on the short drive through an automatic iron gate and up the driveway to the main house.

The chauffeur opened the front door of the house. The old don marveled at the Italian tiles and beautiful dark woods as he entered the English Tudor-style building. It reminded him of a movie star's palace. He had been here before, of course, but every time it was still an experience in how the bigshots lived.

Lorenzo didn't wait for the housekeeper to greet the visitor. He was there when the double doors swung open. The two men embraced briefly, and the godfather ignored the strong garlic odor of his visitor. At only 35, he appeared a fashion plate in one of a closet-full of $3,000 Seville Row suits. Thus his nickname, coined by the tabloid press. Today, it was a double-breasted gray with white pinstripes. He didn't look or act like the Hollywood version of a godfather. He impressed Gattino as the CEO of a Fortune 500 company. That was because he ran the family business more like General Motors than the mob.

"Welcome, old friend," said a smiling godfather. "It's been too long between visits. Your flight okay?"

Like his late father, Lorenzo continued to invest in and control many legitimate businesses, along with the old standard mob favorites of gambling, protection, prostitution, labor, and racketeering. Gattino knew Lorenzo did have some standards. His family stayed out of the drug business. It wasn't a moral thing. It was business, the result of the Jews and Italians merging their talents in the 1960s. He simply wanted to avoid gang wars.

Gattino understood that Lorenzo's philosophy was to let the spick, nigger, and raghead gangs do that shit. *We Italians and our Jew pals are doing fine without all that heat, thank you.*

He also knew that the charming young man seated across the 12-chair formal dining room table was no wimp. He could be ruthless with his underlings, telling henchmen he would blow up their houses if they refused to obey his orders.

He had engineered the violent deaths of many of his own rivals, so he respected the old don because he had never wavered when it came to murder. He knew gang wars hurt business and drew attention to the mob from the media as well as from the law and aspiring politicians.

Although Gattino was from the old school, working his way up from a wise guy to soldier, etc., Lorenzo appreciated the old don's continued contributions to his family coffers. Additionally, Lorenzo liked Gattino because of the respect the old man showed him. The old don had never hesitated in giving him that, even before his father's demise. Thus, he had been rewarded with the underboss title.

Being Lorenzo's underboss had made Gattino more powerful than many other family bosses. Lorenzo understood that respect came from the fact that both men were born killers who never hesitated to whack anyone who was a menace to the family.

Gattino not only got rid of rivals, but he sent a chilling message, because on several occasions the murders were committed with a chainsaw while the victims were still alive. The body parts were placed in the victims' car trunks, and their vehicles returned home.

"Can you imagine the look on the widows' faces when the cops opened up the trunks and asked them to ID their fucking husbands?" the don once told the godfather. They had both laughed knowingly. To them, murder was part of doing business.

Lorenzo wasn't in any hurry to talk business this afternoon. The two mobsters enjoyed a lunch of pasta and hot sausages, ripping off hunks of fresh Italian bread and sipping a rich red Chianti.

The housekeeper who served the two men noted that both had stuffed their napkins in the top of their collars.

I can see Don Angelo doing that to protect his beautiful suit, the housekeeper had thought. *But that old don's suit looks like he got it from the Salvation Army.*

"You know, Godfather, drugs are destroying the Mafia. Along with the drugs has come more money, but also more greed, more violence, and less honor," Gattino said as he wiped his lips with a napkin. "With the exception of you, gone are the men of honor whose word you believed."

After coffee was served, the godfather dismissed the housekeeper.

"We can stay here in the dining room, old friend," Lorenzo said. "We might want more coffee. So what can I do for you today?"

"Godfather, I have a problem. His name is Syracusa. Since he belongs to the Detroit boys, I didn't want to do anything until I consulted with you."

"If you get my permission, what would you do with this wise guy?" asked the younger man. Mafia protocol required permission before a member could kill. That was the first lesson Gattino had learned when he was inducted into the brotherhood so many years ago.

There was a commission, which was the ruling body in settling disputes amongst families and deciding policy, and on each commission there was a boss. Even the powerful Lorenzo would not bypass the commission.

Gattino did not hesitate. "Cut the fucker's balls off, stick them in his mouth, and feed him to fucking alligators in the Everglades."

The response resulted in an understanding smile. Lorenzo appreciated the old don's direct approach. *No bullshit. Just tell it like it is.* "How, Sal?"

"With my saw, but with a dull blade, Godfather."

Lorenzo laughed knowingly.

"He's a fucking asshole," Gattino summed up. "We don't need to fix any pro football games. We have a gold mine in sports betting now. If youse agree with my plan to expand to the Internet, we can do business with the suckers over computers in their homes. So a scandal involving a superstar like Longo couldn't fuck up our business." Gattino was pleased that his boss listened and understood that greed was often the undoing of any criminal operation.

"You do well for our family, Sal," Lorenzo replied. "You have some good old-fashioned common sense. I like the online betting idea, but we still need a few more computer-literate gamblers. "We do not want the liberal media and the law coming down on us over that stupid football player. How did a good Italian boy like Longo get so fucked up? A Notre Dame boy, too. Should've had the nuns that I had in school. You deal with Syracusa. I have already mentioned him to both Jerry Pritzi in Detroit and Abe Goldman in Chicago."

"What about Syracusa's champion in Detroit?" the don asked.

"Sal, sports gambling is your responsibility in Florida. Jerry and Abe have no problem with that. Jerry thinks Syracusa is an asshole, too. He says he'll talk to him."

"What if he won't listen to even Jerry?" asked Sal.

"Sal," softly replied the godfather, as he fondly placed his right hand on the old don's shoulder, "if he's an asshole, give him a pair of cement shoes. Jerry and Abe have no problem with such a solution. Bad publicity hurts their enterprises, too. I don't want you directly involved."

"Godfather, youse maybe think I'm too old to whack that cocksucker?"

Lorenzo realized that he might have bruised Gattino's pride. He affectionately placed his right hand on the old man's shoulder again. "Hell no, Sal. It's just that you are too valuable for any risk. We need you to get that computer shit up and running. So if this bum won't listen to Jerry, then have him whacked. Call in a professional for the contract.

"Now, how about another cup of hot coffee before your ride back to the airport? Hey, Sal, I think Cookie even has some cheesecake to go with it."

CHAPTER 7

"And this is good old Boston,
The home of the bean and the cod,
Where the Lowells talk to the Cabots
And the Cabots talk only to God."

John Collins Bossidy

E. JOHN 'JACK' Cabot III opened his eyes to the glorious early sunshine seeping through the closed blinds of his Key Biscayne penthouse condominium. The woman next to him slept silently.

Several streaks of morning light reached the red silk dress that seemed a bit out of place on the saddle leather sofa of his bachelor's apartment. With his eyes, he followed the trail of the woman's undergarments that led from the sofa to the master bedroom. A smile came over his face.

Unable to sleep, Jack put his feet over the side of the bed and sat up. A wave of dizziness passed over him. He recalled the mistake of opening that second bottle of Dom Perignon, and the three rounds of sex that had followed.

He laughed at Bunny and shook his head. He had at least an hour or two before she would awaken. He pulled a cover over her sleeping body and in the dim light of the morning, started to reflect on his life.

Jack was, after all, a WASP from an old line Boston family with old money, and a strong Republican. He had led Harvard to the Ivy League championship while setting a variety of school and league records that earned him a second team berth as an All-America. He had turned down a Rhodes Scholarship when he was drafted in the seventh round by the Minutemen, because he wanted to prove that an Ivy Leaguer could compete in the IFL.

The Boston draft selection was more of a season-ticket-selling scheme than confidence by Minutemen management that Jack could play in the IFL. He pleasantly surprised management by making the club. His arm was hardly a rifle, nor was he a speedster. He was a basic drop-back pocket-passer. His intelligence and leadership qualities had overcome his athletic deficiencies.

It was something he thought about on occasion, now that he was over 40 and no longer a player. It wasn't a bad life as a general manager. He had no money problems. He did, however, miss playing football.

On mornings like this, pain shot through various parts of his six-foot-three, 200-pound frame. He had been heavily battered from 14 seasons with the Minutemen, mostly as a backup quarterback and a place kick holder.

He smiled there in the darkness as he recalled his rookie year. It was the IFL version of freshman hazing. The players had shown him no mercy, constantly making comments about his looks, his family, Harvard, etc. They called him "rich kid," taunting him about everything and anything.

Ha! He was a survivor, a skill he had learned early on as an only child. His quiet work ethic and ability to laugh with his tormentors eventually won him not only a spot on the roster, but popularity with his teammates and coaching staff. His ultimate acceptance, however, was in his fifth season, when he was voted the team's union representative to the IFL Players Association.

He was amused when he imagined the reaction of both the Cabot and Rockefeller sides of his family tree: "Our Jack a union man. How gauche!" Grandmother Cabot would tell her friends.

Jack had never considered IFL management. He had no stomach to be an assistant coach or ambition to be a head coach. There was never any worry, of course, about money. He could stop working and live well in the manner of a Cabot, and that was even before his parents died and left all their assets to their only son.

It was, however, a chance meeting with Bunny Rubin that had changed his future and led to his present position.

To Jack, Bunny was still a looker. Even at 50, she attracted long, lustful looks from young men who probably fantasized about her long legs wrapping around them. It wasn't easy to keep fighting the clock that moved her toward old age, but she wasn't going easily. She was fighting with all the resources of the rich for both medical and cosmetic help to hold back the clock.

Although they shared Boston as a birthplace, their backgrounds were quite opposite. She would tell Jack of her life in South Boston as one of six kids of Francis and Mary Sullivan. Her father was a beat cop in Southie, and her mother was a clerk at Jordan Marsh. They were staunch blue-collar Democrats and devout Catholics, and her mother had hinted that she hoped her daughter might be interested in becoming a nun.

Jack realized that Bunny Sullivan had been a rebel. Although bright and a quick learner, she despised Catholic schools and their discipline. Even in grade school, she had sensual feelings, and she had the audacity to ask her father about giving up sexual pleasure for the church.

Her father's reply was from his black leather uniform belt. She was 13 at the time but the memory of that strap stinging her bare buttocks was still painful. This explained why she had not been to church since age 17, and she always voted straight Republican.

Bunny was her creation of a nickname, she confessed to Jack. She dreamed of being a WASP lady of means, part of Boston society and the country club set. The nickname was one of those preppie things that helped perpetuate her fantasy.

Initially it had been the booze that loosened her tongue; but as her clandestine relationship became more comfortable, she shared most things with her lover. She told Jack she had never felt this way with her first husband, and certainly not with her second.

Jack believed her. He knew that many thought her a cold, calculating, gold-digging bitch.

That prick Casey at Miami P.M. was always taking cheap shots at Bunny, as well as her husband, he mused. S.R. deserved it, but not Bunny.

Yet when she could get free of S.R. for occasional all-night stands like this, he felt something electric which produced heretofore unknown passions. *Fucking the boss's wife is always risky, but she's worth it. I really like Bunny.*

Bunny freely told her lover how her pretty Irish face, red hair, and shapely size six figure got her a chance in show business. What she didn't say was that she started as an exotic dancer. It was not easy initially to take off all her clothes and dance before a bunch of horny men, but the money was good.

Jack should have been turned off by her admitted use of sex to strategically land some bit parts in TV soaps, a minor role in two long-forgotten action films, and eventually some TV commercials. It had been her marriage to millionaire auto dealer Herman Cohen that gave her the opportunity to do the agency's TV spots for 10 years, Jack remembered. That was how she met Sol Rubin.

Jack had to take a leak. He staggered out of bed and into the bathroom. Even while he watched the hot stream of urine hit the water in the toilet, his thoughts remained on Bunny. *I wonder what her reaction would be if she knew that I was thinking of her while taking a leak?*

Jack remembered that Back Bay Motors Ltd. was a warehouse dealer of domestic and foreign vehicles, including Porsches. It was also a major TV sponsor of the Minutemen, and the owner, Cohen, leased a $200,000 a year luxury box at Gillette Stadium in suburban Auburndale.

The owner had been introduced to Bunny while she was auditioning for the Back Bay Motors TV spot. She had wasted little time in seducing the older, widowed man, gaining the legal title of Mrs. Cohen.

It was this association with the Minutemen that had resulted in the Cohens' invitation to a Saturday night cocktail party on the eve of the Miami-Boston game.

Jack laughed softly. Unfortunately for Mr. Cohen, he was in Stuttgart, Germany, on a business trip to the Porsche factory. Bunny hated cocktail parties, but her husband—to his later regret—insisted, no, *demanded* that she go.

The party was hosted by Rubin in the downtown Boston Coply Plaza Marriott. At the time, he was a bored married man and father of one grown son, Steve. Rubin had made his fortune in computer software, and then had decided he wanted to own an IFL franchise.

Jack remembered vividly that Bob Casey had written: *Rubin had all of the moral characteristics that made him welcome in the exclusive club of IFL owners. He was a multimillionaire, a drunk, a womanizer, a cheapskate, and a tyrant, and he knew very little about pro football. He is grooming his son, who inherited good morals and intelligence from his mother Sadie, to become his successor.*

Steve Rubin was still in college, Jack knew. Casey was correct about the kid's morals and intelligence. He was, of course, very upset about the ruthless manner in which his father had dumped his mother for what he considered a gold-digging Gentile.

Rubin had a big mouth even when sober, which wasn't often after 5:00 p.m., Jack understood. He made the mistake once of telling Casey, "Some rich SOBs want to piss their hard-earned money on running for public office. Not me. I want to be someone. You aren't someone in this life unless you own an IFL franchise. Who knows who's the president of Sun Airlines or General Motors or IBM? But they damn sure know who owns the Miami Sharks!"

That dumb Mick bastard had printed it all in his toilet rag.

"I don't argue that S.R. isn't a good businessman, but the fucker knows less about pro football than the man in the moon," Bunny had told Jack. "I figured I could be a football celebrity, too. A start, you know, would be to let the fucker get into my panties."

Jack laughed as he thought about his lover's candor.

"I had to insist on marriage, even if it meant swapping one old Jewish businessman for another."

Jack knew Rubin was neither handsome nor dashing. He was nearly bald, and he wore a portly size 54 suit over his five-foot-nine frame. Although he could afford the best in clothes, he still patronized the discount stores, which provided all of his ill-fitting and unfashionable suits. His life had been business, business, and business. As a team owner, Rubin treated Sharks employees the way he had treated his workers at his R & R Software Inc.

Surviving in business in the early years had made him niggardly in operation and payroll costs, IFL insiders had told Jack. Even with the Sharks, he hired many temps to fill office positions in order to avoid paying benefits. He once fired a secretary because she wasted too much paper.

He and head coach Don Sherman were described as "the odd couple of pro football" by Casey. Jack smiled. If Rubin did one thing right, it was keeping Sherman as coach and paying whatever the market demanded to get and keep talent. Sherman knew that no other owner in the league would give him that kind of financial support. S.R. wanted a winner.

Jack understood that Sherman could have any head coaching job in the league, but only S.R. would provide unlimited bucks to buy the horses. Thus, Rubin held court in his downtown Miami office while Sherman's empire was the training camp in the adjoining county of Broward at Pembroke Pines.

As far as Jack was concerned, S.R.'s personal life was a mess. He was a slob who exemplified the boredom of traditional Jewish family life. His escape was vodka, especially martinis—and sex with any young woman who didn't mind giving blowjobs.

Rubin had a secret desire, one common to many old, rich men, according to Bunny. That was to have a young, beautiful wife as a showpiece. This explained, Jack reasoned, why S.R. was immediately smitten by Bunny Cohen when they first met at Rubin's cocktail party in Boston.

Jack believed that S.R. hadn't wanted to find a Jewish American Princess, which was why at first he didn't pay much attention to the beauty introduced to him as Mrs. Bunny Cohen. Like Cohen, Rubin found her Boston Irish accent as irresistible as her red hair and the long legs that supported her Miss America body.

"It doesn't take Dear Abbey to know how to charm most men," she told Cabot. "Just smile, show some cleavage, and a little thigh. Encourage him to talk about himself. That's my formula for success."

She was ready, Jack knew, and willing and able to do anything that would please the object of her conquest. *Yeah, and it doesn't help to be a fox who gives BJs.*

Actually, Bunny's pet saying was that a woman had three cavities to receive a hard cock, and she loved all three receptions. Jack could attest to that, so he understood how she had seduced the Sharks' owner so easily.

Jack climbed back into bed while remembering her tale of seduction. He smiled every time she told it. She had finagled an invitation on game day to the visiting owner's luxury box. Seated next to Rubin, she had acted more than a bit brazenly during the second quarter. The two were seated in the front row with a counter in front of them. S.R. was on his fourth martini when she slipped her hand in his lap, lightly grazing his leg near his penis.

Looking into his eyes, she had gushed softly, "Oh, Mr. Rubin, you are absolutely the sexiest man I have ever met." Meanwhile, her right hand had moved up closer to the organ and pressed against it.

In his unexpected excitement, Rubin had needed to brace both hands on the counter as his knees started shaking. It didn't take long for him to think he'd like to explode in her hand. The other guests in the box had attributed his surprised moan to the action on the field below. Unknown to the two at that moment, Boston had just scored on a 69-yard pass from Cabot to wideout Otis Anderson.

Jack wasn't certain whether the story was meant to shock him. It didn't. He was now even more fascinated by a woman who could pull off such a caper successfully. The owner had been both shocked and flattered by the daring act.

"I've got to hand it to you," Jack quipped the first time he heard the story. She laughed at his pun and felt happy that he accepted what she had done to get where she was.

For S.R., it was a case of love at first sight. Following a torrid and clandestine, long-distance romance that was first hinted at by Bob Casey in a column, he was faced with a decision, because on a weekend at New York's Plaza, she had given him the "marry me or leave me" ultimatum.

The owner didn't think twice. He quickly filed for divorce from his wife of 35 years, while Bunny did the same with her husband of 12 years.

The divorce didn't take place until she had secured a prenuptial contract. In it, Rubin made her co-owner of the Sharks and provided handsomely for her life after his death. Rubin's lawyers had suggested the co-owner status to save on the inheritance and probate taxes.

"Your new wife won't be involved in the operation of the business," one of the lawyers had said. "It will give her a little feminist prestige to tout when she trots around the social set. When Steve graduates from college, you can put him on the ownership list, too."

Jack understood that the idea made good business sense at the time to S.R.

The general manager checked to see that Bunny was still sleeping. He remembered how they had met. It was by accident in Boston's Ritz-Carlton.

The visit with her parents was bittersweet. Her father, now a captain, was ready to retire after 35 years with the Boston police.

Her parents would not forgive her for marrying outside the Catholic Church. A divorce, followed by marriage to a second Jew, was impossible for the Sullivans to accept.

Mrs. Sullivan was upset that her daughter wouldn't sleep over in her childhood bedroom, instead of opting to stay at a fancy WASP downtown hotel. Bunny liked the stately Ritz-Carlton because it was old Boston. She remembered when it was difficult for non-WASPs to gain entrance. The Irish had been treated like steerage passengers by the hotel help. She remembered, too, the hotel's rigid formal dress code.

The cab had arrived at the Boston Common entrance to the hotel. The doorman opened the cab door, and Bunny handed him a suit box. It was a warm July afternoon, and Bunny loved returning to her native city like titled royalty.

She had hesitated for a moment to take in the summer afternoon excitement of shoppers and tourists who filled the sidewalks. Then, reclaiming her box and tipping the doorman a crisp five-dollar bill, she walked briskly into the lobby. The Saks Fifth Avenue dress box had obstructed her view. It was an impulse dress she had purchased on a brief shopping trip. Seeing an elevator door open, she had rushed toward it.

BAM!

She had collided head-on with Jack, and was knocked to the lobby floor.

There she was, looking up at me. I helped her off the floor while uttering a flurry of apologies.

"Don't worry, sir, I won't sue," she had told him. "My lawyer isn't very good."

She was shaken, but Jack greeted her dry humor with a smile of relief.

"You, sir, look familiar," she had said as she regained her balance. "You aren't in politics. . .?"

He had cut her short. "No, I'm Jack Cabot, Mrs. Rubin."

"THE Jack Cabot?" She told him later that she had been an admirer of the veteran quarterback and wondered why he had never married. *She thought I might be gay!* In thinking back, Jack admitted that she had always held a certain fascination for him. At first, it was probably because she was from the opposite side of the tracks.

"Mr. Cabot, it was my fault," she told him. She started talking fast to prevent his leaving. "Please let me buy you a drink. I know I certainly could use one." He knew now that she had been buying time and trying to come up with a game plan.

Bunny loved sex, she had confessed to him, but she had used it mostly as a survival tool for her security. Her enjoyment came with a vibrator and a fantasy lover, which on more than one occasion had been Jack. She liked his Brooks Brothers look of a blue, three-button blazer with gray slacks and a red turtleneck.

"I'd like to, Mrs. Rubin, but I have a meeting with my agent," he remembered saying.

She tried to mask any hint of desperation in her voice. "Please, Mr. Cabot, I could really use that drink."

I guess I was truly flattered by the invitation. But I perceived it as a simple social gesture. I wasn't a skirt-chaser. Hell, I've had no trouble getting laid, but I have never become serious with any woman.

Jack remembered that the couple had found a booth in the hotel cocktail lounge, and after the first drink neither showed any inclination to adjourn. The second Chivas and soda relaxed them. By the third round, there was a certain chemistry developing between them. Bunny had surprised Jack with a knowledge of pro football and had flattered him by recalling Cabot's notable game when he came off the bench to pass for three touchdowns in a playoff game two years earlier against the New York Titans.

"How could I forget it?" she explained. "S.R. was rooting for the Titans because he had bet 50 grand on them. You guys were down 14-3, and when you went in, he said at the time he regretted not betting a hundred Gs."

"He wasn't alone, Mrs. Rubin—"

"Please, call me Bunny. All my friends do."

"Well, Bunny, I was just hot that afternoon. The Titans had a rookie right cornerback. I took advantage of his inexperience. You know, I had the advantage of replacing our injured starter, Billy Hermann. You see, the Titans had prepared their defense all week for Hermann—"

"Well, Jack, you brought the Minutemen back for a 24-21 victory. That pissed off my husband! I remember your game-winning pass," she had continued. "It was an improbable 'Hail Mary' bomb that tight end Andrew Johnson managed to grab in the end zone. I was excited, and S.R. was piss—er, upset."

"I didn't see the end of the play until the game films on Monday," he replied. "I was knocked into the turf by two Titan defensive linemen. When I heard the moan from the home crowd, I knew I'd been lucky."

Jack had wanted to change the subject. He wanted to hear about his companion's life and thoughts. He knew she was from Southie. He knew she was Irish and Catholic. He couldn't help but wonder what kind of sex life she had with that old reprobate of a husband.

By now she was thoroughly aroused. After a fourth round of drinks, she became aggressive and gambled. "Jack, will you do me a favor?" He could still remember the smell the Chivas on her breath mixed with the scent of her Joy perfume.

"Sure, Bunny," he replied without hesitation.

She toyed with her glass and, looking into his eyes, said in a sensual voice, "Take me to bed." Not *would you like to*, but *take me*—a command.

Jack remembers how he was caught off guard by the suddenness of the proposal. He was speechless, pondering a reply. Bunny had not given him a chance to answer. Slipping her room card key into his right hand while brushing her left hand against his crotch, she was pleased to find that he was aroused.

"See you in 15 minutes." She had exited with a knowing smile. "We don't want any scandal, do we?"

Bunny was standing in the middle of her suite's living room when he'd arrived. She had a fresh glass of Chivas in each hand. He still remembered that breathtaking Chanel suit in shocking pink. She had kicked off her pumps and stood in stocking feet. The skirt was hemmed two inches above the knees, and her waist-length jacket was partially unbuttoned to reveal a black bra.

He accepted the drink and took a swig. They were, at that moment, like two competitors sizing each other up. If this were Spain, she'd be the matador, and of course, he would be the bull. He couldn't help but laugh out loud about the comparison.

"You're laughing at me?"

He shook his head as she approached and tenderly kissed his lips. He remembered that they recovered long enough to find the bedroom. It was 72 hours before they would leave again.

"I like you," he said simply to the older woman. It was more meaningful than that, of course, but in time he would learn how much.

It was after that weekend of passion in Boston that Jack realized that Bunny had launched her master plan to obtain control of the Miami Sharks.

Rubin considered most women bimbos. He never suspected that his wife was very bright in business, but he was no different from most married men in discussing business decisions with their wives. What he didn't know was how manipulative his wife could be. She was well aware that her husband was grooming his son Steve for eventual control and operation of the Sharks.

In their prenuptial agreement, Rubin had specified that in the event of his death, the ownership would revert to his wife. This was for tax purposes. He figured his widow would enjoy the role of club owner while his son would actually make the decisions and run the operation.

It was a plan that would backfire. Thanks to estate taxes, family-owned sports teams have become increasingly rare. Estate taxes, which are levied on what you owe when you die, were designed to prevent wealthy families from hoarding all the nation's riches.

Jack understood Rubin's problem with estate taxes, and appreciated that Bunny was a heartbeat away from inheriting a pro football franchise.

S.R. had made his decision after seeing what happened to the widow of Los Angeles Dons' owner Barry Sanders. She was being forced by the IRS to sell the Dons to pay the $247 million in federal and state income taxes. The team's value was estimated at $650 million, making it subject to a federal estate tax of 55 percent. That was why S.R. made Bunny co-owner of the Sharks while setting up a trust fund for his son Steve.

Knowing that Steve Rubin was the heir apparent, Bunny figured correctly that her husband didn't want some big-name, high-priced general manager. So she started planting the proverbial seed in S.R.'s mind that he should hire a former big-name player looking for front office experience, one who would work for low pay until Steve was ready for command.

Bunny had told Jack how she helped get him the GM job. The Rubins had separate bedrooms. It was S.R.'s idea, but it was fine with Bunny because he was a very loud snorer. It was an unexpected visit to his bedroom where she had treated him to oral sex, which proved pivotal.

While recovering from the sex, he started thinking out loud about who he should get as general manager. She suggested the veteran player route. He mentioned a few names, but without conviction.

"Honey, what about that Boston quarterback? Jack Kazmier?"

"You mean Jack Cabot," he replied.

"Yeah, him," she said, as if she were more interested in combing her hair. "You need a figurehead for now. I hear tell that this Cabot is from a rich Gentile family, a Harvard boy. He probably would work cheap, because his career as a player is over, and he needs a new career. I read in the *Boston Record* that he was hoping someday to get in the Minutemen's front office."

Jack was surprised the next morning when he got a call from his lover. "Tell your agent to get lost. Tell the Minutemen you have retired. You'll be hearing from S.R. soon."

Jack knew now that Bunny had been right. Now, two years later, he and his lover were concerned about Steve's college graduation next May and S.R.'s plans to bring him into the front office.

#

Bunny uttered mumbling sounds from the bed, which ended Jack's thoughts.

"What time is it, honey?" she asked.

"Time to talk about our future," Jack replied.

Bunny was concerned about how she looked without makeup. It was obvious that Jack didn't care, because he kissed her on the forehead and mumbled, "I love you."

Bunny had other concerns, as well. *Time is running out on my plan.* S.R. was now 72. If he was still alive by next spring, Steve would have control of the club.

"If only S.R. would have a heart attack," she blurted out in frustration. "The team would be ours!"

Jack was momentarily shocked. Yet he was flattered by the "ours."

"I'm only kidding, honey," she quickly added. "All I really need is you."

Jack embraced Bunny, and he too started thinking what life could be like for both of them if something were to happen to S.R.

CHAPTER 8

"The roulette table pays nobody except him who keeps it. Nevertheless, a passion for gaming is common, though a passion for keeping roulette wheels is unknown."

George Bernard Shaw
Man and Superman

B ACK FROM A Miami-New York turnaround, Suzy Peters finished reading the column in *Miami P.M.*, and turned to its author. "Good grief, Bob, no wonder you have so few friends."

Bob just smiled and took a sip from his glass of Chivas. The two were huddled in a booth in a darkened corner of the lounge at Cella's, a popular Italian restaurant in the Miami suburb of Hallandale. The retirement community on the Dade-Broward county line was known affectionately by some senior residents as Lanskyland in honor of the late Meyer Lansky, "the Jewish godfather of the Mafia."

It was a busy Friday night, and there had been a line waiting for tables. When owner Edmund Cella spotted the sports columnist and regular customer, however, the old Italian greeted Casey warmly and ushered the couple to a booth in the lounge. Attired in a white shirt and bow tie, he always wore a white apron. The owner was soon back again with a waitress in tow.

"You gonna have your usual hot sausages with peppers on a bed of spaghetti?" he asked. "I don't need to ask. What about the young lady?"

"She'll have the same," Bob replied without hesitation.

Some of my women's lib friends would have resented Bob's decision-making, but not me, Suzy thought. *That's the role of a man, my dad believed. I get turned off by the new era of wimpy young men who can't make decisions, and those who suggest going Dutch.*

"As for the wine, Mr. Casey?"

" A good Italian red. Perhaps a Bolo. Bring a glass for yourself, Edmund. We are celebrating our engagement. Meet Suzy Mary Peters, known to many as Sky Princess."

Suzy blushed, because it was only Bob who called her Sky Princess.

Cella took a quick look at the woman and sputtered, "You, miss? You're not really gonna marry this newspaper bum, are you? You're too pretty for him!"

"I'd probably prefer marrying you, Mr. Cella, but I understand you have a pretty wife," Suzy replied with a feigned sigh. "So I guess I'll have to settle for this newspaper bum."

Cella laughed. He had only just met this woman, but already he liked her. The owner returned with a bottle of Bolo red wine, opened it, and the trio made a toast to the couple's coming happiness.

The restaurant was divided into a well-lighted main dining room and a dimmer bar lounge with red-leather booths, which the regulars like Casey preferred.

"The food is basic Italian, and after 10:00 p.m. you can even order pizza," Bob had told Suzy in advance. "It's a hangout for the Gulfstream Park crowd during the horse race season, as well as a hangout for Mafia types."

Suzy listened with almost a schoolgirl rapture. *It's obvious that Bob is not only a regular here, but very popular with the owner and the help.*

"Even a hood like Gattino will take his wife here for dinner," Bob said. "This joint is owned by Cella, and while he welcomes mob diners, he doesn't pay 'em any tribute. Rumor has it that the food is so good, the Mafia has let it be known that 'Edmund Cella is one of us,' even though he isn't."

"Honey," Suzy interrupted, "you aren't talking about any relation to that nice Gattino couple we met in Munich, are you?"

"Damn right, Suzy. Oh, I guess I haven't had time to tell you the scoop on Gattino."

"Scoop? Honey, Gattino was on my flight this morning to New York."

Bob quickly filled her in on Hess's report on Gattino.

Suzy gasped. "That nice old man?"

"Aren't you glad you didn't spill any coffee in his lap?" Bob asked with a grin.

"Bobby! That isn't funny."

"I know, Suzy. I remember how he was working me for insider information on the Sharks, especially Longo. Could it be that Longo is in hock to Gattino?"

The subject of Gattino and Longo was tabled with the return of Cella.

"Hey, Mr. Casey, now about this article you wrote about gambling and the Mafia. I don't want no hit men shooting up this booth and spilling your blood all over my nice upholstery. Why you not lay off gambling and the mobsters? Why you not write some nice things about how good a football team the Sharks will be this season?"

Suzy thought the owner was serious, but she quickly learned that the two always exchanged this gallows humor.

"Edmund, old friend, if I wrote such slop, I couldn't afford to eat in this joint. . .much less a *good* restaurant," Bob replied. "Anyhow, I understand this joint is owned by the Mafia. So why would they want to mess up their own joint?"

The owner laughingly waved off Bob's remarks and left, vowing to return with a suggestion for dessert.

"I have a suggestion for dessert, Bobby," Suzy said with an impish grin, "but it's not on the menu."

He had never liked to be called Bobby until Suzy had started and continued to call him that.

"Eat and drink first. Then we can make love all night long," said Bob. "I'm so hungry I could eat one of those Gulfstream claimers."

"Not tonight, lover. I have an early flight tomorrow to New York," Suzy countered.

"It's not until eight a.m.," he protested.

"I have to work that flight, Bobby. That means I have to show up at MIA two hours before the scheduled takeoff. That means getting up at five a.m."

Bob faked a pout.

Like a little boy who was sent to bed without his dessert, she thought. *And I love him all the more for it.*

"Cheer up, Bobby," she said, breaking an awkward minute of silence. "We'll have all Saturday afternoon and night to mess around in Green Bay."

Bob grinned and stared adoringly at her. *Pinch me! I can't believe I'm acting like a lovesick highschool sophomore. I am, because that's the way I feel.*

"Look, honey," she said, changing to a serious tone. "In that column today about sports gambling. . .well, can you explain some of the basics? Our first officer, Vince Lombard, is a big football gambler, and he intimidates me and the other flight attendants with his know-how."

Bob took a long sip of red wine and smiled as he continued to gaze lovingly at his companion. He reached across the table and gently squeezed her left hand, and felt a surge of pride that Suzy was wearing his diamond engagement ring. It wasn't an awesome diamond, because Suzy had insisted he stay under $5,000.

"Okay, young lady, let Professor Casey give you a quick course in Football Gambling 102," he said. "A sports-wagering facility that functions as a business on its own or as part of a casino is called a sports book. An athletic contest often pits teams of unequal abilities. So the line is how the sports book deals with this inequity so that wagers will be placed equally on either team.

"Most Nevada sports books do not set their own lines. They buy lines from businesses whose sole function is to calculate the lines. There are two different betting lines in sports. There is the money line and the point-spread. The money line is simply called 'the line,' and it penalizes those who prefer to bet on a favorite by making them bet a lot to make a little. This is called laying, or giving odds, and it works like this: if you lay eight to five odds that the Sharks will win, you pay eight dollars to place the bet, and get back $13 if you win. That's the way you bet baseball.

"In football and basketball, the point-spread is the thing, along with under-and-over wagering," he continued after taking a quick sip of wine. "The point-spread gives the underdog extra points for the purpose of deciding the bet. Like Sunday, the Sharks must beat the Holsteins by 11 points for Sharks backers to collect. You can also bet a money-liner on football."

"But you said the line was ten and a half points," she interrupted. "How can a team score half a point?"

"They can't, Sky Princess," he replied patiently. "It means a team really has to win by more than 10 points."

"You're doing great, Professor," Suzy said. "Pray tell, how do the bookies make money on this, or is this another tax write-off for the Mafia?"

"Well, Sky Princess, the Mafia makes its money from every bettor. Whenever you place a point-spread bet, you lay 11 to win 10. This means if you want to win $100, you have to wager $110, no matter which team you are betting on. If you win, you'll be paid $210—your $110 wager plus the $100 you just won. This difference is called the house's vigorish, which amounts to a 4.54 percent commission on every point-spread bet made."

"A vigorish? Sounds like an Italian dressing."

Bob laughed. "No, that's just slang for the bookie's commission. There are some other methods to bet on football, such as a teaser or a parlay, but I'll save that for our next lesson."

The waitress arrived with the food.

"This sure beats airline chow," said Bob as he picked up his fork. "Of course, I didn't mean Sun Air's award-winning, first-class cuisine."

"Right. Well, we workers have it even worse. They're called crew meals," she said with a grim look. "Tell me, Bobby, why do you get so worked up about sports gambling? It doesn't hurt anyone. I mean, it's not like drugs. . ."

Bob put his fork down. "Sky Princess, I don't want to sound like a prude but. . .the profit from sports gambling goes to the Mafia so it can support its many criminal activities, including drugs. Some gamblers become addicts and borrow from the Mafia loan sharks. Like Johnny Longo. And all this illegal gambling hurts legitimate wagering such as the parimutuel sports which pay taxes. You know, like Gulfstream Park and Hollywood Greyhound Track."

The couple continued to eat for a minute.

"Okay, so why not legalize sports betting so the states can regulate it just like horse and dog racing?" she asked.

Bob cooled down a bit. He didn't want his passion against gambling to hurt his love relationship with Suzy. "College and professional sports lobby against this, and with good reason," he replied. "More money bet on games would only increase the risks of point-shaving and throwing games. Even though you can bet legally at Florida parimutuel establishments, a lot of money on horse racing is still bet with illegal bookies. Some even operate on the track."

"Why, Bobby?"

"To avoid taxes, for one. If you win more than $600 at a track, you have to fill out an IRS form. Parimutuels don't give their patrons credit. A bookie will. And. . .do you remember that nice, little, old Italian grandfather we shared a table with in the beer hall?"

"Yes."

"Well, Sky Princess, that nice, old guy is one big don in the Mafia. His specialties are murder and gambling. He loves to do people in with a chain saw."

She stared at him. "A chain saw? You're kidding!"

"Afraid not. Now let's eat. Oh, do you want me to pick you up tomorrow on your return to Miami?"

"Thanks, honey, but I have a union meeting to attend," she replied. "I think we may have a strike."

Bob frowned.

"Cheer up, honey, I've been assigned to work the Sharks charter for the season opener in Green Bay on the weekend," she said with a grin. "I'm sure we'll have plenty of time to mess around Saturday before Sunday's game."

Bob smiled.

#

Suzy knew a strike was coming.

Sun Airlines was a coast-to-coast trunk line with a strong route structure in the Sunbelt. Its financial picture was very strong, for it carried little long-term debt and owned a fleet of new aircraft that had high value. However, it had high-priced union help who routinely loved to go on strike. Before deregulation, Westinghouse considered such labor actions to be one of the costs of doing business. Not any more.

Sun Airlines was the nation's sixth largest carrier, serving more than 90 cities within the United States with 56 international designations. Its annual passenger load was 42 million with 43,000 employees.

Suzy knew that since Mike Kelly had been elected president of the Machinists Union, he had become a formidable foe to CEO Westinghouse. Kelly was a labor militant who strongly upheld the agenda of Samuel Gompers: "More." The Machinists Union was not simply representing the skilled mechanics; it had grown in size by adding aircraft cleaners and baggage handlers.

She knew the pilots were the key to breaking a strike. If the pilots crossed the machinists' picket lines, Sun Airlines would stay airborne, because Florida was a right-to-work state.

The Federation of Flight Attendants' contract with Sun Airlines still had a year to go. Militant members such as Mary Rich, however, wanted to join the Machinists Union if they went on strike.

That was why Kelly had been invited to address his probable allies at the Miami Union Hall, and reporter Buffy Zei was on the scene.

#

"Hi, Ms. Rich. I'm Buffy from *Miami P.M.* I talked to you on the phone."

The reporter found Mary talking with Suzy and Ann Parker. It was obvious from what she had overheard that the group wasn't in agreement on wanting to strike.

"Right, Buffy," said Mary. "Glad you could make it tonight. You'll enjoy hearing Kelly speak. He knows how to deal with those management bastards."

Zei scribbled down notes on a pad, while using her pen to point when asking questions. She listened patiently as Mary talked about the struggle of labor and the need for union solidarity.

"I understand your feelings, Ms. Rich, but what about your contract?"

"If the machinists walk, the planes won't fly," Mary replied with confidence.

"Maybe, but what if the pilots don't strike and Captain Westinghouse farms out the maintenance work?"

"The pilots will strike."

"And if they don't, Ms. Rich?"

"The fly boys are good union members. They won't let us down."

"Don't bet on that, Mary," Parker interrupted. "Pilots think they are God's gift to the airline industry, and the rest of us are serfs."

Another female flight attendant joined in. "That's not so, Ann. Only a few of them are jerks. The rest respect the job we do in the cabin."

Zei noted the dissenters and turned to Suzy. "What about you? What do you think you guys should do?"

"Who me?" replied Suzy, playing the fool. "I don't think. I pay my union dues and let our elected officials like Mary make such momentous decisions for me. But I do hope the single girls. . .er, *members*. . .realize that, unlike the pilots and the machinists, we have no fat strike fund. I hope, too, that all our members realize Florida is a right-to-work state. And you know, Captain Westinghouse has been on record saying flight attendants are a dime a dozen."

"Why, Suzy honey, you sound just like a management person," Parker said.

"No, Ann honey," Mary asserted, "Suzy is no management person like some of our members. She won't sleep with Westinghouse. . ."

Parker's face turned red, but before she could reply, the meeting got under way. Zei joined the others on cheap, metal folding chairs in the hall.

Mike Kelly waited on stage. Zei noticed that he was accompanied by three men.

"Who are those guys with Kelly?" the reporter asked Suzy.

"That big guy is Bubba Youngblood," Suzy replied. "The black guy is T.J. Lewis. The third? I'm not—"

"That's Jose Cortez," interrupted Parker. "They're three of Kelly's union musclemen."

Mary introduced Mike Kelly. He received a polite but hardly enthusiastic applause. Zei was impressed by Kelly's style. He stood next to the podium and held the PA mike in his hand. He said nothing for 30. . .40. . .50 seconds. Then he started in a low monotone.

"Fellow union workers. I appreciate this opportunity to be with you tonight. I know that in the transportation business, the various unions have had our differences in the past. Tonight, however, I want to invite you to join our revolution. Because if you don't, we will all, every one of us, become victims of a greedy, tyrannical management. Westinghouse is the Hitler of commercial aviation. If we don't stand as one to fight this monster, we shall perish one by one. This labor action isn't about money and benefits and work rules."

Kelly took a long but calculated pause as he made eye contact with the audience. The flight attendants hung on the speaker's next words, while suspense filled the hall for a brief 30 seconds.

"No, my fellow unionists, it is about survival. *Our* survival. Do you honestly believe that Westinghouse cares about you flight attendants?"

A woman's voice screamed, "Hell, no!"

Like calling "fire!" in an audience, the scream triggered a chant of "Hell, no! Westinghouse has got to go!"

Zei was impressed by the way Kelly so quickly gained control over the audience. As he continued, he reminded the reporter of a TV preacher. *Many of his facts are false. Why is no one challenging him? He's holding this audience in an almost hypnotic trance. I bet if he asked them to drink cyanide, they'd do it willingly.*

Kelly's theme that the unions wanted a whopping 30 percent pay hike was big news. Zei kept asking herself over and over: *How the hell do the unions think Sun Airlines can come up with such money? There are some 42,000 employees. Meanwhile, the company is asking for wage freezes and relaxed work rules. Both sides are crazy. Aren't there any sane people on either side?*

Driving back to the newspaper office in downtown Miami, she realized that all the flight attendants weren't bimbos or mindless union zealots. *That Suzy Peters has a mind. Yeah, a mind of her own.*

#

The woman with that mind, however, was not thinking about union business as she drove home. She was engulfed with passionate thoughts about her lover.

Suzy Casey, she thought. *My, that has a nice sound to it. No Peters-Casey last name for me, thanks. Mrs. Suzy Casey will do just fine.*

She was excited, because after the union meeting, Mary had said Suzy would work the Sharks charter for the season-opener in Green Bay. Suzy knew Mary was doing her a big favor, because she was still junior to most of the carrier's flight attendants. She regretted shooting her mouth off to the reporter.

Now her thoughts shifted back to Casey. She knew he would call at her apartment.

#

Bob Casey's Working Press:
The day Carver
Discovered God

MIAMI—It was called a routine hospital visit. Shari Carver entered Miami Hospital to give birth to the couple's third child.

The normally routine delivery brought the mother near death before surgeons delivered an eight-pound-three-ounce son, Martin Carver. The first name is in honor of the slain civil rights leader, Dr. Martin Luther King, Jr.

"We were so happy that Shari was going to be a mama again; we just took it for granted that all would go well," said the Miami Sharks All-Pro defensive end. "We didn't even ask our pastor to pray. We nearly learned the hard way."

"Crusher" Carver spent the night before the Sharks exhibition with Washington in the hospital chapel. He was pleading . . . begging God to spare his wife's life.

"I promised God that night that I would give up pro football or anything else. If I didn't know before that night, I knew then that my family was the most important thing in my life."

His prayers were answered. I can report happily that Shari is on the road to recovery.

> What is unfortunate is that Sharks coach Don Sherman was critical of Carver's decision to leave training camp to be with his wife.
>
> "It's just a routine birth," said the coach. "Carver needs to be at practice and play in the Washington game."
>
> "At the salary we pay Carver, it is hoped that he will honor his $2.5 million contract," said Sharks owner Sol Rubin. "He owes it to his teammates and the Miami fans."
>
> Isn't it fortunate that Carver has learned that he need only answer to a higher authority to discover the true meaning of life?
>
> "I promised God that my family would attend services regularly at Mount Zion Baptist Church, and we would dedicate our lives to Christ," he said humbly. "I want to thank my teammates, especially Norm Amundsen and the Fellowship of Christian Athletes, for their loving support."
>
> The Sharks players, who rallied to show their love and prayers, crossed all lines of color, nationality, and religion. Even the Rev. Francis J. O'Malley, pastor of St. Vincent's Church and team chaplain, went to the hospital and prayed. Steve Rubin, the owner's son, brought the family rabbi, David Goldstein.
>
> There are those who scoff at religion and the lessons of camaraderie that transcend race and religion in football, but don't tell that to "Crusher" and Shari Carver.
>
> On a long, hot, summer night in Miami, the Carvers learned the true meaning of love and what is truly important in life. It is a lesson from which we all could profit.

\#

Bob arrived at Miami International Airport about an hour early for the scheduled Saturday morning departure of the Sharks charter for the trip to Green Bay. It was a good opportunity to socialize and even get news leads from the coaches, staff, and players.

Larry Bloom had cautioned Bob that Rubin might keep him off the flight because of his gambling column, but both Bunny and the team media relations director had talked the owner out of such a course of action.

One of the early arrivals to the Sun Airlines Sun King Club room was Carver. The six-foot-six, 305-pound African-American had not only played for Duke, but he had graduated with a 3.5 grade point average. He was also an All-Pro and was a quarterback's worst nightmare.

Unlike most of the veteran players, Carver liked to arrive at the airport early. Having missed a flight his rookie season, he vowed he never wanted to face the wrath of Sherman or the hefty fine again.

"What's happening, my man?" Carver asked when he spotted Casey.

"I was hoping you'd tell me, George. Like, are you guys going to cover the spread tomorrow?"

Carver laughed loudly. "You're crazy, Bob. I read that shit you wrote about gambling. . ."

"And?"

"It's probably true," replied the big guy as the columnist and player exchanged high fives. "On a serious note, my man, my wife Shari and I want to thank you for that column you did the other week. It was very touching, you know. . ."

Bob spotted Jorge Cunill sipping on a cup of Cuban coffee. Nearby, a radio guy was taping some of Sherman's views about the Green Bay game. "Hey, Wetback, aren't you taking down any of Sherman's great quotes?"

Jorge almost laughed as he swallowed a big gulp of hot coffee. "Hey, gringo, that's the kind of shit you columnists love."

Jorge already knew he would be dining alone that evening. He was happy that his friend was about to become a married man again. Still, he owed Bob one for the Berlin trip during which the columnist checked the Cunills out of their room after the second day at the Adlon, and had the hotel send their luggage to the airport.

Claudia Cunill thought the prank was funny, which lessened the revenge factor. She had pointed out that last January, during a playoff in Buffalo, her husband had bought drinks for all 63 patrons in the Marriott bar and signed the tab to Casey's room.

The Sharks' normal travel party included the players, coaches, support personnel, the owner, front office personnel, media members, Father O'Malley, and some friends of the owner. The only female passenger permitted on the flight was the owner's wife.

As a rule, most of the cabin crew was handpicked by the airline, with some suggestions from Rubin. Since most of the charter cabin crews were seniors, it would have been easy for some flight attendants to resent Suzy's assignment. But with Mary Rich and Ann Parker among the crew, she was warmly welcomed.

Suzy took some good-natured kidding about becoming engaged when she reported to work at MIA that Saturday morning. The crew admired her ring. She made eye contact with Bob as he entered the DC-10 cabin and headed back to the coach section.

#

Bob was actually excited about the trip to Green Bay. He had trouble keeping his eyes off Suzy, but his mind was still on Longo.

Man, she is a knockout in that navy blue uniform. Is she really going to be my wife? Whew... He had to control pangs of jealousy as he watched the flight attendant exchange banter with the other passengers. She could turn the sexual inferences into humor rather than an incident. She was so impressive that she could even handle that animal, fullback Larry Wargo.

The three-hour flight to Green Bay was uneventful. Bob tried to nap, but it was hard because he was seated on the aisle, and periodically Suzy would slow her walk while making her rounds, and suggestively rub her butt against his arm. She gave no indication while working the flight that Bob was something special.

One of the owner's guests, a banker, even asked Suzi out for dinner. The banker wasn't about to take "no" for an answer. Luckily, Parker came to her rescue and volunteered to be the banker's dinner companion.

It seemed strange to the airport workers in Green Bay to see a DC-10 land there. They gawked as three charter buses, an equipment truck, and the owner's limousine rolled out to the runway to meet the jumbo jet.

It was a warm and sunny afternoon in the Wisconsin city of 85,000, where the tallest building was the ten-story Catholic hospital. The natives were friendly, and most displayed their black and white Holstein colors the day before the game in Kraft Cheese Stadium. Bob was hoping to introduce Suzy to the custom of double bubble at the hotel bar that afternoon.

"Suzy, honey, why don't you take the guest bus over to the hotel," said Mary. "I believe we can secure the aircraft. We'll see you tomorrow morning. We have tickets for the game, thanks to Mr. Cabot, but we'll have to leave at the end of the third quarter to get set up here. You can join us then."

"Thanks, Mary, I really appreciate—"

"Hey, none of that foolishness. This crew is family. Just enjoy the layover, and be sure to take your birth control pills."

Suzy blushed.

Maybe the two lovers thought they were fooling everyone on the trip, because they didn't sit together on the guest bus for the ride to the hotel, and they both picked up their individual preregistered room keys.

Bob had no sooner washed his hands in Room 305 than there was a soft knock on the door. It was Suzy. She was still in her uniform, but she carried a gym bag.

"I left all my stuff in my crew room," she explained.

"So what's in the bag?" he asked.

She opened the bag. Inside there was a sleep shirt and a couple dozen miniature liquor bottles she had liberated from the plane's liquor cabinets. "Aren't you going to kiss me? Or have you grown tired of me already?" she asked.

They embraced with passion. Suzy was warm, and her body odors, mingled with her Chanel No. 5 perfume, smelled wonderful to the columnist.

She knew he was horny, and she was grateful.

She pulled away abruptly from his embrace and moved quickly to the window, where she pulled the blackout curtains.

"What's the matter?" Bob asked, fearing that he might have done something wrong.

"No need to entertain the pedestrians below," she whispered.

"Not with you in your uniform," he said with a relieved laugh.

#

It was a warm September Sunday afternoon in Green Bay. The leaves were just turning colors, and the Sharks, who had grown weary of training in humid, 90-degree weather in South Florida, welcomed the 72-degree temperature at kickoff.

"There is a wholesome, small-town atmosphere about football Sundays in Green Bay," Bob told Suzy.

The Holsteins' faithful fans came early to the stadium, and the parking lots were filled with vehicles and tailgate parties. Cooking fires filled the air with delights of bratwurst and other meats. And the beer drinkers started early, too.

Bob enjoyed his rare visits to Green Bay. Up early in the morning, he and Suzy had taken a long walk through downtown before breakfast.

Having Suzy there kept his mind off Longo.

"This must be a great place to live and bring up kids," Suzy said.

#

Bob and Jorge were in the front row of the press box in the section reserved for visiting media. Both used field glasses while taking notes on yellow, legal-sized pads. Their laptops were untouched, because working for an afternoon paper, they didn't have the early deadlines of the morning newspaper reporters. While their opposition was obsessed with making deadlines, they could roam the locker rooms after the game for the second-day angles that Bob loved to write. Then, with an afternoon game on a road trip like this, they could go back to their motel room and leisurely write on their laptops.

Still, they had a 3:00 a.m. deadline, because *Miami P.M.*'s first edition was on the street by 7:00 a.m. to greet those heading to work. The only negative was not flying home with the Sharks. And now, missing a night with Suzy.

There was a lot of good stuff that could be obtained on the return team charter flight, but instead they were to return home on a commercial flight on Monday. Bob was already feeling pangs about not seeing Suzy on Sunday night. He tried to block her out of his thoughts and concentrate on the game. Then there was the Longo problem to be resolved.

It was a weird game. The Sharks dominated the Holsteins on offense, as Longo was seemingly completing passes at will, but he was having trouble getting the ball into the Green Bay end zone. Five interceptions and three lost fumbles by the Sharks had kept the underdog home team in the contest. Trailing 14-10 with 10:10 to play, the Holsteins moved 86 yards in nine plays for the go-ahead score.

Michael Phillips reeled off a pair of seven-yard runs, and quarterback Gordon Banks followed with a 43-yard scramble as the home crowd of 68,072 got into the game. Banks completed the scoring drive by finding rookie Kenny Edwards in the right corner of the end zone and reaching him with a bullet pass for a 29-yard TD.

Bob and Jorge looked at each other in disbelief.

"Doesn't look like the Sharks are going to cover the spread," Bob observed.

"It doesn't look like they're going to win, either, Bobby."

Bob watched the final five minutes of the game standing along the visitors' sideline with other media members. Trailing 17-14, the Sharks got the ball back on their seven yard line with 1:58 and all three timeouts left.

Longo showed no panic as he started the two-minute drill. His methodical drive up the middle cost them all three timeouts by the time he reached the Green Bay 38. There were 24 seconds left on the clock. Operating out of a shotgun offense, Longo took the snap from the center and dodged two blitzing Holsteins. Downfield, the quarterback spotted Muhammad Johnson open at the 20. He launched a spiral strike to the wide receiver as Johnson sprinted toward the end zone, only to be tripped up by the safety.

There was no yellow flag thrown by the back judge.

"What the fuck!" Sherman screamed. "That's a goddamned foul! He knocked my receiver down, you fucking blind zebra!"

With the game clock stopped by the incomplete pass, the Sharks gambled on one more pass into the end zone. This time, under pressure again, Longo was forced to dump off a pass to Richard Baldwin, who almost broke through for a touchdown. Baldwin was stopped at the Green Bay 6, but couldn't get out of bounds to stop the clock.

As Baldwin hurried off the field, kicker Siegfried von Katzen and the field goal team were poised to race onto the field. All Longo had to do was spike the ball. The scoreboard clock was ticking down, and the crowd was into the count: "Nine, eight, seven, six. . ."

The Holsteins were slow in returning to their side of the line while Longo quickly directed his mates to get in formation.

"Five, four, thee, two," roared 68,000 partisan voices.

Longo took the snap and spiked the football as the official's gun went off.

"I spiked the sucker! The clock should've stopped!" the quarterback yelled at the referee.

The seven-man crew of officials went into a huddle for what seemed like an eternity. The crowd was quiet as they awaited the decision. Von Katzen was in position for the field goal. Players on both sides yelled and made gestures at the huddled officials.

Finally, the referee left the conference, turned on his stadium mike and announced: "Time had expired. The game is over."

Sherman raced onto the field and attempted to reach the referee and his crew trotting off the field. Two burly security guards held him away from the officials.

"You assholes couldn't work a highschool game," the coach yelled at the officials.

Longo, who had completed 37 of 52 passes for 421 yards, had combined with Johnson for an amazing 16 receptions for 232 yards. The 16 catches were two short of the IFL record. One of his five interceptions had resulted in a 93-yard touchdown return by Green Bay's Lionel Jackson.

Sherman was not a happy coach when he met the media in front of the visitors' locker room. He shoved two TV mikes from his face and appeared drained emotionally. "I don't want to take anything away from Green Bay's victory," he began, "but we played like cow shit! You can't give any team in this league eight fucking turnovers and expect to win. We didn't get any breaks from the zebras at the end, but we never should've been in that position in the first place."

Bob McNamara, the radio voice of the Sharks, asked, "Coach, it looked from the radio booth like the back judge blew a pass interference call on that pass to Johnson."

"Yeah, the back judge blew the call big-time," snapped the coach. "What do you expect when the league uses part-time officials?"

That remark would later cost Sherman a $5,000 fine for violating IFL policy in being critical of officials to the media. At the moment, though, he was so angry he would have risked a $50,000 fine.

Bob asked the coach about Longo's performance.

"You saw it," he replied. "You tell me. He passes for more than four hundred yards, and we get only 14 fucking points. But don't blame just him. This was a fucking team loss."

Bob pursued his theme. "Coach, did you observe anything that Longo was doing out there that might have contributed to his eight turnovers?"

"You mean like playing with his pecker?" Sherman snapped. "I read that piece of shit of yours about gambling. You want me to say I think he deliberately threw five interceptions and fumbled three times? Your question doesn't even deserve an answer. Next question."

Jorge asked the coach about Johnson's 16 catches.

"Yes, Muhammad played well. Well, you know what we say about statistics. Statistics are for losers, and that's what we are today. We are 0-1 in the league standings. It's obvious that we have a lot of work to do."

It was quiet inside the players' locker room. The equipment managers were scooping up discarded dirty uniforms, white tape, and towels from the floor. The steam from the shower room slipped into the dressing room. Media members went from stall to stall to talk to selected players such as Johnson, but everyone was waiting for Longo to emerge from the training room, which was off-limits to visitors.

Bob found Carver seated on a stool in front of his locker stall. He was ripping tape off his ankles. He had received a broken nose, but the pain was tolerable.

"Bad day, George."

"We've had worse, Bobby," he replied. "We worked our butts off today on defense. You know, we gave up only one TD. Our offense gave up the other TD and set up their field goal. Don't print that! Use the company line, you know, about how this is a team game, etc."

"No problem, George. What about Longo? Kind of a real bad afternoon, huh?"

"Johnny is too good a quarterback to have such an afternoon. Between you and me, my man, if I didn't know better, it looked to me like he was on drugs out there. I'm no offensive genius. Defense is my game. But. . ."

"But, George?"

"Their defensive line wasn't that good," Carver continued. "They didn't pressure him at all. He just made bad reads or real bad throws."

"You don't say, George."

"Now, my man, don't start making a mountain out of a molehill," the defensive end cautioned. "You ask me what I thinks about his play for the record, and I'll give you the company line. You ask me what I thinks off the record as a friend, and that's another story."

Bob looked around. The two were being ignored. "I'm asking you off the record and as a friend."

"My man, I think Longo bet the spread, and he got more than he bargained for. And that's all I is gonna say because I'm headed into the trainer's room to put the fear of the Lord into that sinner."

Bob had the luxury of waiting after the rest of the media had given up on Longo emerging from the trainer's room. The locker room was nearly deserted when he limped slightly on his left leg.

"Hey, Johnny," came Bob's greeting.

"Not now, Bob. I have to catch the bus—"

"I think we have to talk," the columnist replied. "If not this minute, very soon. I know you have a problem, a big one—"

"Who's been feeding you that crap? I haven't got any problems except with our team being 0-1—"

"Save that line for the *Morning Journal*, Johnny. I'm talking about your business partner, Lucky Syracusa."

"Who? I don't know anyone by that name."

"Johnny, I'm trying to help you. But if you won't take it, then I'm going public."

"Right. You write whatever you want in that scandal sheet, but I've got a bus to catch." The quarterback brushed by the columnist and out of the locker room to the waiting team bus and the long plane ride back to Miami.

He was followed by Carver. The big defensive end glanced at Bob and shook his head, and his expression showed his disgust about his visit with the quarterback. Bob was now convinced that Longo was shaving points, maybe even tossing a game.

If he was going to break such a scandal, then he knew he would have to have solid evidence—evidence that would hold up in court.

#

While Bob and Jorge remained behind the Green Bay press box to file their copy, Suzy returned to Miami on the team charter. It was midway to Miami, at 38,000 feet, while Suzy was in the galley in the belly of the DC-10 checking the warming ovens that she was shocked to find Wargo standing there.

She could smell the beer on his breath, and his speech was slurred.

"Can I help you, Mr. Wargo?" she asked.

"I need another Coors, honey," he replied.

"Sorry, the beer is upstairs," she said, hoping that would get rid of the drunk.

"I know you were dying to be alone with me, little lady, so I sort of speeded things up," he said with a grin.

The inference angered the flight attendant, but she controlled her feelings. "Sir, you know you aren't supposed to be in the galley," she replied firmly. "That's an FAA rule."

"But I'm Larry Wargo. You know, the Sharks' fullback."

"Sir, I know who you are, but—"

He reached for her suddenly and tried to kiss her on the lips. Suzy struggled, but she knew it would be useless as she felt the strength in his arms.

"Come on, sweet thing, just a little quickie for your favorite Shark," he muttered as he placed a hand up her skirt. "Such a nice pair of legs. . . *y-e-o-w!* What the fuck!"

"Oh, excuse me, sir, I didn't mean to spill the coffee," she said, managing to sound truly sorry. The flight attendant stood there with the empty coffeepot as Wargo grimaced in pain from the hot liquid assault on his lap. She hoped his penis felt like it was on fire.

He was furious about being rejected and humiliated by the assault, but before anything else could happen, a voice called out, "You need help down there, Suzy?"

It was flight attendant Chris Gaylord.

"Yes, thank you. A player had an accident," she replied. "I spilled some coffee in his lap. Can you get the first-aid kit and come down here? I think this is a guy kind of treatment."

A smiling Gaylord, whom Suzy knew to be gay, figured out what had happened. He enjoyed the opportunity to pour soda water on Wargo's lap and massage it slowly with a cloth. Gaylord could feel the hard-on as he rubbed the coffee stains out.

The fullback wasn't amused. Wargo had been rendered speechless.

Suzy was angry, but she knew that proving sexual assault would be difficult even if it was against a flight attendant. It would be a "he said, she said" case. In court, what Miami jury would ever convict the star Sharks fullback of sexual assault on any woman? Not to mention the fact that Sun Airlines would probably sack her for causing negative publicity.

Suzy cooled off, and at the end of the flight she made it a point not to be cowed by Wargo as the six-foot-two, 240-pounder deplaned.

Standing next the cabin door, Gaylord bid farewell to Wargo with, "Thank you for flying Sun Airlines." And with a knowing grin, whispered, "You aren't going to be free any time soon in Miami, are you, big fella? I know a great disco joint. . ."

Wargo clenched his teeth hard and said nothing. He had been humiliated enough by that bimbo flight attendant, and now this queer was hitting on him.

Suzy would never have told anyone about the incident. Not even Bob. The Wargo incident bothered her, of course. She was still surprised, remembering her cool response while under attack. He was an arrogant animal. She would often shiver when she recalled his fingers groping her pantyhose and catching a glimpse of his hard-on sticking out of his slacks. Dumping the coffee was strictly a reflex, but it had saved her.

Maybe that was the image which that old tell-all book *Coffee, Tea, or Me?* gave the public.

CHAPTER 9

"Help me, Cassius, or I sink!"
                        William Shakespeare
                        Julius Caesar

Bob Casey's Working Press:
Time for a QB change?
Longo's days numbered

GREEN BAY—With Johnny Longo 36 years old and Eddie Malloy as his backup, the Miami Sharks must start thinking about their quarterback of the future.

Like now.

After a team record of eight turnovers by Longo in Sunday's embarrassing 17-14 loss to the lowly Green Bay Holsteins, Sharks management will have to make some fast decisions.

Longo is playing on a pair of battered knees. I saw him limp out of the visitors' locker room, and I'm wondering how much longer his battered body can survive on Sunday afternoons.

Malloy is in his fifth season and is due to become a free agent this coming winter. He is starting to realize he has a big-bucks future. Surely the job he did in going 5-2 last season when Longo was sidelined with a knee problem tells us this.

The crisis is fast approaching for the Sharks. Longo still believes he has a few good years left. How can Sherman keep both quarterbacks satisfied?

If the Sharks want to designate Malloy as their "franchise" player in order to retain him, they will have to give him a contract worth more than $20 million, by IFL rules. If they are thinking in terms of a "transitional" player, that pact must top $18 million.

For a franchise player, the amount is based on the average salaries of the league's five highest-paid quarterbacks. For transition status, the contract must call for the average of the top 10 quarterbacks. So the Sharks will have to shell out somewhere in the vicinity of $20 million to keep Malloy.

The bottom line question for GM Jack Cabot is not if owner Sol Rubin can afford $50 million for quarterbacks, but whether they will lose other key players to keep two fat-cat quarterbacks.

After Longo's dismal performance here on Sunday, I would suggest that Coach Don Sherman start Malloy in this Sunday's home opener against Eastern Division foe Buffalo.

#

Bob filed his story over the telephone in his room. It was 2:00 a.m. in Wisconsin, but 3:00 a.m. back in Florida. He closed his PowerBook computer, found a cigar, and poured himself a Hennessy's cognac. As he watched the ash appear at the end of the cigar, he called Bloom at home.

"Why the fuck are you calling me at this hour?" demanded a groggy Bloom.

"Larry, I'm building a trap to catch some rats."

"You're what? Oh, never mind. I'm going back to sleep. Have a nice flight home."

"I won't, boss. I'm flying home on United. Sun Air doesn't service Green Bay."

"Gee, Bob, you won't have Suzykins to wait on you on that flight."

"Fuck you, boss."

Larry laughed and hung up.

Bob returned to his drink and cigar as he unwound. He tried to think about Suzy, but his train of thought kept returning to Longo.

I really think I covered a pro game where the quarterback not only shaved points but dumped it, too. I can't believe the coaches won't start thinking the same way after they review the films today. What about the other players? Do they smell a rat, like Carver does? Why the hell did Conte tip me off?

The Sharks' flight home was quiet. The players did not feel good about losing their season-opener, especially to a weak opponent like Green Bay. After beer and dinner, most of the players in coach tried to nap. The coaching staff in first class were busy studying game tapes in their mini-viewers and making notes about player performances for Tuesday morning's team meeting.

Johnny sat alone in the back of the aircraft on the left aisle. He had the two aisle seats to himself and had pulled up the armrest. He had cold packs attached to both knees, and the team doctor had given him a couple shots of Novocaine plus some pain pills. He rejected common sense, and washed down the pills with a can of Coors.

He wanted to sleep. The pain and the thoughts that engulfed him prevented the quarterback from such escapism. He kept reviewing how he could get more action with Syracusa. It was bad enough that he was in the hole to him for $2.5 million, but now the SOB was charging usury interest on the gambling advances. Syracusa had gone from a golfing buddy to a hard-nosed shylock.

He wants my pound of flesh, and he's beginning to get nasty. He says I owe him more than $5 million because of interest on my advances. He says the interest keeps increasing. I just need a couple of big scores, and I can pay back some of that.

He had wagered on the Holsteins to cover the spread—not win—in the Sunday game. *It isn't even easy for a quarterback to manage that. There are too many factors such as legitimate fumbles, dropped passes, and missed calls by officials. That back judge blowing that interference call cost me big-time.*

#

It was a combination of fear and embarrassment that brought Longo to turn to his parish priest for help. The next day, he finished the early morning Mass at St. Vincent's Church in Miami Shores and called on Father O'Malley at the rectory next door.

"Father," Johnny said in a slow monotone, "as you know, I have a problem with wagering."

O'Malley nodded but said nothing.

As Johnny sat across from O'Malley in the Spartan den of the priest's rectory, he knew he needed someone safe to talk to. It had taken a great deal of courage to overcome his shame and make it to the priest's home.

However, Johnny's troubles were bigger than his embarrassment now. He couldn't look the priest in the eyes. He hesitated a moment longer and glanced at three bookcases filled to overflowing. Assorted photos, a Miami Sharks pennant, and a large crucifix hung on the wall.

Johnny took a deep breath, tensely locked his fingers together, and stared at the maroon carpet on the floor. "Some guys think I. . .I dumped the game on Sunday."

"Did you, my son?"

The priest's directness startled him. Johnny looked up. "No, no, no. I didn't do anything bad. I didn't shave points. I didn't try to lose. I just had a very bad game. The harder I tried to win, the more errors I made."

"I want to believe you, Johnny," O'Malley replied. "The problem, however, is that some others are starting to think the worst of you."

The quarterback didn't mean to bare his soul, but he did. "Would they believe me, Father, if I could prove that although I did bet on the game, it was for the Sharks to win?"

O'Malley's mouth opened in amazement. "You *what*?"

Johnny started to sweat, but he had gone too far to stop his confession. "I bet a hundred Gs on the Sharks to win," he said. "I lost a hundred Gs on that game, Father. It's bad enough that I lost so much money, but it's worse now for some to believe that I tanked the game." Johnny's hands started to tremble. He looked around for a place to put his mug, and placed it on the edge of the desk. "Father, I need help. I'm paying a hundred Gs a week in interest to my bookie."

There was a brief moment of silence as the priest seemed to ponder what he was being told. "One hundred thousand dollars a week in interest? Johnny, that's more than some of my parishioners make in five years." O'Malley got up and went to the center bookcase. It opened, and the priest found an open bottle of Hennessy's and poured cognac into a pair of Waterford glasses. "We both need a belt of this, my son," he said as he took a long swig.

"No, thank you, Father. . ." Johnny politely protested.

"Drink it, Johnny, drink it," the priest insisted. It was more of an order than a request. O'Malley handed him a glass of cognac.

Longo didn't argue. The cognac seemed to calm his nerves.

"Johnny, you can't go on this way." O'Malley talked softly as he paced the small room, pausing only for a taste of the cognac in the glass he held in his right hand. "I'm only a priest, not a lawyer. You must think of Martha and the children. I think you have to go the authorities, as well as the league, before you reach the road of no return."

This wasn't exactly the advice the quarterback was hoping for.

"What you have done so far is wrong. So far, however, you only have hurt yourself. And you've financially damaged your family, too. I believe you know this, or you wouldn't be here. I can pray for you, my son, but it is you who must help yourself."

The quarterback nodded and took another swig of cognac. "I think Bob Casey is sniffing around. He goes to church here, doesn't he?"

"This is Bob's parish," O'Malley said. "I regret to say he hasn't been coming since his marriage failed." Before the quarterback could ask the priest the damning question, O'Malley asserted, "Bobby is one of us. He's a good Catholic lad. Maybe not in keeping his marriage or in church attendance, but he is a man of honor, a decent man. You might seek him out. Having a newspaper columnist in your corner wouldn't hurt. It might help."

Johnny pondered the suggestion. "You may be right, Father. I don't need any more enemies than I have already."

"Bless you," O'Malley said. "I will keep you in my prayers."

#

Johnny left the rectory for the short walk to the church parking lot, where he had left his Mercedes sedan. As soon as he opened the rectory door, the bright tropical sun blinded him. His mind was on a cure to his problems. *What I need is a winning streak. Then I can pay back my debts.*

He fumbled for his sunglasses. While he was putting them on, he didn't notice the white Lincoln Town Car pull up to the sidewalk. Two burly men in tropical suits jumped out and grabbed him before he knew what was happening. His first thought was that he was about to be robbed.

"What are you guys doing?" he yelled. "I'll give you my cash—"

"Shut up," said a middle-aged guy in a white tropical suit with a Panama fedora. "Mr. Syracusa wants to see ya."

The other man poked the quarterback in the gut with a .380 Walther PPK. "Get in the back and shut up!" The gunman forced the quarterback into the back seat of the Lincoln.

Longo was scared. It felt like something out of a gangster movie. "Where are you taking me?"

The ride was short. Pushed out of the car by a gunman, Longo came face to face with Syracusa. The two hoods held him slightly. He tried to smile and greet Syracusa, but it didn't work.

Syracusa slapped Longo across his face. "Motherfucker," the gangster said as he grabbed Longo by the shirt collar. "Where the fuck is my money?"

Johnny was struggling to appease Syracusa as the two stood inside what appeared to be an auto repair shop. It was dark, humid, and dirty.

"Take off his right shoe," Syracusa ordered.

One of the hoods pulled off the right brown penny loafer.

"You know I'm good for it. . ." Johnny started, but he didn't get to finish his sentence. He couldn't figure out why Syracusa went down on one knee, and the flash of the hammer wielded by Syracusa was only a brief blur. Then Longo screamed in pain as the hammer smashed on his right foot.

"You've broken my foot," the quarterback moaned as he fell to the concrete floor that was stained with oil and grease.

"No, motherfucker, only a couple of toes," Syracusa snarled as he dropped the hammer to the floor. "I was very careful not to put you on the disabled list."

Johnny was truly scared.

"Now listen carefully, Johnny boy," the gangster continued. "This is a sneak preview of what happens to jerks who can't or won't pay their debts. You owe me big-time, and this ain't no credit union. So I'll tell you what I'm gonna do. You got seven days to come up with a hundred Gs."

"But, but. . ." protested Longo.

"Seven days. If you fail, you may be dinner for some real sharks in the Atlantic," said Syracusa. "Now, boys, take our client back to his car. Seven days, Longo, seven days."

#

Monday was the players' day off. Sherman and his staff were busy reviewing the video of the Green Bay loss and preparing for the home opener. The suggestion that their quarterback deliberately threw interceptions or made fumbles never was a consideration for the coaches. They knew that even future Hall of Famers had bad days, too. "Otherwise, we wouldn't have to play the damn game every Sunday," Sherman was fond of saying.

Rubin didn't sober up until Tuesday morning, so he never missed his wife, who didn't sleep at home Sunday night. He sure missed the 20 Gs he lost Sunday backing the Sharks. He didn't just blame Longo.

"The whole fucking team sucked," he ranted to anyone who would listen. Sherman's game plan sucked, too."

#

Shortly after breakfast in his nearby Hollywood home, Gattino called Greenwich. "Godfather. That prick Syracusa must have gotten to Longo. I understand that fucking Miami newspaper columnist Casey is smelling a rat. If Longo is shaving points. . .you knows. It would probably trigger a congressional investigation. So I need a travel agent who can plan Syracusa's next trip."

"I have just the man for the job," said the godfather. "He's young, and in a way he's from the old school."

"I'm listening, Godfather," Gattino said.

"His name is Jimmy 'The Trigger' Scalise," said the godfather. "He lives on the West Coast but prefers to do business on the East Coast."

"If you say he's the best travel agent, I'll hire him," Gattino said.

The godfather laughed. "You show me respect with your trust, but let me tell you about his credentials." The godfather gave Scalise's background. "Orphaned at an early age, he was trained in crime by his older brother Vito. He was able to avoid prison, but not the draft. He served in the Army in the final months of Vietnam. On one occasion, he stormed a Viet Cong machine gun nest and killed 18 Cong. An officer had to restrain Scalise later, when he was still pumping bullets into the dead bodies.

"Following his honorable discharge from the Army, he returned home to Los Angeles. In addition to robbing stores, he hired himself out as a freelancer, using a Tommy gun, and earning the sobriquet of 'Trigger.'"

"Meaning no disrespect," protested Gattino, "but this isn't a job for some jerk who uses a tommy gun. Tommy guns are old-fashioned."

"Sal," the godfather said with a chuckle, "please let me finish." And he continued. "Scalise quickly developed a reputation as a berserk killer, but he was efficient, so he got 50 Gs per contract. It is debatable whether he often kills for mere pleasure or out of the intense rage that consumes him. He has done several contracts for me by a middleman. He never asked 'why?' or 'who?' only 'when?' So I have taken the liberty of assigning Scalise your contract."

"I have no problems with your selection," Gattino said.

"Now you gotta love this guy," the godfather continued with enthusiasm. "Scalise is a loner. He scoffs at a driver or backups. He trusts no one, which is probably why he is so successful. His choice of a client's departure is the restaurant.

"You know, he loves old-time gangster movies and has a library full of videos of 1930 to 1940 movies. He envied the old-timers using those Tommy guns, despite the problem in concealing them. 'No sawed-off shotguns or fucking Uzis for me,' he told my agent. 'No silencers or any of that fag CIA stuff. I want to hear that rat-a-tat-tat. I would have loved working during Prohibition.'"

Gattino laughed. "Ah, nostalgia. You knows, Godfather, it brings back fond memories to me. Thank you for your help in this matter."

"Remember, Sal, Scalise doesn't know why or what for, only who. No way if he is caught that he can be connected to our family."

#

The season opener at Miami was played in a driving rainstorm. Even without the ailing Longo, it appeared that the Sharks would beat Buffalo.

Bob was bundled in a yellow slicker as he stood near the Sharks bench during the final five minutes of the game. "Looks like the Sharks will win it," he said to a nearby reporter.

As Bob was contemplating a column around the heroics of Miami reserve quarterback Malloy, Snowmen quarterback Jim Frazier hit wide receiver Bobby Blades with 2:03. Blades sloshed 63 yards for a touchdown that gave Buffalo the lead, 22-15.

Bob was rooting for Malloy to come back and pull out the win. *A win will make for a much better column.*

Malloy, who started in place of the injured Longo, was 16-of-28 for 243 yards and a touchdown.

Come on, Eddie old pal. Win one for the columnist.

Malloy started his two-minute drill on the Miami 33. He drove the Sharks to the Buffalo 23. The clock showed 12 seconds left.

The Miami quarterback faded back to pass. Johnson was open in the left corner of the end zone. Malloy put the ball in the air. Some 72,000 voices in Sol Rubin Stadium were stilled as the ball spiraled toward Johnson.

But because of the rain, Johnson slipped on the soaked grass just as the ball was arriving. A Buffalo defensive back, who had been beaten initially by Johnson, recovered and made the interception.

"Damn!" Bob muttered.

"Hey, Casey, you have money on this game?" asked a radio broadcaster.

"Fuck you," Bob replied.

#

"We didn't play well," Sherman told the press conference following the game. "Yes, the rain was certainly a problem. And yes, we do miss Longo despite what you guys think and write. You know, a lot of our guys didn't play very well for the second straight week. This is a reflection on the coaching staff."

"It was my mistake," Johnson said in the somber quiet of the Miami clubhouse. "I had to make that play. When you are in the IFL, you have to make those plays."

Bob and Jorge went back to *Miami P.M.* to write. The columnist was in no hurry to get home, because Suzy was working a five-day trip in the Northeast. When he left the office at about 9:00 p.m. Sunday, he spotted Dom Conte visiting with the newspaper security guard at the employee entrance. Conte followed him into the parking lot.

"Mr. Bloom paid me for my services," said Conte. "Now I have some really juicy stuff. How would you guys like some evidence that links Longo to a bookie? No need to answer, Mr. Casey. I have in my possession some copies of credit card transactions made with South Florida Sports Consultants Inc. The state of Florida lists one Augusta Syracusa as the chief operating officer."

Surprise showed on Bob's face. "You're telling me that Longo used his credit cards to make bets?"

"More important," Conte said with a smirk, "Syracusa was *estúpido* to accept any kind of payment that left a paper trail. So you tell Mr. Bloom to find 20 Gs, and the information is all his."

Conte left Bob speechless for a moment. "You want $20,000 for this information? Come on, Conte, you have to understand that we're a newspaper, not General Motors. And how do we know this stuff is genuine?"

"Listen, hot-shot columnist," said the PI, "if your little paper can't afford this story, then I'm sure the *Morning Journal*. . ."

"Okay, Conte, I'll tell my boss. But I can't promise you $20,000. If we do, it will take a few days, because we don't have that kind of change in petty cash. While I'm at it, why are you being so nice to us?"

"I love *Miami P.M.*," the PI said a bit sarcastically. "It's simple. You get the money. You give me the money. I give you the evidence. Bloom knows how to reach me."

Bob watched the PI slowly disappear into the night, and kept saying to himself, "That asshole Syracusa." The columnist climbed into his Corvette and dialed Bloom at home on the car phone. *Damn! The line is busy. If Conte's stuff is for real, this will be one helluva story.*

After the fourth try, Bloom answered the phone.

"Larry, you won't believe this. . ."

#

The following Thursday night, Syracusa, his gal pal, and two of his soldiers arrived at La Stelle, a four-star French restaurant on Miami Beach. During the winter season, you needed to tip the maitre d' at least $50 with reservations, and $100 without.

"This is like being in Paris," Syracusa boasted to his companions. "This joint has the dark woods, rich leathers, expensive paintings, and fresh flowers on every table and sideboard. Overlooking the main dining room is a balcony where two bookkeepers operate, just like in France."

"But, honey, the menu is in French," complained Syracusa's gal pal when they were seated by Miguel, the maitre d'.

"Youse don't worry, honey, I'll do the ordering for all of us," Syracusa said.

Miguel smiled. The menu was in French, and the women's menu never contained any prices. As always, Miguel had discreetly slipped an English version of the menu inside the main French one so the mobster never looked foolish ordering. Miguel still remembered a Friday night two years ago when Syracusa had entertained six major contractors and their wives. Between courses, a finger bowl of water with a lemon was served. The mobster, mistaking it for an entree, had spooned the bowl dry. A very savvy wife of a contractor had immediately followed his example. The rest had joined in. *Embarrassing a man like Syracusa could be harmful to one's health*, thought Miguel.

Miguel hovered over Syracusa's party as if he were attending royalty. He bowed and scraped, as if the party were blue blood instead of Black Hand.

Syracusa was still upset about Longo. He ignored his gal pal as he complained to his two soldiers about the situation. They just listened and nodded in agreement. On occasion, one or both would add, "Right, boss."

"That puke was lucky I didn't break his fucking hands," Syracusa said. "If I did, he'd be out for the fucking season. Now that he knows I'm serious, we're going to find a big game for him to help me make a fucking killing."

Just before the main course, Tony Salerno, one of the soldiers, excused himself to make a phone call. This should have made Syracusa suspicious, but his 26-year-old gal pal, was massaging his penis under the table. She had no class. She had gone down on him under the table in lesser joints, but she knew he wouldn't want that in this fancy establishment.

The other soldier, Paulie Roma, studied the French menu as if he understood the language. Meanwhile, the gal pal had discreetly unzipped the mobster's fly and had given him a very quick hand job. Roma looked up from the menu to see his boss's face in a contortion, and at first he thought it was a heart attack.

Syracusa's penis exploded in the woman's gifted right hand, and she nonchalantly wiped his penis and her hand in one of the expensive purple cloth napkins.

"You must have studied music, Helena," said Syracusa, breathing hard.

"Why, hon?"

"'Cause you make beautiful music on my organ."

At about that moment, Scalise entered the restaurant. He appeared dapper in a gray, double-breasted suit, designer shirt, and black knit tie.

Obviously, he must be in the arts, thought Miguel as he greeted the patron. The fact that he carried a trench coat over his music case in South Florida should have been a red flag for Syracusa. But the mobster was relaxing after sex and the start of a second $175 bottle of Italian red wine. He was thinking about anal sex with Helena when they got home.

Scalise smiled warmly and shook hands with Miguel, leaving a wad of bills. He then said he would dine only if they had in stock a rare 1972 French Pomard. Miguel was positive he had the wine, but excused himself to check the wine room in the rear of the establishment.

That gave Scalise the time to do his work.

The tommy gun's bark was deafening in the close quarters of the dining room. The rapid fire of .45-caliber bullets cut down Syracusa, his gal pal, and Roma. Scalise used steel-jacket hollow-point ammunition, which exploded in the victims, splashing blood and flesh over the booth and wall. It was all over before shocked and screaming patrons could hit the floor.

Scalise calmly reloaded his weapon and walked quickly to the men's room. One quick burst cut down the informer. The hit man calmly dismantled his submachine gun, placed it in its case, and walked out the door to where the valet parking lot attendant had his rental car running. He thanked the kid, who had his headphones tuned to rap music and was oblivious to the gunfire, gave him a crisp $20 bill, and drove slowly past a dozen police cars with flashing blue lights, which were converging on the scene.

#

Miguel was upset somewhat by the incident, but realized that the publicity would help business during this slow season. He owed the hit man, who had asked him to check out the wine cellar for a rare wine. When questioned by police, he glanced at the crisp $100 bills that had been pressed into his hand by the gunman. There were 10 bills.

"I'd like to help, Detective, I really would. It all happened so fast. Well, the gunman was a dark-complexioned Latin. He wore blue jeans and a black leather jacket. He certainly wasn't the kind of person we would welcome to this restaurant."

The Miami Beach police termed it "a drug-related incident," because the two dead soldiers were known traffickers. And since the murders happened late in the evening, they weren't reported on the 11:00 p.m. TV newscasts, and the *Miami Morning Journal* buried the story inside its late edition Metro Section.

This, of course, was a story made for *Miami P.M.* It was the lead.

Mob gunman denies four their desserts

\#

Bob huddled with Bloom in the ME's office most of Friday.

"Hey, guys, what was the name of that restaurant where the shootings took place?" asked Mary Jane Williams, Bloom's secretary.

"Why do you care?" Larry wanted to know.

"I want my husband to take me there to dinner. I mean, would a Mafia don eat at a crummy restaurant?"

"Aren't you scared to go to a joint like that?" Bob asked.

"Hell no!" she asserted while emptying the ashtrays. "The Mafia is very careful not to piss off law-abiding citizens by killing us. I mean, the Mafia doesn't want any bad press."

"Mary Jane, when I worked in New York, there was an incident in 1992 at a Manhattan restaurant where two couples were gunned down by Mafia hit men. The hired guns were from Las Vegas and were looking for members of the Colombia family. The four people they killed were tourists visiting New York from Norwalk, Ohio."

Between cigars, coffee, and a deli lunch brought in by Mary Jane, both newspapermen mulled over their next move. Larry had agreed to pay Conte the $20,000 for his evidence, but it was still premature to go to press accusing the quarterback of being a gambler with Mafia connections.

"With that sucker Syracusa dead, it will make our task harder," Bloom lamented. "But it won't change anything for Longo. Hell, the Mafia will still want its pound of flesh."

Bob groped for a match to light a fresh cigar. "Maybe, maybe not," he offered. "What if Syracusa's loan-sharking and bookmaking operation was a ruse? I mean, according to Major Hess, Gattino is the gambling don for this territory."

"Does that mean Longo could walk away scot-free from his gambling debts?" the managing editor asked.

"I haven't a clue, boss," Bob said. "But I think it is time for me to corner Mr. Longo and have a long chat. Once we get those credit card slips, we can squeeze his nuts."

"Right, Bobby. But go easy on this one. The fact that four people are dead should raise a red flag. You don't want to make Suzy a widow before she's even married, do you?"

#

The morning news was very disturbing to Longo. He put down the morning newspaper and almost knocked over a cup of coffee. His face turned ashen. The couple had been sparring over the cost of braces for their oldest child.

"What's wrong?" Martha asked her husband as she finished the breakfast dishes.

"Nothing," he replied, obviously upset. "Why does something have to be wrong?"

But something *was* wrong. If he had problems with Syracusa, what next? He started to feel fear. *These SOBs play hardball. Who will come collecting next? Will they be willing to settle for me shaving a few points? Or will they pressure me into dumping a game?*

#

St. Vincent's Church was packed the following Monday morning for Syracusa's funeral. It was a lavish affair, and Father O'Malley was scheduled to perform a Mass of requiem.

"Father, I can't believe you're giving that Mafia hood a formal church burial," Bob scolded the priest in a phone conversation.

"Robert, if Mr. Syracusa has sinned, God will punish him," replied O'Malley. "He was a member of this parish. I would do the same for you, too."

The columnist calmed down. He knew that the godfather had ordered a lavish funeral as a goodwill gesture to the Detroit family.

What he didn't know was that Gattino had informed the priest earlier that the kin of the late Syracusa had deposited $100,000 in the St. Vincent's bank account. The money was just in time for the school building project. O'Malley considered this heaven-sent, and could easily cloud his mind as to who had made such a generous contribution.

Cardinal Murphy had threatened to bar a church funeral, but had given in to a passionate long-distance telephone plea by the parish priest. The cardinal had cited Canon Law 1184, which stipulated that funeral Masses would be denied to "manifest sinners" who had not shown some signs of repentance before death. In this case, it seemed that the Mafia dead got the benefit of doubt.

"Your Grace, if Mr. Syracusa was not a Catholic in life, we should have told him, 'You're no good.' Don't say it now, when the family is going to get hurt. He did not die instantly, so I feel he had time to reflect and repent."

When informed of the generous gift to the church school, the cardinal pondered his decision for a generous 60 seconds. "I think you are probably correct, Father. Mr. Syracusa did have time to reflect and repent. Give him the benefit of doubt."

"It was a nice Mass," observed Mrs. Gattino. "I love Father O'Malley, but. . .it would have been nicer, you know, if we had an Italian priest. . ."

CHAPTER 10

"Do ye hear the children weeping, O my brothers?"
E.B. Browning
The Cry of the Children

LONGO RETURNED TO the lineup in week three and sparked Miami to a 42-3 rout of the hapless Titans in New York. That took some of the heat off the Sharks' quarterback. The following week in SRS, the 1-2 Sharks entertained the Boston Minutemen—who held a surprising 3-0 record—in a crucial Eastern Division game.

Bob was happy that it was a 1:00 p.m. kickoff, because it meant he would be able to have a late dinner with Suzy after writing his game column. The way things had started out for the Sharks, it appeared that Casey would be able to write most of his piece by the halftime intermission.

Thinking of getting out of Sol Rubin Stadium early, he started to write a ripper about the Sharks after they fell behind 27-0 with 4:32 left in the half.

The Sharks partisans not only were filling the stadium with catcalls and boos, but a quarter of the 72,000 spectators had already left for the exits.

Bob stopped watching the game and was hitting the keys on his PowerMac G4. He slowed only when the Sharks finally got on the board with an 87-yard touchdown drive when Longo hit Johnson in the corner of the end zone with an 18-yard pass. Von Katzen's place kick was followed by his 48-yard field goal as time expired in the first half.

"Hey, amigo, we're only down 27-10," chided Jorge.

"That's wonderful, Wetback," Bob said without stopping his typing. "Tell me, how many IFL teams have come back from 27-0?"

"Not many," Jorge replied.

"The correct number is two," Bob said. "Two in the whole history of the IFL. And they didn't have that stiff Longo at quarterback."

Runningback Richard Baldwin, however, helped spoil Bob's original column. Baldwin, a five-foot-ten, 240-pounder dubbed "The Bowling Ball" because he ran low and hard, rumbled for 149 yards and four touchdowns in a fantastic last half comeback. He carried the football 14 times, including second-half touchdown runs of 5, 15, 22, and 55. His final TD came on the run from the Boston 45, but von Katzen shanked the extra point kick. This gave Miami a 37-33 lead with 1:12 remaining.

With each Sharks TD, Bob had shouted "Oh, shit!" and hit the delete button on his laptop. This only produced laughter from Jorge. Bob finally pushed aside his computer and picked up his field glasses as the game came down to what would be a wild finish.

What's the spread on this game? Miami by 10 1/2? Someone with money on the Minutemen could win big today if the Sharks win by less than the spread. Could Longo be. . .?

The Minutemen didn't fold after taking the ensuing kickoff in the end zone for a touchback.

Starting from the Boston 20, quarterback Danny Ryan was knocked out of the game by Miami linebacker Brutus Neswiacheny, who drew a 15-yard roughing-the-passer foul. Ryan was then replaced by Dan Cavanaugh.

Bob used his field glasses to scan the Miami bench. He was trying to see if he could detect any emotion from Longo.

If the gamblers have their way, pro football will be as honest as Roller Derby.

#

Standing on the sidelines, Longo felt good. Win or lose, his money was safe because he had managed to place 20 bets of $5,000 each on the Minutemen. *And there isn't any way the Sharks can cover the spread.*

Longo felt great. He didn't feel tired, and the old body didn't ache. He got into the team leadership thing as he exhorted the defense to dig in.

It will be great getting a payoff Monday, rather than trying to hide from the damn hoods. Still, I have to worry about Syracusa's pals. Do they have my paper? Why haven't they come after me? Maybe I better stick 10 Gs of my winnings in Martha's checking account. That should get her off my case for a while.

Longo watched the new opposition quarterback complete a 16-yard pass, benefit from a 34-yard pass-interference call, and move the Minutemen to the Miami 12.

That Cavanaugh isn't bad. Still has a lot to learn, but he shows he can handle the pressure of the two-minute drill. God, I wish I was 23 again.

#

Everyone was standing in the press box. The crowd was hushed as Cavanaugh took the snap and faded back to pass. He fired a bullet to a receiver in the center of the end zone.

"Sack the motherfucker!" Johnny yelled, trying to act as a team cheerleader.

Brutus Neswiacheny—clearly holding the intended receiver—

broke up the pass. The gun sounded. The crowd went wild. Cavanaugh was in a rage as he screamed at the game officials, all to no avail.

Johnny laughed. He nudged Johnson. "Hey Muhammad, Brutus got away with a big one."

"Those zebras have to be blind, or maybe they have some money on the game," the wide receiver said. He was kidding.

Johnny laughed heartily as he joined the players for the trot to the locker room.

#

"At one time, it was one of the most disappointing games I have been involved in," Sherman said from inside the Miami locker room. "I really commend our players for the way they came back and hung in there today. It was a highly unusual game."

Johnny was in a good mood. In front of his locker stall, the quarterback told a throng of reporters, "As a team, we withstood this, and no one gave up. I'd like to get back in a situation where we don't need the last half excitement." Johnny, who had been booed in the first half, completed 26-of-42 passes for 325 yards and one touchdown.

"Johnny has toughness for a gray beard," Sherman said. "He certainly displayed it today. He threw the ball well in the second half, despite being battered around quite a bit in the first half."

#

By the halfway mark of the 16-game IFL regular season, the Sharks were 6-2 and tied with Buffalo for first place in the Eastern Division. The earlier loss to Buffalo could be costly for Miami if both teams ended in a tie in the standings. The Sharks had a chance to even things up during Christmas week in Buffalo. That was the end of the regular season, and the following week the IFL playoffs would begin that would lead to the World Bowl.

Considering that he had love and Longo on his mind, Bob was surprised that he could still grind out a daily sports column. His love of Suzy, however, had a positive effect. His latest concern was whether to have a formal church wedding because of his divorce.

"Maybe one of your Mafia pals will make a donation to the church on your behalf," Suzy said. She was kidding.

"No, Sky Princess, on *your* behalf," he replied. "You are the one living in sin right now."

On the first Sunday of November, the Sharks were scheduled to play in New Orleans. Miami had two home games—the New York Titans again and the Los Angeles Dons—before the big Thanksgiving Day game in Dallas. The Jazz had won only once, and this was expected to be a piece of cake for the Sharks.

Bob and Suzy were looking forward to the layover in New Orleans, but the flight attendant was concerned that this might be their only time together for a while. The Machinists Union was set to vote Sunday on striking Sun Airlines, and there seemed little doubt that Kelly would get the votes for his strike.

Muhammad Johnson drove his purple Porsche 911 with Florida license plate SHARK 85 through the Liberty City ghetto neighborhood en route to Miami International Airport. The car radio was blaring a rap music number from a CD. His body ached from assorted injuries from seven years as a wide receiver in pro football, as well as Sunday's recent additions. He felt at times that he wanted to quit. *Where else could I make millions catching a football?*

So on game day, when the pain began to engulf him, he went

to Daniel Barker, M.D., and the team doctor provided some pain pills and a shot of Novocaine. *This morning, I'm going to get some real medicine.*

Johnson pulled into the deserted parking lot at Union Hall, which was conveniently across the street from the Sun Airlines' maintenance facility at MIA.

He was early and hoping his man would be, too. He spotted T.J. Lewis leaving the employee gate and walk slowly toward the union building. While Lewis and Johnson were both African-Americans, their backgrounds were vastly different. The player knew Lewis was a local Liberty City kid. He knew he was a union representative and thus excused from airline work.

"Nice car, Muhammad," Lewis said while sliding into the passenger seat. "Frankly, I dig my Mercedes roadster better."

Yeah, that fucker is making big bucks as a drug dealer.

"Hey, man, you mothers looked like you were all high yesterday."

"Cut the shit, T.J.," Johnson implored. "You got some shit for me? You knows, I really need it bad."

"Now bro, you knows T.J. is your main man. I have here some real good shit fresh off the plane from Colombia." Lewis, who was dressed in a company mechanic's uniform and baseball cap, opened up his lunch box and pulled out a large plastic bag of white cocaine powder. "Who say it don't snow in Florida, Muhammad?"

Johnson fumbled for his wallet.

"Cool it, bro, you don't need no green to gets the white. Not from T.J. Your bro here just needs a little favor."

"Like fixing him up with a white Sharks cheerleader," Johnson quipped.

"Hell no, brother! I can always find a white bitch that wants to do her liberal thing and fuck a nigger. No, Muhammad. Whats I needs is a chance to meets some of your friends. You knows, like at parties and such. In return for your cooperation, I will render unto you an unending supply of white happiness. You can call it a professional courtesy."

Johnson knew what Lewis wanted. He was looking for new customers, and the All-Pro would be the Pied Piper. He didn't like the role, but the opportunity of free cocaine was overwhelming. *Anyhow*, he rationalized, *if people want drugs, they will get them from someone. So why not Lewis?*

"Sunday. After the Buffalo game. There's a party in Plantation. That's in Broward County. Here, give me your pen. Here's the address. Dress is casual but neat. Talk like a ghetto nigger. The rich, liberal honkies dig that shit."

"Thank you, my main man," Lewis said with gusto. "Now, are you stiffs going to cover the spread Sunday against Buffalo? We got a hangar pool going. Everybody healthy? How about Longo?"

"Fuck you, mother," Johnson snapped. "I'll help you sell drugs to the honkies, but I won't help you compromise the great game of pro football by givin' you insider information."

The wide receiver smiled when he saw Lewis was momentarily stunned. Then both men laughed.

"I admire a man of integrity," Lewis said as he left the Porsche. "Now don't you go sniffing until you get home. Don't want no honky pig pulling you over."

Johnson hit the gas pedal and enjoyed the sound of the tires squealing as he headed out of the lot and home to his $3.5 million country club home in Plantation.

#

Larry Bloom was pondering the lead story for Tuesday when Millie Locastro walked into the managing editor's office and curtsied. "Well, boss, this will come as a real shock, but I have your 144-point headline."

"They caught the serial rapist?" Larry replied sarcastically.

"No, we're still hoping he attacks the mayor's wife in time for the second edition," the city editor said in an equally sarcastic manner.

"I hope the rapist has better taste than that, Millie. Tell me what you have that's worth our 144-point lead?"

"Zei has a blockbuster on Sun Air—"

"Not Buffy Zei!" Larry interrupted. "Not that Harvard Business School intellectual in business Zei? Let me guess. Sun Air is eliminating peanuts on all flights of less than a thousand miles."

"Boss, please. Call up Sun drugs on your computer."

FEDS SAY SUN AIR FLIES COKE
by Buffy Zei, P.M. Staff Reporter

MIAMI—*Creative cocaine smugglers are causing tension between the U.S. Customs Service and Sun Airlines, threatening their drug-fighting alliance.*

Calling the presence and amount of drugs found aboard Sun Airlines' flights "disturbing" and "a threat to flight safety," Customs officials have told the airline that they believe employees and contract workers are responsible. Customs also threatened the Miami-based carrier with $15 million in fines.

Sun Airlines' CEO Bruce "Bud" Westinghouse responded by threatening to pull out of the six-year-old anti-smuggling alliance, which costs the airline $13 million a year for the 1,000 security people it employs to combat smuggling.

The trouble began when Customs Commissioner Eleanor Holmes sent a letter to Westinghouse last month.

"We are now witnessing a disturbing number of incidents in which we believe that airline employees/contract workers have secreted narcotics in sensitive electronic areas of the aircraft cockpits and air vents," she wrote. "As you are surely aware, safety is an additional factor in these incidents."

The incidents included the discovery last year of "dope on a rope" on 10 Sun flights to Miami from seven Latin American countries—464 pounds of cocaine dangling from fishing lines in the floor air vents. Some of the drugs had fallen against hot parts of the plane and burned.

Relationships between Customs and airlines have historically been fragile. A get-tough Customs policy of multimillion-dollar fines and seizures of aircraft failed to solve the problem in the 1980s. In the 1990s, Customs toned down its approach to airline drug smuggling. If airlines cooperated and tightened their security, Customs agreed to tread more lightly with the fines.

The drug problem seems to be worsening now, as drug smugglers get more creative and airline employees get in on the action. Customs is caught between its mandate to stop drugs and its need for a good working relationship with the airlines.

And the implications are obvious.

At a time of heightened concern about terrorists and safety, the best airline security experts are unable to keep cocaine out of the sealed compartments of jetliners flying from Latin America.

"Now we're finding drugs in these planes," Mrs. Holmes told Westinghouse. "In this environment, it could be explosives."

More recently, cocaine has been found in the cockpits of Sun jets: 60 pounds in a Houston flight and 32 more on one to New York.

Robin Martin, vice president of corporate relations for Sun Airlines, said the letter from Mrs. Holmes took them by surprise.

"All of a sudden we get a letter that's quite critical, but with no specifics, from the commissioner of Customs," Martin said. "Rightfully, the president of this operation wants to know, 'What the hell is going on?'"

Mrs. Holmes now says she should have handled things differently. "I had a follow-up conversation with Mr. Westinghouse," Mrs. Holmes told Miami P.M. "I said, 'Look, if I've offended you by surprising you, perhaps what I should have *done differently was to call you on the phone. "I apologize if I've upset you by the approach I've taken to bring this to your attention."*

Sun officials dispute that their security has suffered any breakdown. They contend that last year's spate of seizures was a temporary penetration that has since been halted.

But Customs documents reviewed by Miami P.M. show that no other airline has had so many serious problems. Seizures of drugs stashed in sealed compartments on Sun planes have mounted from 10 two years ago to 25 last year and 30 in the first six months of this year.

"We are deeply concerned that those drug-related incidents may be symptomatic of a general breakdown in Sun Airlines security operations," Mrs. Holmes wrote.

Customs is now considering penalties for Sun. Customs has issued a six-month moratorium on fines and told Sun that any fines would probably be reduced or wiped out in mitigation proceedings.

Westinghouse's displeasure with the idea of penalties was clear in the tone of his response to Mrs. Holmes: "I am extremely disappointed by your letter... We are mystified as to why you have chosen to call the program's success into question."

"Okay, you sucker," Judge Hugh Glickstein demanded, "I want to know who is responsible for sending that hearse to my chambers and having the driver inform me he was there because my love life was dead." He toweled his neck from the tennis workout and sat on the court bench next to Bob at the Miami Yacht and Tennis Club.

Captain Dick Norton and attorney Jim Walden, drinking cans of Coors and relaxing before the rubber match, made no response.

"It was probably Walden," Bob said, breaking the silence in which the others were fighting to hold back laughter.

"Why me?" protested the attorney.

"Because Jim knows how you love to fuck defense lawyers in your court," volunteered Bob.

"Only female ones," Glickstein responded.

"We should all have more pussy to choose from, now that Bobby is getting married," Walden said. "Think of all those frustrated Sun Air flight attendants who will miss their Bobbykins."

"Especially Mary Rich," Dick interjected.

"Mary who?" Glickstein asked.

"Purser Rich," Dick explained, "is a Sun Air legend for giving blow jobs in the galleys of DC-10s. Although she does have standards; she only offers her service to first-class passengers."

Bob started to shake his head frantically. "I want it on the record that I have never received a BJ from Mary Rich."

"Dick must be happy that he's getting in shape now," Walden said. "If Sun Air goes on strike, he will be walking the picket line."

"Not me! Remember, I am now chief pilot and management. I hope the pilots don't honor those crazy union machinists."

"The union isn't so crazy," Bob said. "The Mafia calls the shots. Sorry about that, Your Honor. As I recall, you tossed out the FBI evidence against the Sun Air union two years ago."

"You have this Mafia thing about everything," the judge said without displaying any emotion. "I agree that the mob had probably infiltrated the union, but the FBI presented a very flimsy case. Despite your newspaper's attack on my character, we are still a nation of laws in which guilt must be proven beyond a reasonable doubt."

Bob laughed uncontrollably in remembering the *Miami P.M.* editorial blasting Glickstein. "I could have given our editorial writer better stuff, like how you cheat on line calls—"

"What's Suzy going to do if there is a strike?" Dick asked Bob. Before the columnist could respond, Walden interrupted.

"She has a meal ticket in Bobbykins," Walden snarled. "She can retire early—to the bedroom."

Bob knew the remarks about Suzy were just friendly kidding

by his weekly tennis pals. So he didn't react. "I honestly don't know. Suzy has a mind of her own, but I can find plenty of things for her to do if she's out of work," the columnist responded.

Glickstein, Walden, and Norton laughed heartily while Bob's face turned crimson.

"Okay, shitheads, let's play our rubber game, with the losers buying dinner at the club."

Concentrating on tennis helped take the columnist's mind off his passion for Suzy, as well as the Longo caper.

Still, he pondered. Patterson was on vacation in Hawaii, and Bloom lacked the authorization for the $20,000 to get the bank card receipts from Conte. As big a story as it might be, Larry wanted to make sure he didn't rush into it without covering all bets. Walden, who was also the *Miami P.M.* attorney, had cautioned Bloom and Bob that even if the receipts were legitimate, proving they were for betting, much less betting on Sharks games, would require stronger evidence to hold up in court.

CHAPTER 11

"Money, it turned out, was exactly like sex. You thought of nothing else if you didn't have it, and thought of other things if you did."

James Baldwin
Nobody Knows My Name

AFTER GATTINO HAD Syracusa eliminated in the Miami Beach restaurant hit, the gambling don didn't want any association with the quarterback. Conte, who had been on the take from Gattino while a policeman, realized that Gattino wasn't interested in collecting the quarterback's gambling debt to Syracusa. If Gattino whacked Longo now, it would only be to protect the family's sports betting operation that could be compromised by a dirty quarterback.

He didn't want to deal with the quarterback, who might know he was free of Syracusa's debt. But Longo's wife had no way of knowing of any of these matters. She would be perfect. *Yes, I'm sure she wants to save her husband.*

That was why he contacted Mrs. Longo by phone.

Martha Longo was both shocked and scared when Conte said that her husband owed the mob $2.5 million. He claimed Johnny had refused to pay. If he didn't pay, Johnny could end up in the trunk of a car.

Conte, however, said he was willing to make a deal with her. "Listen, lady, you could pay off the money on an installment plan," he suggested.

"Where would I come up with nearly three million dollars?" Martha asked.

"Take a second mortgage on your house," he replied. "Lady, I don't give a fuck. How much is your hubby worth to you alive?"

Martha had the presence of mind to buy some time. "I can get some cash. . ." she started.

"Get it, lady, and then meet me at the Flamingo Motel," Conte interrupted. "Room 222. And please, don't be a dumb broad and go to the cops."

"I can't make it until Friday," she pleaded. "I need time to get the cash."

"Friday," he replied.

#

Martha managed to scrape up $50,000 by cashing in some stock. She had to charm a bank vice president to get the 50 grand in small bills by saying that it was an anniversary present.

She wore a simple black dress accented with a pearl necklace. Only a gold and stainless steel Rolex gave evidence of a higher financial position in society. She remained a striking woman at 36. Even after three kids, she retained a shapely size-eight figure. She was a brunette with shoulder-length hair. When she started to talk, people compared her to a young Lauren Bacall.

Martha was nervous but composed as she drove her husband's black Mercedes sedan rather than the family van. She felt safer in the big sedan as she drove into the seedy section of Miami. She frequently touched the gym bag on the passenger's seat.

She knew that the address was not in the best part of the city, so she had packed a five-shot snub-nosed .38 S&W Chief's Special in the gym bag with the cash.

That damn Johnny! How could he put me in such a situation?

Martha kept telling herself that she should seek help, but she was thinking more of her three kids than her husband.

She thought about the meeting with trepidation as she drove through Miami's mean streets to the Flamingo Motel.

My goodness! This must be a whorehouse. Look at all those hookers hanging around outside. How could any woman sell her body?

Martha avoided the lobby and went up the back stairs. The door to 222 was slightly open. She could hear voices, which turned out to be from the TV. But she still knocked on the door.

"It's open. Come on in," replied a male voice.

Conte had been drinking. She could smell it on his breath. She didn't know, however, that he was mixing his liquor with an occasional snort of cocaine.

He stood there in a stained white tank top undershirt and dark trousers. He put down a cheap cigar to greet his visitor. "You got the mortgage money, lady?"

"Yes. It's here in the bag."

"Good," he said with a smile that showed yellow teeth. "You want a drink?"

This guy was once a Miami policeman? "No. No thank you. I've got to go."

"Hold your horses, lady. We have to talk. You'd better have a drink."

Conte filled a plastic bathroom cup from a bottle of cheap gin. He added a splash of tonic and passed the cup to her. She took a sip from the cup. The strong taste of the cheap gin made her shiver. The smoke from the cigar was bothering her sinuses.

"Look, honey, I'm doing all I can to save your husband's ass," he began. "This token payment, you know, can only go so far. Now, as the middleman in this deal, I deserve a fee."

"A fee? You have all the cash I could scrape up right in that bag."

Conte took a long swig of booze. She shivered when she realized his eyes were undressing her. He closed in on his prey. He ran his left hand across the front of her black dress, stopping to squeeze a breast.

Martha shivered again from the assault. He made her feel cheap and dirty. She wanted to run, but she was too scared—not for her welfare, but her husband's.

"You know what I mean. You don't need no cash for the service charge. I'll be happy, you know, to take it out in trade."

"You're crazy, mister. I'm not interested in having sex with you."

Conte grinned and refilled his cup. "Oh, I think you will. Or maybe you don't care if your husband is wearing cement shoes." His sinister grin reflected confidence.

"You. . .you have the money. There will be more. . ." she stammered.

"I know there'll be more. That money is for the boss. I want a service charge for seeing that it gets to the boss. No service fee, no delivery."

It was warm, and the old-fashioned window AC unit couldn't handle the workload in the room, which had a musty smell along with the cigar smoke. Martha felt cold. She was attempting to come up with a solution for this problem, but it was clear that to save her husband's life, she was going to have to submit to this foul-smelling, despicable gangster.

Before she could speak again, Conte had put his hand on her right leg and had roughly worked it up to her crotch. He smiled.

She trembled as he opened the belt on her dress and fumbled with the buttons before it slid down to her ankles. She knew she could do nothing but submit. With one hand and one motion, he yanked down her black panties and pantyhose.

Martha felt naked to the world and humiliated. She knew, however, that she would submit to this bastard to save her husband's life.

Martha was prepared to go willingly to bed, but Conte didn't know or really care. He slapped her hard across the face to establish his control. Then he tossed her onto the bed.

The cheap springs squeaked as she felt the weight and smell of a man in need of a bath, a shave, and mouthwash. He pounced upon her, and rammed his penis hard inside her. It hurt. He didn't wait. She just lay back with her legs spread, and this man breathing hard as he plunged himself rapidly into her. No foreplay. It didn't matter; she couldn't get wet if she wanted to. She closed her eyes. He had both hands against her breasts. He exploded quickly inside her.

"You bitch!" he screamed. "You made me come early." Conte was in a rage. He started beating Martha with his fists. "You're going to give me a fucking blow job for that," he asserted as he poured himself another cup of booze. He then took the half-full gin bottle and forced some of it down her throat. "This should make you more playful."

He had become a staggering drunk. His speech was slurred, and he was no longer in control of his actions. He poured more gin down her throat, and then tickled her vaginal area with the bottle.

Terror gripped her. Martha prayed for deliverance. She felt sick to her stomach from the cheap gin as well as from the thought of oral sex with this. . .this animal.

The combination of booze and drugs had caused Conte to forget his original purpose of making money. His mind was fried with thoughts of wild sex with this beautiful, upscale woman.

"Now let's see how good head you can give," he said.

Martha reached for the gym bag. She was reeling from the booze as well as the beating. "Take this damned money, and let me go, or else I'm calling the police. . ."

Conte laughed. He slapped her twice across the face. He was attired only in his tank top and socks. He held his limp penis in his right hand and pushed it toward her mouth.

Martha was crying. He forced it in and she bit it. Bit it hard.

Conte screamed in pain. "You fuckin' bitch!"

She was now truly scared. She felt helpless and alone.

"I'm going to stick this piece of metal in your mouth," he asserted, going for a Walther PPK .380 in an ankle holster. "This will be a blow job on hot lead!"

Then he flung the gym bag at her. She saw him coming like an enraged bull. He was staggering and trying to get a gun out of the holster on his ankle. She remembered the .38 in the bag.

Martha struggled frantically with the zipper but pulled the gun from the bag before Conte could draw his weapon. Shaking, she pointed it at him.

He laughed. "You don't have the balls to use the gun."

She needed both hands to steady the .38. She pulled the trigger. Martha was surprised at how little noise the pistol made. Just the slight kick of the .38 as it went *pop, pop, pop, pop, pop* and *click*.

Conte gave a surprised look as the first round hit him in the chest. It wasn't potent enough to knock him down. The second one did before he could reach and raise his weapon. He was sprawled on the floor at the foot of the bed, and she had to sit up on the bed to direct the final three rounds into his body.

Martha Longo's eyes were moist. She had lost some of her composure. *I didn't mean to kill him! Oh, my dear God, what have I done?*

She sat on the bed for almost an hour looking at his body and her empty pistol. It was a nightmare. *Oh, God, let me wake up.*

She thought about calling the police, but remembered her children. *Would the police believe me? Would the state take my kids? How would it look to hear about their mother in a cheap motel with that. . .that horrible gangster?*

#

Later at the Miami Hospital Emergency Room, she used a phony name of Mary Klimkiewitz—a name the hospital would surely mess up—and paid cash.

A sympathetic female E.R. doctor noted on the record that it appeared to be a brutal date-rape case, and police should be notified.

It had been a busy night in the E.R., and the paperwork fell in the cracks of the hospital system.

Martha was still shaking when she arrived home. Johnny was in his den watching game films. The maid had the children in bed. She slipped into the house and into the master bathroom, where she drew bath water and quickly pulled off her clothes. She rolled them into a bath towel and knew she would put them in the garbage.

The soap and hot water relaxed her, and she tried to wash away the memories of killing a man. As a devout Catholic, she couldn't excuse her act of self-defense. She needed a priest.

I have to get to church early in the morning. Maybe Father O'Malley will hear my confession.

#

It didn't take long for Gattino to get word from family friends in Vegas that Longo was weekly betting a bundle that the Sharks would cover the spread.

The don didn't like the news. Not that Longo had occasionally won. *Hell, suckers like Longo never get even. They think they can beat the system. Not even insider help can help Longo.*

Gattino's concern was that Longo was betting on his own games. This could be big trouble if the quarterback was exposed. The don didn't want some congressional hearing hurting his business.

Some of the don's bookies could be burned by Longo's spread-breaker actions, but the vig and spreading out the action between Miami and other cities still made Sundays profitable for the Lorenzo family.

Gattino was now truly concerned that Longo was a loose cannon that would blow open a fix or a point-shaving scandal. The don knew the godfather was right. They couldn't risk a traditional hit.

Now that that cocksucker Longo was in need of a big score, he would be hot to trot again next Sunday. *We have to make it look like an accident. Maybe the brakes on his car. Maybe blowing up the team plane with him on it.*

Gattino laughed out loud.

That would be a fucking hoot. Blow up the team plane! I wonder what the fucking IFL would do if they lost one of their fucking teams?

I wonder if the IFL has a disaster plan?

CHAPTER 12

"It is a dangerous thing to reform anyone."

Oscar Wilde

Bob Casey's Working Press:
Meet Joey: He's your
friendly sports bookie

MIAMI—I don't know Joey's last name. I don't even know if Joey is his first name. I do know that he is a sports bookmaker, operating in the shadow of this newspaper's building right here in downtown Miami.

Joey does not fit the bookie stereotype. He is only 31, clean-cut with short hair, and he dresses in the latest L.L. Bean style. His build is not the least bit threatening, and he impresses you more as a businessman than as a Mafia soldier. He's not even Italian. He's Polish.

"My wife is Italian," he says with a sly grin. "That's the only reason I'm in the family business."

The family business he refers to is the Lorenzo family out of New York. He reports to someone who represents gambling don Salvatore "The Saw" Gattino, a resident of neighboring Hollywood.

Please, don't call him a bookie.

"I am a sports consultant," he insists.

Joey will take your action on football, basketball, hockey, or just about anything else you care to wager money on. He even has some action on local high school games.

"Sports betting is for suckers," Joey admits. "Only the house makes any money. That's because we charge you to bet your money. Everyone thinks they can beat the system. They never do. The suckers all get caught up by greed, and they self-destruct."

I asked him if he wasn't hurting his business by insulting the customers.

"Naw," he said. "The cigarette companies print warning labels on their products, but that doesn't discourage smokers. The same is true in my business. Betting is a habit, an addiction."

Most of Joey's business is with blue-collar folks. He doesn't discriminate. He is an equal opportunity bookie . . . er, consultant.

"My average client spends $200 a week," he said. "Their biggest problem is keeping this from their wives. Some can control their habit. Others can't.

"Everything is done by credit. My new clients are introduced to me by old ones. There is no paperwork, since the action is all phoned into Las Vegas."

What happens if a sucker gets in over his or her head?

"I try to be reasonable," said Joey. "I try to work with a client."

If he can't or won't pay?

"They do eventually," asserted Joey. "Otherwise, I send Rocky and Vito to pay them a visit. They can be very convincing. Last week, this guy was in the hole $6,500. Rocky and Vito returned with his used truck that my client had signed over to me."

So what's the line of Miami at New Orleans on Sunday?

"Your paper says Miami by 12. I can offer between 10 and 14. I have several sources, you know."

Do you think any games are affected by the betting?

"You mean fixed games or point-shaving?"

Right.

"Hey man, if the word gets out, you better believe it. Hell, the Sharks looked like they got the word in the opener against Green Bay."

You aren't suggesting that any players in the IFL would do such a thing, are you?

"If the word gets out, believe it. I thought Green Bay had gotten the word because of all the heavy action on the Sharks.

"I understand that some of my fellow consultants handled several 10 G transactions from one Miami gentleman. He must have been a real Sharks fanatic, because he backed them and lost everything."

Do the cops hassle you?

"Naw," he replied. "They know folks like to bet on sports. Hell, I have several law enforcement types as clients. No big action, you know. Cops are human. Some like to bet, too."

Joey can tell you plenty of tales of the woes of the suckers who gamble away their weekly paychecks, and even their savings.

"I had a regular a couple of years ago who blew his brains out with a .357 Magnum because he was losing all the time. He was a class guy. He wrote me a check for the $1,600 he owed and left it on the table before shooting himself."

Do incidents such as this bother him?

"Naw," he said without hesitation. "Sports consulting is a business, like banking. Do you think bankers give a damn when they foreclose on a house and put a widow lady and her four children out on the street?"

I asked for his advice on betting $100 on the Miami-New Orleans game.

"Take the hundred out to Calder Race Course," he said. "They don't take any 10 percent vig, and I trust the four-legged animals more than those two-legged ones on the Sharks."

#

"Tell me the truth, honey. You made this column up, didn't you?"

Suzy was seated on the floor with her back propped up against the sofa in the living room of her one-bedroom apartment. She was covered only by a mini robe. She had just finished reading Bob's column while nursing a Scotch and water.

Bob walked slowly out of the bathroom. He had a towel around his neck, and a long cotton robe was soaking up the shower water that his initial toweling had missed. He picked up a glass that she had mixed for him from the end table.

"I'm not that good a fiction writer, Sky Princess," he said. "Now if you saw a Tom Edwards byline on such a story, you'd be right to be suspicious."

"Why would a bookie give a newspaper columnist an interview like that?" she asked, waving the folded newspaper at her lover.

"Maybe he thinks it's good for business," Bob replied. "The cops don't care. They claim they do, but they don't. They're too busy running prostitution stings with policewomen to nab the Johns."

"Bobby, did you get busted by some wicked policewoman?" she asked in jest.

"That'll be the day," Bob responded. "Stings are popular with the women libbers, you know. Truth is, the politicians think gambling is harmless, and that it's a possible cash cow for the state and local coffers."

"Isn't it?" she asked.

"Remember that the state lottery was supposed to aid education in Florida?" he explained. "Now there's a push for casino gambling."

Bob affectionately patted Suzy on the head. "Let me borrow your paper. I want to read what Jorge did for an advance on the Jazz game."

#

The machinists were preparing to strike Sun Airlines Sunday. Mike Kelly wanted T.J. Lewis to captain the coming picket lines, but Lewis had other business concerns. Anyhow, he wasn't as gung-ho about the strike as was the militant union leader, Kelly, because grounding the Sun Air fleet would stop his source of cocaine.

I can't get mad at my main man Kelly, you knows, because he lets me do my thing. So he can do his thing, which is striking the honky airline. But without my help.

Lewis was a product of Miami's Liberty City ghetto. He was athletic, and probably would have excelled in high school sports even at five-foot-ten and 165 pounds. He was physically solid, working out several times a week. He could bench press 300 pounds. Because he toted an Uzi, he avoided physical confrontations. He was feared and respected in Liberty City, and this overcame his plain features and dark ebony complexion with most of the women in the community. He was drawn into drug dealing simply because he wanted a job. He had started at age 10 as a lookout for the "Miami Boys," a teen gang of drug-running African-Americans.

Why not? Whitey wasn't hiring any black kids for anything but burger-flipping jobs. Then he found out that success meant more than money. It meant respect.

He couldn't even remember the man who recruited him, but he'd been impressed with all the gold and the BMW. The tough laws mandating a prison term for anyone over 18 in possession of an illegal drug had opened the door of opportunity for the ghetto young.

He knew this had influenced heroin dealers in New York to start using kids as runners, and the practice had continued south to Miami.

The little fuckers are also easy to frighten and control.

Lewis, however, was ambitious. By the age of 15, he was working at the retail level in his neighborhood and at Miami High School.

He had sold cocaine, and even some marijuana, and he was prospering and surviving because he didn't do drugs.

"Like the president's bitch say, 'Just say no to drugs,'" he'd love to tell his street pals. A lot of kid dealers were cocaine users, too. Thus, they would accept their cut from the main man in drugs, rather than cash. Not Lewis. He worked only for cash. But the introduction of crack changed the drugs for cash deal. That's because most dealers don't like crack.

"Cocaine is the drug of choice by the middle-class honkies," Lewis told Jose Cortez while they were unloading a shipment from a Sun Airlines DC-10 that had just arrived from Colombia. "Those whiteys are racists, and they don't like us niggers or you spicks hanging around them. So we have to get more white kids as runners."

"That's why you is kissing that pro football player's red nose, T.J.?"

Cortez nicknamed Kelly "La Oficina." The Cuban had a sense of humor. He and Lewis were almost the same age and had worked at the airline for three years. He was an escapee from Havana, and his dark complexion, wavy black hair, and sneaky smile gave him a handsome but sinister look. It was he who kept the Latino union members in line while drawing $30 an hour as a mechanic.

"You got it, man," Lewis replied as he crawled through the luggage hold of the jumbo jet. "I'm now a big nigger in white society. You know, you have to be a sports celebrity for any whiteys to give a fuck about you. Now that I can get those fuckers their white shit, they'd let me move into their neighborhood."

"But not next door, amigo," suggested Cortez.

Lewis laughed. Then he smiled as Cortez found the wooden crate marked Colombian coffee. The two men worked the crate to the cargo door, where it was transferred to a Sun Air truck.

"Careful, Jose! That's not some fucking passenger's suitcase, so don't bang it on the ground."

The two men laughed.

"Well, T.J., that would be the first time it ever snowed at MIA," Cortez said.

"Yeah, I get your drift, man," replied Lewis. He didn't mean it as a pun; but when both men realized that it was, they laughed heartily.

The African-American and the Cuban got along well, which wasn't usually the case in Miami. Lewis liked Cortez because he was a good listener. Cortez was a follower. He liked a strong man who would make the decisions.

After they unloaded the crate of cocaine, they broke out a six-pack of Budweiser in the cab of the truck. Cortez drove and listened as they drank from the cans. They were headed to a deserted supermarket in Liberty City, where they would drop off the cocaine to the teenaged members of the crew. Crew members sold to retail customers, who worked on a consignment basis. Credit in drug selling was called "fronting."

This evening, the two airline employees had 10 kilos of cocaine.

"How much is our shit worth tonight?" asked Cortez.

"Oh, I'd estimated it on the street at around a million," replied Lewis.

This resulted in a shrill whistle by the Cuban. "And each kid has a week to sell the junk or return it or the cash to you in Liberty City."

"Right on, man," Lewis said. "It's the same with your operation in Little Havana." Then he changed the subject. Mellowed by the second can of beer, he became talkative. "My mother's been dead for 20 years now," Lewis said as the truck left MIA for the short ride to Liberty City. "She died this very week 20 years ago. I was only eight when she passed away. I only knew Mama when she was sick. My older sister took it very hard, because she and Mama were very tight. My grandmother took us in. I don't know, nor do I give a shit, who my father is."

Cortez listened with respectful silence as he sipped on a beer.

"My sister Bettina was bright and did well in school. She could speak well and everything, not like me. She could do everything, you knows. Like with math and sciences, too. She went to college. Got one of those federal jobs, you knows. She has one of those GS ranks with the IRS. Would you believe that my sister is a fucking IRS agent? When grandmother died, Bettina brought me to live with her and her husband.

"He was a state trooper. A bit of an Uncle Tom, but I liked him. They had a nice home in Miramar, but I just couldn't adjust to his ways. I was a street nigger. You know, not an Uncle Tom going to one of those fancy suburban whitey schools. So one night I just took off and moved back into Liberty City. And here I am."

Lewis told Cortez that he had to take a short nap and then pay a visit to Plantation. The Cuban laughed.

The truck with its expensive cargo in back rolled toward its Liberty City destination.

"Those pigs, you know, won't like you black guys coming to Plantation. They'll think you is some breaking and entering type. . .probably shoot you first, and ask questions of your survivors."

After Cortez dropped him off at his posh townhouse in Coral Gables, Lewis exchanged his mechanics uniform for the Brooks Brothers look. In a white mock shirt, navy blue blazer, and tan slacks complete with black penny loafers, he climbed into his Mercedes roadster with a *Support Your Miami Police* bumper sticker, and drove onto the Florida Turnpike en route to the Fort Lauderdale suburb of Plantation.

Despite the camouflage, Lewis did get stopped before making his delivery to Johnson. It was dark, and the street numbers of the houses he sought were hidden by shrubs off the roadway. It was his erratic driving along Country Club Drive that attracted the attention of Plantation officer Cathy Custer.

"Oh, shit!" Lewis screamed out loud when he spotted the flashing blue lights in his rearview mirror. "I've got a fucking load of shit in the trunk, and this pig is going to hassle me." Lewis managed to remain cool and pulled the Mercedes over as the police cruiser pulled up behind.

The officer ran the Florida tag over her radio. "I have a light blue Mercedes with Florida tag Poppa-Poppa-Juliet-Ten-Zebra-November."

Lewis cursed his luck under his breath. *Fuck, the pig is a bitch!*

From the rearview mirror, he watched the female officer approach his vehicle. *Probably expects to find a drunk behind the wheel. Or more likely a car thief.*

"Good evening, sir," she said. "Would you mind exiting your vehicle very slowly and bringing your license and registration with you?"

Lewis complied and displayed no panic or telltale signs that a cop looks for in a bad guy. "Did I do something wrong, Officer?" he asked in his very best Uncle Tom tone.

"What brings you to this area tonight, sir?" she asked after he passed her his license and registration.

"I was looking for my friend's home, Officer. You knows, Muhammad Johnson, the football player. We were college roommates, you knows."

The police dispatcher reported over the officer's radio, "Poppa-Poppa-Juliet-ten-Zebra-November is registered to T.J. Lewis of 12244 West Lakes Drive, Coral Gables. His DL is current, and he is a safe driver."

"Ten-four," Custer responded on her hand-held police radio. "Well, Mr. Lewis, sorry for any inconvenience. I can tell you how to get to Mr. Johnson's home. . ."

Lewis smiled, thanked the policewoman, and climbed back into his Mercedes. He waved to the departing police cruiser, and then removed the 15-shot Glock 9mm automatic from his jacket pocket, turned on the safety, and put it under the driver's seat.

#

Bob and flight attendant Chris Gaylord were seated at the lobby bar in the downtown New Orleans Marriott. The two men nursed drinks as they waited for the rest of the Sharks charter crew to join them.

The crew members announced on the flight to New Orleans from Miami that they would take Bob and Suzy to an engagement dinner at the world-famous Antoine's in the French Quarter. Suzy was in her room still, trying to decide what outfit to wear to dinner, so she dispatched Bob to entertain the crew. Gaylord had connections at the 150-year-old restaurant. This explained why on this Saturday night they had a reservation for 10 at 8:00 p.m. This was quite a feat, even for regulars.

The connection was named Charles, a middle-aged captain, and he was very interested in young Gaylord.

"Isn't Charles a bit old for you, Chris?" the columnist asked.

"Not at all, Mr. Casey," the male flight attendant replied. "He's only 18 years my senior, and he keeps in very good shape. You know, he's from Paris and. . ."

"I know, he speaks perfect French," Bob interrupted.

"You're making fun of me," Gaylord protested.

Bob countered with a slight smile. "I'll look forward to meeting Charles tonight. Maybe he can read the menu to me. The last time I dined at Antoine's, the menu was in French."

"Not any more," Gaylord said. "Charles said that has been changed. You can now have a menu in English."

There were only 10 people in the lounge at 7:00 p.m. There was no hurry for the rest of the crew to meet here, as it was about a brisk ten-minute walk from the hotel to the restaurant.

Two other men at the bar had been there since 1:00 p.m., drinking and watching college football on TV. The two were Ranger sergeants from Fort Polk. They were in town for Sunday's game, and from their size, the two 28-year-old sergeants could be mistaken for Sharks players at the team hotel.

Booze and boredom had taken their toll, and the soldiers were looking for a combat situation. Observing Bob and Gaylord for a few minutes, they nudged each other. Then they walked slowly to the end of the bar where Bob and Gaylord were seated.

"Is this a fag bar?" one sergeant asked in a loud voice, addressing the bartender.

"I don't understand your question, sir." the bartender replied.

"Is this a fucking fag bar? Like, do you serve fucking fags here?"

"Sir, please watch your language," the bartender responded, but in a very meek manner.

"Yes, sir, this here is a fag bar," the other sergeant asserted. "Lookee here, I've found two faggots. Aren't they cute?"

Gaylord's face turned ashen.

Bob turned to face the militants dressed in Army dress green and combat boots. "Why don't you guys sit down and enjoy your drinks," he said in a calm voice.

"The old fag is giving you an order, Sergeant," the other sergeant said. "I betcha he's one of those Vietnam draft dodgers. Probably spent the duration in Canada."

"You idiots were not even alive during the Vietnam War," Bob said, starting to lose his cool.

"Who the fuck you calling an idiot, you fucking queer?" one of the soldiers shouted. "Is that little cocksucker with you the one that you're going to fuck in the ass tonight?"

Bob stood up. "When I was in the MPs, we'd shut you turkeys up quick with our nightsticks."

"This here old fag claims he was an MP," Tucker said. "You were in our Army, fag?"

"Yes, soldier, I was in the Army. Apparently they aren't teaching military courtesy any more."

"What rank were you, fag? A latrine orderly?"

"First lieutenant. So you blowhards can call me sir."

The two drunks roared with laughter. And in unison, they proclaimed, "The fag was an officer!"

The bartender discreetly dialed 911, bypassing the hotel security because his experience told him that there was about to be one violent but very, very one-sided fight.

Bob wasn't looking for a fight. He sized up the situation, but there was nowhere for him and Gaylord to go. The only exit was past the two drunken soldiers.

One sergeant moved to grab Gaylord, but Bob jumped between the two. "You want to fight, asshole, why not try me?" Bob couldn't believe he was sticking his neck out to defend a gay guy. He didn't ponder the situation; he just reacted. *Probably my old military police training.* "Sit down, soldiers!" Bob gave the order in his best first lieutenant's manner.

The two rednecks laughed.

Before he could make another move, they grabbed him. Bob got off a good roundhouse right that staggered one sergeant. The second sergeant, however, pinned him against the bar. Angered by Bob's initial blow, the second sergeant delivered a crushing right to the left side of the columnist's head. The blow staggered him, and he felt the sting of pain. He couldn't move from the vise-like grip of the other, and he resigned himself to a beating.

Crack! The sound of two heads meeting echoed through the bar.

Bob was released, and as he fought to stay on his feet against the bar, he looked through blurred vision to see his two assailants being mugged by George Carver. The awesome six-foot-six, 305-pound defensive end had cracked the two men's heads together with one quick move. He locked both their heads in a pair of forearm grips and smashed them against the bar. Hard, but not hard enough to result in any serious injury.

While he was using the two rednecks as battering rams, Carver turned to Gaylord and Bob and asked in a calm manner, "You guys okay?"

#

Seconds later, two uniformed New Orleans cops arrived on the scene. One was a black sergeant, the other a younger white patrolman.

"Freeze there, mister!" the sergeant ordered Carver. "You, slowly lower those two men you are holding. . ."

"Shall I arrest the big guy, Sergeant? Shall I read him his rights?" said the white patrolman excitedly, obviously eager for an arrest.

"No, Officer. First, we'll find out what the hell is going on here," the police sergeant said.

Carver dropped the two stunned rednecks not so gently to the floor.

Bob said, "Let me explain. . ." Bob caught sight of the ID tags of Sgt. Willie Davenport and Patrolman E.M. McDowell. Bob figured correctly that the veteran Davenport's experience would make him go slow before drawing any conclusions. This was, after all, a posh hotel, and you never knew who the patrons might be.

"Why, you're George Carver, the football player!" exclaimed the rookie cop. "Sergeant Davenport, this here is the All-Pro defensive end for the Miami Sharks."

Davenport shook his head in frustration. "All right, folks. While my football expert calls EMS, I want to know what happened here."

"I'm Bob Casey, a sports columnist with *Miami P.M.*, and this is my friend Chris Gaylord, a flight attendant for Sun Air. We were about to have a drink with Mr. Carver when those two thugs interrupted. They were drunk and rowdy, and called him the 'N' word."

The veteran sergeant shook his head in disbelief. "You mean to tell me, Mr. . . . "

"Casey, Sergeant. Bob Casey."

"Yes, Mr. Casey. You want me to believe that these two men were dumb enough to call Mr. Carver a nigger?"

"Yes, Sergeant, that's the truth. The booze probably affected their judgment."

"Probably. How did you get injured, Mr. Casey?"

"I went to Mr. Carver's defense," he replied. "I don't like unfair fights. I mean two against one isn't fair."

"Right, Mr. Casey. I feel certain that Mr. Carver needed your help in such a matter."

"That's the truth, Officer," Gaylord volunteered.

"What happened here, barkeep?" the sergeant asked, obviously not believing Casey's version.

"It's just like the gentlemen said," the bartender replied.

"Those two men insulted the big black man, and the white guy came to his aid?" Davenport repeated. "That's unbelievable."

Davenport took a deep breath. Bob figured that the sergeant realized everyone was lying. At last Davenport asked Carver for his version of the brawl.

Bob wondered if Carver would lie, too.

"That's the truth, Sergeant," the defensive end replied in a humble and sincere manner. "These two white guys called me a nigger. Then they attacked me. Said something about my mama, and this being a white bar, and us niggers weren't welcome."

Bob fought to keep from breaking out in laughter.

"They being two big dudes," Carver continued with a straight face, "I sure appreciated Mr. Casey coming to my aid. And I sure appreciate the arrival of you officers. In fact, I'm sure Mr. Casey will want your names for his popular sports column in Miami. I can see the headlines now. 'Hero officers rescue Sharks player.'"

From the look on the sergeant's face, it was obvious that he didn't believe one word of the witnesses or the victims. "McDowell, you can attend to those two suspects until the EMS arrives. When they awake, read them their rights, cuff 'em, and charge them with assault, disorderly conduct, and destruction of private property."

"How about adding a hate crime to that list?" Gaylord suggested.

Bob gave Gaylord a look that indicated he should keep quiet.

"Now, bro," Carver said, putting his arm in a comradely manner around the sergeant's shoulder. "I have here four tickets for you and your partner for tomorrow's game. These white soldier boys were just a bit drunk and foolish. Maybe if you could see them sobered up and shipped back to their post. . .well, you knows, I think justice will be served. The Lord, He works in wondrous ways sometimes."

Davenport shook his head, but he couldn't refrain from a grin. "I think I get the picture. It was that male flight attendant that the good ol' boys were after. Well, Mr. Carver, you are probably right about justice being served. I think it's fortunate for those two soldier boys that they didn't call you a nigger. Otherwise, I'd be investigating a double homicide."

Bob watched the black policeman and the black football player as they exchanged knowing glances and shook hands. They were both macho in their own professions, but they also understood the pain of bigotry—even when it wasn't about race.

#

Mary Rich arrived with most of the crew in tow. "My God, Bobby, what happened to you?" She didn't hesitate as she gently pushed Bob down in his seat, ordered a towel and ice from the bartender, and played nurse. Suzy was shocked, of course, but everyone made light of the matter. Everyone except Gaylord.

"Mr. Casey is a very courageous man, Suzy," he said. "You should be very proud of him."

Antoine's was crowded. In fact, the line of people waiting for tables stretched out onto the sidewalk at 713 St. Louis Street. The Gaylord party of 10 did not have to wait. It was welcomed immediately and with some flourish, and shown to a table in one of the restaurant's 15 rooms.

Inside the ironwork-adorned building, they were in a world of white tile floors, slowly turning antique ceiling fans, and the hustle of captains, waiters, and busboys. Charles was certainly impressive with his Parisian accent and dashing good looks.

"Welcome to Antoine's," he said. "All friends of Mr. Gaylord are special. May I suggest the oysters Rockefeller as an appetizer, followed by the filet de boeuf marchand de vin. . ."

The group included Dick Norton, First Officer Jeff Altier, Flight Engineer Vince Lombard, and Mary. The good food and wine relaxed the columnist as he glanced occasionally at the love of his life.

He was thinking about the famed baked Alaska dessert and sex with Suzy—not exactly in that order—when a waiter came to his seat. "Are you Mr. Casey with the Miami newspaper?"

Bob nodded.

"You have a phone call. The caller says it's urgent."

Bob excused himself. "Don't anyone dare touch my baked Alaska," he called as he headed for the telephone. It was Jorge.

"Sorry I missed your bash tonight, Bobby, but I've been working OT," said the Sharks' beat writer. "It seems Muhammad Johnson missed a team meeting after practice tonight."

Bob glanced at his watch. It was only 11:00 p.m. in New Orleans, but it was midnight in Miami. It was too late for any work on Sunday's column, but he knew without asking that Jorge had a story. "Is it an exclusive?"

"The *Journal* guy was out doing the French Quarter," Jorge replied confidently. "I was lucky. I just stumbled on it as the crowd of coaches and Dr. Barker were entering Johnson's room. I just followed the crowd. Boy, was Sherman pissed when he found me in the room. But he was smart enough to try and put a 'The Sharks are family and will stick by Johnson throughout his ordeal' spin on it.'"

"Great job, Jorge! Nothing I can do at this hour except go back, finish my dessert, and go to bed early."

Jorge chuckled. "If I need to get you before breakfast, whose room are you in tonight?"

"Suzy's. It's 1103. Call me at seven. We have some work to do."

Bob returned to his table just in time for the serving of the baked Alaska.

"Anything important, Bobby?" Suzy asked.

"Just business, Sky Princess. I'll tell you later."

Gaylord stood and, with his brandy snifter raised, offered a toast. "To our Sun Air gal Suzy and her soon to be husband Robert. May they have a long and prosperous marriage. May God bless them both."

Purser Rich got so smashed that she ended up in bed with Lombard. Gaylord would spend the evening at Charles' quaint French Quarter apartment.

\#

In another part of the hotel, Sol Rubin passed out dead drunk in his suite. Down the hallway, Bunny Rubin was on her hands and knees as Jack Cabot was ramming his penis up her rectum. She shook with excitement and moaned with delight.

"Harder, Jack! Up my ass! Fuck me! Oh, honey, I'm exploding!"

It was just as Cabot was coming that the ring of his bedside phone startled the lovers. He climbed off Bunny. His penis was wet and dripping as he grabbed the phone. That was how the Sharks' general manager learned about Johnson.

\#

In Room 1049, Johnny Longo was having trouble sleeping. He was like a drug addict without a fix. He wanted to bet, but he was still waiting to learn what had happened in the Syracusa matter. No one had contacted him. *What does this mean?*

Then there was the call Thursday from the bank about the mortgage payment being two months late. *Thank God for that Minutemen game!* He had taken a sleeping pill when he prepared for bed, but it wasn't working. His roommate, runningback Richard Baldwin, fell into a deep sleep right away. A trip to the bathroom and a second pill worked.

\#

The Sunday afternoon game in the New Orleans Superdome was too close for comfort for the Sharks. Bob knew this should be a two-or three-TD laugher, but he no longer trusted Longo.

The fucker is dirty, and I'm going to prove it.

Bob watched as Longo hooked up with Baldwin on a 60-yard touchdown pass with 1:42 remaining to lift the Sharks to a 32-28 victory over the Jazz. It was a rather lackluster effort for the Sharks. In such mismatches, it is hard enough to get the favorites emotionally motivated. The Johnson caper hadn't helped.

The game wasn't important. His job was the Johnson drug caper.

The Sharks had squandered a 17-6 lead, missed dozens of tackles, and had to rally against the worst pass defense in the IFL.

Rhett Hood's fifth field goal—tying his career high—a 37-yarder with 7:09 to go, gave the Jazz a 28-25 lead, and Miami took over on its own 7 with just over two minutes to go. Longo, who was 17-of-24 for 265 yards, found Baldwin for the winning touchdown.

#

"As a quarterback, you like to get in those situations, because they're good tests," Johnny told Cunill following the game. "If you pull it out, you feel good."

Working against defensive back Tom Foley, Baldwin had run a slant from the right, caught the short pass in full stride, and blew past safety George Bush. He outraced a pair of defenders to the end zone for his first passing TD of the season.

"We called that play a few times earlier," Johnny said. "Baldwin was the first option, and he was open."

#

Throughout Sunday, Bob had been scrambling to put together a column about what happened to Johnson.

Bob Casey's Working Press:
Don't ask why Johnson did it:
Ask who sold him the cocaine

NEW ORLEANS—Muhammad Johnson is in a drug rehab center somewhere in this land.

As readers of this newspaper learned first, the All-Pro wide receiver of the Miami Sharks was found in a stupor in his room at the Marriott early Saturday night. His roommate, offensive tackle Norm Amundsen, found Johnson in the room after the receiver failed to show for a team meeting.

Coach Don Sherman issued a terse statement before Sunday's victory over New Orleans. "We are concerned for the health of Muhammad. He has volunteered for drug treatment, and our prayers are with him. We hope he'll recover fully and be able to rejoin this football team as soon as possible."

Sharks owner Sol Rubin, on the other hand, was critical of both the New Orleans police and IFL security.

"How could they let this happen to one of my star players?" Rubin asked. "I blame this city's decadent culture for Johnson's problem. If the New Orleans police did their job, we wouldn't have drug dealers roaming the streets freely.

"When is our new commissioner, Pete Wilson, going to get tough on the players union, which protects its members who use drugs? The union coddles drug users while Wilson looks the other way.

"Our esteemed commissioner thinks gambling is pro football's biggest problem," Rubin said. "Bull! There's nothing wrong with an occasional friendly wager. Everybody does it. Wagering is recreational. It is also legal in some states. But drug use is an epidemic in this league and could spell doom for our game unless action is taken."

Well, Sol, as usual you're out in left field, which isn't good for anyone who claims to be a football man.

Don't blame the New Orleans cops. Not that they're perfect, you understand. There is one helluva crime problem here, and part of it has to do with corruption in the police department. The new police chief, Ronald Gibbs, promises changes.

The bottom line, however, is that Johnson didn't get his cocaine in New Orleans. He got it in Florida.

This wasn't Johnson's first time. Sources tell me he's been snorting for at least two years. This time he just overdid it and came close to killing himself.

The players union isn't perfect, but it didn't sell or encourage Johnson to do drugs.

Yes, drugs are a problem. Yes, illegal sports gambling is a problem. So I guess it is better to have a commissioner who is half right than all wrong. As for Wilson batting .500, well that's great in baseball, baby, but not if you are talking vice in football.

As for gambling, New Orleans is another city where the politicians have duped the public into believing that casinos mean prosperity. Right. Just ask the citizens of Atlantic City. As for the Armstrong Park casino here, you can ask Rubin about it. I understand he dropped five Gs there Saturday at the baccarat table. You could say that the owner found this game the pits!

The question is not why Johnson got hooked on drugs, but who is selling it in Miami?

I have no sympathy for a millionaire athlete who has it all, including a nice family, exotic cars, and a home in Plantation. Defenders of Johnson see it as some kind of racist plot, maybe even a CIA one. Some see him as a victim of ghetto disadvantage and lack of a loving father.

Hold it right there! Johnson isn't a ghetto kid. He grew up in suburban Minneapolis where his father is a high school basketball coach and his mother is a registered nurse. His mama even ran for the city commission—as a Republican!

What Johnson needs is a swift kick in the butt for betraying his family and friends. It is about time he became a man and set a leadership example for other young people.

While other African-Americans may have excuses for doing drugs, Johnson has none.

I hope his near-death here Saturday night scares the hell out of him, so that he comes back clean and once again becomes the football talent that Sharks fans have cheered and loved.

CHAPTER 13

*"For muter, though it have no tongue, will speak
With most miraculous organ."*

William Shakespeare
Hamlet

SUN AIRLINES FLIGHT 1242 was the last to fly Tuesday. Bob had to spend an extra day in the Big Easy. All the Monday flights were booked because of a Baptist convention. The Boeing 727-200 from New Orleans to Miami was operated by a management crew, and it was filled with stranded airline employees seeking to return to their home base of MIA.

Bob was pleased to make this flight, as all the other carriers were booked solid because of the machinists' strike against Sun. Many of the employees were in uniform, and the talk, of course, was about the strike.

While he had taken no formal poll, it seemed to him that on Flight 1242 most of the flight attendants supported the machinists, but the cockpit crews did not.

His thoughts, however, weren't on the strike except in how it would affect Suzy. *I can easily support her. No problem, since we are almost man and wife.*

Now that the Johnson caper was old news, his thoughts turned to Longo. *That bastard is dirty. I know he's shaving points, and I know he's dumped at least one game, and he'll do more if he isn't stopped.*

#

Landing at MIA, Bob noted from his porthole view the Sun Airlines' aircraft neatly lined up and under security guard protection. There was an eerie silence as he exited the jetway into the Sun section of the airport, which normally would be bedlam. There were no passengers milling about.

The ticket counters were marked *closed*. The arrival and departure of Sun Air flights were listed as *canceled* on the TV monitors. Outside, a conga line of union pickets in Sun Airlines' machinist uniforms were joined by uniformed flight attendants. They carried strike signs, and on occasion chanted, "Westinghouse is anti-union. Westinghouse has got to go. Hey, hey. Westinghouse has got to go."

Suzy had told Bob that Kelly was seeking a 32 percent wage hike over three years. He was also demanding stock and wanting four union members to be on the board of directors.

Previous Sun CEOs had always given in to the unions. Before deregulation, it was considered part of doing business, and after the new contracts were signed, the airline passed the cost on to the public in increased airfares. Deregulation changed all of that. New no-frills, low-cost carriers seemed to open for business every month, and they weren't burdened with the debt or high-priced union help that Sun and other established carriers were.

Bob smiled and was impressed with Suzy's knowledge of the airline industry. *It's a shame she'll be out of work for a while. But it'll be nice to find her home every night.*

According to Suzy, Westinghouse would not cave in to Kelly's union. The CEO had his own reorganization plan, Suzy asserted.

"In a right-to-work state like Florida, Westinghouse is about to test the waters," she said.

A uniformed Metro-Dade airport cop stopped Bob. "Mr. Casey, a Major Hess of the Miami P.D. would like to see you. He's parked out front in a white Ford Crown Victoria."

The tropical heat hit Bob as soon as he left the air-conditioned terminal. He quickly removed his blue blazer as he felt sweat form on his forehead. Then he jumped into the front of the white Ford. "What's happening, Leroy?"

Leroy paused a moment to light a fresh Camel. He took the first drag and watched the smoke mix with the cool air provided by the car's AC. He offered the pack to Casey, and soon both men were filling the front seat with smoke as Leroy pulled out of the parking space.

"I remembered that it was your turn to buy lunch Monday, and you stood me up," the major said. "The office gave me some shit about how you couldn't get out of New Orleans until today."

"You're picking me up at the airport for a damned free lunch?"

"Hey, Bobby, we city employees only get paid twice a month. So how about eating Cuban? Then I'll drop you off at your home or office. . ."

"How do you know my Vette isn't parked here?"

"Your receptionist said you left it at the dealer for service, and you had to take a cab to the airport."

Bob shook his head. "Talk about living in a police state. Cuban, it is."

However, Bob knew that this pickup and lunch was more than Leroy being a good guy. The major wanted to talk business.

"You want to talk before lunch, Leroy?"

Hess's CIS unit 700 radio was spewing out routine calls on the department's unique "Q" signals system. This was in contrast to the more popular 10 signals system employed by most Florida law enforcement agencies.

"QTH, 700?" the female dispatcher's voice asked.

"This is 700," replied the major over his hand-held radio. His serious expression betrayed that this wasn't a routine call. He answered with his location. "My QTH is MIA."

"What's happening, Leroy?" Bob asked.

The major motioned for the passenger to be quiet.

"Seven hundred."

"Seven hundred," Leroy said. "QSK."

"Seven hundred, 143 requests you meet him at the Flamingo Motel, 2203 Biscayne Boulevard, regarding a Signal 14. 143 is holding a Signal 45, a probable Signal 31." A signal 14 was an investigation, a 45 was a dead on arrival, and a 31 was a homicide.

"Buckle up, Bob." Leroy turned on a flashing blue light on the dashboard. He gunned the Ford 380-horsepower Interceptor engine and, with an occasional blast of the siren, headed downtown.

"So much for lunch," Bob quipped.

The columnist felt a rush of adrenaline as the unmarked Ford moved through the slow-moving traffic. Even the flashing blue lights and occasional blasts of the siren didn't help much in the parking lot-type traffic.

"Will you tell me what the hell is going on?" Bob asked.

"Later," replied the major. "Later."

The two men remained silent with their own thoughts as the unmarked Ford battled the city traffic.

Thirty-five minutes later, Leroy stopped at the sleazy motel. Three marked police units, an unmarked CIS unit, and the Dade County Medical Examiner's van were parked helter-skelter in the parking lot. Yellow tape proclaiming *Crime Scene* blocked the rear stairway to the second floor.

Investigator Carlos Baptiste greeted the major.

"What have you got, Carlos?" Leroy asked after having quickly exited the Ford.

"A Signal 31, sir. Guess who? A former member of this department."

"Cut the shit, Carlos! Who's the victim?"

"Dominic Conte."

"How?"

"Shot to death."

"When?"

"Last night. The medical examiner says. . .ah, about 2100 hours."

"Where?"

"Upstairs, sir. Room 222. It's one of those rooms you rent by the hour, but the manager says Conte took it for the night on Friday. It appears the victim was having a party. Empty booze bottles, some cocaine residue, semen stains on the sheets, and, would you believe, someone bit his pecker. You want to see the room?"

"Hell, no!" Leroy asserted. "I don't want my name on the crime scene list. I'll read your full report later. For now, I'm going to lunch."

"Lunch?" Bob asked, a bit surprised.

"Lunch, Bob."

Bob was in shock. His best lead to Longo's gambling caper was dead. "Was this a Mafia contract job, Leroy?"

"I don't think so," Leroy said. " Not unless Mafia hit men are using .38-caliber Smith & Wesson five-shot Chief's Specials. Whoever did him in emptied the chamber. There were five rounds in his chest and stomach. Right now we haven't a clue, much less a suspect."

Bob realized that the shooting death of a man, even an ex-cop, in a sleazy motel was not worthy of coverage by the *Miami Morning Journal*.

That rag is into international news, especially stuff from South America. It could be argued that homicides such as this were routine fare in South Florida. So what was so special about this one?

As soon as Leroy and Bob reached El Rick's, Bob excused himself to call Bloom from a pay phone.

"Well, look at it this way, boss, it saved the company 20 Gs," Bob said. It was gallows humor, because Bob knew Conte's death derailed a direct connection to Longo.

"That should make Patterson happy, but it doesn't help us one bit," Larry said. "We know Longo is dirty. But how do we prove it?"

"Find Conte's killer," the columnist suggested. "I think playing this story for all it's worth will help in that direction."

"Right. That's why Conte's slaying is our 144-point head, and the airline strike has been moved inside," Larry said.

#

Over lunch, Bob was shocked to learn that the purpose of the meeting had been Conte.

"A little snitch told me that Conte was doing a bit of blackmailing and trying to establish a minor freelance sports gambling operation," Leroy said as he took a bite of a Cuban sandwich. "I thought this might interest you, old pal, because one of his victims was Johnny Longo."

"Small world, Leroy," was all Bob could reply. His first thought was Longo. "Did that fucker Longo waste him?"

Leroy laughed. "You really have a hard-on for that wop QB, don't you?" Conte's death interested Hess, too. "Well, Bobby, it didn't look like a mob hit or one by some hooker. Conte still had his watch, ring, and wallet with all the cash and credit cards inside it. A mob hit would be far more professional."

Bob frowned. "It couldn't be Longo. The fucker was in New Orleans over the weekend, and he flew to New York after the game for a TV commercial shoot."

"We know that, Bobby. But where was Longo Friday night? That's the time the medical examiner has placed as the time of death."

#

EX-HERO COP SHOT DEAD
IN ROACH MOTEL
by Tom Edwards, P.M. Staff Reporter
MIAMI—City police today were scrambling to find the
killer of a former hero detective who was found shot to death

Tuesday night, lying in a pool of blood in a sleazy, second-floor room at the Flamingo Motel, 2300 Biscayne Blvd.

The dead man was Dominic J. Conte, 42, a member of Miami's finest for 16 years before leaving the department four years ago to work as a private investigator.

Miami policeman Maj. Leroy Hess said while there are no suspects or motive yet for the murder, police believe it is gang and gambling related.

A maid at the hotel discovered the body at about 11:00 a.m. Tuesday. The medical examiner determined the time of death to be Friday evening.

A night clerk said Conte had registered at the hotel Friday at about 5:00 p.m. under an assumed name and asked for a room on the second floor, near the stairs.

Police said Conte's bullet-riddled body was found on the floor in the middle of the roach-infested motel room. Both the TV and the AC were operating.

Conte, who held several department citations for street work, rose to lieutenant after 10 years on the force. His specialty was organized crime. His resignation came with suddenness during a scandal involving rogue cops. Some 12 members of the department were indicted, but no charges were ever brought against Conte.

Police personnel records reveal only that Conte resigned from the department to pursue more lucrative civilian work. Although vested in his city pension, Conte chose to withdraw his contributions, along with the city's matching funds.

Hess said that the murder weapon, which has not been recovered, was a .38-caliber Smith & Wesson "Chief's Special" revolver.

"This was once standard issue to detectives," Hess explained. "Now all our personnel carry automatics. We do know, however, that the five slugs recovered did not come from any weapon registered to the victim."

> Conte's Walther PPK .380 was found in a holster on his right ankle. He had a PI license to carry a concealed weapon.
> "There are no signs of forced entry, but the bed had been used," said the major. "We did recover a bottle of gin, a bottle of tonic, and two glasses. They are being checked for prints. There also are signs that drugs were involved."

#

Wednesday's editions of *Miami P.M.* had hardly reached the street before the story gained reactions.

"No, no, no, Godfather," Gattino protested over the phone at his Hollywood home. "I didn't have a fucking thing to do with this Conte's death. Why? The fucker worked for us. He's been working for us since he was a patrolman. He was our contact with Casey, the newspaper fucker. I was using him to sic Casey on Longo and maybe scare the shit out of the quarterback and put some heat on Syracusa. I don't know who whacked him, Godfather. It couldn't be one of us. Like who would use a pussy piece like a .38 revolver?"

Lorenzo agreed with Gattino. The godfather was in the den of his Greenwich estate, and he had just read the *P.M.* story, which had been faxed to him by Gattino.

"Our travel agent did a nice job clearing up that Syracusa matter," Lorenzo said. "The Chicago and Detroit families have assured me that there is no problem over that matter. In fact, I just got off the phone with Pritzi in Detroit and Goldman in Chicago. They thought Conte was one of our soldiers, but they assured me a few minutes ago that they had no reason to put out a contract on him. I believe them. Now what about the Longo matter, Sal?"

"Godfather, as you know, I followed your advice about not trying to contact or collect any money from Longo. That stiff doesn't owe us a dime. Syracusa was dealing on the side with people in Vegas. I don't think the Vegas wise guys are going to risk their asses by admitting they were doing business on the side with Syracusa, do you?"

"Fuck no! And the million or two bucks they're out will teach them a fucking lesson without us having to use any strong-arm stuff. Pritzi and Goldman agree."

Gattino was briefly relieved. Not for long, though, because the godfather added a very big "but."

"But we are all concerned, you understand, that no scandal comes out of this Longo matter. We do not want any heat on our sports gambling operations. I think, Sal, if you have any concerns about that asshole Longo dragging us into the spotlight, he should be dealt with quickly."

"You mean whacking a star IFL quarterback?" For even as ruthless a man as Gattino, he was a bit fearful of the risk of such a hit.

"But no travel agent shit," said the godfather. "A real accident. Something that won't look even a bit suspicious. Like an auto accident."

"Or maybe a plane accident or. . .?"

"You got the skinny, Sal. Just do it, and don't bore me with the details."

Maria Gattino poked her head into the bedroom that had been converted to her husband's office. "We eat in 30 minutes," she said and left without waiting for an answer.

"Yes, Mama, I'll be there," he said.

"What the fuck you say?" Lorenzo asked.

"Sorry, Godfather. It was Maria. She's fussing about dinner."

Lorenzo laughed. "You're lucky, Sal, to have a woman like Maria. She's a saint. Give her my love. Tell her I'm shipping down some of her favorite Brooklyn cheesecake. Now you take care of the Longo problem. Make sure it is an accident."

In the old days, thought Gattino, *I'd cut off that Longo's balls and stuff them in his mouth.* The godfather, of course, was right. An accident would be best, because once a guy was addicted to gambling, he was like a drug freak.

While eating dinner, Gattino pondered various ways to create a fatal accident that would clean up the Longo mess. He had some ideas. After dinner, he would make some phone calls.

#

Bob needed a stiff drink. He was visibly upset about Conte's murder and the failure to obtain those credit card receipts. He drove the yellow Corvette so quickly from the dealer's service center to Peters' apartment that he didn't bother to take the top down.

Why is it that the expensive convertibles rarely have electric tops? A $40,000 car, and I have to manually put the top up and down! He figured he should save some of his energy to console Suzy, who would be out of work for a week.

"Hi, honey!" A smiling Suzy rushed into his arms before he could even close the apartment door.

"What makes you so cheerful, Sky Princess?"

She thrust a glass of Chivas and water into her lover's hands. "I've got great news!"

"Well. . ."

"I got promoted today. I'm no longer a mere flight attendant. I'm management. I've been promoted to an in-flight supervisor. I got a nice pay hike and even an office at MIA. More important, I can and will work during the strike."

Bob took a gulp of Scotch. "You? You a traitor to the union movement? I would never have thought that you would desert your blue-collar pals on those picket lines. What are Rich, Gaylord, and Parker going to think?"

"I was up for the promotion before the strike. I wanted to surprise you so you wouldn't think I was marrying you as a meal ticket. As hard-nosed a union person as Mary is, she told me she understood. Just as important, she assured me that we were still friends. But she said if I ever wrote her up on a flight, she'd beat the shit out of me."

The lovers laughed.

"So, Sky Princess, what happens Thanksgiving Eve on the Sharks charter to Dallas? Is the team going to fly Delta?"

"Heck no," she said. "Mr. Westinghouse has approved the charter. Management types will crew it, including me. How does that grab you, big boy?"

"Actually, Suzy, I was hoping Gaylord would make the trip. That way I know we could get reservations at the best restaurant in Dallas."

"Chris and Anne are both going to work the flight, but we won't need Chris to find a good restaurant."

"Why's that, Sky Princess?"

"You know we'll have turkey on that flight."

"Really?"

"Sure." She smiled sweetly. "You're going to be on that flight, aren't you?"

Bob faked a frown and made a menacing move toward his lover. She retreated slowly toward the bedroom.

"I'll show you who the turkey is," he asserted. "As soon as I catch her I'm. . ."

Suzy stuck her left hand out of the doorway and playfully waved her white bra. "Come and get it, Mr. Turkey," she purred. "Do you prefer a breast or a leg?"

#

In the Sun Airlines executive suite at MIA, Westinghouse was at that moment planning more than just the Sharks charter flight. He was maneuvering to get most of his equipment back into service without the striking machinists.

"The pilots are the key to this matter," Westinghouse told Dick Norton, his chief pilot. "If they don't choose to honor the picket line, we'll be up and flying again in 72 hours. If they do, I have a flow of new-hire pilots on their way."

"What about the flight attendants, Captain Westinghouse?" Dick asked. "Like the cockpit crews, many of them are honoring the picket line."

The CEO gestured toward the city lights blinking outside his office's panoramic window view. "Out there, Dick, are thousands of men and women who would almost work for free to become flight attendants. One or two newspaper ads, and our personnel department will be swamped. Flight attendants are a dime a dozen. Remember, our flight attendants are still under contract. If they don't honor it, we will hire replacement workers."

Dick nodded his approval. Then he asked who would service the aircraft.

"I've already signed contracts with Air Support Systems, a private airline maintenance firm right here in Miami," Westinghouse explained. "They employ non-union machinists, many of whom were victims of the death of Eastern, Pan Am, Air Florida, and few other major carriers."

"Wonderful, Captain Westinghouse! But. . .our pilots?"

"That's your challenge, Dick. You pilots may belong to a union, but you don't associate with the grease monkeys and cabin waitresses," he said with a knowing smirk. "Even though the pilots' union has a fat war chest in the event of a strike, history has shown the reluctance of your colleagues, as well as those with other carriers, to support a long strike."

Dick nodded.

"As important, since we have been aware of Mr. Kelly's intentions for such a long period, we have assembled a reserve of non-union pilots. They have been certified to fly our equipment. Others are the kids drooling to move up from the commuter carriers, along with some recently retired Air Force talent. I've had them in training in New Mexico at the Lufthansa training base there. Sort of a little international mutual defense pact, so to speak. I think our pilots should understand that if they don't honor their contract with us, we can hire replacement workers. I think they'll have second thoughts about jeopardizing their six-figure salaries and benefits just for a show of brotherhood."

Westinghouse then briefed Dick on the strike spin for the media.

"Our public stance is that we are family and care about all our employees," he said. "Make it clear that we have an obligation to America's flying public. No hard-nosed shit about Kelly or the union. I've told Martin, our PR guy, that he can leak some of our fat-cat machinists' salaries. And, of course, keep mentioning Kelly's 30 percent demand."

Dick knew Westinghouse had studied the cause and effect of the strike that had proven fatal to Eastern in the 1990s. The pilots had honored the picket lines, and as a result eventually joined the unemployment ranks of 40,000 other Eastern workers. He felt certain the lesson of that disaster would be understood by his pilots, some of whom had come over from Eastern as well as Pan Am.

"As for the Sharks charter on Thanksgiving Eve," he added, "I want you to command it. We'll say that that's our goodwill gesture for our home team fans."

"One more thing, Captain Westinghouse," Dick said. "Some Sharks players have been quoted as saying that since they also are union members, they won't cross the picket lines to fly our charter."

Westinghouse laughed. "Dick, that's pure bullshit, and you of all people should know that. Those millionaire players aren't going to inconvenience themselves to support a bunch of grease monkeys. With the strike on, no other carrier has free equipment to fly an extra loss-leader pro football charter when they can fill up that equipment with full-fare passengers."

Dick was impressed. He knew Westinghouse wasn't the typical airline executive. He just might beat Kelly and his union boys. *Now I have to recruit a cockpit crew for the Thanksgiving flight. I wonder if I can convince Lombard to cross the picket line?*

#

Week 10 of the IFL season saw the Sharks still tied with Buffalo for the East lead with 8-2 records.

The hapless New York Titans came to Miami that second week of November with a 1-9 record, which was reflected in the 13 1/2-point spread with Miami as the favorite. By late Saturday, however, bettors placing calls to their neighborhood bookies were learning that the odds had dropped to 10 1/2.

"What the hell is going on here?" asked Mary Rich, a repeat date of Vince Lombard, at dinner Saturday night at a blue-collar restaurant in North Miami.

"Most likely," Vince said as he studied his bottle of Budweiser, "the syndicate just banged the Sharks."

"Why, Vince?" asked Mary.

"Hell if I know," replied the engineer. "But it's the Good Fellas job to know. I got a sneaky suspicion that I should take the Sharks despite the 10 1/2. But what the hell, the smart move is to back the Titans. Eleven points are a lot to overcome in a pro game."

A Sharks season ticket holder, Vince was trying to keep his mind off the airline strike by filling it with pro football. He had also had the hots for Mary since New Orleans. *I could marry that woman. Oh, my God, what am I thinking!*

Since working the Sharks charters, Vince had gotten on a first-name basis with most of the players and coaches. Mary was a devout Sharks fan. She would consider it treason not to support the Miami team, regardless of the odds. So she bet $100 on the Sharks to cover the spread.

"Where'd you get the whole yard, honey?" Vince asked. "You raiding your savings or. . .or you thinking about going back to work?"

"Yeah, I guess it was rather dumb to bet a yard," she said. "And maybe I'll have to go back to work."

#

Gattino, of course, had changed the course of the morning line.

"You must remember the old axiom in pro football, that 'on any given Sunday, any team can win in the IFL,'" he told his soldiers. "Keep in mind that no team in the history of the IFL and the point spread has ever gone undefeated against the spread.

"Even more obvious is the fact that bad teams will cover spreads.

It always amazes me when gamblers can't understand that even good teams like Miami and Buffalo can lose—and at home, too."

Gattino knew partisan football fans found it hard to bet against their hometown team. *That's why so many suckers bet on the favorite home team even when they have to give a lot of points.* Unlike college teams, pro coaches rarely run up the score. That was why the QB kneel frustrated fans who needed a couple more points to cover the spread and win their wagers.

#

Bob was glad the Miami-New York game was a 1:00 p.m. kickoff in SRS, even if it meant not sleeping in with Suzy on Sunday morning.

As was his custom, the columnist arrived two hours before kickoff. The press box was rarely crowded this early, with the exception of the visiting media. It was a chance to chat network with the visiting writers. He wandered into the media lunchroom, poured himself a paper cup of coffee, and found Sam Cohen, a columnist for the *New York Examiner*.

Bob grinned when he spotted Cohen, who looked like a New Yorker on vacation in Florida. He wore a bright flowered sport shirt with its tail hanging out. It covered a pair of cheap, dark brown slacks. The outfit was brilliant in that it captured the mindset of New York sports fans. He chewed on an unlighted stub of a cheap cigar and was reading *Miami P.M.* when he spotted Casey.

"Hey, Slick, how come your rag doesn't have the Beloit-Monmouth score?"

"The who?" asked Bob as he seated himself at Cohen's table.

"Beloit-Monmouth. College football. I got a yard bet on Beloit."

"If your betting skill is as good as your predictions in the *Examiner*, I'd say Monmouth won," Bob said. "Didn't you pick the Titans to challenge for the East title?"

"Hey, Slick, I like long shots. I'm 64, and I need a big hit so I can retire early. The Titans were long shots. What can I tell you? If I could pick pro football, I wouldn't be in the newspaper game. So, tell Sammy boy about Longo and Johnson. Is Longo over the hill? Is Johnson going to find God and come out of drug rehab in time for the playoffs?"

Bob danced around the Longo story, stressing the quarterback's age and injuries, but gave Cohen all he knew about Johnson.

Cohen nodded, jotting a line or two in a reporter's notebook with a cheap ballpoint pen. "Now, my young friend, I have a scoop for you."

Bob was mute. Could Sam know about Longo's gambling problem?

"Your general manager and the wife of your favorite owner are messing around," Cohen said in his pronounced New York accent with a harsh chuckle.

"Not Jack Cabot and Bunny Rubin? No! Rubin is old enough to be his mother." Bob really wasn't shocked, but he didn't think it worthy of his column.

"Not quite, Slick, not quite. I have no proof, of course, but I have it from a very, very reliable source. My source says the two are fucking each other's brains out."

"Since when did Bunny Rubin have any brains?" Bob replied in a most sarcastic manner.

"Listen Slick, you underestimate that Rubin broad. She may act like a bimbo, but underneath that well-preserved body is the mind of a Rhodes Scholar. I say this realizing that she is, after all, Irish. Just because she married a Jew, she couldn't improve her mind that much by a ceremony. Anyhow, we all know Sol Rubin is a shmuck."

Cohen's tip on Cabot-Rubin was worth some investigating. Bob, however, filed it away in his mind. His main mission remained to find out if Longo was shaving points while tossing a game or two for the Mafia. The death of Conte made it a real challenge.

#

Bob and Jorge were seated in the *Miami P.M.* section in the middle of the first row of the stadium press box. Jorge was finishing up on a feature on kicker Siegfried von Katzen while Bob used his field glasses to watch both teams warm up on the lower field.

"Jorge, is there any truth to a rumor that Cabot and Mrs. Rubin are a number?"

Jorge stopped typing in the middle of a sentence. "What? Where did you get that shit? From our society columnist Marcia Levin?"

"No, Jorge. I just was wondering. . ."

"No, Bob, in your case, *hoping*," replied the Sharks' beat writer. "Hey, amigo, until you met Suzy, I thought *you* were going to make a play for old Bunny. She does have one helluva body, that's for sure. Well, if this is true, we know any suspicion that Cabot never married because he is gay is unfounded."

Bob laughed.

The more the columnist thought about it, what difference did it make who was committing adultery? There were far more important matters, including a murder that just might implicate the Sharks' star quarterback.

Hell, Americans even elected a well-known adulterer president, so who would give a damn about the wife of a football team owner?

#

The 68,334 partisan spectators, who had come in the spirit of a Roman circus crowd to see the lions devour the Christians, were shocked almost as much as those gamblers who had backed Miami by giving a lot of points.

As Bob expected, the Sharks jumped to a 14-0 lead with two touchdowns in a 2:27 span of the first quarter. Miami took the opening kickoff and marched 68 yards on 14 plays in over seven minutes. Longo capped the drive with a four-yard TD pass to McCafferty. Baldwin, the fullback, then doubled the margin with a 71-yard scamper to give Miami a 14-0 lead.

A 45-yard field goal by Stan Jankowski put the Titans on the board, but Longo led an eight-play, 74-yard drive that was capped by Baldwin's four-yard run to make it 21-3.

New York quarterback Billy Strock responded with a four-yard TD pass to Cleveland Byner that made it 21-10 with 3:37 left in the first half. Jankowski added a 33-yard field goal following an interception of a Longo pass to cut the deficit to 21-13 with 1:51 left in the second quarter.

But Longo had executed the two-minute offense to perfection, leading the Sharks 75 yards in eight plays. He found McCafferty for a 33-yard gain to the New York 8 before the two hooked up again with 14 seconds left for the score and a 28-13 lead that made the fans as well as the gamblers feel confident.

"Longo doesn't look over the hill to me, Bobby," observed Cohen as he sipped on a Coke and munched a hot dog in the press lunchroom during the intermission. "He's completed 16-of-25 passes for 179 yards in the first half."

"More important, Sam, he's covering the spread of 11 1/2," Bob quipped.

The fans as well as the gamblers loved it, as it appeared that the rout was on. Even the New York writers loved it because it meant they could start early on their early edition stories. Some, like Cohen, started writing on their laptop computers, only to find that the Titans wouldn't throw in the towel.

New York took the second-half kickoff 73 yards in just over two minutes, and Strock capped the drive with an 11-yard pass to James Turner to make it 28-20 with the extra point. After getting the ball back, Strock completed three passes for 72 yards, capped by a 25-yard strike to Jackson in the middle of the end zone. The Titans went for the two-point conversion to tie, but defensive end Carver sacked the quarterback, and the Sharks still led 28-26.

The Sharks settled for a pair of von Katzen field goals and a 34-26 advantage. Bob couldn't believe the New Yorkers had taken the lead with 13:10 to play as Strock capped a 17-play, 77-yard drive with a nine-yard scoring toss to tight end Mike Jackson. Strock then scrambled for the two-point conversion that tied it 34-34.

That quieted the partisan crowd. There were even some scattered boos as the Miami defense unit trotted off the field.

"Fuck you!" screamed Sharks All-Pro linebacker Brutus Neswiacheny as he headed for the sideline. "Why don't you fuckers come down here and show us how to play defense."

"No use yelling, man," Carver said as he checked his right hand, which was beginning to swell slightly. He had banged it against a lineman's helmet on the two-point conversion play. "Those assholes can't hear you, anyway. Man, I need a breather. Where did the Titans come up with this offense?"

Johnny, however, surprised Bob. The quarterback directed a 10-play, 57-yard drive for the go-ahead score. Richard Baldwin converted a 3rd-and-3 with a three-yard run, and Longo snuck for two yards on a 4th-and-1 before hooking up with rookie wide receiver Don McCafferty on a six-yard TD pass.

The Sharks public relations director announced over the press box PA that it was the 32nd fourth-quarter comeback engineered by Longo that could end in a Sharks win. Bobby left for the field with most of the writers assigned to locker room interviews after the Sharks retook the lead. He stood on the sidelines near the Miami bench.

Miami was up 41-34 with 3:01 to play, and Bob was already thinking about a column based on the comeback by the Sharks.

Was this the way this game was supposed to go? This should have been a rout. What's going on?

The scoreboard clock was running down under a minute, and the Sharks had the ball on the New York 11. The Titans' last offensive series had ended when Carver sacked their quarterback on a fourth down situation from their own 22. The Titans were out of timeouts, and everyone including Sherman expected Longo to kneel down twice and end the game.

The fans were heading for the exits and the parking lot. With the exception of loyal fans such as Lombard and Rich, the gamblers in the crowd were booing. What happened next caught everyone—especially the Titan defensive unit—by surprise.

Johnny took the snap under the center, and instead of kneeling down, he sprinted out with the football and headed around the left end.

"What the hell?" asked a surprised Bob.

Both his own teammates and the Titan defenders were frozen as they watched the quarterback romp into the end zone with 16 seconds left.

The officials were so startled that it took almost 30 seconds before the referee signaled a touchdown. Von Katzen's placement made it 48-34.

"Unbelievable," was all that Bob could say.

"That wasn't the fucking play! What the fuck is going on here!" Sherman screamed into the face of Longo as the quarterback returned to the sideline.

"Remember, Coach, you let me call my plays. Anyhow, we owe this to our fans."

"Fuck the fans, Longo! Fuck the fans," screamed the head coach. "You could have fumbled the ball, and we could have lost the fucking game."

"But we didn't, Coach," Carver pointed out as he patted Longo on the head.

#

Father O'Malley, in his role as the Sharks' chaplain, managed not to hear the profanity that was commonplace on pro football sidelines. He was shocked by Longo's last touchdown. The priest feared the worst. He knew that Longo's unwanted touchdown had to do with the gambler's morning line.

Those like Mary and Vince, who had taken the Sharks minus

10 ½ points, were rewarded as von Katzen's ensuing kickoff was returned only to the New York 32 as the gun sounded.

Mary was so excited she jumped up and hugged Vince. "We made money!" she screamed.

"That we did, my love," Vince replied as he made the sign of the cross and blessed Longo. "Let's celebrate, Mary. I'm buying dinner."

Rubin was drunk, as usual, and had to be carried from the owners' box by a couple of front office flunkies. He didn't know he had made $10,000 until he sobered up Monday morning.

Bunny winked at Jack as her husband was carried out to the limo for the ride home. As soon as she saw S.R. tucked into his bed, she would rush to Cabot's apartment.

#

Johnny was happy, too, because he had just scored $100,000 on that play. He, too, needed 11 points or more to beat the spread.

Bob didn't know that, of course, but like some reporters at the game, he smelled a rat.

Naturally, that was the first question put to the quarterback after the game in the Miami locker room.

"I felt we owed it to our loyal fans," a smiling Johnny said without hesitation.

"You mean the gamblers who needed 11 points to beat the spread?" Bob snapped.

"Was that the spread?" the quarterback replied, feigning innocence. This drew a brief roar of laughter from the reporters. "No, I wanted our loyal fans to have some boasting rights against all those snowbird New York fans."

This resulted in more laughter. Bob felt his case wasn't going anywhere, so he sought out Sherman and some Sharks players. Not one, not even Carver, would criticize the quarterback.

"Look, Casey, Longo calls his own plays," Sherman asserted. "You heard those boos. Maybe Johnny wanted to shut up the boo-birds. Instead of writing all that negative shit, why don't you write something nice about us tomorrow? We are 9-2 and still in first place. Would you rather be covering the Titans? Then you could kick their asses every week, like that fucking yellow journalist Cohen."

"He's not yellow, Coach. He's Jewish."

Bob's quip broke up the media conference, and Sherman stalked off to his office.

Sam Cohen put his arm around Bob. "Hey, pal, what're you trying to do, kill my circulation in Chinatown?"

Bob grinned. Then he placed one of his $10 cigars in Cohen's breast pocket. "See you at the playoffs, Sam. Enjoy your flight back to the Rotten Apple."

"What's to enjoy, Bobby? Since Sun Air is on strike, I have to fly on USAirlines. And I'll miss my Sun Air frequent flyer miles."

CHAPTER 14

"Abandon hope, all ye who enter here."

Dante Alighieri
Inferno

B OB WAS IN a sullen but fighting mood as Week 11 of the IFL season approached. It was hard to concentrate on Sunday's home game against the Los Angeles Dons with so much on his mind. Suzy, of course, was always on his mind. He was beginning to feel frustrated about the Longo caper and the public's apathy to organized crime's control of sports betting. So it was understandable that he mentally filed the Rubin-Cabot romance investigation under *things to do when I have nothing else to do.*

"Why do you take things so much to heart, Bobby?" Suzy asked.

He studied an empty glass of Chivas in his right hand, waved it toward the waitress, and held up two fingers on his left hand. Then he returned to the conversation in the corner booth in the dimly lighted lounge at Cella's. It had become their favorite restaurant, especially on Friday nights. This would be the couples' third round, and he was relaxing and talking, and talking, and . . .

"It makes me angry, Sky Princess, that so few people are upset that Longo can get away with thumbing his nose at the league, just because he covered the spread. The world is sick. Can't anyone see the evil in illegal sports gambling, or even *legal* sports gambling? My God, last year we ran a story about some highschool basketball players in upstate New York shaving points on their own games. Where the hell can kids find a bookie to take action on highschool basketball? And why isn't the public outraged?"

"Because everybody likes to gamble," Suzy said. "Heck, even Father O'Malley uses Tuesday night bingo as a fundraiser. My straight-laced mom plays the New Jersey lottery every week. We even have an office pool on the World Series and the World Bowl."

"I'm sorry, Sky Princess," he said as he reached across the table and squeezed her right hand. "I'm Mr. Motor Mouth tonight."

"Don't be sorry," she replied with a reassuring smile. "I like to hear what's on your mind. Heck, you listen to me blabber all the time about my job and my problems. So tonight it's your turn on the couch. And Dr. Peters is all ears."

Two fresh Chivas and waters arrived via Rose, the grandmotherly waitress, who treated only her favorite customers with total disrespect.

"A third round, and you haven't even eaten," Rose barked. "You trying to get Suzy drunk so you can take advantage of her?"

"I hope so, Rose," giggled Suzy.

"Let's order dinner," Bob said agreeably. "At Rose's age, by the time she finds the kitchen, it could be breakfast."

Rose rattled off in her monotone laced with a Brooklyn accent, "I've already ordered it. Two orders of sausages and roasted green peppers over a bed of spaghetti. And a bottle of Bolo. Red. At room temperature. Okay? Okay."

The couple laughed.

"Some night, we should fool Rose and change our order," Suzy suggested.

"I tried that once, Sky Princess."

"And?"

"She accidentally dumped a drink in my lap."

"Accidentally?" Suzy said as she started to laugh uncontrollably. "What did Edmund do?"

"Right! Accidentally," said Bob, who joined in the laughter. "Do? Hell, Edmund's afraid of the old waitress. She once threw a dish of hot pasta at him when he criticized her. That was more than 10 years ago. Since then, he hasn't dared to give her even a dirty look."

The good food and booze had mellowed the couple by the time they left the restaurant hand in hand. There was a chemistry between the two which seemed to get stronger every day. They never tired of each other's company or became less attentive after sex. In their own ways, both had given thanks to God for bringing them together. Both believed strongly in marriage, even though Bob's first marriage had failed.

Bob was pleased that she wanted to be near him. This was in contrast to his ex-wife, who had hated football and thought that reporting sports was little more than macho recreation. She had never understood why he worked such crazy hours. She thought his weekend trips to cover road games were simply party time that excluded her.

Hell, she never even read my columns. She boasted that she read only The New York Times.

#

Suzy understood crazy hours and knew that, as a flight attendant, business trips were mentally and physically draining. She was fascinated by Bob's work, and as an avid reader, she appreciated his craft.

"He's very bright and has a tremendous sense of humor," she told her parents. "Oh, he's not perfect. I kind of like that, too. He reminds me a lot of you, Dad. I mean, he's really a nice guy when you get to know him. He's no wimp. And he certainly doesn't believe in women's liberation. He treats me like you treat Mom. What more can a girl ask?"

#

Since Bob had no way of reading Suzy's mind, he harbored a fear that she might eventually become disenchanted with him. There was, after all, a 10-year age difference, not to mention the fact that she was a beauty. Even though he was highly successful and well paid, at 40 he realized that he was undergoing a minor mid-life crisis. He had tried to blot out middle age with B & B—booze and broads—until his chance meeting with Suzy. She was his dream girl.

Most importantly, he felt comfortable with her in all aspects of life. She wasn't a complainer, and she never nagged. Like him, she was a loner. And they were content to enjoy each other's company.

#

Bob had gotten tickets for Leroy Hess to Sunday's Sharks game, and the major insisted on buying brunch because of the 4:00 p.m. kickoff. While Leroy's two teenaged sons took repeated trips to the buffet line at the Miami Marriott, the two men had a chance to talk business.

"Gattino's bookmakers had to be pleased by Syracuse University's 33-21 win over Miami on Saturday in the Orange Bowl, even though Syracuse had more than covered the spread of 7 ½ points," said Leroy as he ordered his second Bloody Mary.

"How can that be, Leroy?" asked Bob.

"In addition to the 10 percent vig, they made money on every bet," the major said. "They also made money on the sucker bets, such as the under-and-over, the parlays, and the teasers."

Leroy knew from organized intelligence that the godfather in

New York was pleased both by Gattino's figures as well as his own good fortune with smart money tactics.

"The godfather has inside connections on college campuses and pro camps," continued Leroy. "Because of his position, he was able to get first shot at the Las Vegas lines for all college and pro games for the coming week."

"Leroy, you are a closet of information today," Bob said, obviously impressed.

"The first shot by the legal books in Vegas goes to a select clientele of big-time players known as wise guys," Leroy continued his report on the education of the young henchman. "Our intelligence shows that the godfather loves that term. He can afford betting lines that the average bettor would never see. Since wise guys such as the godfather have made a big dent in the official opening Vegas line on Sunday night, they will continue putting up big bucks with their inside information, figures, and sharp power ratings."

Bob was fascinated. He just listened in awe.

"From midday to late Friday, many lines are adjusted," the major continued. "Plenty of public money originates from those who are visitors to Vegas for the weekend. Wise guys such as the godfather, however, get down early for the weekend action. They have seen the public action fluctuate all week. Now they prepare for some big moves on the weekend card. If they see a line being bet on the wrong side of their figures, they will go after that line.

"On pro football Sundays, like today, the godfather probably places his money down 30 minutes before the 1:00 p.m. East Coast and 4:00 p.m. West Coast kickoffs. A change of up to three points just before game time should be a tip-off that the smart-money guys have made a dramatic move.

"The godfather probably put his money on the underdogs, because he feels that a small underdog should be a solid favorite, and a large underdog even has a chance to win outright or keep the game real close."

"I need a refill," Bob said.

"Yeah, one for the road," Leroy said. "By the way, I have some information about your favorite quarterback. . ."

On the drive to Sol Rubin Stadium, Bob knew the column he would write would be so potent that it would need a read by the newspaper's lawyer, Jim Walden. His concern was that the publisher might try to spike it. *But my contract won't let him, as long as I get Walden's approval.*

At the stadium, Bob had a chance meeting outside the press gate with Fred Vercini, a sports columnist with the *Daytona Beach Democrat*.

"I understand that Jack Cabot was in my neck of the woods yesterday," Vercini said. "Our police reporter told me that he was a visitor at Tomoka State Prison."

"Interesting," said Bob. He really wasn't excited about Cabot, because of the Longo caper. "Thanks for the tip, Fred."

If Bob had followed up on the tip, he would have learned that on Saturday, Cabot flew aboard the Sharks' Lear jet into Boca Raton, where he took a taxi to the Sayfie Clinic. There, the GM checked out Muhammad Johnson for the day. The two continued a flight to Daytona Beach, where in a rented Lincoln Town Car, they drove to the Tomoka Correctional Institution, about 12 miles west of the city.

Jack had a lot on his mind, including the possible scandal with Longo, and of course Bunny's fixation on gaining control of the Sharks. The GM was consumed by his passion for this woman, but at the same time fearful that she might do something drastic like shoot her husband.

He tried to put the subject out of his mind and concentrate on the more immediate problem of trying to save a star player.

Johnson did not have a clue about what was happening. He was happy to escape the clinic life and his drug rehab for a day.

"You should be pleased that Coach Sherman placed you on the injured reserve list," Jack said. "By not suspending you, Sherman has kept you on the payroll as long as you undergo drug rehab."

"I appreciate that, Mr. Cabot," said a humble Johnson. "I hear tell, however, that S.R. was furious about the decision."

Jack and Johnson made polite talk for the rest of the trip. When the car pulled into the prison parking lot, the wide receiver believed he was going to give a talk or something to the inmates. Tomoka was located in a wooded area. The prison appeared more like a military camp than a state prison.

Still, it was a stark and foreboding sight. Johnson glanced at the fences topped with razor wire, the guard towers, and thought that for many men, this was where they would finish their lives.

Jack checked in with a receptionist behind a glass window.

Johnson didn't like the atmosphere. The two visitors were admitted through an electronic gate, where they were met by a uniformed guard who escorted them to the warden's office. The ugly yellow walls absorbed most of the light and made the corridors appear even more depressing. Johnson realized that the Sayfie Clinic was a grand hotel in comparison to this joint.

Warden John Harding greeted the visitors. "Gentlemen, I'm honored to meet two greats of pro football. I understand you want to visit with inmate Thompson."

Johnson was surprised but said nothing.

"That's correct, Warden," Jack replied. "I thought Thompson and Johnson might have a chance to visit."

"It's not a visitors' day," said the warden. "But I have no problem with that, Mr. Cabot. I want you to know I appreciate you volunteering to visit with our inmates in the Sports Club today. Most, you will find, are still pro football fans. They'll appreciate the Sharks media guides, programs, and other material you have already FedExed to me. I'm sure they'll look forward to the Sharks highlight film you brought, too." The warden used a desk intercom. "Jefferson, will you please escort Mr. Johnson to the library to visit with inmate Thompson."

A uniformed guard escorted Johnson to the library without conversation. There was a brief stop, as the two had to wait for another guard to electronically open a sliding door of bars. Then came a silent walk down a dimly lighted corridor to a door marked *Library*.

Rufus Thompson wore a blue denim shirt with his inmate number on it and blue jeans. He sat on a plain wooden table with four wooden chairs nearby. He nodded to the visitor as the guard left them alone in the deserted library.

Johnson was surprised to see the former running back, who had once sported an Afro. He now had short hair with gray at the edges. He tried to size up Thompson while trying to figure out why he was here.

"Sit down, boy," Thompson ordered.

Johnson seated himself on a chair, looking up at the inmate.

"What did you say your name was, crackhead?"

The hostile greeting surprised him. "What do you mean, crackhead?" Johnson snapped.

"Boy, you're a fucked-up crackhead," the inmate continued. "I can see you're headed for this joint, motherfucker."

Johnson stood up. He wasn't going to take any abuse from some convict. "What kind of shit is this, bro? I didn't come here to take any shit from a fucking felon, much less one who pissed away his pro football career back in the 1980s." He was sorry for his words, but he was angry. Before he could soften his next words, he was knocked back into his chair by a powerful right-handed push from the inmate. It was obvious that Thompson was still in shape.

"Who we talking about, boy?" Thompson asked. "You or me? It's your black ass that's gonna follow mine here to this fucking cesspool. You still have a chance to save your sorry ass. I still have five more years to go before I is eligible for parole."

Johnson struggled to get up from the chair. He was confused and upset. *Why am here? What the hell is happening?*

Instead of taking his anger out on the aging black inmate, he took it out on the Sharks' GM. "That fucking honky Cabot," Johnson snarled. "That motherfucker brought me here—"

Thompson slapped the wide receiver hard across the face with his right hand. "Shut your mouth, nigger! I played against Cabot when he was with the Minutemen, boy, and he ain't no honky, you understands? You know, he's the only one from the Sharks organization who still stays in contact with me. He found a job for my wife. He makes a monthly contribution to my commissary fund. So don't you badmouth my main man, you understands, boy?"

Johnson was stunned by the confrontation. He was not about to let anyone, even a fellow African-American, get away with calling him a nigger, much less a boy.

Maybe a guard would arrive and end this ridiculous confrontation. None came. Instead, he was forced to listen to a lecture—no, a sermon. He thought about fighting back, until he noted the muscles bulging under that shirt.

"Look at me, bigshot," Thompson said. "I was once a bigshot, too. Drove a Porsche. Wore a Rolex. Had more pussy than one man deserves. Now I was only making $245,000 a year, but that was 1980s bread. Then I got hooked on shit. You know, I had all the excuses of why I was using it. Then when it became more and more expensive, I made a deal with the man to start selling it, too. I fucked up big-time, you knows. I made a sale to a Miami narc, and here I am."

"I'm sorry," muttered a suddenly contrite Johnson. "What's that go to do with me, man? Hey, I'm sorry some fucking racist cop busted you—"

"The cop that busted me was a bro. He didn't cut me no slack because I was a bro. I know now that I was wrong. You get a lot of time to think when you're inside here."

"Hey, man, I haven't sold any shit," protested the visitor. "I just needed it to handle the pressures of football. Everyone on our team uses some kinds of shit. . .pain pills, Novocaine, booze."

Thompson shook his head. "Listen, crackhead, life is about freedom. You knows the chair your black ass is in? That's the best it gets in here. I'd love to be able to put my ass into one of those big, soft, comfortable recliners. In here, you either sleep in your bunk, sit on a straight chair like that, or you stand. You dig my drift? Think about that, boy! Think about spending 10 years here without ever being able to sit in a comfortable chair."

It didn't seem like such a big deal to Johnson, but then he slowly realized that there were many more freedoms and comforts that were not to be found in Tomoka. *Man, I've heard all the lectures about drug abuse, but here I'm getting a view from the horse's mouth, so to speak.*

"Now, boy, you are here today so I can show you what life will be like if the polices catch your sorry ass doing or dealing shit. We is going to get a grand tour of this prison, and you is going to meet some mean brothers. They would be the first to fuck you up your young black ass when you come through those gates. You think you is tough because you play football. Fuck! We got guys in here who would cut your throat for a cigarette.

"Life is hell here, boy. It's getting even worse, because the public is pissed about crime. That's why we have no air-conditioned cellblocks, no more TV, and no more weights room. Think about that when you leave here today. Because you can walk out of here today, and I can't."

Johnson didn't learn until later that Thompson was a member of a jail program in which veteran inmates tried to scare the hell out of visiting teenagers before they could become criminals. Thompson wasn't sure if such tactics would work on a worldly adult such as the Sharks' wide receiver, but he had suggested the idea to

Cabot. The general manager figured that Thompson's fame as a former player might make it work.

At the same time, Jack had gambled that Johnson's middle-class background had spared him the ghetto life and penal experiences. Cabot was right.

#

Thompson's shock treatment indeed scared the hell out of Johnson. When he was discharged from the clinic for a weekend at his Plantation home, Johnson's first thought about why he wanted to become clean and sober from drugs was found in the den. It was an oversized, leather recliner.

He remembered he had hidden a bag of coke in a bookcase. He recovered it, looked at the bag. . .and went to the bathroom where he flushed the bag down the toilet.

#

Week 12 would be a short week for the Sharks who, after the Dons' game Wednesday afternoon, were scheduled to fly to Dallas for a nationally televised Thanksgiving Day game with the Texans.

Bob found it difficult to focus on covering the Dons, since they were almost as bad as the Titans. He really wanted to finish off the Longo matter.

He juggled his thoughts between Suzy and the coming Monday morning editorial meeting with Walden, Patterson, and Bloom while trying to find an angle on the Sunday afternoon game in SRS.

When the columnist reached his seat in the front row of the press box, he found Cunill typing on a new tangerine iBook laptop. "Hey, Wetback, happy birthday."

Jorge stopped typing. "Gringo. . .thanks for my birthday present. It's really cool. You shouldn't have."

Bob brushed off his friend's gratitude, grabbed a flip card, and pulled a yellow legal-size pad and a pair of field glasses from his computer carrying case. "What you doing, amigo?" he asked Jorge.

"Writing the game story," replied the sports reporter. He was only kidding. He was working on a feature for later in the week. Jorge knew that he could probably write most of this Sunday's game story as soon as the first half ended.

"That's easy for you beat guys," Bob said as he searched for his tape recorder. "We columnists really have to struggle with the meaning of today's Sharks victory."

Both men laughed.

"You know, Bob, I would love to be on TV. Look at Jon Swift of Channel 5. As a sports anchor, he comes here to eat free and watch the game. Then he goes back to his studio for a two-minute show on the six o'clock news, where he shows a 30-second film clip done by one of his reporters in the locker room and reads the rest of the IFL scores. And that sucker is making $500,000 a year just because he has a pretty face."

"Right, Jorge. Then Channel 5 will flood its market with promos showing Swift interviewing Sherman. What a joke. The BBC has it right in England. They call anchors such as Swift 'news readers.'"

"Oh say, amigo," Jorge said after he glanced around the area to make sure they were alone. "You going to visit with the guys with the shiny shoes tomorrow?"

"Yeah, at ten in the morning."

"Wear a shirt and tie, Bob. I mean, if you own any."

Bob shot Jorge a bird just before the playing of the national anthem.

"Oh, my God," moaned Jorge. "Another local rock singer is set to make us cringe with his modern rendition of the national anthem."

"Right, Jorge," Bob dryly replied. "Probably another Castro agent impersonating a wetback refugee."

Jorge pretended that the insult hurt and returned the bird salute to his companion. Then they both exchanged grimaces as the rock singer's attempt at singing the anthem sounded like fingernails scratching across a blackboard.

\#

Bunny watched from the owner's box, as her husband got rowdy and drunk before the intermission. She exchanged knowing glances with Jack while continuing to entertain the dozen assorted guests in the box. Bunny was growing antsy as the new year approached, because she knew that in the spring Steve Rubin would graduate from Stetson University and move into the front office.

If only something unfortunate would happen to S.R. That would end my problems. His will leaves me the team and a trust fund for Steve. If that kid comes to work here, Sol will flip-flop the deal. Having money is no big deal. A lot of rich folks get respect only from their bankers. A pro football owner is somebody in the news, a celebrity. Wouldn't it be a dream to own the Sharks and have Jack for my husband instead of that slob Sol?

\#

The game went as expected. By the game-ending gun, Jorge had his first edition story finished with the exception of the final statistics.

SHARKS SNACK
ON WIN-STARVED
DONS BY 35-10
by Jorge Cunill, Miami P.M. Sports Reporter
MIAMI—Johnny Longo threw for 176 yards and three touchdowns in the first half before leaving Sunday with a hamstring injury. Rookie Roosevelt Roots had a career day with 160 yards and a pair of scores, as the Miami Sharks cruised to a 35-10 rout of the Los Angeles Dons.

Miami (8-4) remained tied with Buffalo (8-4) in the East-

ern Division as the Snowmen also won 42-7 over Jacksonville.

Miami, which is 16-3 in its last 19 meetings with Los Angeles, embarks on a three-game road trip with games at Dallas on Thanksgiving, then Indianapolis, and Buffalo before its season finale in Rubin Stadium against Kansas City.

Longo limped off the field following a 19-yard scoring pass to Roots that opened a 21-3 lead with 15 seconds left in the first half.

"On the last touchdown pass I called, we didn't even have it in our play book," Longo revealed. "I just told the outside guys to run to the corners. I had a feeling they would bite on it. I said over and over that no one could cover this kid, Roosevelt Roots."

"He's remarkable, he's absolutely remarkable," Sharks coach Don Sherman said of Roots. "He never ceases to amaze me. His rookie presence has done a lot to rejuvenate our offense since we lost Muhammad Johnson."

Longo, who got a head start to the locker room, was holding his right hamstring after the TD pass.

"It's sore," Longo said of the hamstring, the same one that forced him to miss a pair of games last season. "I'm glad it wasn't the knees this time. It happened on the play before the touchdown. I was not sure how bad it was. After I threw the pass, I felt it. It didn't pop like before. I'll have to take it a day at a time. It's not like it was before."

Roots entered the game with 10 catches for 113 yards and one score this season, but Longo found him four times for 108 yards in the first half. Roots, whose 160 yards are a career high by any Sharks rookie, caught an 18-yard scoring strike from backup quarterback Eddie Malloy midway through the third quarter to make it 28-3.

#

It was the first time in five years now that Johnny had not bet on an IFL game. It wasn't that he didn't want to. Oh my, how he wanted to! Not even his wife's latest tirade had doused his uncontrollable urge to gamble.

He was a marked man, of sorts. No one was willing to handle any of his action. Unknown to the quarterback, Gattino had put the word out throughout the country that Longo would not be served. It didn't take any small-time bookie to figure out the connection between Longo and the hit on Syracusa. The inability to bet on football bothered Longo more than the hamstring.

Gotta get some big action for Thursday's game, because it's gonna be on national television and there will be a lot of money bet on it. But how am I going to do it?

#

Meanwhile, Gattino was trying to figure out a scheme that would eliminate Longo without calling attention to the Mafia sports betting empire. Then he had an idea. He called Anthony "Little Tony" Tenuto, the son of an old Brooklyn pal of his who controlled the Transportation Employees of America Union (TEAU), headquartered in Chicago.

Tenuto moved in high social, business, and political circles and was president of the 100,000-member TEAU. Tenuto was once acquitted on charges that he had swindled $2.4 million from the union pension fund. *His old man would have been proud of the kid*, thought Gattino.

Tenuto owed Gattino for helping in negotiations between the Chicago and East Coast families. The East Coast families—the most notable of which was the Lorenzo family—had handed over complete control of union organizing as well as Las Vegas gambling in exchange for full control over sports betting and the Atlantic City casinos.

"Tony. Sal Gattino in Hollywood."

Tenuto was surprised at the Sunday afternoon call that interrupted his watching the Chicago Pandas-Green Bay Holsteins telecast. But he treated the old don with all the respect of his office.

The two mobsters exchanged small talk about their families and the weather. Following a respectful time, Tenuto ventured to ask the caller: "Don Gattino. To what do I owe the honor of your call?"

"Tony. I have a small favor."

"Just ask it, Don Gattino. You were a good friend of my late father. And you have been my friend, too, in helping to solve our little jurisdictional conflict."

"You have influence with the Mick labor leader of Sun Airlines?"

"You mean Kelly, Don Gattino?"

"That's the man, Tony. His boys are on strike, but I think management is about to take some serious action."

"Kelly is a dedicated unionist," replied Tenuto. "He thinks he's calling the shots. He doesn't know that our guys have been stealing cargo and baggage at will from that airline. That's good, because he can honestly defend his union boys from the cops as well as the press."

Gattino paused briefly. "Tell me, Tony, if Sun Air starts flying again tomorrow and it breaks his strike, do you think he would be a bit pissed or really fucking pissed?"

"Really fucking pissed, Don Gattino. He'd do almost anything to get even. His boys are crazier than the longshoremen when it comes to getting even."

Gattino paused again. "Pissed enough to blow up an airplane and make it look like an accident?"

#

Monday arrived dark and dreary with what would be an all-day rain. Westinghouse's replacement workers, along with some pro-company types, crossed the picket lines at Sun Airlines stations around the system.

Among them were chief pilot Dick Norton and flight

attendants Chris Gaylord and Ann Parker. They had to cross a picket line that included Brutus Neswiacheny, the Sharks All-Pro linebacker.

"I'm a member of the players' union," he told reporter Zei while posing for television and still shots with strikers. "We players know about repression from management as well as low pay. I am proud today to stand with my brothers and sisters in the union movement."

Bob, who had dropped Suzy off at Sun Airlines headquarters en route to his crucial 10:00 a.m. meeting, laughed at the idea of a guy who made $5.5 million annually walking with blue-collar guys on a labor action. That was because he knew that after the media left, so would Neswiacheny. He had to prepare for a 10-minute speech that evening to benefit Miami Children's Hospital, for which his agent had obtained a $10,000 fee.

Only a token number of flights would leave MIA that Monday, but they would be filled with passengers who were eager to take advantage of what Sun Airlines advertised as its Turkey Trot fares, such as $199 round trip from Miami to New York. Almost immediately, Sun Airlines reservation lines became backed up as holiday-bound travelers quickly responded to the cheap fares.

The boldness of Westinghouse's action caught Kelly by surprise. However, the union leader didn't panic. This was a war, and Monday's event was only another battle. Tuesday would be another day. This was a big test for the power of unions. All of America would be watching this strike. So would the management of other commercial carriers who believed cheap labor was the road to prosperity in the era of deregulation.

"The fucking people are rushing to fly for the cheap fares," Kelly told a mechanic walking the line in front of the employees' entrance to Sun Airlines' mechanical facility. "Whatever happened to union solidarity? Some of those fuckers buying those cheap seats today are retired union workers. I can't believe those people."

Kelly, however, realized that what the union needed was some adverse publicity about the airline that would scare the shit out of the flying public. And it needed it quickly. Something so horrible that it might even get the FAA to shut down the carrier. Such happenings would strengthen the union's bargaining position with Westinghouse. That might even get the SOB run out of office by his board of directors.

#

At the Sharks' practice facility in Pembroke Pines, Sherman damned the IFL schedule-maker for not giving Miami its bye the Sunday before a Thanksgiving road trip.

"There's no reasonable way you can come off a Sunday game and prepare for a game Thursday on the road," Sherman told Jorge Monday morning. "Buffalo doesn't have to play a Thanksgiving Day game. I can't control the schedule. So we have to forget about the schedule and think only about beating Dallas.

"Time's running out, Jorge. We'll have only three games left Thursday. If we win on Thanksgiving, we have a mental edge on Buffalo. They don't play their Week 14 game until Sunday. It probably will come down to our final meeting, but I'm not looking past Dallas."

Jorge asked about injuries, then questioned Longo's status.

"Johnny took a pounding Sunday," said Sherman. "I'm waiting for our trainer's report. I may let him watch Malloy take the snaps in what's left of the week. Come game day, I'll have to determine if Johnny is healthy enough to start."

#

The wise guys, of course, were equally interested in Longo's status.

The official IFL injury report didn't come out until Wednesday, but the wise guys figured Longo would be listed as "probable" and that he would start.

The odds-makers would favor Dallas because of the Texans' home field advantage, but the announced spread would be key for the wise guys.

CHAPTER 15

"Every editor of newspapers pays tribute to the devil."
                                                La Fontaine

BOB HATED MEETINGS. He considered them a waste of time. That was why he never coveted an editor's position. Most newspaper editors spent most of their workdays at meetings trying to guess what the news would be while sending reporters out to confirm that the editors guessed right. Editors were so mesmerized by packaging stories with photos and graphics that they routinely sent reporters out to make the story fit the package. May God help the reporter whose digging enterprise came back with the opposite of the prepackaged theme.

Larry was from the old school of newspaper editors. He loathed meetings, considering them inconsequential.

Monday's meeting, however, was different. It was in a brightly lit room full of expensive furnishings. There were dark furniture woods, $2,500 leather chairs, and oil paintings on the walls.

This was the P.M.'s boardroom, and it was rare that any editorial personnel under the rank of assistant managing editor ever graced the premises. It was next to publisher Patterson's office on the fifth floor. This was a much more formal meeting than those run by

Bloom two stories below, in the plain pipe rack of an editorial meeting room.

Bob shocked the people he passed en route to the fifth floor. The columnist drew second looks, since he was attired in a tan gabardine business suit, white button-down-collar shirt, and a conservative striped tie. He had followed Larry's advice about "dressing for success" because he knew that this column was going to be a hard sell.

Patterson greeted Bob. The publisher was no fan of the star sports columnist, whom he considered a muckraker. Bob was not the kind of person that Patterson would ever invite to dinner at his Miami Lakes Country Club. His father-in-law, Andy Lyon, loved Casey's work. *Why couldn't my father-in-law be the owner of responsible newspapers like The New York Times?*

"My God, Casey, you really do own a suit and tie!" Patterson exclaimed sarcastically.

Bob felt the urge to give a one-line comeback, but thought better of it. Instead, he just smiled at the publisher and replied, "Thank you."

"Nice tie," Larry said as he gently tugged on it. "I hope this isn't your noose."

Patterson sat like a ship's captain at the head of a walnut table. Seated to his right was Walden, whose black leather pilot's case had been placed on a chair to the lawyer's left. Also seated at the table were executive sports editor Chris Sciria and Bloom.

Walden appeared to be the Hollywood version of a corporate lawyer. He wore a three-piece, $1,200, gray pinstriped suit, a white button-down shirt, and a plaid bow tie. His $14,000 gold Rolex showed his success, while his nearly bald head and the remaining white hair and metal frame glasses showed his age.

Bob couldn't help but wonder how one tied a bow tie. *He looks so different in his tennis attire.*

The publisher's secretary distributed paper copies of Casey's undated column as the publisher opened the meeting with, "I think we've all read this a few times."

Everyone nodded.

Then they began reading the column. Even Bob read it again.

"While I personally do not agree with all that Bob writes, I realize that his personal services contract gives him quite a bit of editorial freedom. In this Longo gambling column, I appreciate that he was professional enough to wave a red flag before it was printed. I do, however, have concerns about it. So I invited Jim to join us. The ultimate decision, however, will be my call."

Bob sat quietly and showed no emotion. He fought back a yawn, because he was bored by the procedure. He knew, however, that the ultimate decision on this matter would not be made by the publisher, but by his father-in-law. Bob loved old Andy Lyon, whom some considered a tyrant as a boss, and whom most considered a modern-day yellow journalist. *Love is strange*, he thought, *or how the hell could Lyon's daughter marry a nerd like Patterson?*

While Bob and Walden were friends and tennis competitors, the lawyer always put business before friendship. He was, however, the ultimate corporate attorney. That was reflected in the list of his firm's major clients, which included *Miami P.M.*, Sun Airlines, and the Miami Sharks.

Walden shuffled a yellow legal pad filled with longhand notes along with a marked-up copy of the column. The best advice that the attorney had ever given Bob was, "Always destroy your notes and tapes after you have finished a column." The reason, according to Walden, was that, "They can be used against you in court. Notes and tapes can be interpreted by the plaintiff's attorney to prove their case."

The attorney cleared his throat and checked his notes on the legal pad. He acted more like he was in court rather than with a client in the sanctuary of his boardroom.

"I must say Mr. Casey doesn't pull any punches in this one. Even though I don't agree with everything he writes, I happen to be a fan of your sports columnist. I don't doubt for a moment that what you say, Mr. Casey, is probably true about the gambling.

The police evidence does support your charge that Mr. Longo is involved in illegal sports gambling.

"It is the murder allegation that concerns me. That, too, may prove very true. But for now, we aren't on very solid ground if we suggest that Mr. Longo could be involved in a murder. This is a very serious charge, and it isn't—at least at this moment—supported by the police. Also, I'm concerned about the allegations against Mr. Rubin. He's very active in community affairs. I don't think we should offend members of the Jewish community—"

Larry interrupted Walden with a brief fit of uncontrollable laughter. "Excuse me, counselor. It doesn't offend me," said the managing editor. "Rubin is a drunk, a womanizer, and a big-time gambler. That is a matter of record. As for the murder accusation, we're simply tightening the noose around Longo. Hell, Bob's column is dynamite. He's close to Major Hess and on top of the murder investigation. This is the kind of copy our readers love. We're talking about a world-famous quarterback involved in gambling and murder. It has the makings of another O.J. Simpson story. It'll boost our street sales and get us national attention."

Bob was impressed by Larry's passionate defense of the column.

"And a damned expensive lawsuit," Patterson asserted.

"You're right on that, Jack," Walden agreed.

"Gentlemen, you forget that we often benefit from such suits by increased circulation," Larry asserted. "Mr. Lyon believes in including a generous line to cover libel suits in our editorial budget. Mr. Lyon believes that the mission of *Miami P.M.* is to raise hell and sell newspapers."

Patterson said nothing, but he seethed inside when Bloom quoted Lyon. He resented the strong relationship between Bloom and his father-in-law that gave the managing editor control over the editorial product of the Kangaroo News Ltd. daily. He knew, too, that his father-in-law was a fan of Casey's.

"What do you think, Chris?" the publisher continued, trying to act impartial but at the same time seeking an ally. He didn't get it.

"I agree with Larry, Mr. Patterson," said the executive sports editor. "This is a red-hot column. I think it's great that we're taking a stand against illegal sports gambling. We've been sued before, but isn't truth the best defense against libel?"

Walden smiled. "Mr. Sciria. Does that mean you'll discontinue running morning lines in your sports section?"

"No, Mr. Walden."

"I thought not."

"I don't think you really understand the newspaper business," replied the executive sports editor. "We run a lot of things we personally don't agree with, because our readers demand them. I don't smoke, but if I owned a convenience store, you bet I would carry cigarettes. That's just good business sense."

Patterson waved his hand and asked for quiet. "Why should we run this column and risk being sued, Bob?"

"Because, Mr. Patterson, we want to raise hell and sell newspapers. Isn't that what Kangaroo News Ltd. is all about? We're a tabloid in a highly competitive market. This is one of the few remaining two-newspaper cities in America. We stay in business because we are more daring than the old lady down the street, the *Morning Journal*."

It was this passionate statement that triggered Bloom and Sciria to clap politely. This did not please the publisher, though, who felt he was losing the battle.

But Patterson was a survivor who made all of his decisions by trying to figure out what Lyon would want. While he rarely agreed with the old man on any issue, Patterson knew that his job was only as secure as his marriage. He knew that someday Lyon would be dead, and the media empire would be split between his two sons and daughter. Because his wife was submissive and preferred the country club to the office, Patterson would be a major player.

My first official act will be to can Bloom and Casey. But for now, I'll play the game.

"Jack, you know that being sued is part of tabloid newspapering," Larry said. "Even when we lose in court, the publicity helps circulation. I ask you: Can Johnny Longo risk going to court? Longo isn't some innocent victim. He's dirty. He's at least fixing games."

Larry's stand convinced Bob that the ME would go over the publisher's head to fight for the column.

God, what a treat, Bob thought, *to be a fly on the wall and witness a session between Lyon and his asshole son-in-law.*

"Okay, gentlemen, I need time to think over this call," Patterson said. "I'll make a decision before Thursday."

Casey, Sciria, and Bloom headed for the elevator.

"Bobby, enjoy Dallas, and have a happy Thanksgiving. Say hello to Suzy. I'm going to make a call to the land down under," was Larry's parting remark to Casey.

Bob smiled in victory. "Why am I not surprised?" He pulled out his cigar case and handed one Churchill to Bloom, while preparing to light another for himself.

As Bob's cigar began to smoke, Sciria grinned. "Hey, here we are at the old Boston Garden, and Red Auerbach is celebrating another Celtics' victory. Methinks this Auerbach will have to exit by the stairs, because they won't let him on the elevator with that smelly stogie."

"I'll be out at the Sharks' camp if you need me, Larry." With that remark, Bob happily headed for the stairway and climbed down five flights while savoring the rich taste of the imported tobacco.

#

Larry strode off the elevator and into his office. Before seating himself, he picked up the phone and dialed the Kangaroo News Ltd. corporate headquarters in Sidney, Australia. He was pleasantly surprised in spite of the time difference when the CEO answered on his private line.

"Mr. Lyon," he said. "Good day from your Miami property. I was wondering if you were willing to risk a lawsuit to raise hell and sell some newspapers?"

There was a brief silence, and then a slight chuckle before Bloom heard the voice with the Australian accent reply. "Okay, Larry, tell me what your ace sports muckraker is up to now, and how much this one is going to cost me. . ."

#

Patterson phoned Bloom at 9:00 a.m. the next morning.

"After thinking about it, I guess we should risk a lawsuit to run Casey's column on the pro football player. Run it Thursday. That should boost our holiday sales."

Larry wanted to protest, but thought better of it. He had won the war, so why worry about a little battle. Lyon had made the decision for his son-in-law. Patterson wanted to save face and had therefore ordered the column buried in a Thanksgiving Day edition that would probably be only half the normal daily circulation of 550,000.

#

Bunny Rubin took off her designer sunglasses, sipped on a tall glass of iced tea, and read the typed resumé of a soldier of fortune. It wasn't a resumé that one would submit to a personnel office for an average job. The applicant, however, wasn't applying for an average job.

She was determined to become the owner of the Sharks. *I can't wait any longer. Sol isn't going to croak with a heart attack. And his damn son will be out of school by May.*

It was a balmy mid-afternoon at the Green Turtle Café at Duck Key. Bunny and a man, who had identified himself as Klaus Müller, were having lunch at a picnic table on an open back porch overlooking the Atlantic Ocean.

The Green Turtle was a shanty with a liquor license that served tasty, local cuisine and was a popular eatery for folks of all classes.

Bunny had spotted Müller's classified ad in Combat Elite magazine, and had contacted him a month earlier. She couldn't believe this was happening so fast. She took her time studying the resumé.

My God, who would offer such a resumé? Here was a native of the old German Democratic Republic, a former captain of the DDR Olympic ice hockey team, a college graduate who spoke four languages—German, English, Spanish, and Russian—and a former officer in the DDR secret police. *Almost unbelievably, now he is working for our country!*

Müller had a Prussian military look. He appeared 10 years younger than his real age of 52. He was lean and mean at six-foot-one and 190 pounds.

He displayed a fresh crewcut and wore aviator style sunglasses, a polo shirt, and khaki slacks. Muscles bulged under his tight shirt. On occasion, he would still automatically click his heels together as he did when he first met Bunny in person this noon. This, Bunny had observed.

What she couldn't see was the Walther PPK .380 carried in an ankle holster on the man's right leg. His English was almost flawless, but on occasion he betrayed a bit of an accent of his native German tongue.

"You're an educated German, an old jock, and an ex-soldier," Bunny began. "You served in the old East German army and later worked for a police agency. You also work for an agency in the United States. That doesn't tell me a lot about your ability to do my assignment."

Müller smiled. After a sip from his glass of Beck's, he reassured her. "Well, Frau Rubin, I admit to being a member of the Stasi. That was the DDR's version of the Nazi Gestapo. When things started to change, I was recruited and joined your American CIA. I keep busy doing freelance work for your agency. In fact, I just returned from an assignment in Central America."

Bunny shook her head in disbelief. "How did you go so quickly from working for the Communists to working for us?"

"I am a professional," he said simply as he poured a head on a glass of beer. "I am not a foolish romantic or even a patriot. I am, you might say, a mercenary who can adapt to any political persuasion, as long as I'm paid decently."

What Bunny didn't know was that this man lunching with her would be in prison if the German Federal Republic ever found him. Müller was a ruthless and proficient policeman who had on occasion infiltrated the West German government.

When it became obvious to him that the days of the DDR were numbered, he had offered his services to the CIA. The Americans were delighted to have a man of Müller's background, because he knew the inside operations of former East German allies such as Cuba, North Korea, Vietnam, and China.

Müller had no major weaknesses such as drugs, booze, women, or men. His only passion was money: money that he could sock away in both Swiss and Bahamian banks for his early retirement. He was, after all, getting a bit old for this line of work. He was using his leave time from the agency to do a little freelance work.

Bunny Rubin couldn't believe that she was really plotting the murder of her husband. But she was actually excited by the danger. *Even though I've suggested getting rid of Sol to Jack, he isn't taking me seriously. He is too moral, too principled. Jack wouldn't understand my passion to become a team owner at any cost. He'd call it murder. It really is just a business move.*

"So," said Bunny after taking a bite from her chef's salad. "I'm not looking for a spy. I'm looking for someone. . .er, a little more basic, like a professional hit man."

The man behind the aviator glasses smiled slightly but showed no other emotion. "You know that movie character, James Bond? Well, I am a German version. I am licensed to kill by the United States of America."

"I'm impressed, Mr. Müller, if that is your real name," she said dryly. "I have an assignment for you, if you can handle it."

Bunny was not the least bit scared by meeting this stranger. She had already taken a risk by sending him $25,000 in a complicated cash transfer that ended in some Bahamian bank. She didn't want to get burned by hiring some Miami cop impersonating a hit man. This former Commie cop was the right choice. *A moonlighting CIA agent, no less. What a trip!*

Müller, on the other hand, figured that the woman was serious by her 25 Gs statement. She was a celebrity, so she would pay his fee in full when he completed it. He hadn't the least doubt of that.

"You took a risk, Frau Rubin, by sending an unknown man $25,000, did you not? I guess that is a risk common to you Jewish business people."

Bunny kept her cool. "I'm not Jewish. I'm Irish. I married a Jew. I want you to eliminate the Jew in my life. Can you handle such an assignment?"

While Müller was an equal opportunity hit man, the DDR had indoctrinated him well on the state's line of the evils of the international Jewry in business, etc. That was one of the good reasons for the former Berlin Wall—to protect decent DDR citizens from Jewish capitalism.

Müller knew that Bunny wasn't Jewish. He had used the agency resources to run a complete background check. He even knew she was sleeping with Cabot. He had merely wanted to see her reaction to being called Jewish.

Ah, the Amerikaners. Such hypocrites. They condemn the Nazis for killing Jews, but they think of their own Jews as niggers.

"True, there was risk in losing $25,000," Bunny explained. "I believed you to be a person with bigger goals. That's why you will get the remaining $75,000 when the job is done."

Müller had no moral conscience. Killing was a business to him. The Germans and the Americans paid him to kill. Did God differentiate between murder for the state and that of private enterprise?

While this Rubin matter was not state business, the money seemed good. He was much too smart to think about blackmail later. He wasn't greedy enough to blow a good deal with the

Americans. *A bitch like Rubin would probably put a contract out on me.*

They finished lunch. Then Rubin gave the German a photograph of Sol Rubin, along with a description.

"I want this to look like an accident, Herr Müller. No Mafia-style shooting. Can you do that?"

"You mean like an auto accident?"

"Not exactly. How about a plane accident, Herr Müller?"

The German struggled momentarily with the use of *plain* or *plane*. "What is the plain accident, Frau Rubin? You mean you don't want anything exciting?"

"Not plain, Herr Müller. I'm talking about an airplane. Flugzeug." Rubin was glad she remembered something from her highschool course in German.

"Ah, ja, Frau Rubin. Flugzeug. A small one or. . ."

"Big. A commercial jet. A gross Flugzeug. A DC-10."

For a moment, the German was speechless, but that was all the emotion he betrayed. "Anything is possible for a price, Frau Rubin."

"If you do the job, I'll double your $100,000 fee," she said.

"This means there will be other casualties besides your husband."

"That's business, Herr Müller."

"Ja," he replied. "What aircraft are we talking about?"

"A Sun Air team charter. A charter of the Miami Sharks football team."

"Interesting," he said with a slight smile. "Do you ever fly with your husband?"

"Unfortunately, yes. Well, damn it, I don't plan to be aboard when he goes to hell."

"How soon?"

Now Bunny was excited. "Next month," she said, almost breathless. "Yes, next month. That way I'll make sure I'm not a passenger. We have a trip to Buffalo."

Müller clicked his heels and offered a short bow. "It is nice doing business with you, Frau Rubin," he said. "So as not to call attention to the transfer of funds, I suggest that you make them in monthly installments of, say, $20,000."

"No problem," she said. "No problem."

About the same time in Sun Airline's empty union hall, Kelly and Danny O'Brien were dividing a large pepperoni pizza and a pair of six-packs of Budweiser at a table on the auditorium stage. O'Brien had been dispatched from Chicago by Tony Tenuto of the TEAU to plant a seed in Kelly's mind about the need to create a safety crisis among the public for the carrier.

Tenuto was too smart to get personally involved in setting up the sabotage of a commercial airliner, even when it was a personal favor to a fellow don, Sal Gattino. He did, however, send his top lieutenant, O'Brien, for two important reasons. First, he trusted the Mick. Second, the two Micks should interact better. He did make it clear to O'Brien that this assignment was very, very important family business.

"You know, Michael, me boy, you could lose this strike if Westinghouse is successful with his scabs," the man from Chicago said. "He's already got some flights off the pad, and with the lucrative holiday season coming, seats will be scarce coming into Florida. You don't think even old-time union folks will care if they have to fly down on a scab carrier, do you?"

O'Brien was one of the few non-Italians who had risen to power in the Chicago family. Maybe it was because the godfather, Abe Goldman, was Jewish. Probably it was because he was a good union organizer, and Tenuto liked him.

It was his gift of blarney and salesmanship that he used on the Miami union leader, because he knew Kelly was oblivious to the Mafia's control of the TEAU. Tenuto felt that Kelly was more valuable out of the loop.

"True. Union solidarity isn't what it used to be 30 years ago," Kelly said while popping open a fresh can of beer. "That fucking Reagan started all our problems when he fired those air controllers back in 1981. Him a good son of Eire, too."

O'Brien lit a cigarette and used an empty beer can for an ashtray. "To tell you the truth, Michael, there are concerns in Chicago about your handling of this strike. Now, I like you. You're smart and dedicated to our cause. But. . .we don't want to lose this one. No way, no how. If we lose the Sun Airlines battle, we could lose the whole war with the airlines.

"Now if Westinghouse keeps planes in the air, slowly the tide will turn against us. Action is needed. And very quickly."

"Like what, Danny?"

"A disaster, lad. Show the world that Sun Air isn't flying safe jets. Show the world that it needs your mechanics back. A big disaster. Yeah, that would do it."

There was a minute of silence as Kelly pondered the suggestion. "For Christ's sake, Danny, what do you want me to do, blow up a DC-10?"

"Bingo!"

Kelly was shocked into a moment of silence. "You gotta be shitting me, Danny. That would be mass murder."

"Call it what you want, my friend, but if such an event did take place—and I'm not suggesting it—Sun would be grounded. Then, you know, Westinghouse would have to settle the strike—and on your terms."

Kelly grabbed another beer. Although he was a fanatical union leader, he was still a licensed commercial airline mechanic. The thought of destroying an airline was foreign to him. To destroy it with people on board would create a problem for his Catholic faith. Still, he knew O'Brien had a point. Such an event could turn the tide in favor of the union.

"Perhaps we could create a scare that would do the job without any loss of life," was Kelly's alternate solution. "You know, those cargo doors on the DC-10. . ."

"We have near-crashes almost daily in commercial aviation," O'Brien interrupted. He was losing his patience. "They don't make the six o'clock news or the morning papers." O'Brien reached into his flight bag and produced a quart of Irish whiskey.

Kelly smiled appreciatively, excused himself, and found two glasses in the men's room. He returned just as O'Brien opened the bottle.

"You know, Michael, I am a native of Belfast," O'Brien said after a swig of whiskey. "What most don't know is that I once served with the IRA. I did a lot of things that were not nice by me dear old mother's standards. It's never easy to kill. It is harder yet when the victims be women and children. You do that in a war, lad. That's what we have in Ireland. There is no crime in killing in a war, now is there? You are called heroes and get medals."

Kelly didn't believe what he was hearing. He hated the British, but killing women and kids?

"Well, this is a war we have here. A war between the working man and the capitalistic bastards. So I'm asking, lad, do you have what it takes to be a soldier of the TEAU in this war?"

The two men were slowly getting drunk. The whiskey unlocked some of the black secrets of the former IRA member. Kelly listened in awe, because he considered any IRA man a patriot. The thought of killing women and children, however, continued to bother him.

O'Brien revealed that he had been caught in London while his IRA unit was conducting a series of bombings. He made a dramatic escape from the British police, fled to the United States, and settled in Chicago where Irish-Americans hailed him as a hero. IRA supporters in Congress protected him from being returned to British authorities, and he found work as a baggage handler at O'Hare, where he became a gung-ho TEAU member.

"The rest is history, Michael," he said, lifting his glass in a toast. "To the English. May they rot in hell."

Kelly automatically lifted his glass, but he was already thinking about the cargo doors. He remembered an incident seven or eight years ago with a DC-10 in Detroit when he was a mechanic assigned there.

"Give it some thought, Michael, me lad," the man from Chicago said. "A big win for us against Sun Air could move you up the ladder of the TEAU. I know Mr. Tenuto has his eyes on you."

Kelly nodded and said he would consider the matter. The already unpleasant thought had made him sicker than the hangover he expected.

#

At International Football League headquarters in midtown Manhattan, Commissioner Pete Wilson had summoned Paul Dungan to his office ASAP. Dungan, a Miami private investigator, was under contract to the IFL and assigned to the Sharks. His job was not only in team security but also to complete background checks of business and social contacts of Miami players.

Dungan had to take a 6:00 a.m. Continental flight to Newark, and then bus over to Manhattan in order to make the 10:00 a.m. meeting. He wasn't looking forward to this trip, because he was already on the commissioner's shit list for not being aware of Johnson's coke problem. Now this Longo matter had probably created havoc among the league executives.

Dungan was a retired Chicago cop. At six-foot-one, 245-pounds with wavy red hair and a red nose, he was the stereotype of a big-city Irishman. He still had a sense of humor, but a bullet wound in the gut had ended his boozing and brawling days forever. The wound during a drug bust had ended his career two years early, but he was drawing a pension and an IFB salary.

Wilson's career was in corporate law. He, too, was the stereotype of the corporate lawyer. He wasn't even a football fan when the owners recruited him to replace the retiring commissioner.

He was a Yale graduate who had lettered in tennis at Ole Eli. He married into a prestigious New York law firm and rose rapidly to become a senior partner. Maybe that was why the players disliked him and columnists like Casey and Cohen made fun of him in print.

"Sit down, Mr. Dungan," said the commissioner after the receptionist had shown the PI into the spacious executive office in the corner of the 12th floor overlooking Park Avenue. "I won't waste our time with chitchat. I want to know what the hell is going on in Miami."

"In what particular area, Mr. Commissioner?" the PI asked in a respectful tone.

"What area? For God's sake, man, we pay you good money to stay on top of things in our Miami franchise. I'm talking about the matter of Mrs. Sol Rubin and Jack Cabot."

Dungan was shocked into momentary speechlessness. *The commissioner isn't concerned about drugs or gambling in his Miami franchise? Only about an affair between the owner's wife and the GM? Amazing!*

"Yes, Mr. Commissioner, I am aware of the affair." Dungan slowly told what he knew of the affair.

"You didn't inform Mr. Rubin?"

"No, Mr. Commissioner."

"Why not?"

"Because, Mr. Commissioner, I work for the IFL, not Mr. Rubin."

Wilson smiled slightly. "I think, Mr. Dungan, you could very well have a long and lucrative career with the league. You have done the right thing by not telling anyone except me about this embarrassing matter. You know, Mr. Dungan, the IFL has to set a high moral standard, and a matter like this could be disturbing to some of our TV sponsors."

"You may also be aware, Mr. Commissioner, that Mr. Rubin is a compulsive gambler and bets at least $10,000 a week on Sharks games," offered the PI.

"Everyone has a little gambler in him," replied Wilson. "Mr. Rubin can afford to bet. Betting on pro football is as American as apple pie, if you know what I mean. I don't think we have a problem with our players, do you? I think they make too much money to risk getting involved in a scandal, don't you?"

Dungan shook his head to both questions. *I guess I am about to become a yes man,* he thought.

"What I want you to do is continue surveillance on Mrs. Rubin and Mr. Cabot. Get pictures, etc. Well, Mr. Dungan, I won't tell you how to do your job. You can treat this like a major divorce case. Any questions?"

"No, sir."

"Good. Um. . .you didn't ask why I need this information."

"That's not my department, Mr. Commissioner. I worked with an intelligence unit when I was in the Army during Desert Storm, and I just follow orders. I don't ask questions."

"I like your thinking, Mr. Dungan," said the commissioner, who rose to indicate that the visit was over. "As a token of the league's appreciation, your annual salary has been increased by $10,000."

"Thank you, Mr. Commissioner. Thank you, sir."

Being a yes man sure has its rewards.

CHAPTER 16

*"Heap high the board with plenteous cheer, and gather to the feast,
And toast the sturdy Pilgrim band whose courage never ceased."*

Alice Williams Brotherton
The First Thanksgiving Day

GOING INTO WEEK 12 of the 16-game International Football League season, the American Conference's Atlantic Division was a four-way horse race with only the New York Titans out of the competition.

The standings as of the day before Thanksgiving looked like this:

ATLANTIC DIVISION

Miami Sharks	8	4	.667
Buffalo Snowmen	8	4	.667
Indianapolis Hoosiers	6	6	.500
Boston Minutemen	5	7	.380
New York Titans	3	9	.250

Coach Don Sherman didn't appreciate Thanksgiving Day games. It was a Dallas tradition, and of course the TV contract needed two games on that holiday. This year the IFL schedule made the Sharks the Dallas Texans' foe.

The Texans were first in the National Conference's Central Division, with a 10-2 record. Although he wouldn't say it for the record, Sherman was upset because the Snowmen not only didn't have to play until Sunday, but it was a divisional match against the hapless Titans in Buffalo.

The gamblers made Dallas their morning line favorite, but not with great enthusiasm. The spread was 3 ½ points.

In Hollywood, Gattino was on the phone to his gambling lieutenants to ensure that the action was spread fairly evenly. This meant shifting some of the action between Texas and South Florida. That way, no bookmaker was top-heavy with one team. Regardless, the Mafia would make money because there was always the vig, the crazy under-and-over betting, and other betting combinations.

Although the machinists were still on strike, and some pilots and flight attendants were honoring the picket lines, Sun Airlines' flights were booked and overbooked for this holiday weekend. Westinghouse had rejected requests from two vice presidents to scrub the Sharks charter and put that DC-10 on the heavily traveled Miami-New York La Guardia route.

Martin had convinced Westinghouse that the Sharks charters were positive public relations during this stormy period of labor discontent. In addition, the corporate public relations veep got Westinghouse to increase an advertising blitz on television, including the network coverage of IFL games. As a result of the extra revenue, the network had asked its game announcers to plug the airline.

Norton, however, had the challenge of getting pilots and engineers to cross the picket lines. He felt confident that he could sell his fellow aviators.

Dick and new flight attendant supervisor Suzy Peters assembled their respective cockpit and cabin crews on Wednesday for the DC-10 that would fly the Sharks charter to Dallas/Fort Worth. Suzy had assigned Parker and Gaylord, along with six new-hires, to work the cabin. Mary Rich, with the rank of purser, had finally agreed to cross the picket line.

As was his custom, Bob arrived about 90 minutes before flight time. In the holiday traffic, it took him an hour to drive to MIA, and another 20 minutes to find a parking space on the roof of a parking garage.

The columnist had to pass through a machinists' picket line in front of the Sun Airlines entrance. Inside, the terminal was bustling with passengers and flight crews. A smiling red coat greeted him at a portable podium, and checked his name off a list on a clipboard, while another red jacket escorted him to a private waiting room for charter passengers. Some players, coaches, team personnel, and camp followers had already arrived. He wanted to talk with Father O'Malley, but he was surprised when he spotted Muhammad Johnson talking with George Carver.

"George, Muhammad," the columnist said with a cordial smile. "To what do we owe the pleasure of Muhammad's visit today?"

"I'm cleaning up my act, Bob," replied the wide receiver. "I've found Jesus. I've been discharged from drug rehab. If I pass my tests next week, the commish will reinstate me. Coach Sherman said he'll welcome me back."

Carver, the defensive end, playfully placed his powerful right arm around the neck of the five-foot-eleven, 185-pound wide receiver. "If this brother fucks up again, Bob, I promise you I will personally break his neck."

Amundsen, the offensive tackle and president of the Sharks' chapter of the Fellowship of Christian Athletes, joined the group. "Muhammad has joined the FCA, too," Amundsen said. "If he lets us down this time, I feel certain our Lord will not forgive him his sins the second time around."

"I promise I won't stray from the flock anymore," Johnson said. He sounded sincere. "I've been born again. God bless you, Bob."

"God bless you too, Muhammad," said Bob as he excused himself. He didn't feel comfortable among the Bible-thumping players.

Bob didn't see Father O'Malley, so he settled down to visit with offensive coordinator Moses.

#

O'Malley had tried to leave early, too. He had his over-night bag packed, and he was looking forward to his trip with the Sharks to Dallas. He was pleased that Bob and Suzy had invited him to join them for dinner that night.

He found a line waiting for confessions, so he entered the booth at St. Vincent's, hoping the sins of his parishioners were few and mild.

"Father, forgive me for I have sinned."

The voice was that of a young boy, probably a young teen.

"How have you sinned, my son?"

"I. . .I. . .I have abused myself, Father. I play with myself."

The priest could sense the shame by the sound of the young man's voice.

"You mean you masturbate, my son?"

"Yes, Father, I do that, too."

"Why do you do that?"

"You see, I'm going steady. An', you know, Barbara gets me all excited like. I really like her. I wouldn't do anything bad like having sex with her or anything. She's a proper Catholic girl."

It was hard for O'Malley to give advice about sex. He had no sexual experience with either sex. *God save me. I did have those yearnings as a youth—and the sexual revolution of the 1960s challenged the Church on so many sexual issues.*

He was aware that many women in his parish practiced some form of birth control, while others probably even had abortions. The difficult part for the priest was dealing with unmarried teenagers having sex.

The priest cleared his throat. "If masturbation keeps you from sinning with Barbara, or any other young lady, then you have my understanding. You are behaving like a good Catholic by refraining from sex outside of marriage. Now go home and say a dozen Hail Marys."

"Thank you, Father. I do try hard to be a good Catholic."

"Bless you, my son. Go with God."

O'Malley thought that that was the last confession, and he had prepared to leave the booth. The opening of a door followed by footsteps clattering on the tiled floor signaled that he wasn't finished yet.

"Father?"

It was a mature woman's voice, sounding almost as sexy as Lauren Bacall.

"Yes, my child, I am still here."

"Thank heaven. I thought I might have missed you. . .forgive me, Father, for I have sinned." The voice sounded familiar, but he made no effort to identify it. Otherwise, why have the sanctuary of the confessional booth?

"How have you sinned, my child?"

There was a silence of about a minute. Then: "I've killed a man." The woman's voice was faint, and it was choked with emotion.

The declaration had blindsided the priest. His reply was one of shock. "You say you've done what?"

"Father, I killed a man. Shot him down in cold blood. Pray for me."

Before he could reply, the woman lost her composure and began to sob.

"Father, do you hear me? I killed a man. Oh God, somebody help me!"

It was then that O'Malley recognized the voice. It was Johnny Longo's wife Martha.

#

On the fifth floor of Miami Police Headquarters in the Criminal Investigations Section, Leroy Hess was already on his third cup of coffee Wednesday morning. A bright tropical sun poured in the corner office overlooking the Miami harbor. He fumbled through the clutter in his desk drawer to find a bottle of Excedrin and popped three pills into his mouth, downing them with a swing of tepid coffee.

"Damn retirement parties," he muttered out loud.

Leroy stared hard at the paperwork in front of him. He pushed all of it aside to concentrate on the homicide, a typed report he would read for the third time. It was the report of the shooting death of Dom Conte.

The major picked up the phone and summoned the Homicide Section commander, Lt. Roberto Martinez. "I've read your Conte case report several times, Roberto. It's good work. I'm concerned about the prime suspect. We're talking a big-time name as a suspect here. We don't have any witnesses placing him at the crime scene, only a witness that spotted his car leaving the scene. That doesn't place the subject behind the wheel."

"True, Major. But I believe we have established enough circumstantial evidence to show who terminated Conte. Plus, we have established that the suspect has a million reasons to become a trigger man. If we collar the suspect and put the fear of Old Smoky in him, he just might confess to try and cop a plea." Old Smoky was Florida's electric chair at Raiford Prison.

Knowing that most homicides are solved within the first 48 hours, usually because there is a well-known connection, Leroy couldn't argue with Martinez's logic. The major had already agreed with the media that Conte's murder was a mystery, and he had even figured it might be a mob hit disguised to look like an amateur job. The Mercedes leaving the scene, however, was more than circumstantial.

"I wish the witness could give us an ID of the driver, even the sex of the driver," Leroy said. "I'm not knocking your work, Roberto, understand. I just want to make damn sure we're right. Otherwise, you know, this could be another Simpson caper, and the victim in this case is hardly a beloved citizen. I do not want this division or this department to become the laughingstock of the goddamned liberal media, if you catch my drift."

"I do, sir."

"Good. Now get a warrant for the arrest of Johnny Longo. Don't make the collar until tomorrow night. That's when the Sharks' plane returns from Dallas."

"Couldn't we have the Dallas P.D. make the collar, Major?"

"Why? Do you want to waste time trying to extradite him from Texas? He'll come back on that flight. Metro Dade police will make the collar at MIA, since it's in their jurisdiction, and then they'll turn the suspect over to us."

"But, sir. . ."

"Roberto, you really don't think Longo is a serial killer who will strike again, do you? He probably believes he has gotten away with first-degree murder. Won't that cocksucker be surprised. . .oh, and Roberto, be sure our public information officer sees that our friends at *Miami P.M.* get this story as an exclusive. Remember, we're hero cops with that rag, not pigs like we are with that fucking liberal *Journal*."

#

It was a routine flight from MIA to DFW for Dick and the crew of the DC-10. Charter flights were informal compared to regular commercial flights. Most of the flight attendants were regulars on the Sharks charters, but the labor action had changed that for this flight.

With only 128 passengers in the wide-body aircraft, even the passengers in the cabin section didn't have anyone seated next to them. Sol and Bunny Rubin, GM Jack Cabot, and Sherman and his coaches were all seated in the first-class cabin. The only players seated up front were Longo and George Carver, and this was because of their seniority, not their value to the team.

Bob and Jorge were seated on the right aisle in coach. Bob had the aisle seat, and several times during the flight, Suzy would go through the cabin on her rounds and deliberately brush her butt against Bob's shoulder. Despite their relationship, Suzy did not give any evidence aboard the aircraft that Bob was any different from any other passenger. The columnist understood that this was her job; the brush was just a message that she was thinking about him.

"You and Suzy break up?" Jorge asked with a silly smirk on his face. "She hasn't even spoken to you during the flight."

Bob gave his companion a dirty look. His mind was on Father O'Malley. The priest had appeared a bit shaky when he had arrived, moments before Suzy had closed the passenger door to the jetway. Well, if something was bothering the padre, he would find out that evening at dinner.

Up front, Sherman and his assistants went over the game plan for Thursday's game. It seemed strange to Suzy to see the macho head coach wearing bifocals as he studied the playbook.

Longo, of course, had no idea that at this moment in Miami, the police were seeking a warrant for his arrest for Conte's murder. He was busy going over the first 15 offensive plays with Moses, the offensive coach.

Rubin was on his second martini while Bunny read *Cosmopolitan*. She was intrigued by an article entitled "Why Old Women Seek Young Lovers." A quick glance at Cabot seated next to Dr. Dan Barker, the team physician, made her tingle with excitement. She was looking forward to being in Jack's arms this evening. At times, however, her thoughts were on the East German/

CIA hit man, whom she had contracted to pay $100,000 in cash to terminate her husband.

How will he do it? Well, I have to be prepared to act like the grieving widow.

#

On his way to the first-class lavatory, Sherman stopped at Cabot's seat. "Jack, I haven't had time to thank you for getting Johnson to clean up his act. We can really use him, if he passes his league drug test Monday."

"I'm glad you're happy, Coach, because S.R. is pissed. I don't think he wants to pay Johnson's full salary."

"Tough shit," Sherman replied as he patted Cabot's shoulder. "You know, for a third-string quarterback, you've become one helluva GM."

Both men laughed.

#

Fullback Larry Wargo spent the entire flight trying to hit on the flight attendants. He avoided any possible contact with Suzy, and had been shot down cold by Parker.

He had, however, set up a score with Nancy Hill, a naive, redheaded, new-hire flight attendant from Casper, Wyoming. At 22, Hill was very excited about being a flight attendant and meeting fascinating people like Wargo.

She spent the remainder of the flight daydreaming about being married to a famous football player.

#

Dick landed the DC-10 smoothly at DFW. The aircraft was parked near a maintenance hangar, where a convoy consisting of a Lincoln stretch limo for the Rubins, three buses—two for the coaches and players, a third for the media and camp followers—and an equipment truck were parked. The flight attendants boarded the third bus, which was already full.

"I don't expect you to get up, old man," Suzy informed Bob, who was seated in the rear of the bus, "so I'll just sit on your lap."

Passengers nearby laughed and clapped. Bob's face turned a bright crimson, but he placed a reassuring and loving arm around her waist for the quick ride to the DFW Marriott.

#

At dinner Wednesday night, Bob, Suzy, and O'Malley took a taxi to Joe's Steak and Chop House in downtown Dallas. Joe's was an upscale steak house with a warm, cozy atmosphere. The owner, Joe Dunn, greeted the trio at the door.

"Oh, Father O'Malley, we're pleased to have the Miami Sharks' team chaplain as our guest tonight," said the owner. "You know, Father, we were booked solid for tonight because we're having a cigar party. Brother Robert, however, said it was your birthday tonight, and he and Sister Susan wanted to treat you. As a good Catholic myself, I could hardly disappoint a priest—even if he is the chaplain for the opposing team."

"Thank you, Joe," a subdued O'Malley replied. "I feel blessed to be here with Brother Robert and Sister Susan." After the owner had gone, O'Malley shook his finger in mock anger at Bob and Suzy, trying hard not to laugh at the ruse they had used to gain entry to such an interesting restaurant. "I don't know the exact penalty for impersonating a brother and a sister, but if we are ever found out, I fear my final parish will be near the Arctic Circle," O'Malley said.

Bob and Suzy laughed. Then Bob cleared his throat and said, "You know, Father, Suzy and I have been putting off talking to you. We need some advice because we want to get married in the Church in June. If possible, we'd like to bring you to New Jersey to do the ceremony. So maybe you can help me in my divorce status. . ."

The waiter brought a bottle of French champagne. "Compliments of the house," he explained.

"Boy, being members of the clergy has its perks," observed Bob. "It's a bottle of Moet."

"You won't think so tonight in bed, Bobby," Suzy said. Before she had finished the sentence, her face was crimson. "I'm sorry, Father. . ."

The old priest smiled and laughed. He patted Suzy reassuringly on her hand. "You made a telling point, Suzy. I'm glad you understand. I know you are good Catholics who want to marry in the Church. I will do my best on your behalf with Cardinal Murphy."

The priest was well aware that the unmarried couple—his good friends—would be sleeping together shortly. He knew the Church's view on such conduct. It was hard for him to find fault with a couple who were obviously in love and planned to marry.

Following an enjoyable meal and an after-dinner cognac, the three returned to the hotel.

"Thank you for a pleasant evening," O'Malley said. "God bless you both." They took the elevator to Bob's room while the priest headed into the lobby bar. He needed a stiff drink as he mulled over the shocking confessional of Martha Longo.

#

Down the hall in Room 348, Nancy Hill answered the soft knock on the door.

Although the young flight attendant had followed the request of Wargo to remain in her uniform, she had changed into a fresh one. She was so excited about the thought of this romantic encounter with a football star that she couldn't even order a room service meal.

Wargo had slipped out of his room after bed check. He wore

shorts, a T-shirt, and moccasins, and as Hill would soon find out, no undershorts.

"You wore your fly-girl suit," he said with a boyish grin.

"You asked me to, Larry, and. . ."

"Good, good, let's get to it, Suzy," he said as he dropped his shorts to expose a very large penis.

"I'm Nancy. . ." she mumbled as she stared at the erection. This would be only her second sexual experience. Her first had been several romps in the front seat of a pickup truck with the captain of the junior college baseball team.

Wargo was thinking of banging Suzy Peters, not Nancy Hill, as he pushed the woman onto the bed, pushed up her skirt and slip, and shredded her panty hose. The football player was like a horny bull. He pulled open her blouse, and tore off her bra. His ham-like hands fondled her breasts, and before she could speak, his large penis tore into her. It hurt.

"Please be gentle. . ."

Wargo didn't answer. He was breathing hard as he lay on top of her in the missionary position. He was both heavy and strong. His fantasy was that this was Peters under his command.

Hill realized this encounter was pure sex with no affection. She tried to react, hoping to achieve an orgasm, but it was over too quickly for that. She felt Wargo explode inside her.

Wargo quickly climbed off the bed. He grabbed a pillow and used the case to wipe his wet and dripping penis. "You were great, little lady," he said as he pulled on his shorts. "Got to hustle. Big game tomorrow. Got to get my beauty sleep."

Hill never had a chance to say a word. Wargo was out the door and back to his room. She lay on the bed in the same position he had left her. She felt cheap and used. It was her fault, she realized, for hoping for romance when she fell under the spell of this football celebrity.

#

It was by chance that Dungan found himself in the hotel lobby shortly after 11:30 p.m. Wednesday, when Bunny and Jack Cabot made a brief appearance together en route to the bank of elevators.

"I'll see you in the morning, Jack," Bunny said. "I have to check something at the front desk."

Jack took the elevator, and Dungan followed its climb to the fifth floor. *That's his floor, and his suite is 502.* Dungan knew that from the team roster. About two minutes later, Bunny returned and took the elevator.

Three, four, five. . .bingo! The little lady is getting off at five, not seven, which is the presidential suite for the Rubins. The security man smiled and checked his watch. *I'll give that bitch 30 minutes before she gets the surprise of her life.*

#

S.R. had been sound asleep for about two hours when the ringing jarred him awake. He had a splitting headache, and he fumbled to answer the phone. "Who the hell is it?" he demanded.

"It's Paul Dungan, Mr. Rubin. Sorry to bother you, but we have a problem. It's Mrs. Rubin and Mr. Cabot. . ."

Rubin was hung over from his dinner of six martinis, but his recovery was amazing as he checked the second bedroom and found his wife's bed unused. "Where the fuck is Bunny?" he yelled out loud. He quickly pulled on a pair of slacks and a sport shirt. He was still in his slippers, and he groped to find a pair of shoes. But Dungan was impatient, so the owner went on the mission wearing his slippers.

Ten minutes later, Dungan and a visibly shaken Rubin arrived outside Suite 502. Dungan knocked several times on the door.

"Who is it?" Jack asked, his voice displaying irritation.

"It's Dungan, Mr. Cabot. I need to talk to you."

"At this hour?"

"It's important. It will be only a minute, Mr. Cabot."

The door opened. "This had better be important. . ."

Dungan pushed the general manager aside and stormed into the suite. He never slowed until he opened the bedroom door. S.R. followed, and the scream he heard was that of his wife.

Bunny was naked, and Dungan had a strong grip on her right arm.

"You cheap, fucking, Irish whore," screamed S.R. as he unloaded a right hand into her face. Fueled by his anger, his punch staggered Bunny, who could feel her left eye starting to swell.

Before S.R. could make another move, Jack grabbed the owner and flattened him with a roundhouse right. Rubin was trying to get up from the rug when two burly hotel security men arrived in the room and subdued the general manager.

"Thanks, boys," Dungan said as he assisted S.R. to a chair. "You okay, Mr. Rubin?"

"Fine, I'm fine. Thanks, Dungan." The owner looked at Jack, who was now handcuffed. Bunny, who had put on a robe, joined her lover on the sofa. "Cabot," S.R. said slowly. He shook slightly from the ordeal, and was trying to control his rage. "You're fired. I don't even want you in our fucking team hotel. I promise you, you'll never get a job in this league again."

Jack betrayed no emotion.

You can only act that cool when you have money, and work is only a hobby, Bunny thought. *Jack must come across to S.R. like the WASP country club gentleman who has just lost a tennis match, instead of the SOB who was caught in bed with his wife.*

"I respect your wishes, S.R. Sorry about hitting you. You should've hit me, not Bunny."

The reply angered Rubin, but he took his wrath out on his wife. "As for you, you whore! You're out in the street, too. Don't bother trying to fly home with the team. Don't come home!"

Bunny's left eye was red, and her vision was blurred. Although the injury hurt, she wasn't going to break down and cry. She was embarrassed, of course, but she was far from defeated.

The timing was bad, but she still had several aces in her hand. She felt certain that Jack would take care of her if she lost the war. But she wanted the ownership of the team. Being the wife of a Pilgrim blue blood would be icing on the cake. Did this old Jew asshole think he was going to cast her out in the street like some stray, unwanted cat?

Bunny stood up. She surveyed the living room like an attorney in court before addressing the jury. She gave Jack a brief, affectionate nod for coming to her defense. In a calm and rational manner, she put her tormentors on the defense.

"Gentlemen, I think it would be prudent if you left quickly before I dial 9-1-1 and file a police report against all of you for trespass and assault. My lawyers will resolve the personal matters between me and my husband, but they'll also involve you and your hotel in one helluva suit."

"To whom do you think you're speaking?" Dungan demanded.

"Certainly not to a real cop. You have no legal right to break into a hotel room and assault Mr. Cabot and me. And if we're held any longer, we can add kidnapping to the charges."

The two hotel men exchanged glances and tried to act hard-nosed, but they knew the woman was right. Another knowing glance, a nod, and they headed like sheep for the door without further comment.

"Gentlemen," Bunny said. "Before you leave, will you be so kind as to remove the handcuffs from Mr. Cabot? Thank you."

Dungan was surprised at the woman's cool cunning as he unlocked the cuffs. He had obviously underestimated her, but the bottom line was that he had cast his fortune with the man who signed the team payroll checks, and he had no doubt that he would be rewarded by S.R. as well as the commissioner.

Jack was impressed by his lover's strength in this embarrassing situation. *No tears. Her cool but aggressive attack silenced even her husband.*

Well, not quite.

"You fucking whore, you won't get a fucking penny from me," asserted S.R. "How could you do this to me, after all I've done for you?"

Bunny smiled. "As they say, Sol, we'll see you in court."

Dungan was quick to lead the retreat and to calm the owner. "Let them have the suite for tonight, Mr. Rubin," he said. "You have the facts and the witnesses. No sense creating a stink that might result in some bad press."

As angry as he was, S.R. knew Dungan was right. Anyhow, he was tired, and his jaw ached. His pride was hurt by this betrayal, but he would get his pound of flesh. *I'll break both of them!* As a businessman, he knew better.

As soon as the door slammed, Jack embraced his lover. "You were fantastic," he said softly and with admiration. "Don't fret about money. The Cabot women never end up living in Southie."

The suggestion staggered her. "Are you talking about marriage?"

"Why not, honey? It might not be as much fun after we're married, but. . ."

Bunny was pleased by her performance, thrilled by Jack's proposal, and upset at her hired German hit man for not doing his job before this incident. *If something happens to S.R. now, I certainly would be a suspect.* However, she had no intention of ending her quest to become the sole owner of the Sharks. She had worked too hard and made too many sacrifices to get this far. She consoled herself that she would never have to have sex again with that fucker.

Tomorrow I have to contact that Hun bastard and tell him to hurry. I can't wait to get rid of that fucking old man.

Her thoughts and the pain from her eye injury faded into passion as Jack kissed her gently over the injured eye while his hands worked their way up her bathrobe.

#

As a new day dawned back in Miami, the holiday issue of *P.M.* came out in the morning with a limited press run. Casey's column would prove to be a real shocker.

> *Bob Casey's Working Press:*
> *Longo's gambling capers:*
> *It's time for investigation*
>
> DALLAS—*The question this International Football League season is not will the Miami Sharks win or lose, but will they cover the spread?*
>
> *It should be obvious to any football fan over the age of five that quarterback Johnny Longo has shown a direct involvement in the point spread of most Sharks games this autumn.*
>
> *Now I offer damning evidence that Longo may have lost more than $3 million in illegal sports gambling bets, some of which may have been bet against his own team.*
>
> *Maj. Leroy Hess, commander of the Miami Police Department's Criminal Investigation Section, tells me that he has traced large money transfers between Longo and slain mobster Augie "Lucky" Syracusa. There also may be a connection between Longo and murder victim Dominic Conte, a former rogue city cop turned PI.*
>
> *While Hess continues his investigation, no one in authority in the Sharks organization or the International Football League seems to give a damn.*
>
> *Why hasn't the owner, Sol Rubin, or Coach Don Sherman taken any action? What about IFL investigator Paul Dungan? Why hasn't IFL Commissioner Pete Wilson asked for an investigation? Why isn't the FBI involved?*
>
> *I'll tell you why.*
>
> *Rubin himself is a sports gambler. Admittedly, he's a piker by Longo's standards. You won't have Rubin turning on a spotlight that might catch the owner in its glare, too.*

As for Sherman, he has never met a pro football player who was immoral. Not even reformed druggie Muhammad Johnson has been criticized by the coach. Before Johnson, however, Sherman doesn't even remember Rufus Thompson, the former star Sharks running back who's doing prison time for selling drugs.

As for Dungan, he's too preoccupied with finding blue-collar bars with TV dishes that aren't paying the league a royalty to be concerned about fixing games and/or shaving points.

As for Wilson? The commish is the toady of the owners. He sees, hears, and speaks no evil about pro football.

The FBI, as you may recall, was once headed by J. Edgar Hoover who claimed there was no Mafia. Today's FBI agenda seems to consist solely of hassling political activists, not using its resources to combat the Mafia, whose gambling is corrupting American sports.

Will it take another Black Sox scandal to force pro football to find a commissioner of baseball's Judge K. Mountain Landis' stature and get rid of the gamblers in uniform?

That's exactly where Longo and his ilk are leading the IFL.

Johnny Longo is corrupting pro football. Worse, he may even be a murderer.

So can somebody out there please tell me why Longo is still in uniform and still a starting quarterback?

#

The wake-up phone call jarred Bob and Suzy awake at 8:00 a.m. Thursday. It was already 9:00 a.m. in Miami.

"Bobby, what the hell am I doing in bed with most of my clothes on?"

"I love that green blouse and khaki skirt, Sky Princess. But those knee-high nylons don't cut it with the miniskirt."

She pulled up the covers to look, before realizing she'd been had. "Bobby Casey, I hate you!" she screamed as she rolled against him with her fists flying.

Bob stopped her. He took her in his arms and, looking into her eyes, stated, "I love you. I don't think I would have a life without you."

"I love you, too. You, Bobby, you are my life until death do us part."

While Suzy prepared for the day, the desk phone started ringing like a rapid-fire rifle. It was the reaction to Casey's column. The first caller was Hess.

"I didn't interrupt your sex life, did I, Bob?"

"I hope this call isn't costing us Miami taxpayers."

"Listen, yellow journalist, the Miami P.D. is about to save your fat ass and make your column today look like a prize-winner."

"What the hell are you talking about, Leroy?"

"You'll see, Bob. You'll see. You owe me more than a cheap lunch on this one. This should be worth a dinner at a five-star joint. Oh, and have a happy Thanksgiving, you turkey."

Bob didn't have time to ponder Hess's call, but he knew the major well enough to know that he may have bagged Longo on some rap. That would be great. The phone rang again, and Bob picked it up.

"You fucking, cocksucking, yellow journalist. We'll see you in court." That brief message came from Longo before he slammed the receiver down.

Guess you could say he's a bit pissed. Wonder what Hess is planning for Johnny boy?

The phone rang again as Bob was shaving.

"You want me to get it?" Suzy asked.

"No, I'll be there," he said as he left the bathroom with a face full of shaving foam. "Yeah," he said, picking up the phone.

"Bob. George Cockerill here. Under the circumstances, Mr. Rubin doesn't think it wise for you to fly home with us following the game today. Also, I think you will have to make other travel arrangements for the rest of the season."

Cockerill was the Sharks' public relations vice president. He was being hounded by media calls from the eastern states as Casey's column had made the wire services, and was being quoted on radio and TV sportscasts.

"George, I don't know how to break this to you, but I always fly home commercial. In fact, I'm booked back to MIA Friday morning on Continental. Furthermore, you can tell your drunken boss to go fuck himself, too."

"I'm sorry, Bob, but—"

It was Bob who banged down the receiver. As soon as he did, it rang again.

"We've hit the jackpot!" It was Bloom calling from his Miami home. "I've already gotten calls from radio talk shows looking for you. What do you bet Larry King's rep will call, too?"

"Larry, Hess called me. Said he might have some good news regarding this column."

"Maybe this has to do with the tip the Miami PIO called to Locastro about a bust late tonight of a big fish," the ME said. "We were advised by the Miami PIO to have a reporter and photo team on the scene. But the PIO wouldn't go beyond that."

"Great, Larry."

"Well, enjoy your turkey dinner. I'll be watching that 3:00 p.m. kickoff after my dinner. See you Friday afternoon. Say hi to Suzy, and don't put her meals on your expense account!"

That produced a chuckle. "Such a managing editor!"

Ring! Ring!

"Bob Casey?"

"This is he."

"Hi. I'm J.J. Brown, a sports writer with the *Dallas Star-Gazette*. I was wondering if you had anything to add to your *Miami P.M.* column this morning. I've only read the A version, but you sure stirred up a hornets' nest."

"No, J.J., I've nothing to add at this time. Thanks for the plug. Have a happy Thanksgiving."

#

Damage control was quickly under way. Sharks media relations veep Cockerill was issuing the blanket statement, "It is not our team policy to respond to allegations made against an individual player. What we have is a speculative column in a tabloid newspaper that offers no facts to sustain the allegation. Coach Sherman will play Longo today because Coach Sherman believes that this is just another case of yellow journalism."

In his White Plains, New York, home, IFL commissioner Pete Wilson was directing the league's media relations and legal staffs in handling the fallout from Casey's column. Wilson did not want a gambling scandal, not with negotiations under way with the major networks over the new five-year television contracts. He wasn't pleased by the intrusion on his Thanksgiving holiday that would keep him on the phone most of the day.

CHAPTER 17

"Coming events cast their shadows before."
                                    Thomas Campbell

THANKSGIVING DAY WAS gloomy in the Dallas/Fort Worth area. It was to be a harbinger of things to come. It was a cool 52 degrees, and a light rain fell intermittently. The raindrops splashed against the windows of the three charter buses on the ride from the Marriott to the stadium. Bob and Suzy sat together near the rear door of the third bus and watched the rain in silence.

Bob and Suzy had discovered that it wasn't easy being in love. It was difficult to focus on work and the daily routine without their minds constantly returning to each other. It was hard for either to imagine life without the other. The couple still felt the warmth of last night's passion and companionship. Both, however, felt a bit empty because they wouldn't be together again until Tuesday.

Five days can seem like an eternity to separated lovers. Suzy's London trips would start with the 8:20 a.m leg to LAX the next day. She knew that all the fun of a London layover would be missing without Bob there. Suzy would return to MIA on the charter flight with the Sharks while Bob would write a Friday column in the hotel room that would also feel empty without Suzy. It would be hard to write, but he would try to get her out of his mind for the couple of hours required on the PowerBook. Because of the strike and her management position, Suzy had scheduled herself for a Miami-Los Angeles-London-Miami week.

"Will you miss me, Bobby?"

Her question broke the silence of the couple's thoughts.

"Not if you bring me back a box of Cuban cigars from London."

Bob had this almost gallows humor when it came to being serious, but she had finally come to realize that this was really a facade that masked his deep love, passion, and devotion to her. She no longer felt threatened by any of his banter. In fact, she had learned to enjoy it and participate in it.

"It's against the law to bring Cuban cigars into the U.S. Anyhow, I don't know if I'll get to downtown London on our layover."

"There's always the duty-free shop at Heathrow."

"You must think we flight attendants are rich. Do you think we can afford to buy thirty-dollar Havana cigars and risk our jobs smuggling them through U.S. Customs?"

"Sky Princess, if you don't have the money, offer your body," he replied coolly. "But at least demand the fifty-dollar Havana Churchill. . ."

Suzy snuggled against Bob. "You know you'll get the cigars. What else do you want me to bring back?"

"You."

"Now that's the right answer, Bobby boy, even though you put me second to your damn stogies."

"You know I will miss my Sky Princess."

"I know, honey, and I will miss you something terrible, too."

#

Two police motorcycle officers led the parade of three buses into the stadium parking lot. It was two hours before game time, and the lot was filling rapidly with fans, many of which were setting up cookouts. The coaches and players exited the two forward buses and disappeared down a runway and into the bowels of the stadium to prepare for the game. The camp followers and flight crew had tickets for the game, but the flight crew would have to leave for DFW after the third quarter to prepare the aircraft for the return flight to MIA.

Climbing off the bus, Bob put down his portable computer bag and grabbed Suzy. He kissed her gently on the lips. "I love you very much."

"Have a bad flight on Continental," Suzy said with an impish grin. "I understand that their flight attendants all wear combat boots."

The columnist laughed and waved goodbye as he caught up with Cunill en route to the press gate. He checked for his working press badge. It was tied with a string around his belt.

"Hey, Mr. Celebrity," said Jorge. "You going to make the Larry King Show?"

"He hasn't asked me yet, Jorge," replied Bob. "I think it's a toss-up for Friday night between me and the president."

"You win, amigo. King is a football fan. You know he once did pro football on Miami radio. He'll probably ask you too many questions about football that you can't answer."

The sports writer was right about Bobby's celebrity status. Print and electronic guys asking for comments on the Longo column mobbed him in the press box. He didn't shy away from any opportunity to give his view about the evils of organized crime's illegal sports betting.

The only media members that shunned him that afternoon were from the rival *Miami Morning Journal*, the American Television Network, which carried the game telecast, and Bob McNamara, the voice of the Sharks.

Even McNamara was apologetic to Bob. "I'd love to have you on our pre-game radio show, but my management won't let me."

"You mean Rubin won't let you," replied Bob. "I understand, Mac, because we have sacred cows in our business, too."

Bob liked McNamara, who also understood the difference in their media. Like all team broadcasters, McNamara was paid by the station but under contract with the team, so it was team management that had the final say on the broadcasters. As McNamara had once said over a beer on a road game: "Remember, Bob, the New York Yankees fired Mel Allen and Red Barber for telling it like it was."

#

Among those watching a network interview on Thanksgiving were gambling don Gattino in Hollywood, godfather Lorenzo in Greenwich, Connecticut, and IFL commissioner Wilson in White Plains, New York. Obviously, they weren't pleased with the notoriety of the Longo matter.

"Don Gattino."

The voice was cool and formal. The gambling don was chilled by the godfather's call.

"What is the situation concerning that Longo matter? He is fast becoming a national embarrassment. You know our family doesn't like this kind of publicity."

"Neither do I, Godfather. I have taken steps to terminate the problem."

"The travel agent?"

"No. I have followed your advice, Godfather. It will be an accident."

"Good, Sal. Make it happen soon. Please pay my respects to Maria."

Gattino hung up the phone and strode to the liquor cabinet. He poured himself a six-ounce belt of Scotch and gulped it down in three quick swallows. *That Tenuto has to come through soon, or else I will have to get Longo a pair of cement shoes and dump the cocksucker in the Everglades.*

"Oh, Sal dear, did you see who's on TV? It's that Irish boy who writes the newspaper column. You know, the one we met in Munich last summer. He was with that nice young flight attendant."

#

Dungan had finally returned the commissioner's call. He wanted to tell him about the incident with Bunny Rubin, but all Wilson wanted to talk about was the Longo matter.

"This is your number one assignment, Dungan. I want you to run a background check on that fucking yellow journalist. But at the same time, let's get every bit of dirt on Longo. If he is dirty, I want to be the one that crucifies him in front of the free world."

"Mr. Commissioner, there is another matter. It concerns the Rubins and Cabot, and—"

"Forget that matter for now, Dungan. We'll talk about it later. Right now, your job—your *only* job—is Longo and Casey. Get cracking!"

Before the security man could respond, the line went dead.

#

The ATS interview with Casey was watched with interest and mirth in Sydney by Andy Lyon. "That Casey is hot shit!" he yelled out loud with the glee of a little boy getting a birthday present. *That asshole son-in-law of mine almost scrapped that column. Thank God I had the sense to put Bloom in Miami as M.E.*

#

Bunny and Jack watched the telecast from the GM's suite. Remembering the invasion a few hours earlier by her husband and the rent-a-cops angered her.

Now she felt even stronger about her lover, who had put up his fists in her defense. The memory of Jack's roundhouse right knocking S.R. across the living room floor was invigorating. She realized that Jack never needed to work, and he could support her in a queenly manner, too.

Regardless, she hadn't wasted all these years getting into a position to own a pro football team just to blow it at this juncture.

Jack and Bunny watched TV, and later the Sharks-Texans game. Throughout Thanksgiving Day, Bunny repeatedly tried to contact the German mercenary on his cell phone, but to no avail. She was concerned that he might do his thing, and the cops would be suspicious of her because of the hotel incident. In spite of the risk, however, she wasn't scared and was now more determined than ever to get rid of her husband.

Maybe it would be just as well to blow up Sol on the return flight. That would make it easy.

Jack marveled at Bunny's cool under combat conditions. She had been humiliated by being caught in the nude in his bed, but had stood tall throughout the ordeal. Even this morning, she had called the front desk to keep the room for that night while calling Continental for a flight back to Miami on Friday.

"I got us booked on the 1:05 p.m.," she said, hanging up the phone. "It wasn't easy because of the holiday traffic and Sun Air being on strike. We do have two first-class seats, and better yet, I charged them to S.R.'s Platinum American Express card."

Bunny also called attorney Jim Walden at his Coral Gables home.

"Sorry to bother you at home, Jim, but we need to talk Friday. Yes, I know it's a goddamned holiday weekend, and your office is closed. For what I pay you on a retainer, I believe you can afford to buy me dinner. While you're feeling sorry for yourself, think about the potential business for your firm if you got all the Sharks' business, too."

In a honky-tonk bar on a dirt side road about three miles from DFW, Jose Cortez and T.J. Lewis stood out from the folks with cowboy and cowgal outfits. The jukebox kept up a steady stream of country and western music, while the two union reps nursed bottles of Budweiser at a corner booth. The bar was a hangout for airport and airline blue-collar employees, but noticeable by their absence were the strikers from Sun Airlines.

"Jose, my man, you look like shit this morning," said Lewis.

"You drive like a fucking cowboy, amigo," said Cortez. "Why didn't you drive your Mercedes instead of that fucking truck?"

"We made it to the airport on time, didn't we?" replied Lewis. "Now, are you damn sure your wetback pals at DFW are going to let us in the American employees entrance? I don't want us to be seen by any of our pickets in front of the Sun Air entrance."

"Relax, bro," replied Cortez in an imitation of what he called ghetto-speak. "A couple of those American guys have a lot at stake, too, if that fucking Sun Air flight reaches its final destination tonight."

"If it doesn't make it, Jose, we'll be back in business in a few weeks, free of any hassles. Kelly should be happy, too. Our mechanical efforts should aid the union cause and bring a speedy settlement to the strike. You know, man, like on the union's terms."

Cortez took a long swig from his bottle and burped.

"Sounds just like a DC-10 going off the radar screen," said Lewis with a sinister laugh.

"I'll drink to that, bro," said Lewis. "Hey, beer girl! Two more Buds over here."

#

The game was a few minutes from the opening kickoff at 3:05 p.m. Central Time, which meant that the Miami writers were still working on deadlines against the 4:05 p.m. Eastern Time back home.

"It's times like this when I love working for an afternoon rag," Jorge said as he connected his laptop computer to the rented telephone assigned to the two *P.M.* sports staffers. "You know, we should work for the telephone company. Do you know that the fucking phone company charges us $350 to rent this phone for a few hours?"

"Not *us*, Wetback," Bob said. "They charge Bloom. What do you want us to do, use carrier pigeons?"

Bob was sorry that he and Suzy had missed Father O'Malley's morning Mass. The phone calls had kept him occupied, and he wanted to explain his absence to the priest, who was a guest in the owner's box.

"Hey, Bob, did you happen to notice that Cabot and Mrs. Rubin aren't at the game today?"

"Nope. Why is it important? They can't punt, pass, kick, catch, or block."

Jorge strongly believed that something was going on between the general manager and the owner's wife. He had no proof, but it was those telltale signs in the way the two reacted when they were together in public. It really wasn't a big deal. It might make for a juicy note in a gossip column.

The writer, however, couldn't understand what a fox—granted an *older* fox, but nevertheless a fox—could see in S.R., other than money.

"I know you think Mrs. Rubin is a bimbo, amigo, but I'm not so sure. I don't think a smart guy like Cabot would be interested in that old lady if she was just a piece of ass. I mean, Cabot is a middle-aged version of a matinee idol. Hell, Bob, even an old fart like you could find a young, foxy lady, so figure how fussy Cabot can be."

The two men laughed.

"I understand Wargo got laid last night," Jorge said as he checked his lineup flip card.

"Who was his victim?"

"A flight attendant. One of the new ones on the charter."

The news of Wargo's latest conquest drew little interest from the columnist. "How you'd get the scoop so quickly?"

"Oh, Mr. Wonderful told most of his teammates at the team meal," Jorge said.

"What an asshole!" Bob exploded. "Can you imagine, Jorge, that poor girl on the flight home? Every Sharks player will be mentally undressing her and fucking her. I hope some Dallas linebacker puts Wargo's ass on the golf cart today."

Bob couldn't help but wonder how many men mentally undressed and fucked Suzy at 33,000 feet. *Why is it that flight attendants attract this kind of sexual harassment? Is it some kind of sexual mystique? The dream of screwing a flight attendant in the first-class lavatory is for many men the ultimate fantasy. Hell, I guess I've experienced the same fantasy.*

Now that he was about to marry a flight attendant, it was a different story.

The ring of the *Miami P.M.*'s press box phone jarred Bob out of his thoughts. He quickly reached over and picked up the receiver. It was the executive sports editor.

"What the hell are you doing working on a holiday, Chris? Don't give me that crap about letting the poor sports copy editors have the holiday with their families. You're just worried about overtime and getting yelled at by Bloom."

Sciria laughed. "You talk like some bigshot columnist. You going on the Larry King Show soon? Look, we have a big Friday paper. All those department store ads, you know. Naturally, our deadlines have been moved up. So write like we're an a.m. rag. I need your horseshit column by 10:00 p.m. And tell Jorge that we need a Longo denial story as a follow-up to your Thursday column."

"No problem, Chris," replied the columnist. "Jorge is flying home with the team. He wants to sleep with his wife tonight. He can write his game story and a Longo tear-jerker on the way home and file it as soon as he's in the Miami airport."

"Well, why don't you do the same thing, Bob?" asked the sports editor. "Or did Suzy dump you already?"

Bob laughed. "I've been bounced from the team plane by management."

"Now that's a shocker," the sports editor replied in an amused tone. "Wonder why?"

#

It appeared to Bob that the Dallas-Miami game was to be a repeat of the last three in this intraconference rivalry. Miami jumped on top. Dallas tripped and stumbled. Dallas righted itself. But in the last three games, Dallas fell short. The holes the Texans had dug in the past were simply too deep.

So it appeared that Miami would make it four straight. The partisan home crowd of 68,897 sat in silence throughout the first quarter as the Sharks took a 10-0 lead. Longo was sharp. *Bam!* Richard Baldwin ran around the right end for nine yards. *Whiff!* Longo zipped a pass through the Dallas defense to wide receiver Otis Clark for 14 yards.

The Sharks' first drive went that way, covering 82 yards in 15 plays. The drive stalled, however, at the Dallas 12, and Siegfried von Katzen kicked a 30-yard field goal.

On that first drive, Miami kept the ball for nearly eight minutes. When Dallas finally got the ball back, the Texans kept it for less than a minute. Dallas, in fact, would go three-and-out on its first four series.

Miami scored again with 3:18 left in the first quarter when Longo found a streaking, open, rookie reliever—Chris Nicholls—down the middle for a 31-yard touchdown pass. Von Katzen's placement made it 10-0.

"Hey, that rookie Nicholls is going to challenge Muhammad Johnson for the starting spot," Jorge said.

"Miami held the ball for 11:33 in the first quarter, Jorge," replied Bob. "Is this going to be a Sharks rout?"

In the game's first 12 minutes, Miami outgained Dallas 154 yards to zero. Thus, it was easy for Bob to see why the Sharks scored the game's first 10 points.

"You know, Jorge, Sherman's game plan always calls for them to script the first 15 plays," Bob said. And on their first two drives, it looked as if the game had been scripted just for them. They played so easily that they made it look like a midweek practice.

Things changed in the second quarter. Dallas kept the ball for 11:12 in the second quarter, gaining 130 yards and holding Miami to five yards. And, most importantly, Longo would leave the game for good with 7:14 left in the first half.

The veteran quarterback suffered a concussion on a series of hits. Two in particular were smashing blows, one by linebacker Ken Murphy, and the other a combination of tackles by Murphy and J.B. Gardner.

"Did you see that hit, Bob?" Jorge excitedly asked, seeking confirmation.

Both he and Bob turned for a replay on a TV monitor above press row one. It showed Murphy grabbing Longo from behind while Gardner pulverized him with a direct blow in front. Longo could not recover from the assault. He limped to the bench, and a towel was draped over his head while Dr. Barker attended the quarterback.

Miami led by 10-7 at the intermission despite losing Longo to injury.

When the Sharks quarterback was helped off the field and replaced by Eddie Malloy, Bob quipped, "Well, Longo can't fix this one."

"That's no way to talk about an injured gladiator, Bob," said Jorge. "You've got to admit that he was having a good first half."

It was not Longo's absence that got the Texans going so much as Dallas' offensive awakening. Anderson finally began to find running room open receivers.

Still, Miami took a seven-point lead when Wargo shocked Dallas with a trap run around the right end on a third-and-5 play. Wargo just kept going, scrambling 27 yards for a touchdown that lifted the Sharks to a 17-10 lead with 10 minutes and 28 seconds to play.

Both teams floundered for a while, but then Dallas, with 6:36 left, had a solid chance to tie. The Texans had driven all the way to the Miami 10, but once there, Anderson was intercepted by linebacker Brutus Neswiacheny.

"I think Dallas is up a creek," Jorge said.

Miami was up by seven and could play ball control, attempting to run out the clock, or at the very least go three and out, punt, and put Dallas in a deep hole with little time left.

But all of a sudden, the Texans got the ball back. On Miami's first play after the Dallas turnover, Malloy was intercepted by Herman Corn.

The partisan crowd was on its feet for the final telling drive. The Sun Airlines flight crew were the only patrons to exit the stadium after the third quarter for the van ride back to the DFW.

"One of these games, they're gonna let me stay 'til the end to see who won," Parker complained.

"You can read about it in the newspapers," Suzy said.

"In the *Miami Morning Journal*?" Parker responded.

"For that remark, Ms. Parker, you can forget working first class," Suzy said, feigning a mean grin. "You will work coach." Suzy gently grabbed Parker's sleeve to slow her down from the rest of the crew. "Hey, Ann, is there something wrong with Nancy Hill? She looks like hell today, and she hardly talks."

"Nothing I know of, Suzy. Maybe it's a sign of being overworked by you management types. But I'll talk to her alone on the flight back."

"Why don't I let the kid work in the galley," Suzy suggested. "Then maybe you can visit her after your rounds in coach."

#

Bob and Jorge grinned when the game went into OT, because they saw the pained look in the *Morning Journal's* Roberto Castro as he struggled to make the first edition deadline in Miami. Castro had to make an 8:00 p.m. copy deadline for his paper's state edition.

Dallas took the kickoff to start the overtime period and drove 78 yards in 13 plays. Rhett Hood's 29-yard field goal won it 20-17.

"Hey, Jorge, what was the spread on this game?" Bob asked.

"Three and a half points, Señor Casey. It never ceases to amaze me how the mob knows how to make the spread so accurate in pro football."

#

Casey and Cunill joined the horde of media in the visitor's locker room. Sherman, who always opened his post-game press conference with his own thoughts before accepting questions, made it clear that he would not comment "on any speculation stories in the tabloid media about any of my players."

Sherman had his back against the wall just inside the locker room, and pushed away a TV camera and a reporter's tape recorder which he considered to be too close to his face.

Sherman's general thoughts on losing to Dallas were, "We should give credit to the Texans for what they did. We both had some opportunities, but they capitalized better on theirs. We played fair and square. We had our chances, but we didn't take them.

"Still, it's a very bitter loss. I can't think of one that hurts more than this. This was an important game. Tell me one that isn't. But it hurts, and if I'm showing it, I can't help it." When asked about the impact on the postseason aspirations of the Sharks, Sherman responded, "We're worse off now than we were before this game. We have to wait until Sunday to find out how Buffalo makes out. We certainly ain't dead. We're not going to roll over, and we're not going to whimper about something that wasn't done or something that went wrong. We didn't do well enough, including myself. It takes a special kind of person—and that's why these guys are

Sharks—to come back after this kind of disappointment. So we'll go back to Miami and regroup for next week's game."

"Coach. What about Longo?" The question came from a Dallas TV reporter as his camera crew zeroed in on the Miami coach.

The coach, shading his eyes from the bright camera lights, replied, "You mean about his injuries today?"

"No, Coach. About his betting on pro football—"

"Fuck you, you cocksucker!" Sherman showed his rage as he stalked out of the meeting. "Ask that yellow journalist Casey about it."

Sharks PR man George Cockerill quickly announced: "Coach Sherman's conference is finished. You may go into the players' room now."

The defeat may have upset their head coach, but for the most part the players were not drowning in tears. It was stuffy in the room now crowded by the media. Players answered questions while sitting on a stool or while dressing in front of the locker stalls.

Longo's stall area was vacant, but reporters crowded around his backup, Malloy, who had just arrived from the training room and was wrapped in only a towel.

Bob was trying to stick his tape recorder through the huddle of reporters. It was difficult to hear Malloy, because he talked facing his stall while putting on his underwear.

It was both wet and cold, and resulted in a brief discomfort like taking a big bite of frozen ice cream. The large container of Gatorade and ice cascaded down over Bob's head, soaked his corduroy sport coat and khakis, and splattered on his penny loafers.

"What the fuck!"

That was Bob's initial reaction to the ambush, and by the time the columnist turned to confront Longo with the empty cooler, he was fighting mad.

"That yellow piss is for you, you fucking yellow journalist," screamed the quarterback. His face was crimson, and he was shaking with rage. "Now I'm going to knock the shit out of you!"

No one was sure who made the first move. But there, rolling on the floor in the locker room were the quarterback and the columnist. Johnny was in better physical condition, but his injuries left him almost on a par with Bob, who had been trained at the Army Military Police School at Fort Gordon. As brawls go, it was quite tame. It mostly consisted of huffing and puffing. The players and reporters stood and watched until assistant coaches Jim Moses and Tris Carta rushed into the room to subdue the brawlers. Meanwhile, photographers and TV cameramen got some great shots and footage.

Attracted by the commotion, Sherman arrived on the scene. Brutus Neswiacheny, the All-Pro linebacker, had Longo in a protective bear hug while George Carver was helping Casey off the floor.

"Johnny," said the head coach in a stern manner, "you get the hell out of here at once. Get on the bus. I'll talk to you later. Oh, and for Christ's sake, don't you stop to talk to anyone."

Johnny recognized that the tone in Sherman's voice meant that the coach didn't want him to discuss the order. The quarterback glared at the columnist, but quickly walked out of the room.

Sherman knew what had happened as soon as he looked at the Gatorade-soaked Casey. The columnist's jacket displayed a torn left sleeve, and there were bloodstains on his polo shirt from the bloody nose he had received in the scuffle.

Bob realized that the coach was upset by his column on Longo, too, but he was bright enough to know that this assault was big-time trouble. So his manner was patronizing but sincere.

"You okay, Bob?" the coach asked.

Bob nodded as he held a handkerchief to his nose to stop the flow of blood. The Sharks' trainer came to Bob's aid with a towel and ice.

"You have my apology for this incident," Sherman said. His tone was sincere. "I don't agree with all you write, but no member of this team will act like a thug. I can't condone what Longo did. I promise you that I'll take the appropriate action."

Sherman, Bob understood, was partially grandstanding for the media. The coach had enough problems without being fried in print and on the air. He resented Longo putting him in this position. He had no love for sports writers, and Bob sure had castrated Longo in print. The coach, however, must suspect that Longo was dirty, but he didn't know to what extent. In the good old days, he would have suspended the quarterback on the spot. But not in this era of a strong players' union and a milquetoast commissioner.

The trainer assisted Bob to a table, where his nosebleed was quickly stopped. The team doctor gave him a quick look too, and told Bob to take a hot shower. The trainer offered a team warmup suit to Bob for the trip back to the hotel. The columnist turned down the offer, thanked the trainer and doctor, and met Jorge at the locker room entrance.

"I have your laptop, final game stats, and play-by-plays, gringo," Jorge said. "The Dallas PR guy sent an assistant to drive you back to the Marriott. You look like you just went over Niagara Falls in a barrel."

"Thanks, pal," Bob said. "Don't miss the press bus, or you won't be in Miami in a few hours."

"Oh, amigo, I can't tell you how much I enjoy my birthday gift," Jorge said. "I get a lot of kidding about this tangerine iBook, but—"

"Forget it. Use it in good health on the plane."

#

Back at the hotel, Bob spent 20 minutes in the shower. He didn't think there would be enough hot water in the entire hotel to erase the cold from the Gatorade dunking. He was still angry about the assault.

How shall I handle this? Should I blast Longo and the Sharks?

He could hear his room phone ringing, and knew it would probably be Sciria and Bloom reacting to the early TV reports of the locker room assault.

Fuck 'em. They can wait for a few minutes while I ponder the way to handle Friday's column.

The hot water relaxed him, and he began to think rationally.

No, damn it. I think taking a low-key approach will work better. I can't appear to be seeking revenge. No, let Longo's action speak for itself.

The message lamp was flicking red when he returned to the bedroom wrapped in a towel. Before he could react, the phone rang again. It was Bloom. He was laughing but trying to show concern for his columnist's misfortune.

"You made the network, Bob. You look like a drowned rat."

He could laugh now. The hot shower had tamed his anger over the incident. "I'm putting in for a new set of clothes on my expense account this trip," he said.

"Now I know you're feeling better, Bob. Let's see. A very used polo shirt, sperm-stained khakis, and a pair of cheap tennis shoes."

"Like my beloved imported corduroy jacket," Bob replied. "More important, how do you want me to handle my roll on the floor?"

"You name it. You lived it, Bob. We won't let our staffers become public punching bags."

"Right, Larry. Look, why don't I play it cool in my column. I can let the editorialists and the champions of our rights in the Pro Football Writers Association carry the banner against the evil Sharks Empire. I think I should just mention it in a light-hearted way. I don't want to get every guy on the roster to zip their lips because ol' Bob is the bad guy out to get their quarterback."

The managing editor laughed. "You've got it, Bob. I want to read it first. I'll be in my office in a couple of hours. I'll be waiting with bated breath for your prose."

#

Bob Casey's Working Press:
Sharks' QB sacks sports scribe

IRVING, Texas—I may have made pro football history here Thursday when I was sacked by Sharks quarterback Johnny Longo.

Longo, who wasn't healthy enough to finish the Thanksgiving Day loss to the Texans, apparently wanted to prove that my column in Thursday's Miami P.M. was all wet.

You could say that this was a sure bet waiting to happen.

I mean, why else would he share a cooler of Gatorade with me in the Sharks' locker room? Considering his less than potent throwing arm this season, what were the odds of him hitting even a fat, old sports columnist like me?

I was wrong about Johnny's arm. He can still hit a big target from at least a yard away.

Maybe his career as a quarterback is almost all washed up, but I don't see a future for Johnny in pro wrestling.

I should know, because I went to the mat with him in the Sharks' locker room. I think Johnny took a gamble to engage an Irishman in a brawl. We have a lot more experience in such physical encounters. But we prefer neighborhood bars, not locker rooms.

Sharks coach Don Sherman stopped the match in the first round. He was apparently concerned for the safety of his quarterback.

I haven't seen the match films yet, but I'll be surprised if I lost.

Whatever. I'm hopeful of a rematch. Vegas. National television. Maybe a cool $30 million purse. It could be a benefit. A benefit for Gamblers Anonymous or retired Mafia dons.

Now I have a question for another gambling guy, Sharks owner Sol Rubin.

How will you tell Johnny that his decline has been frighteningly rapid, and there's no way you can pay him next year what he wants, or thinks he's worth?

Or in language the QB will understand: "You're not worth the gamble."

The morning line favorite to replace Longo next season will be backup Eddie Malloy. But Rubin could opt for some blue-chip college kids in the spring draft.

Despite the loss to the Texans, I still believe the Sharks have enough talent to remain in the eastern horse race, and they should finish in the money again this season.

It's next season that Rubin will have to part with some big bucks to get a quarterback to replace Longo.

#

Bob finished his column on the Macintosh PowerBook's 14.4-inch screen and connected the modem to a phone line to dispatch his Friday gem back to Miami. He called the sports department to confirm that the column was in the newspaper's computer system. It was.

"I'm going down for a drink in the lobby bar. If you or Larry need me, I can be reached there."

"Right, Bob," replied sports editor Sciria. "Enjoy your Gatorade on the rocks."

"Fuck you. May your system crash on deadline."

Considering his ordeal, Bob was in a good enough mood. He knew that the hotel bar would be nearly empty on Thanksgiving night. He was even surprised to find it open.

He thought of the bar at the Adlon Hotel in Berlin last August, when a similar visit had introduced him to Suzy Peters.

What were the odds of such a happening? Something like this could happen only in a movie. Oh man, I miss that woman right now. It's going to be hell going to bed alone tonight.

CHAPTER 18

"I wish you all the joy that you can wish."
William Shakespeare
Merchant of Venice

"M R. CASEY, EXCUSE me, Mr. Casey, would you like someone to talk to? I'd be pleased to get you a cup of coffee over at the Salvation Army canteen."

Florida Highway Patrol Lt. Bill Sanders' voice jolted Bob back to the present, to reality. He was at the scene of a major disaster, a major news story, and he was a newspaperman.

Bob turned and said in a calm voice, "Thank you for your kindness, but I have a job to do here, too. Maybe you can find me a couple of rescue workers, maybe one who is a Sharks fan."

The PIO nodded as Bob headed toward the crash scene. The uniformed trooper stayed at the newspaperman's side and escorted him through the organized bedlam of the rescue mission to the makeshift rest area for policemen, firemen, divers, and others. Bob had to blot out the tragic death of Suzy. He would do anything to keep his mind busy.

He called Bloom on his cell phone. "Larry, save a hole for a column."

The managing editor didn't know what to say except, "Yeah, sure. . .okay, Bob."

\#

GRIM HUNT IN GLADES
FOR DOWNED SHARKS' JET

The 144-point headline was the tabloid's stark cover page of *Miami P.M.*'s first edition. If people that Friday morning were unhappy that the rest of the paper was the Thanksgiving edition, no one in southeast Florida bothered to complain. The early edition sold out after an initial press run of 200,000.

Before the day would end, the normal 550,000 press run would have broken all *P.M.* records, with 2,215,000. People were lining up outside the circulation's loading deck to buy papers before they could be loaded into a line of delivery trucks.

Inside, readers found the lead story on Page 3.

TEAM OWNER, COACH SHERMAN BELIEVED VICTIMS
by Tom Edwards, Miami P.M. Staff Reporter

MIAMI—*Rescue squads worked through the early morning hours today in snake and alligator infested swamps in the Everglades to retrieve the living and the dead from the crash of a Miami Sharks charter jumbo jet early this morning.*

First light this morning revealed terrible scenes of chaos and destruction after the worst disaster of an American professional sports team in the history of aviation.

A Sun Airlines DC-10 with a crew of eight and 142 passengers crashed while trying to land at Miami International Airport, after the jumbo may have been disabled in mid-air by an explosion.

Police said there are survivors.

The injured were pulled from the wreckage, and they have been taken to hospitals throughout South Florida.

Among the missing and presumed dead are Sharks team

owner Solomon Rubin, 72; his wife Veronica, 52; General Manager Jack Cabot, 42; head coach Don Sherman, 55; and numerous players. The players' names are being withheld, pending notification of next of kin.

"We have seen nothing like this before," one rescue worker said, with a white handkerchief covering his face. "It is bizarre and sickening."

Early reports say that the jet broke into four sections after hitting the swamp, and the first-class section was turned into a fireball on impact. The cockpit, coach section, and tail section were found scattered in the swamp.

Rescue workers had to battle through darkness and swamp water. By late morning, some 50 bodies had been recovered, a police spokesman said.

"Our first priority is to look for survivors, of which we have found several," said the spokesman.

Rescue workers' vehicles have struggled to reach the doomed jet, which went down in the vicinity of Alligator Alley.

#

"Joe Scherr just called, boss," City Editor Locastro told Bloom. "He's at MIA. Says a couple of people missed the flight."

"Who, Millie?" demanded the M.E. "Damn it, woman, no games. Who?"

"Mrs. Rubin and Jack Cabot."

"Where are these lucky suckers?" Larry demanded to know.

"Joe says they're flying in this evening from Dallas."

"What time?"

"Should be here by nine p.m."

"I want art, Millie. Close-ups. Portrait stuff. With emotion. Call in the photo chief for it."

"He's at the crash site, boss."

"Call him and tell him to cover it. That's our lead art for

Saturday."

#

Before darkness Friday, investigators listed those known dead, or missing and presumed dead, at 108 out of the 150 believed to be aboard the doomed aircraft. The report was reduced to 105 when three other people surfaced who were not on the flight.

Bunny and Jack Cabot arrived together Friday night on a Continental flight from DFW. Buffy Zei was assigned to cover the return of the lucky passengers.

With the exception of Zei, reporters who mobbed the couple at MIA didn't think it strange that the two were together. They had been scheduled on a Friday morning flight, but Bunny wanted to dress the part of the grieving widow. At Neiman-Marcus, she bought a $1,200 black suit for her return as a widow. And a pair of designer sunglasses hid her black eye.

"I'm in a state of shock," she told the reporters who cornered her outside the jetway in the main terminal. "I should have been on that flight. . .sitting next to Sol."

There was a 30-second pause while she fumbled for a handkerchief. Jack passed his to the widow, who dabbed away her tears. It was brief enough that no one noticed the black eye. She played the role well, Jack thought, as she led the questions away from her personal loss, to her concern for all those aboard the plane. In the harsh glare of TV lights and flash camera poppings, Bunny gave a smashing show.

"Are you the Sharks' owner now?" a reporter asked.

"I am a widow now," she replied. "I'd rather have my husband alive."

"What's going to happen to the team for the rest of the season, Mrs. Rubin?" another reporter asked.

"Excuse me, but I haven't even considered any business matters. I just want to see Sol's rabbi, and do what is necessary. . ." Breaking into uncontrollable sobs, she was comforted by Jack and her stepson,

Steve Rubin, home on his Thanksgiving break from college. They guided the widow away from the horde of reporters to a limo outside.

"Mr. Cabot," yelled Zei. "How did you and Mrs. Rubin manage to miss the flight?"

It was a question the rest of the media there wished they had thought of.

"I was scheduled to scout a college game Saturday," he called back.

"Right. And what about Mrs. Rubin?"

"She suffered a severe migraine headache Thursday. She even missed attending the game. Considering the tragedy, I think she's holding up bravely, don't you?"

Zei also spotted Bud Westinghouse in the crowd. After the horde of news people departed, she cornered the Sun Airlines CEO.

"This was the first major crash in Sun Air history," he said. "And it was probably sabotage."

That caught Zei's attention. "What are you saying, Mr. Westinghouse?"

"Look, Ms. Zei, I am devastated by this. My heart goes out to the loved ones who were on board. I don't know any more than that there may have been, you know, a bomb of some sort. . .uh, that kind of thing that, uh, caused the crash."

"Who would do such a thing, Mr. Westinghouse?"

"I wouldn't put it past Kelly and his union thugs. . .oh, don't print that. . .Just say we are awaiting a report from the FBI and NTSB, or something like that. You know how to word it."

Normally, Zei would have used that union quote. But not this time. She had the feeling her future would be better served by pleasing Westinghouse. She did have an exclusive interview, plus the arrival story. That would impress Bloom.

#

A disheveled Bob arrived at the office Friday evening.

"Yes, Mary Jane, I do need a shower and a shave," he said to the secretary who greeted him. "But for now I need a pot of coffee to keep me from falling asleep at my computer."

Larry came out of his office. In a rare show of public affection, the M.E. embraced Bob. "I'm sorry, Bob. We. . .we all are."

"I know, boss," he said, choking a bit on his words. "I have a column to write."

"So I hear, my friend," Larry said softly. "I feel certain it will be a good piece. Go to it. We'll talk later."

Bob surprised the sports staffers by this rare appearance in the department. He had a cubical for an office, but he wrote most of his columns at the scene, on the road, or at home. This Friday, he did not want to be alone. He wanted the noise and the people to keep his mind off Suzy. Realizing the situation, the embarrassed staffers avoided him.

In his cubical, he turned on the machine, but before it finished warming up, Scherr, the city police reporter, tapped him on the shoulder. He didn't consider Bob's state of mind at the moment.

"Sorry. . .hey, Bob, what kind of football team do they have at Raiford?"

"Huh, what. . .Joe?" Bob said, irritated. "I've got a column to write and. . ."

"Your Thursday column has been vindicated," the police reporter continued without encouragement. "The Miami P.D. is charging Longo with murder in the first degree. He's under guard at Fort Lauderdale General."

"Thanks for letting me know, Joe," Bob said, his voice softening.

Even being informed that he had won a Pulitzer Prize couldn't have cheered the despondent columnist. He was fighting depression with work and trying to blot thoughts of Suzy from his mind. He was too tired to carry on a conversation with anyone, and only the hot coffee was keeping him awake.

"Did you know the cops were waiting for Longo at MIA? Millie got a tip. We had an exclusive story. Now. . ."

Bob wanted to forget about Longo. Longo only reminded him of Suzy. He was tired, and he had to concentrate. He turned his back on the reporter, opening his notebook and turning on his tape recorder. *Man, I smell. I really need a shower. But first . . .*

He started slowly tapping the keys as his mind constructed a column. His pace picked up, and he soon was engulfed in the column.

Bob Casey's Working Press

MIAMI—It was bound to happen. The odds were stacked in its favor. The only thing surprising is that it took so long.

Pro and major college sports entered the jet age at the end of World War II. Until that time, athletic groups traveled by train and bus. In the early 1970s two college football teams were involved in air disasters.

Less than a mile off Alligator Alley, in a no-man's land of swamp, there is the wreckage of what once was a Sun Airlines DC-10. Among the dead, missing, and injured are members of the Miami Sharks family.

The Sharks thus became the first American major league sports team to become the victim of an air crash. By commercial aviation standards, this is not a major crash. I mean, there weren't 300, 400, or 500 souls killed.

Just a mere 105 dead.

Because the mere 105 are pro football coaches and players, however, they are well known by South Florida fans. Unlike the unknowns who have died in other air disasters, these victims are more like our friends and neighbors.

"I carried out the body of Muhammad Johnson," Miami fireman Tom Bush told me. "I recognized him as the Sharks' wide out."

Bush was seated on the pavement of Alligator Alley, his back propped against a fire truck. He was soaking wet from sweat and swamp water, as he took a well-earned cigarette and Gatorade break.

"We waded up to our necks in some parts to get to the coach section," he recalled. "It was still dark. Oh, I guess it was about 4:30 or so this morning when we found the plane. Before I reached the front of the coach section, I bumped into an object. I thought at first it was a gator, and I was scared enough to let out a cry.

"Another fireman's lamp lit up the object. It was . . . what was left of a man. He was burned to a . . . a crisp. I threw up. And, mister, I've seen a lot of horrible things in my profession."

You wonder to whom that burned-out body belonged? Was it owner Sol Rubin? Was it coach Don Sherman? Was it one of the assistant coaches or players? Or flight attendants Nancy Hill or Suzy Peters?

There were many heroes in the swamp Friday. First there was the pilot, veteran Sun Airlines Chief Pilot, Capt. Dick Norton. He is credited for a belly flop landing of a stricken aircraft that resulted in the saving of at least 50 lives.

Then there are flight attendants Mary Rich and Ann Parker. They struggled through a night of terror in that black hell to keep up the survivors' spirits while awaiting the rescue units.

Rescue workers tell how Father Francis J. O'Malley, the team chaplain, consoled the injured and extended the final blessing to the dead, some of whom may not have been Catholic. It was in this gentle priest's arms that Johnson died.

As you read this, the search for the unaccounted passengers will continue. Among these will be players and coaches we all know.

There were some fortunate people who missed the doomed flight. There was the owner's wife Veronica "Bunny" Rubin, who was saved by a nasty headache. And there was GM Jack Cabot who was scheduled to scout a college game in Texas.

There were at least two players who had permission to remain with their families in the Dallas-Fort Worth area over the long weekend.

Miami P.M. staffer, and my dear friend, Jorge Cunill, is a known victim. We had flown the doomed flight to Dallas together, but I remained behind to write about the Sharks-Texans game. It is hard, very hard, as I write this column to realize that I have lost my best friend in a dreadful Florida swamp.

Bush finished his cigarette and put on his gear. A hot, bright sun bathed the rescue site. It would be more hot and hard work. The fireman was ready to return to the swamp and the gruesome job of finding bodies.

"It's like finding the bodies of your own kin," he said softly. "But it's my job, and I'll do it."

Air travel, statistics show us, is safer than ground transportation. That doesn't dull the impact of any major air disaster.

Athletic teams will continue to fly. The more flights there are, the greater percentage of similar disasters there will be. That's tomorrow. Today we mourn for what was once a great pro football team.

God love you all who did not survive. May you rest in peace.

#

Bob was just about to send electronic copies of his column to the sports and managing editors when he was tapped on the shoulder again. Thinking it was Scherr, he didn't turn. "Yeah, Joe, what the fuck do you want now?"

"What do you mean *Joe*?"

Bob spun around in his chair when he heard Suzy Peters' voice. "Suzy! Suzy! Oh, my God. . .I don't believe it!"

She pounced on him before he could stand. She felt his warm tears against her face as they kissed and hugged. She didn't mind his beard or even his BO. She just wanted to hold him like this forever.

"How? Why? What. . ." Bob's questions were fired as if from a machine gun, while he kept touching her to make sure she was real and alive, and not some cruel daydream.

The drama attracted Bloom and other staffers. They were excited, and all started asking questions in unison.

Suzy, who was in her Sun Air uniform, waved her left hand. It was then that Bob noticed that her right hand was in a plaster cast.

"Cool it, folks," she said, while wiping tears from her cheeks. "Let me tell you what happened."

What had happened, she explained, was that after leaving the stadium at the end of the third quarter, the crew was met by a van to take them to DFW. Suzy was seated in the second row of the vehicle next to the sliding door. She had her hand on the door frame when the van's driver slammed the door shut.

"I screamed, and my hand hurt like hell. The door cut the skin, and it started to bleed and puff up. I wanted to kill the driver. I was in a lot of pain, and I was crying and hysterical. They rushed me to the nearest hospital."

Like all hospital emergency rooms on a holiday, Dallas Medical Center was short-staffed, and the waiting room was packed.

"Sun Airlines' crew regulations prohibit a sick or injured person from continuing on their scheduled flight," she said while holding hands with Bob. "I wouldn't have even been permitted to deadhead back on the charter if I had been treated for my injury on time. Gosh, as a lefty, I can at least do paperwork."

The audience laughed politely and let Suzy continue.

"Well, you know about hospitals. . .it was almost midnight Dallas time before a doctor looked at my X-rays and pronounced that my hand was broken. While I realized that this would keep me grounded for a few weeks, I figured that it would give me a chance to surprise Bob back at the hotel. I only had my uniform and my purse. My crew bag had been put on the flight during the confusion."

"Honey, why didn't you call me?" Bob asked softly.

She patted her lover on the shoulder. "I suppose I should have. But hell, I wanted to see the expression on your face when you opened the door. . .then it took forever to get a cab at the hospital.

When I arrived at the hotel, I went up to your room. I knocked and knocked and knocked. And no Bobby. So I called you from the house phone. No answer. I went to the desk. . ."

Larry interrupted. "Your dumb boyfriend left without checking out. So as far as the hotel was concerned, he was still registered there."

She frowned. "Yeah, I thought maybe he was shacking up with some Continental or Delta bimbo. No, not really. I was worried. So I took a room. I was exhausted, and my hand was throbbing. It was. . .it wasn't until mid-Friday when I woke up that I learned of the tragedy. I had to buy a ticket and fly out this evening on Continental. I made a call at the airport, but the newspaper operator told me you were out on an assignment. So. . ."

Larry hugged the woman. "If you had been in that first-class section. . .well, God works in strange and wondrous ways, Suzy. I'm glad you broke your hand."

"So am I," Bob said as he gently kissed her cast.

The couple excused themselves and walked through the city room to the elevators, holding hands. The reporters and desk editors stood and clapped politely. This was an event that Bob and Suzy would never forget. It was more emotional, of course, for Bob because he had accepted his lover's death.

"I'm too tired and wired to even drive," he said. "Mary Jane, will you call us a cab?"

The secretary made the call.

#

Both the FBI and the NTSB were represented at the crash site. The agents waited patiently until the rescue units had accounted for all of the passengers. If the crash was an accident, the investigation would be solely that of the NTSB. If there was sabotage involved, the FBI would join in the probe to find the criminals responsible. While the agencies waited to comb the wreckage before it would be hauled to a remote hangar at MIA to be reassembled for clues, survivors were interviewed by agents from both agencies.

#

Early Saturday morning, Westinghouse visited Norton in a private room at suburban Hollywood Hospital.

The captain's location had been kept secret to prevent a media circus at the hospital. As an added precaution, the hallway was under the watch of two security guards. Dick's left leg was in a cast and suspended by a wire pulley system. The pilot was dozing, and Westinghouse noted the bruised face with the blackened left eye. The doctor had said there were some internal injuries, and he was listed as serious but stable. The doctor indicated that Norton would survive.

"Hey, old buddy."

Dick turned to greet the CEO. "Hello, Captain Westinghouse."

"They treating you okay, Dick?"

"Can't complain."

"Got a real looker for a nurse," Westinghouse said with a grin.

Dick nodded. "My wife noted that on her visit last night."

"I brought you some newspapers, Dick. The media is making you a big hero. Rightly so. That was one helluva landing."

"I learned that from the Detroit adventure. But I wasn't as successful in this landing as I was in DTW."

"We were very lucky in DTW. Lombard told me that he thinks it was another case of a bad cargo door. What do you think?"

Dick pondered the question. "It sounded about the same way. I thought they fixed the locking device on the 10 cargo doors."

"They did, Dick. Not after our mishap, but after the DC-10 disaster over Madrid."

Dick coughed slightly and pointed to a pitcher of ice water on the nightstand. Westinghouse poured a glass and helped the pilot take a couple of swallows.

"If it was a case of history repeating itself, why didn't the door blow when we took off from DFW?" Dick asked. "We flew most of the way at 390, but it didn't happen until our approach to MIA."

Westinghouse nodded. "You're right. If it was a bad cargo door, it would have blown leaving Dallas."

"So..."

"So, Dick, maybe Lombard was right when he said it sounded like a bomb blast."

"Captain Westinghouse, you aren't suggesting that some SOB bombed my flight, are you? Why? For God's sake, why would anyone want to blow up a plane full of pro football people?"

A nurse entered the room. "You'll have to leave now, sir," she said. "Captain Norton must rest."

Westinghouse got up from the bedside chair and glanced at the young nurse, who was poured into her white duty uniform. *A perfect 10*, he thought. "Your wife was right, Dick."

The two men laughed.

"What's so funny?" asked the nurse.

"Nothing," both men replied in unison.

In the lobby, three men in conservative business suits and shiny shoes stood out from the other visitors, who were attired in tropical sports clothing. The oldest of the trio had thinning white hair and wore glasses. He spotted Westinghouse getting off the elevator.

"Mr. Westinghouse?"

"That's me."

The man in the Brooks Brothers three-piece gray suit held out his hand. "Good morning. I'm Morris Meeker, special agent in charge of the FBI's Miami Office. I've been looking all over for you. Let's have a cup of coffee."

Meeker and Westinghouse found a table in the corner of the lobby coffee shop.

"Mr. Westinghouse, as I understand it, you are a licensed DC-10 pilot as well as CEO of Sun Airlines."

"That's right, Mr. Meeker."

"And your airline had a similar accident about eight years ago over Detroit. Our agency isn't into this matter officially yet, but if it becomes a criminal case, we will be very much involved. Do you have any problem with that?"

"No, Mr. Meeker. If it was sabotage, I want you to nail the bastards who did it."

"Sabotage, you say?"

"Yes, Mr. Meeker. Sabotage. And I'll bet this cup of coffee that you'll find the SOBs in our union hall."

#

There were those who believed that the crash would provide fuel for the union to blame Sun Airline's out-of-house maintenance deal, but Kelly knew that that strategy could be a double-edged sword. That was because, until two weeks ago, it was his union that did the work. If anyone was going to question Sun Airline's safety, it had to be someone outside the union. In any event, Kelly was by trade an aviation mechanic who took pride in his skills when he was just a worker.

He had concerns, too, that some disgruntled member of his union might have somehow sabotaged the aircraft. That was a chilling thought. If true, it would not only be a terrible scandal for the union, but he kept thinking of those 105 dead people. The thought occurred to him, too, that the former IRA agent might have had his hand in this.

He was in his office at the union hall when Zei found him about to open his third can of Budweiser.

"What can I do for you, little lady?"

"Offer me a beer."

Kelly laughed and found another can in a plastic cooler on the floor. He popped open the top and handed the beer to the reporter.

She took a short swig of the ice-cold beer. Kelly was the complete opposite of Westinghouse, yet she sensed some similarity in their dedication to their work. She kind of liked the union leader.

"My editor wants a quote or two from you about the crash."

Kelly motioned for her to take a seat next to his desk. "Our members," he said slowly, choosing his words carefully, "share the grief of the loved ones of the, uh, passengers and crew. Even though there is a labor action between this union and Sun Airlines management at this time, we strongly believe that there is no connection between our labor action and the tragic accident." Kelly took a long swig of beer. "That's it, little lady. That's all I have to say at this time."

Zei was impressed by Kelly's statement. She was beginning to understand how a man with just a highschool education had become a union leader. He was not about to say anything that would embarrass his union or its cause. It would seem that in Kelly, Westinghouse had a formidable foe.

Leaving the office, Zei encountered several men picking up new picket signs that declared: *SUN AIR FLIES DEATH JETS.*

#

In New York, Commissioner Pete Wilson called an emergency session Monday with all the International Football League owners. Casey, who was dispatched to cover the meeting, took a 7:05 flight out of MIA to New York's La Guardia Airport and arrived at the Plaza Hotel just as the meeting was commencing.

Bob spotted Cockerill, the Sharks' media relations director, chatting with a dozen New York media members. Cockerill was one of the lucky passengers who had escaped with hardly a scratch. He and GM Cabot had made the trip to Manhattan, and the PR man was complaining about the shortage of hotel rooms here.

"Well, this is the Christmas season," explained a *New York Mirror* reporter.

Cockerill spotted Bob. "Bob. Glad you could make it. I hope you have a hotel room. We're staying out at the airport."

"My God, George, you are the miracle man," Bob said with sincerity. "I'm glad you survived. It must have been a horrible experience."

"It was. I don't want to think about it for now. Oh, here, Bob, this is a copy of the IFL's Disaster Plan. The owners have just started to meet. Mrs. Rubin isn't here, of course. Our club is represented by General Manager Cabot."

Casey found a seat in the lobby of a meeting room. He read the IFL Disaster Plan:

Definitions
As a companion to the insurance policy that takes effect if IFL players are lost in a common accident (so-called Disaster Plan), the following procedures and definitions will be observed:

1. Lost Player
A lost player is deemed to be one killed, dismembered, or incapacitated for the remainder of the season in a common disaster.

2. Disaster
A disaster is deemed to have occurred when a team loses 15 or more players in a common accident.

3. Near-Disaster
A near-disaster is deemed to have occurred when a team loses less than 15 players in a common accident.

Bob shook his head. Only a bunch of lawyers could have written such a document. *It's the death of 14 players, so isn't a disaster, it's only a near-disaster.* He read on.

Procedures
If a team suffers a near-disaster, it will be required to play out the season, provided that the team will have priority on all waiver claims for the remainder of the season. In addition, all reacquisition rules

(i.e., rules covering players who have been traded, assigned via waivers, or terminated by the near-disaster club) will be suspended, and such club will be under no restrictions on returning players to its Active List from its Injured Reserve List.

If a team suffering a near-disaster loses any of its quarterbacks, it will be permitted to select the number of quarterbacks it lost from other teams' quarterbacks that will be returning to those teams. The maximum restriction will be two quarterbacks (i.e., if a club loses one, it selects one).

The team may select only from teams that have three quarterbacks available to play (either on the Active or Reserve List), which teams may protect two quarterbacks.

The near-disaster club may select no more than one quarterback from another club. Any quarterback selected under these procedures will revert to his original club the following year.

If a team suffers a disaster (15 or more lost players), the Commissioner is empowered to determine whether the team must continue or cancel its season. If the season is continued, the procedures covering near-disasters (see above) will apply.

If a team's season is canceled due to a disaster, it will have the first selection in the succeeding draft and will be allocated players from other teams at no cost under the following procedures:

* Each of the other teams in the League will protect two players from its Reserve List. List only (including all categories)—injured, retired, unsigned draftees, etc.

* Thereafter, each of the other teams will protect 32 from its remaining total pool (Active and Reserve Lists).

* All other clubs in the League must make their lists of unprotected players available to the disaster club, and the disaster club will then select one player from each club in any order the disaster club desires, until the disaster club has replaced the exact number of lost players.

If the number of players exceeds the number of other clubs in the League, the disaster club will be permitted to select more than one player per club, provided it has first selected at least one player from all other clubs.

After each selection from another club, that club immediately will protect an additional player from its total pool.

The Commissioner will have the power to review the circumstances of each disaster or near-disaster and to adjust the above procedures in whatever manner he deems appropriate, subject to approval of the Executive Committee.

Insurance Coverage

The insurance is business interruption coverage. Home team coverage is the home team's share of gate receipts plus actual rent paid. Visiting team coverage is the visiting team's share less travel expenses saved. These amounts would be paid directly to the teams.

The television/radio coverage covers all the network contracts. If any payments were made, they would be paid to the League and shared equally. These payments would offset any reduction in rights fees paid by the networks, which would also be shared equally.

It does not cover any cost of acquiring additional players or payments to players or their families. The players' medical plan includes life insurance with double indemnity payable to the player. The players' pension plan has disability provisions, and the players would be covered by workers' compensation.

Each club is invoiced for its portion of the annual premium, which is based on the prior year's receipts. The premium is adjusted each year on the basis of actual receipts. The IFL is then invoiced for the postseason premium.

#

Meanwhile, in Miami, the fight for control of the Sharks franchise was about to begin. Most observers assumed that Steve Rubin, at age 21, would become the youngest IFL team owner in league history.

Jewish custom was that a funeral would take place the day following a death, but there were extenuating circumstances, since Rubin's body had not yet been found.

After the Monday funeral service for his father at Miami's Temple David, young Rubin found his stepmother among the throng of departing mourners.

"Bunny, we have to talk at length on Tuesday. I've decided to forgo the remainder of my senior year at Stetson University in order to assume control of the team. There are a lot of decisions to be made right away regarding the rest of the season, and. . ."

Bunny was attired in a simple but designer $3,500 long, black dress. She wore a wide-brimmed black hat with a black veil.

She pushed back her veil to reveal two red eyes and tear-streaked makeup, but she spoke clearly and strongly, not as a weak, grieving widow. "Assume control?" The reply was cold and confident, and the tone in his stepmother's voice alarmed Steve.

"Why yes, Bunny. It was my father's team, and—"

"Slow down, Steve. I don't think you understand the situation. Your father, my beloved husband, has left me the team. I am the sole owner of the Miami Sharks."

Young Rubin couldn't believe what he was hearing. "My dad. . .uh. . .he told me I would inherit the team. I have a copy of his will."

Bunny softened her tone. "That, Steve, is an old will. When we were married, your father changed his will to provide for me in case something happened to him. I didn't ask for it. He insisted that I inherit the team.

"Of course, Steve, there will always be an executive position for you with the Sharks. Just as soon as you graduate. It is, however, my intention to operate the Sharks as the sole owner." Bunny didn't dislike her stepson. She was sincere in offering him an executive position.

The young man, however, felt a mixture of anger, betrayal, and suspicion. This was no place for a scene, not outside the temple, not minutes after his father's funeral service. He was almost speechless. Before he could answer, a group of mourners arrived and engulfed the widow.

Sadie Rubin had attended the service. She was almost unnoticed, except by long-time family friends. This was understandable, since she was not the grieving widow, but the ex-wife. She came out of respect for her family. Sadie was not a businesswoman. She came from an upscale Chicago Jewish family. She was educated and well traveled, the opposite of her ex-husband.

Her late father, Herman Stearn, was a lawyer, and Sol Rubin had been one of his upward-bound clients. Stearn had thought as a lawyer, not as a father, in manipulating the courting and eventual marriage of Sol and Sadie. Because of the family, she had learned to look the other way when it came to her husband's womanizing. They really never had much in common except the same last name and the children. She was, however, shocked when Sol dumped her for the shanty Irish gentile.

Young Rubin, shaking and flushed, met his mother just before she entered a black limo. "Mother, you won't believe this!"

"What's wrong, Steve?"

"That bitch, that Irish, gold-digging whore! I. . .I think she's stolen my football team."

CHAPTER 19

"The old order changeth, yielding place to new."
Alfred Lord Tennyson
The Passing of Arthur

POLICE HOLD SHARKS' QB
FOR MURDER OF EX-MIAMI COP
by Joe Scherr, Miami P.M. Reporter

FORT LAUDERDALE—Miami Sharks' veteran quarterback, Johnny Longo, is under arrest today on a murder charge. He is under police guard in Fort Lauderdale General Hospital, where he is recovering from injuries sustained in Friday's crash of the team charter into the Everglades, it was learned exclusively Saturday by Miami P.M.

Longo is being held on charges by Miami police that he shot and killed former Miami police lieutenant turned P.I., Dominic Conte last month in the room of a sleazy Miami motel.

The arrest confirms an exclusive report by sports columnist Bob Casey in Thursday's Miami P.M.

Longo is being treated for head and internal injuries.

Listed in critical condition, according to a hospital spokesman, he is in the hospital's Intensive Care Unit.

The quarterback was taken to the nearest trauma center shortly after being removed from the wreckage of a Sun Airlines DC-10 in the Everglades early Friday morning.

Miami Police Maj. Leroy Hess, commander of the Criminal Investigations Section, said his agency had requested Dade County police to take Longo into custody after the team charter landed at Miami International Airport.

"Fort Lauderdale police are holding Mr. Longo under hospital arrest until such time as he can be returned to our jurisdiction," Hess said.

Hess told Miami P.M. that police have a witness who connects the quarterback to the shooting death of Conte in the Flamingo Motel on Biscayne Blvd., Miami.

"We believe the shooting death of Mr. Conte was the result of a rather substantial gambling debt incurred by Mr. Longo," said Hess.

Alex Ford, the Miami attorney and sports agent representing Longo, said he could not comment on the charge until he read the police report and talked with his client.

Jack Cabot, the Sharks' general manager, said, "Under our system of government, all men are considered innocent until proven guilty in a court of law. We hope this is true for even a celebrity football player. For now our main concern is the speedy recovery of Mr. Longo from that tragic crash."

#

Bob and Suzy celebrated her good fortune and their love at Cella's Italian Restaurant in Hallandale.

Seated in their favorite booth in the lounge corner, they could chuckle at Rose's effort not to be her normal, bitchy self. Finally Bob could stand it no longer. He summoned the waitress.

"Rose. Suzy and I appreciate your love and concern for our

good fortune. Now, until you come to our funerals, we would appreciate it if you changed back to your same old, bitchy self."

The waitress's expression didn't change. "Sounds to me like you guys are looking to stiff me out of my tip."

As Rose left, the couple broke into laughter.

"You're rotten, Bobby. How could do that?"

Their laughter died away as they thought about how Suzy had missed the doomed flight.

"If I had, you know, been on the flight back to Miami, I would've kept Ann up front with me," she said with tears flowing down her cheeks. "We would've been in the first-class jump seats. . .instead of those. . .two silver wingers."

Bob looked his lover in the eyes. "Sky Princess, it was fate, or even God's will, that spared you from that flight. I don't think it was an accident."

"I'll be okay, honey. I just need to go to the powder room. I must look a mess."

While Suzy washed her face in the ladies' room, Bob thought about Scherr's story on Longo. *I know Bloom wanted a follow-up for Monday. I'd better get hold of Hess tomorrow at home. God, there are so many angles for a columnist to follow because of the crash.*

He watched Suzy cross the floor from the restroom area, dressed in a simple button-down white blouse and a short navy blue skirt. It was almost like her flight attendant's uniform, he thought. He realized how much he loved this woman, but for now he just wanted to rip her clothes off and attack her. He shared this thought with her when she returned to the booth.

"Hey, buster, you aren't getting away without buying me dinner tonight. Let's find Rose and eat."

#

On the other side of the restaurant, Sal and Maria Gattino were dining. The don had picked up a street sale *Miami P.M.*

"You aren't going to read that newspaper while we eat, are

you?" asked his wife.

"Now, Maria, I just want to check the headlines," he replied. "It's company business." The don read the Longo story. *Son of a bitch. That fucker is alive! If he lives, he'll blame my sports gambling organization for killing that cocksucker Conte. What will the godfather say? And worse, what will he do?*

Gattino ate and listened politely to his wife's small talk while plotting a way to eliminate Longo before he could talk to the cops. *Pulling the plug inside the hospital could be done*, he reasoned. *It takes one insider who needs money, or maybe one up-and-coming Mafia soldier to get inside.*

The don, however, wasn't sure what had caused the DC-10 crash. Was it simply an accident, or had his Chicago connection come through? Either way, Longo had survived. If the crash was traced to the Mafia, the shit would really hit the fan.

Mrs. Gattino wanted to talk about a church project, and he wanted to plan a hit. *A wife can be a pain in the ass at times like this.*

"Sal, you aren't eating all your pasta. Drink some red wine. It's good to prevent heart attacks. . .that look on your face. No good with food. Drink your wine."

#

The first Sunday morning of December found Bob and Suzy attending Mass at St. Vincent's. It was a bit embarrassing, because they arrived in the church parking lot almost in a dead heat with Martha Longo and her children.

Mrs. Longo glanced at the couple and said nothing, but concentrated on shepherding her three kids toward the church.

"Isn't that the sports columnist, Mom?" a young voice asked.

"Yes," replied Martha Longo. "Now keep moving or we'll be late for Mass."

Bob felt strange about being in church again. Suzy had insisted. How could he refuse after what was a major miracle that spared Suzy's life? He respected Suzy's strong faith and wished he could be as ardent a Roman Catholic as she was. While his lover was a true believer, she did not suffocate him with her fervor, a trait he appreciated.

Bob had been a pillar of the church as a boy. He had even served as an altar boy and attended Catholic grade and high schools.

It was Sister Noreen who had started him on his newspaper career when she appointed him editor of the monthly school paper when he was in seventh grade. She was a hard taskmaster. She had made him write and rewrite and rewrite his copies. He had disliked the old nun at the time, but later came to appreciate the writing discipline she had instilled in him.

There were also those slave-driver Jesuits at Fairfield University, who had molded his character. In this era of moral decay, he was beginning to appreciate more the old-fashioned morality he had been taught by his parents and the church. He did not know it, of course, but it was these values that Suzy had sensed early in their relationship. His ill-fated marriage and divorce had soured him on Catholic morality, but Suzy was fast restoring his appreciation for it.

Father O'Malley served Mass. He abandoned his original sermon, and he realized that there might have been some in the Church administration who wouldn't approve of his style that Sunday. The priest, however, felt strongly that God would understand, and that was the bottom line, as far as he was concerned.

The sermon was on understanding the crash of the Sharks charter. It was more of a eulogy to the coaches and players he had known for so many years. His tribute to Muhammad Johnson was especially moving and brought tears to many of the female faithful seated in the pews. He recalled the final hours with the wide receiver, a man of a different faith, who had overcome the sin of drug abuse and proclaimed he was a born-again Christian.

"Mr. Johnson was a hero. He sacrificed his life so that I might live. During the crash, he covered my body with his. It was he who suffered the deadly effect of all the flying debris. This was a black Baptist man who didn't hesitate to make the supreme sacrifice to save the life of a white Catholic man. Can there be any better testimony to the folly of racial and religious bigotry in God's world?

"Remember, it was Jesus who made that initial sacrifice on the cross. On another dark Friday morning, it was so apparent, oh so very apparent, that Muhammad Johnson truly practiced what it means to be a Christian."

Bob was touched by the sermon. Thinking as a newspaperman, he realized what a great, tear-jerking column this would be. He was already organizing it in his mind for Monday.

#

On leaving the church, O'Malley greeted the couple at the main entrance.

"We didn't think we'd see you serving Mass today, Father," Suzy said. "It was a wonderful sermon."

"My way of thanking God for his mercy, my child. We also gave thanks last Sunday for you missing the flight. As for you, Bob, I'm pleased to see you at Mass once more. I think we need to visit with Cardinal Murphy about your annulment. Oh, before I forget, we need to talk soon. Perhaps tomorrow."

"Well, Father, I'd like that, but I'm up to my neck in alligators because of the crash. Can we. . ."

"It is very important, my son."

Bob sensed the urgency in the priest's voice. "I have a luncheon date. How about later Monday afternoon? Say about two, Father?"

"Two will be fine, Bob. We can have tea and dessert, also."

The two men shook hands. The couple left holding hands. The priest knew that Suzy was responsible for bringing Bob back to the Church.

I'm certain the cardinal will approve the annulment. After all, Bob's wife deserted him for a Protestant lawyer.

The priest quickly finished greeting the exiting parishioners, then retreated to the parish house for Mrs. O'Neill's good Sunday dinner and a couple of strong drinks. He had a lot on his mind, including the Longo and Johnson matters. He could not even hint about Martha Longo, because she had confided to him inside the confessional booth.

Johnson was a different matter. The dying football star had given O'Malley a deathbed statement, and maybe Casey would know how to deal with it.

Bunny wasted little time in taking control of the Sharks. She called a meeting of the surviving and healthy front office staff at the club offices on Monday afternoon. Cabot returned from the IFL meeting that morning with a report that the commissioner was waiting for a player head count before he would declare the Sharks a disaster or a near-disaster. Since most of the front office did not travel to road games, they were secure, along with Cabot and PR veep Cockerill.

Tuesday morning, Bunny visited Dungan at Hollywood Memorial Hospital. The security agent didn't know what to expect, since he had informed her husband about her affair with Cabot. He felt helpless in the hospital bed with both legs in casts suspended by wire pulleys. The crash, of course, had prevented him from reporting the incident in Cabot's suite in Dallas to the commissioner. Maybe the bitch was here to plead for his silence to prevent a scandal. *That would be a cold day in hell!*

Unlike her late husband, Bunny did not believe in management by fear. Her management style would be to over-pay every employee. Therefore, even those who might hate her would never dream of leaving the Sharks' organization. She would also provide so many perks and benefits that everyone from a vice president down to the mailroom kid would become a gung-ho loyalist for life.

Her first test would be with Dungan. She greeted him with a

smile and passed him a deli bag and a six-pack of beer. "There's a couple of corned beef on rye sandwiches and assorted goodies here," she said. "I thought this would be a welcome break from the hospital food."

Dungan accepted the two packages and didn't know what to say. So he said nothing.

Bunny didn't waste time. She pulled up a chair next to the bed so that her face was only a foot or so away from Dungan's. She was close enough that he could breathe in her expensive Joy perfume and appreciate the expensive makeup that made rich broads look 10 years younger.

"Paul, I don't believe in beating around the bush. As you will soon find out, I am the sole owner of the Sharks. I didn't appreciate your action back in Dallas, but I realize you were working for the commissioner as well as for my late husband. Now, as I see it, you have two choices. One, you report back to Wilson and even try to create a public scandal. I will survive any scandal, but you, my friend, would find that my fellow IFL owners would put enough pressure on Wilson to make you a liability.

"Unless you plan to write a telltale book, make the talk show rounds for a brief fling, and try to find work as a PI, I have a better idea. Work for me."

"Is this some kind of a bribe, Mrs. Rubin? You want to buy my silence?"

Bunny pulled out a pack of cigarettes and lit up a Moore.

"Smoking isn't permitted in here, Mrs. Rubin."

"Smoking, dear Paul, can be hazardous to one's health. So can making the wrong decisions in life. No, I don't want to bribe you. God forbid that I would try to corrupt a man of your high moral principles. I'm here to offer you a job. The offer won't be repeated. The Sharks need a vice president of security. At, say. . .$100,000 to start. . .plus a car. . .plus perks. . .plus the loyalty of a cop to the police department."

Dungan almost choked trying to digest the hundred Gs annual salary. In his analytical mind, he realized all too well that Rubin's affair would only wound the woman, and in the end she would prevail, because she was now a pro football team owner.

"Well, Mrs. Rubin, I guess you bought yourself a security veep."

"No, Paul. I want you because you are good at what you do. When I remarry, I'll expect you to look after my interests in the same manner you did for Sol. Meanwhile, you get well. As of this moment, you are on the Sharks' payroll, and I'll have your secretary notify the commissioner of your new employer."

Bunny left Dungan to ponder his good fortune. A hundred Gs. A car, a secretary, and a title as a veep. He had changed his mind about his new boss. She was no bimbo. This was a smart lady who knew what it took to succeed in business.

#

Later, at the Sharks' offices in downtown Miami at her first meeting as owner of the team, Bunny assured the staff that it faced many rewards and a promising future. The staffers were surprised at how knowledgeable she was of the team operation and of their particular functions.

"I am promoting Mr. Cabot to team president. He will continue to function as general manager," she announced. "Our first major decision is how to replace Coach Sherman. I have offered Coach Moses a three-year contract to rebuild our team.

"I will leave all player personnel decisions in the hands of Mr. Cabot and Coach Moses. But remember, people, I am the one who'll sign the checks."

The staffers permitted themselves a polite laugh. They were trying to size up their future under S.R.'s widow. Many had considered her just a bimbo who had married a rich, old man. In coming weeks, however, she would prove to be a knowledgeable businesswoman who knew how to motivate her employees.

"Until I have the opportunity to meet with all of you individually, I will tell you only this. I have ordered an immediate 10 percent pay hike for all Sharks front office employees."

This was greeted with a collective sigh and polite applause.

"Our immediate problem, people, is determining our participation in the remainder of the season. With such a huge tragedy only a few days old, I do not want to appear heartless—but I feel certain the dead and injured would want us to try to finish this season. Mr. Cabot and Coach Moses are working on solving that problem at this moment. We know this is a business. I won't try to finish the season if the team we field would be an embarrassment to our dead and wounded comrades.

"I recognize and appreciate all your efforts during this terrible time. I won't forget them. While I have not been able to attend every funeral, I have asked Father O'Malley, our team chaplain, to organize a non-denominational memorial service for Thursday. Meanwhile, we all have a lot of work to do."

Bunny had indeed made an immediate and highly positive impression on the rank and file. The days of the penny-pinching, tyrannical rule of Sol Rubin were history. There were understandably more than a few workers who couldn't help but be pleased by the crash.

Now these people owe everything to me, and they know it.

#

Jack and Moses knew that trying to rebuild a pro football team in two week's time was an exercise in futility. They set up camp in the conference room, adding easels to hold team rosters, and a bank of extra telephones. Cabot and Moses had a good chemistry, which was necessary in a general manager and team coach.

Moses, a long-time assistant, had no ego problem about Jack making major personnel decisions. Jack, like Bunny, had that special gift for working with subordinates and making it appear that it was a team effort.

"Our decision by tomorrow, Jim, is to determine if we are going to be a disaster or a near-disaster team," said the new club president. "I think our first crisis is replacing the coaching staff."

Moses shook his head. "Jack, we both know we're talking next season."

Jack nodded in agreement.

"Right," replied Moses.

"Jim, you and I know that the IFL owners and coaches aren't going to be happy to help us rebuild," Jack said. "For the record, they shed tears over the disaster, but pro football is a business, and no one looks forward to having us raid their roster."

"You know, Jack, when we don't finish the season, it will make another playoff spot available," the coach said. "The fucking Titans won't appreciate the loss of the league's No. 1 draft pick, either."

Wilson and the owners took a lot of heat, too, for not postponing the schedule the Sunday following the Thanksgiving Day disaster. As Bob would later observe in a column, "What else would one expect from a league that wouldn't even cancel its games on the weekend that President John F. Kennedy was assassinated in '63?"

The Mutual Broadcasting System, which televised Monday night games, was concerned about what had appeared to be a ratings buster on Week 17: the Miami-Buffalo showdown for the Eastern Conference crown.

MBS president David Peterson called Wilson on Monday morning and asked that the IFL give the network a replacement game.

"If the Sharks don't finish the season, we will provide MBS with a comparable replacement game," said Wilson. "If they do, we cannot afford to risk a public relations disaster by swapping games."

"Well, Mr. Commissioner, let me remind you that MBS also has the rights to this year's World Bowl. A rebuilt Sharks in the Bowl..."

Wilson laughed. "No way in hell, Mr. Peterson. Even if the Sharks finish the season, I don't see them winning any of their three remaining games. If they do, they'll become a Cinderella team. Viewers love Cinderella teams."

#

Then there was the Mafia.

"How the hell can we create a morning line on a rebuilt team with less than a month left in the season?" asked Gattino.

#

The final body count of the DC-10 crash was 105 dead and 45 survivors. The NTSB was moving the wreckage to a hangar site at MIA to begin the task of reconstructing the aircraft. The first-class section was a lost cause because it had exploded, but bits and pieces would still be sought. The remainder of the carrier—cockpit, coach section, and tail section—was in remarkably good condition. The black box, which was really painted orange, was found to be in good working order.

Bob knew that since the captain and flight engineer had survived, they might be able to help in the coming investigation in determining the cause of the crash. He wanted to speak with Norton as soon as the captain was able to receive visitors. Dick might help shed some light on who had really done this.

Bob had filed the death of his friend, Jorge Cunill, away in his mind as he dealt first with Suzy's situation. But now he felt angry about Jorge, and he vowed to himself to get the bastards who caused the crash.

#

Surprisingly, the crash had not hurt Sun Airlines' business. Christmas was approaching, and by offering bargain fares between the Northeast and Florida, the public ignored the crash in favor of cheap seats.

Westinghouse was pleased. Martin explained to his CEO that outside of the carrier's main headquarters, remarkably few people connected that carrier with the crash.

"That's because the media referred to it as the crash of the Sharks charter," Martin said. "Some people even believed that the team owned and operated the DC-10."

While Kelly figured that the holiday shutdown would do the most damage to Westinghouse, the result was proving to be the opposite. The carrier kept adding flights as more pilots returned, and others were recruited. Regular flight attendants started to return, too, sensing that the airline was actively recruiting silver wing replacements by the hundreds.

Because of her injury, Suzy was temporarily grounded, but she was coordinating recruiting trips and teaching training classes at the Sun Airlines Academy.

As in past similar disasters, the media raced to be first with the cause of the crash. Thus on TV, radio, and in print, there were a flurry of speculative stories, some fueled by irresponsible charges from groups who had their own political agendas.

A Miami Spanish TV news station charged that the DC-10 was shot down by a Cuban MiG fighter. Another Miami TV station claimed that the DC-10 was a victim of friendly fire, hit by the accidental launching of a Navy missile from a U.S. submarine in the Atlantic Ocean. Miami's talk radio shows had all kinds of conspiracy theories, most of which were laughable.

Reluctant as he was to take advantage of the disaster, Kelly realized that his union was losing the war with the airline. He reacted with leaks suggesting that the non-union maintenance was responsible for the crash. He spread rumors about non-English speaking mechanics being certified by the FAA.

This prompted Westinghouse to order Martin to leak hints that the striking mechanics sabotaged the aircraft.

Some members of Congress didn't wait to learn the facts from the NTSB investigation before calling for congressional hearings as well as touting the need for new laws.

Bob had his own idea of who was responsible. He didn't have any facts, just a gut feeling. Such feelings weren't admissible in a court of law, but he knew that they would be read and considered by the court of pubic opinion.

Anyhow, the columnist was on such a roll after his Longo revelation that he could have claimed that the president had a gay lover, and *Miami P.M.* would have run the story.

He followed the old Hearst technique to create a story when there might not be one. "It's called 'the denial story,'" he explained to Suzy. "A reporter calls the mayor and asks if the mayor is beating his wife. If the mayor denies it or issues a 'no comment,' the reporter has a story. Actually, I'm not that much of a yellow journalist, because I called FBI Special Agent Meeker, who made the mistake of saying 'no comment.'"

Suzy shook her head. "Bobby, you're bad."

#

>Bob Casey's Working Press:
>Did Mafia gamblers down Sharks' jet?
>MIAMI—Is the FBI investigating a Mafia plot in the downing of the Sun Airlines charter carrying the Miami Sharks?
>FBI Special Agent Morris Meeker would neither confirm nor deny such an investigation. He would only say, "I have no comment at this time."
>This columnist has reason to believe that the Mafia sabotaged the DC-10 en route from Dallas to Miami early Friday morning in order to wipe out quarterback Johnny Longo.
>Why?
>The Sharks' quarterback was in the red to the mob for an estimated $2.5 million in gambling debts, according to Maj.

Leroy Hess, commander of the Criminal Investigations Section of the Miami police.

It was Hess who broke the Dom Conte murder case with Longo's arrest two weeks ago on a charge of first degree murder. Longo, who was seriously injured in the crash, is under police guard at Fort Lauderdale General.

While Miami's finest have no jurisdiction in the crash, Hess believes the Mafia should be considered a prime suspect.

"Illegal sports betting is a multi-billion dollar operation by the Mafia, and the mob doesn't tolerate unlucky gamblers who can't or don't pay up," said Hess.

"Mr. Longo, our investigation shows, was seriously in debt for illegal sports gambling. We also have reason to believe that the late Mr. Conte was involved in illegal gambling involving Mr. Longo. We believe that this is why Mr. Longo met Mr. Conte at a Miami motel and shot him dead in cold blood."

Would the Mafia blow up an entire commercial jet just to kill one man?

"Why not?" asks Hess.

Indeed, why not?

What if Longo was so badly in debt that the only way he could get out of it was to (gasp!) shave points or even throw a game or two?

What about the late Sharks' owner, Sol Rubin? He had a history of betting big-time on sporting events. Maybe he owed the Mafia, too, and the mob decided to make it a doubleheader hit.

Hess calls Sal Gattino, a Hollywood senior citizen, the don of East Coast gambling operations for the Lorenzo family of New York. Maybe the FBI should talk to Gattino.

"Sports bookmaking is a nationwide scandal, and it is controlled by the Mafia," says Hess. "Law enforcement lacks the resources and sophistication to keep up with the mob. Worse, politicians discourage law enforcement's efforts, because they see sports gambling as a revenue cash cow for government."

Even pro sports leagues have taken the position that it is okay for its players and coaches to participate in *legal gambling, as long as it doesn't concern their own sport.*

In the beginning, Longo did not bet on IFL or Sharks games. Gambling, however, is an addiction. Like any addiction, it grows and grows, so that eventually it knows no borders.

International Football Commissioner Pete Wilson still insists that players are paid too much to become involved in illegal gambling and wouldn't jeopardize their careers by shaving points or even throwing a game.

"When there are billions of dollars bet on pro football, there is a lot of incentive to shave points and dump games," Hess said. "Mr. Longo should be a prime example of this evil."

Okay, Special Agent Morris Meeker, the ball is in the FBI's court. Does your agency have the guts to go after the Mafia?

#

The second week of December was a typical one for South Florida during this time of year. There was blue sky with a few scattered white clouds, and a bright, warm sun, and the temperature was 82 degrees with only 30 percent humidity. It was hardly the kind of weather that reminded folks that Christmas was only two weeks away.

The media continued to feed on the crash as the NTSB tried to determine if it was an accident or sabotage.

Dick Norton's experience with the cargo door accident over Detroit and interviews with Lombard and the cabin crew resulted in keeping initial focus on the rear of the DC-10. Fortunately for the investigators, the coach section and tail section had survived the crash in good condition.

There were, however, political considerations. The FAA and NTSB had been involved in a feud over DC-10 cargo doors since the Detroit incident. The NTSB recommended to the FAA that the door should be rendered "physically impossible" to close incorrectly, that modifications should be made to the floor and vents, and that the floor strength should be increased. The response at the FAA, as well as at the manufacturer, was to ignore all the proposals. Eventually, the FAA began to urge airline manufactures to make the NTSB's recommended changes.

What bothered Dick was that if the cargo door was the culprit, why hadn't the crash happened on takeoff from DFW? He also knew Sun Airlines had followed the NTSB recommendations to strengthen the DC-10 floors in its fleet to withstand the decompressive effect of a 20-square-foot hole appearing in the fuselage.

"That DC-10 cargo door is like a bank vault when closed," Norton told NTSB investigators. "It would take an explosive device to blow that sucker open that late in the flight."

Thus, the investigators started their work in the vicinity of the cargo door, where experts found traces of a mini explosion. If the bomb theory held, the FBI would immediately go to work on the sabotage case.

Meeker had already gone public by asking for help on the Miami Field Office Home Page on the World Wide Web.

CRASH OF SUN AIRLINES FLIGHT 169
Miami Field Office
On the early morning of Friday, Nov. 28, Sun Airlines Flight 169, carrying 142 passengers, including members of the Miami Sharks football team, crashed in the Florida Everglades while en route to Miami. There were 45 survivors out of 150 on board. Information from the public is always critical to the ability of law enforcement in solving such cases. A special toll-free line—1-800-245-0169—has been established for this purpose. If you should have any information, please call at once. All calls will be kept in the strictest confidence. Or E-Mail Miami@fbi.gov on the web.

#

Naturally, the special agent did a slow burn when Casey's column was brought to his attention. *If that crash is the result of sabo-*

tage, Meeker knew only too well, *it will appear to the public that the FBI had been prodded into the investigation by a newspaper.* If it was sabotage, his fondest wish was that it would not be connected to the Mafia. Otherwise, the media would become insufferable. Still, the agent knew that it was possible for the Mafia . . .

Meeker's thoughts were interrupted by a phone call from an FBI mole inside the NTSB.

"Morris," said the mole. "It's still an unofficial call. My boss will give you the word. But take it from me, we have a case of sabotage. Early indications show that the cargo door was blown by an explosive device. It will take days before we can identify the device, but. . ."

#

Gattino received word before the *Miami P.M.* arrived at his Hollywood home the following afternoon. He ripped Casey's column out of it before his wife read the paper. His face turned crimson with rage as he ripped the newspaper page into little pieces.

That fucking Mick writer is becoming as big a problem as Longo. Maybe I should have both of those cocksuckers terminated. Fuck the FBI. Those guys are assholes. Longo is gonna be history.

The mobster regained his composure as he picked up the phone and, after finding a California number listed in a black book under *Travel Agents*, he made a call.

Gattino lived a modest life in a modest suburban Hollywood neighborhood in order to avoid the media spotlight. He followed the mob code of avoiding hits on law enforcement and media people as smart business. He would concentrate his effort on eliminating Longo before the quarterback started talking to the cops in hopes of copping a plea in the murder caper. If the cops could connect Conte to him, Gattino knew that they might uncover enough to bring charges against him.

#

It was quiet in the St. Vincent's rectory office, where Father O'Malley and Bob sipped tea and went through the formality of small talk between old friends. Bob knew this wasn't a social visit, and he was a bit hyper because of all the developments in such a monstrous story. He knew the priest well enough to know that O'Malley couldn't be rushed.

O'Malley faced one of his biggest challenges as a servant of God. He knew who had killed Conte, but he was prevented from making it public.

While realizing the privilege between parishioner and priest, how could he remain mute and let another man be convicted of a crime he didn't commit? While he pondered that heavyweight dilemma, he would provide his friend with the last words of Muhammad Johnson.

"Robert," he began ever so slowly. "Perhaps I should have gone to the authorities right away with this information, but maybe it will be better served by telling it to you."

Bob promptly set down his teacup and saucer. He nodded for the priest to continue.

"Johnson, you know, had a drug problem, and the young man had beaten it."

"Yeah, I know that, but. . ."

"Be patient, Robert."

"You're right, Father. I'm sorry."

"Johnson told me he believed that the drug dealers were out to get him, and that they had somehow sabotaged the plane."

"That makes no sense, Father."

The priest raised his right hand for silence. "Johnson feared that the drug dealers believed he might talk to law enforcement, or that he had already done so in order to be reinstated by the team."

Bob wasn't pleased by the news, because he really felt that it was the Mafia. He didn't want to offend the old priest by shrugging it off. *What if this is true?* "Did he give you any names, Father?"

"Yes. Yes he did. But his speech was slurred. He mumbled the initials of T.D. or T something. He kept asking why a bro would do such a thing."

Bob recommended the priest give that information to Hess. It didn't appear to the columnist that drug dealers, whoever T.D. or T something might be, were capable of sabotaging a commercial jet.

"Oh yes, Bob. He did mention something about T.D. or T something working for Sun Airlines."

That got Bob's full attention. "Father, I strongly suggest you tell this information to Major Hess ASAP! I'll ask him to come out here so that you don't have to go downtown."

O'Malley nodded.

Bob was thinking like a newspaperman. He knew Hess wouldn't leak the allegations, and if they did turn out to be fact, he would have the blessings of the major along, with a helluva story.

"Was there something else?" he asked the priest.

"Yes, Robert, but I think it should wait for another time."

Even when the priest headed for the liquor closet and poured them both a stiff drink of Irish whiskey, Bob didn't sense that O'Malley carried a burden within him that would be a dynamite story on the Conte murder.

O'Malley took three quick swigs to empty his glass before Bob could make his first taste. Bob was surprised to see the priest return to the wet bar and refill his glass.

"Robert, you and I have been friends for a long time. . ."

O'Malley paced the room slowly as he talked. He removed his metal-framed glasses and wiped them with a white handkerchief. He reminded the columnist of a country lawyer preparing to make his case in front of a jury.

"I respect a free press," he continued. "I admire your work as a journalist. I know you to be a man of principles, a good Catholic. I understand that a journalist has an obligation to the public. So you must understand that my work and my obligation is under a higher authority."

Bob said nothing. He felt as if he were in church, and the sermon was beginning. He felt a bit uncomfortable.

"Robert, I know. . .I know that Johnny Longo did not kill that man."

"Father! How do you—"

"Quiet, my son. I know, but I can't tell you how. I face a giant moral and ethical dilemma. Perhaps I have even gone too far to share this knowledge with you, a journalist. But as one, you have the investigative skills and resources to get to the truth. You cannot let Mr. Longo be convicted of a crime he did not commit."

Bob didn't ask for a refill after he downed his whiskey. He got up from the chair, strode across the room, and poured himself a refill. He was stunned by O'Malley's statement. The priest wouldn't lie, of course, and he spoke as one who really knew the truth.

"Robert, old friend, I understand that this may mean admitting you were wrong in print. But I know you as a man of honor who will do the right thing. And will it be any less a journalistic accomplishment if you do solve the killing by revealing the real killer?"

Bob remained standing. His mind was already in motion reviewing the case against Longo. What did the priest know? And how? If it wasn't Longo, who could it be? Could the killer be someone O'Malley knew? He had more questions, and no answers.

"Father, I appreciate your position. I, too, want justice. I'll start looking into the matter at once."

O'Malley escorted his visitor to the front door. They shook hands. "Bless you, my son. And remember the lesson in John 7:32. 'And ye shall know the truth, and the truth shall make you free.'"

#

Bob looked at his watch. It was 2:28. He drove his yellow Corvette onto the parking lot that served as I-95. It was at times like these that he was glad he had insisted on an automatic transmission instead of a stick shift.

It took nearly an hour in the bumper-to-bumper traffic before he pulled into the visitors' parking lot at Miami Police Headquarters.

Hess looked up from a desk overflowing with paper reports. He had his dress shirt sleeves rolled up, and his tie hung limp, exposing a white T-shirt under the two unbuttoned holes.

"Jesus, I thought you'd be hanging around your new G-men pals."

Bob pulled up an office chair. "You got any of that free taxpayers' coffee left, Leroy?"

Hess went to a table and poured two mugs from the coffeemaker. He handed one to his visitor. "It's black, Bob. You taxpayers failed to fund our sugar and cream appropriation this week."

Both men laughed.

"What would you say, Leroy, if I told you that Longo didn't knock off Conte?"

Hess betrayed no emotion. He took a sip of coffee. "I'd say you're probably right, Scoop."

"Huh. How's that again? Then why the fuck are you holding him?"

"My guys have built a good circumstantial case," explained the major. "We even have a witness who saw Longo's Mercedes leave the scene. Call it a gut feeling, you know, of a cop who's been involved in too many homicides, but I don't think he shot Conte."

"Why is that, Leroy?"

"A macho athlete doesn't waste a creep like Conte with a five-shot .38 revolver. He would probably beat the living shit out of him, not shoot him. If Conte was the Mafia bookmaker or loan Shark, Longo would know damn well that killing a soldier wouldn't solve any problems.

"No, I don't buy your published theory that the Mafia sabotaged the Sharks' jet to terminate Longo or even Rubin. I'd pin that rap on the fucking Sun Airlines union punks."

What the major said made sense. The columnist was having a bad Monday. *First O'Malley, now Hess.*

"Okay, Sherlock," said Hess, "tell me why you no longer think Longo is the bad guy that you claimed he was in your rag."

"I can't reveal my source, Leroy, but—"

Hess slammed his right fist hard on the desk. Papers scattered. "Goddamn it, Bob, spare me that newspaper bullshit! I can have you tossed in the slammer for withholding evidence."

"Fuck you, Leroy! I have a man—a man of unquestioned character—who has confided in me that Longo is innocent. Is he? If he is, then who wasted Conte?" Bob leaned forward toward the major's desk. "I have some other information. Father O'Malley said Muhammad Johnson told him before his death that the drug dealers were out to get him. They were afraid he would blow the whistle on them. He even mumbled some names. I told the good priest you might drop by the parish and take a statement. Maybe the drug dealers sabotaged the plane."

Hess noted O'Malley's name on a yellow legal pad. He tossed his pen aside. "I had one crazy caller today who suggested it was one of those dead sports writers who caused the crash with his laptop computer. Mafia. Drug dealers. Next, someone will blame the CIA. Okay, I'll visit O'Malley myself."

"When, Leroy?" Bob asked with urgency in his voice.

"This evening, Bobby. As soon as I have dinner. Yeah, I'm interested, even if we can collar only one dirtbag drug dealer."

CHAPTER 20

"By gaming we lose both our time and treasure—two things most precious to the life of man."

Owen Felthman

It WAS MORE than a week before Martha Longo was permitted to visit her husband. She didn't bring the children. Fort Lauderdale General listed the quarterback's condition as critical. He suffered a broken right leg and arm, internal and head injuries, along with minor burns.

Johnny had plenty of time to think in the hospital. He remembered starting gambling even before he became a freshman at Scranton, Pennsylvania, Catholic Central High School. It was small stuff then. He had placed his first bet when he was nine. After school, he would go to play in a local park—baseball, stickball, tag, the normal kids' games. When young Longo saw the older kids pitching quarters, he wanted to become part of the action. By the time he left, he had lost $11. He stole the money from his sister's piggy bank.

Feeling guilt and shame, Johnny refrained from gambling again until age 14, when it was flipping cards, playing pinball, and organizing school betting pools. His competitive personality that had made him a three-letter winner also made it easy for him to organize his own sports pool. It was small stuff at first. He eventually built it up to a $1,000-a-week operation that netted him a vig of $100 each week.

Damn! I couldn't stand prosperity, so I'd often blow the hundred bucks on gambling.

There was no moral disgust for him, Johnny realized. His Church, his parents, and even the state-sponsored gambling schemes. His father had played the state lottery, and his mother was an ardent bingo player Tuesday nights at the Catholic parish. He wasn't afraid to take chances. *But it was this trait that gave me success as a highschool and college quarterback.*

There was plenty of money for me to bet on games at South Bend, where the starting quarterback for Notre Dame was a national celebrity. There were all kinds of boosters, businessmen, and others who were happy to loan me money.

He knew the big lie was that college athletes got paid in education and free room and board. *We make millions for our schools, but under National Collegiate Athletic Association rules, we can't receive one penny or else we cease to be amateurs.*

I never lacked anything during my four years on campus. I had the use of a new convertible from a South Bend auto dealer. He recalled the red Mustang with the big V-8. *What an ass wagon! I could charge my clothing purchases at several upscale South Bend stores. Hell, everyone was doing it.*

He smiled as he was reminded of how he was treated during his weekend visit to Notre Dame during his senior year in high school.

First he was flown to South Bend on a booster's private jet. He was then provided with a female student escort, a real knockout who that Saturday night provided him with his first sexual experiences, including oral sex. *Man, I really thought I was in love. How dumb was I? Did I truly believe that by signing a letter of intent, she would become my campus sweetheart?* Instead, he later learned, she had provided the same incentives for a dozen or more highschool All-Americans who visited the campus that autumn.

Then he met Martha Klimkiewitz.

Johnny reached for a glass of water. He downed the glass and let his mind wander back to his sophomore year. Martha was a Notre Dame cheerleader and 4.0 student. She was the fifth child of a Polish family of eight from Utica, New York, and she was a devout Catholic. *She held onto her virginity until her junior year, when she was convinced that I wanted to marry her.*

As a coed, Martha had cover-girl looks to go with her brain, and she never seemed in awe of Longo's jock status on campus. Her father was a highschool football coach and math teacher, and she was able to talk technical and strategic football with Longo.

As his mind drifted back to those happy days when gambling didn't dominate his life, he realized what a fool he had become. He was ashamed of the way he had treated Martha.

Combined with his injuries and arrest, the quarterback began contemplating suicide. Still, the need to gamble consumed him. He wanted to bet on this week's football games.

There's no hope. I've lost my reputation, my family, and my self-esteem. There's no other way out. He felt himself sinking into a deep black hole. *Could I kill myself? What else is there? If they pin that murder rap on me, or even if they don't, I'm fucked, just like O.J.*

His thoughts were interrupted by the visitor walking into his room. It was Martha.

He looked so helpless, like a little boy, she thought as she observed the casts, bandages, and IV attached to Johnny's battered body. Both eyes were blackened, and his face was swollen and showed scratch marks. With all that had happened to their marriage this season, she didn't know what to say when she pulled a chair up to the bed.

"Johnny?"

"Is that you, Martha?"

"Yes, Johnny, I'm here. How you doing?"

"Not too good, Martha," he said. "You, uh, know, the cops think I killed some hood in Miami. I didn't kill anyone. You have to believe me, Martha. I'm a gambler, but I'm not a murderer."

Martha started to cry as she embraced her husband on the bed. She gently kissed him several times on his battered face.

"I know you didn't kill that evil man, Johnny. And you aren't going to pay for a crime you didn't commit. Your attorney said you are to talk to no one, and don't give a statement about the charge. He will be in to see you tomorrow."

"Martha, what do the kids think? I mean, the media has me convicted. And, you know, their peers can be so cruel. . ."

His concern for their children touched Martha. It rekindled her deepest feelings for her husband. As soon as she had seen him in that hospital room with guards outside, she had forgiven him for his recent abuses. After all, he had never been physical with her before the gambling problem had escalated.

"Johnny, the children love you. Hell, they've survived when their playmates picked on them when you had a bad game or the Sharks had a bad season. You are in their prayers every night. As you are, you know, in mine."

Martha tried to concentrate on small talk, but she continued to be consumed by guilt for killing Conte. *I'm a murderer. So how can I damn Johnny for his gambling? I deserve to be abused by Johnny. That is my punishment for being a sinner.*

#

Meanwhile, Mrs. O'Neill, the housekeeper, escorted Leroy into the rectory office of Father O'Malley.

"I appreciate you coming to see me, Major Hess," the priest said in greeting. "Will you share some coffee or tea, or perhaps something a bit more spirited?"

"A Scotch and water would be fine, Father."

Leroy was only kidding. But before he realized that the priest thought he was serious, the policeman was treated to the liquid treasures inside the bookcase bar.

"I only drink Irish whiskey myself, Major," O'Malley said as he passed the glass to the policeman. "However, I try to appeal to the drinking likes of all mankind. In these days, I guess you would call it being politically correct."

Leroy laughed. Normally, he wouldn't accept a drink on duty, but he realized that no purpose would be served by saying that he had only been kidding.

O'Malley passed him a large ashtray. "Light up, if you have 'em, Major. Bob Casey says you smoke Camels. I'm a cigar man myself."

Leroy quickly pulled out a pack and lit one. He liked the old priest. "And what else did Mr. Casey tell you about me, Father?"

"Goodness, Major. Bob admires you. He says you're an honest cop, a brilliant detective, and a fine human being."

"Really," replied the policeman. "What else did he say?"

"Well, Major, he also says you owe him lunch tomorrow."

"Okay, Father, enough of your Irish blarney. What service can I provide today?"

O'Malley related the deathbed confession of Johnson during which he had hinted that drug dealers were involved. Leroy took notes in a small spiral notebook. He felt that there was information there worth harvesting. Even if the drug dealers didn't down the plane, he might be able to put some of the bastards behind bars.

"Thank you for the information, Father. It may be more useful than you can imagine. Oh, by the way, I understand Johnny Longo is one of your church members."

"Yes, the Longo family attends services here, and their children are in our church school."

Leroy put his notebook slowly back into his sport jacket's inside pocket. "You wouldn't have any information, you know, that could be useful to our investigation, would you, Father?"

The priest blessed himself with the sign of the cross. "I will not lie to you, Major. What I know is privileged information. I cannot, and will not, violate my sacred trust as a priest. I can tell you, however, that. . .that Johnny Longo did not commit murder. Perhaps you may find that it wasn't a murder at all."

Leroy displayed no emotion. He knew that the priest couldn't betray his trust, but he appreciated his sharing information that he had suspected all along: Longo did not kill Conte. *So who did?*

Leroy was formulating a game plan as he said goodbye at St. Vincent's, and that plan included Casey's column. Hess returned to Miami Police headquarters and called his counterpart, Major Robert Kelly. Despite the last name, the major wasn't Irish. He was an African-American. Kelly commanded the Special Investigations Section, which handled vice and narcotics. He took Hess's information and farmed it out right away to his narcotics lieutenant.

Oh, the power of the press!

Hess called for a meeting with his investigators in the Longo case. He knew the homicide detectives wouldn't like what he had to say, but fuck 'em. Then he called Casey.

Bob's column for Wednesday was another blockbuster. Bloom acted like a kid in a toy store with carte blanche. The column earned the page one headline, which keyed to the item in the sports section.

> *Bob Casey's Working Press:*
> *Did drug ring down Sharks'*
> *jet to quiet WR Johnson?*
> *Team chaplain tells of WR's heroic sacrifice*
>
> MIAMI—Did drug dealers down the Miami Sharks' DC-10 charter in order to silence wide receiver Muhammad Johnson?
>
> Maj. Leroy Hess, Miami police commander, tells me that he is probing a tip from the Sharks' chaplain, the Rev. Francis J. O'Malley of St. Vincent's Church, to that effect.
>
> O'Malley told his congregation on Sunday at St. Vincent's that Johnson saved his life by using his body to shield the priest from flying debris when the aircraft crashed into the Everglades.
>
> It was an emotional sermon that brought tears to the eyes of those in attendance at the Miami Shores Catholic Church.

Here was a young African-American, a gifted athlete who had everything to live for, who sacrificed his life for an older white man of a different religious faith.

I blasted Johnson in the past for his drug problem. Now let me be the first to praise him for his ultimate heroic sacrifice. His sacrifice must not fade from memory.

We must establish some way to remember this man's courage to fight back from drug addiction and his bravery in the final hours of his young life.

"Before Mr. Johnson died, he provided Father O'Malley with the names of the drug dealers we can consider possible suspects in the tragic crash of the team charter," Hess said. "Our agency is at this moment acting on that information."

Hess requests any person with information in this case to contact his office. Your identity will be protected, and it could even lead to a substantial reward.

Johnson, an All-Pro wide out, had been suspended by the Sharks after he passed out before a team meeting for a game in New Orleans in September.

Under the players' association contract with the IFL, Johnson voluntarily placed himself in a drug rehab program at the Sayfie Clinic in Boca Raton. Thanks to Sharks GM, now president Jack Cabot, and the late coach, Don Sherman, the WR received support while he fought to become clean of drugs.

To show their faith in his efforts, Sherman and Cabot took Johnson on the team plane to Dallas for the Texans game on Thanksgiving Day.

In a twist of fate, new Sharks head coach Jim Moses survived the crash, because Sherman asked Moses to visit with Johnson in the coach section to tell him that he would be reinstated and activated on Monday.

"If it was drug dealers who did this, then they should get the electric chair," an angry Moses asserted. "Drug dealers are nothing but animals."

> "To honor Johnson's memory, the Sharks organization has created a new Comeback Award that will be awarded annually to a player who overcomes great odds to make the team. Meanwhile, our prayers are with the Johnson family in Plantation."

Moses' statement reflects the way most of us feel about Johnson. "He is a credit to his race—the human race."

God love you, Muhammad. Rest in peace.

\#

Dick Norton's suspicions about the cargo door led the NTSB's technicians to determine that a small explosive device was responsible for blowing open the door. In calling in the FBI, the NTSB said that it was because of criminal sabotage.

"We have all kinds of crazies out there who might want to blow up a commercial jet," Special Agent Meeker told Norton when he called to thank him for the break in the case. "No one, however, has claimed responsibility for this mass murder."

Meeker had invited Norton to visit him and provide any more technical help that he could. The agent was surprised when the next day Dick hobbled into his office on crutches, his right leg in a cast.

The FBI's Miami Bureau resembled a stockbroker's office, except that the shirt-sleeved agents seated behind a sea of desks with computers packed handguns. Meeker had a private office, and it was Spartanly furnished and contained a wall of photos, including one of Meeker shaking hands with the agency director in Washington.

Dick and Meeker sipped from paper cups of coffee as they talked.

"It is my opinion that the bastards who planted the bomb had a good knowledge of DC-10 aircraft," the captain said. "This was a highly professional job of sabotage. The bomb was obviously set off by a timing device. But why, and by whom?"

Meeker smiled. "Being a detective isn't so easy, hey, Dick?"

"That's for certain. That's for damn certain, Morris."

"Now we have every clown in the media running speculation stories," Meeker said. "Did you see *Miami P.M.* today? That Bob Casey, a mere sports writer, is suggesting that drug dealers did it. Why? Because some old priest took it as gospel from a dying junkie that his dealers wanted revenge. Next, someone will suggest that it's a CIA conspiracy."

Dick didn't debate the issue. He wouldn't tell the special agent that Casey was a long-time tennis pal. It would take away all the fun of listening to Meeker rip Casey for prodding law enforcement. Dick realized the positive effect of a vigilant press in gaining action.

"Well, Morris, even the mainstream press has jumped the gun on this crash. Did you see this story in the *Miami Morning Journal*?"

The agent shook his head. Dick pulled the first section of the *Journal* out of his battered, black pilot's case.

> *DID U.S. MISSILE DOWN SHARKS' JET?*
> *by Morris Katz, Journal Washington Bureau*
>
> WASHINGTON—The Navy tested two Trident D-5 missiles off the coast of Florida over the Thanksgiving weekend. But a Pentagon spokesman said Tuesday that it "stretches the imagination" to think that the missiles might be involved in downing a Sun Airlines DC-10 carrying the Miami Sharks football team early Friday morning.
>
> *The NTSB is examining commercial pilots' reports of possible missile flights Thursday and Friday in the South Florida area . . .*

Meeker handed the newspaper back. "Once we announce the bomb as the cause of the crash," said the agent, "every whacko radical group will claim responsibility. Already the conservative Cuban radio here is blaming it on Castro. But we must have a press conference Thursday. That's what both our bosses in DC want."

"What time, Morris?"

"They suggested 2:00 p.m. Meanwhile, I have work to do."

Meeker assigned agents to check out every possible lead, including the striking mechanics, the Mafia, drug dealers, radical groups, and even the military. He stopped short of considering Castro's Cuban government a suspect.

#

"Bubba" Youngblood panicked when he read Casey's column. He called T.J. Lewis.

"Man, they know. They know it was us who blew up the plane."

"Shut the fuck up, Bubba," rebuked Lewis. "The law ain't got a clue. If they knew, we'd be in the joint. And don't ever talk like that over an open telephone line. You never know if the line is bugged. Our only fear is that we are low on white stuff, and our clients are getting nervous. If Kelly doesn't make a deal with Westinghouse, we may have to invest in some mules as a temporary measure to bring in junk."

Youngblood still wasn't convinced that the FBI wasn't about to collar him, but he felt better after talking to Lewis. *If T.J. ain't scared, why should I be?* "What about that news guy? He can keep making trouble. . ."

Before Youngblood could finish, Lewis said, "Listen, man, Jose and I have a plan to shut up the fuckin' honky writer. Trust us. You stay cool. We haven't got a thing to fear as long as we keep cool and quiet. You understand?"

"Yeah."

"Good."

#

At *Miami P.M.* on Wednesday afternoon, Bob enjoyed a cigar in Bloom's office as the two discussed the game plan for the continued coverage of the Sharks' disaster.

"I understand Bunny Rubin is attempting to field a team under the IFL disaster plan to finish the season, Bob."

Taking a long drag on his cigar, Bob exhaled a cloud of smoke and said, "No way. There is no way anyone can field a replacement team in a week or even two weeks after such a disaster. In basketball, baseball, hockey. . .maybe. Not in football. If this were a major league baseball team, it would be different. Baseball is a game of throwing, catching, and hitting. There are no complicated systems to learn on offense and defense, no relationships to develop between quarterback and receivers, and. . ."

#

It wasn't until he attended the funeral Mass for Cunill at St. Vincent's that Bob realized the finality of the death of his friend and co-worker.

Bob fought hard to manage his emotions. He was glad that he had Suzy at his side throughout the service. He was soothed by Father O'Malley's eulogy and pleased by the turnout that packed the church.

He saw the black-clad Mrs. Cunill and her two children. She was surrounded by a horde of relatives and dignitaries from Miami's Cuban community. Even Castro from the *Morning Journal* was there.

Near the end of O'Malley's eulogy, Bob broke down and cried unashamedly. Later, he consoled the widow.

"I'll get the scum who killed Jorge," he said softly. "I will never rest until he is avenged."

CHAPTER 21

*"There was the door to which I found no key,
There was the veil through which I might not yet see."*
Omar Khayam
Rubaiyet

Bomb!

MIAMIANS AT LUNCH were greeted by hawking newspaper sellers waving Thursday's first edition of *Miami P.M.* The copyrighted story contained a byline by the rising star reporter of the afternoon daily.

FEDS HUNT BOMBERS
OF SHARKS' AIRCRAFT
by Buffy Zei, Miami P.M. Reporter

MIAMI—The National Safety Transportation Board has determined that a bomb caused the November 28th crash of the Sun Airlines DC-10 that carried the Miami Sharks football team, Miami P.M. has learned exclusively.

The NTSB will turn over the criminal hunt to the FBI in a press conference scheduled by both agencies this afternoon at Miami International Airport.

> *This newspaper learned that NTSB investigators discovered evidence of an explosive device that had blown open the cargo door of the aircraft as it prepared to land at MIA in the early hours of November 28.*
>
> *Now the question is no longer "how" but "who planted the bomb?"*
>
> *The suspects range from disgruntled, striking Sun Airlines employees to organized crime to drug dealers to radical groups.*
>
> *Spokesmen for both agencies declined to comment.*
>
> *FBI agents, however, are at this very moment conducting an investigation that is headed by Special Agent Morris Meeker of the Miami office.*

Meeker obtained a copy of the tabloid at a traffic stop en route to work. He was furious about the news leak, although he knew the early release of the cause of the crash would hardly hamper his investigation. It concerned him because it was apparent there was at least one disloyal agent working this case.

The leak, however, had come from Dick, who wanted to show his appreciation for Zei's coverage of the non-English speaking mechanics scandal.

In a bit of irony, to double-check Zei's anonymous source, City Editor Locastro had asked Bob to see if his pal Norton could confirm it. Dick had a difficult time not laughing when he got the call from Bob at his Hollywood home. Dick, a conservative Republican, had no love for the liberal *Miami Morning Journal*, so he took great delight in scorching the morning paper.

In addition to the editors at the *Journal* and the area TV and radio outlets, there were others upset by the scoop. And it wasn't because *Miami P.M.* got the story first.

"What does that fucking yellow rag mean with that shit about the FBI investigating the mechanics?" *If the fucking FBI gets wind of that, my ass will be shit. No one will believe we didn't do it.*

Mike Kelly kicked chairs and knocked over a cup of coffee in a temper tantrum at union headquarters when he read the story. His anger, however, was also about that meeting with the former IRA patriot turned union officer.

Two of his union assistants, Jose Cortez and T.J. Lewis, laughed when they read the story. They had laughed earlier, too, when Casey accused drug dealers of downing the plane.

"Hey, Mike," said Lewis. "Calm down, boss. The Jewish press is just anti-labor. Hell, they're blaming everyone for that crash. That crazy honky Casey has already blamed the Mafia and the drug dealers. Next will be the CIA."

The phone on Kelly's battered wooden desk rang. Cortez answered it.

"It's for you, boss," said Cortez. "It's Mr. Tenuto from Chicago."

Kelly took the receiver. The two labor lieutenants saw Kelly's mood change. "Thank you, Tony. Thank you." He hung up the phone. The fax attached to the phone started humming, and an excited Kelly grabbed the sheet of paper. He read it quickly and exploded into a quick step that resembled a jig.

"Hold the fort. I'll be back soon. I have to pay a visit to the *Morning Journal*. I have a story for that rag. Yes, sir, a great story."

#

In Hollywood, Don Sal Gattino was on the phone with the godfather.

"Sal, we have to stop all this shit about the Mafia being investigated in that team plane crash," asserted Angelo Lorenzo. "I'm getting heat from Jerry Pritzi in Detroit and Abe Goldman in Chicago."

"How do we do that, Godfather?"

"We find the cocksuckers who blew up the plane and deliver

them to the cops. Or we find someone that we can frame and let them take the rap. I don't give a goddamn about who takes the fall, as long as they aren't family. Maybe you can pin it on one of the nigger radical groups, or even the Ku Klux Klan. First, though, get rid of that fucking Longo. He is a ticking bomb ready to explode. He'll blow us all away with the cops, just to save his ass from the electric chair."

"Godfather, as we speak, Mr. Longo may soon be history."

"Not the LA travel agent?"

"Capisce, Godfather."

#

Jimmy "The Trigger" Scalise arrived at the employees' entrance of Fort Lauderdale General Hospital as the shifts were changing at 11:00 p.m. He was attired in a green scrub orderly's outfit, with a stolen hospital ID furnished by one of Gattino's soldiers. The elderly hospital guard didn't even take note of an orderly carrying a violin case. The guard had his mind on a portable TV set and the eleven o'clock news, waiting to see if his lottery number was a winner.

Scalise kept his cool when two of the reporting shift workers kidded him about his case. "I play in the Fort Lauderdale Symphony," he said. "That's why I need this job."

He had a gift for staying cool, and a sense of humor that put people at ease. At the same time he did not dress or act in a manner that might cause anyone to remember him being at the scene. Since being given the assignment, Scalise had cased the hospital by day and by night. By pretending to be an orderly for two straight nights, the nurses on duty had no reason to question him.

Longo's room was in a corner on the fifth floor. Scalise uncased the Thompson submachine gun and placed it on a wheeled dining cart, covering the weapon with a tablecloth.

Ever so slowly, he nonchalantly pushed the cart toward the

officer seated outside the prisoner's room. The veteran hit man knew that he had to act fast. He wouldn't get a second chance.

Officer Don Polanksi was bored by the guard duty. He was taking a catnap, which proved beneficial to his longevity. Having no desire to terminate a cop, Scalise used the wooden butt of his weapon to knock out the policeman. It was quick. A crack on the head as wood met flesh, a muffled moan, and the sound of the falling officer hitting the floor. Experience gave Scalise the skill to control such a KO from being fatal.

Scalise pulled open the room door and was surprised to see what he believed was a real orderly at the side of the patient. He didn't hesitate. The Thompson spat out a lethal dose of lead poison that cut down the orderly and ripped through the man in the hospital bed.

The hit man stepped out over the downed officer, replaced the Thompson in the violin case, covered it with the tablecloth, and wheeled it down past the nursing station. He was surprised to see the nurse's back, as she appeared glued to the monitor of the computer.

She glanced around briefly. "Oh, orderly? Will you check the TVs down the hall? I think they have a war movie on."

"Yes, ma'am, they did. I turned the TV off."

"Thank you, orderly."

Scalise took the stairs down. He went down at a trot and arrived at the employees' entrance. The old guard was still glued to the TV.

"Good night," Scalise said.

"Yeah, have a good one," replied the guard, who never moved.

As he drove from the scene in a rented white Chevrolet sedan, he heard the sirens and saw the flashing blue and red lights of a convoy of Fort Lauderdale police units converging on the hospital.

A good night's work and an easy 50 Gs.

He drove straight to a motel near the Miami International Airport. The following morning, he stopped at a private post office to mail the violin back to LA. After turning in his car and checking in for his flight to LAX, he strolled to a newsstand and bought a copy of *Miami P.M.* He liked its coverage of crime news.

DRUG LORD SLAIN BY
HIT MAN IN HOSPITAL

"What the fuck . . .?"

Scalise momentarily forgot himself. No one in the bustling airport terminal appeared to notice his loud exclamation. He quickly turned to page three of the tabloid.

DRUG DUO GUNNED DOWN
IN LAUDERDALE HOSPITAL
by Joe Scherr, Miami P.M. Reporter

FORT LAUDERDALE—*A notorious drug lord held under police arrest following a high-speed chase, and a gang member posing as an orderly, were cut down early Thursday morning in a hail of machine gun bullets in a fifth-floor room at Fort Lauderdale General.*

A Fort Lauderdale police officer, Don Polanksi, was also injured after being hit over the head, apparently by the bogus orderly.

Shot dead were Vincent "The Snake" Manning, 38, of 1805 Ocean Drive, Palm Beach, and Robert Holmes, 22, of no certain address.

Even though police say that they found the room riddled by .45-caliber bullets, the noise of the shooting apparently did not attract the attention of the hospital staff until almost 20 minutes after the double homicide.

Police say they have no witnesses and no description of the killer, who was believed to be a hit man.

A police spokesman said, "This is being treated as a drug gang killing. The killer was either acting for a rival drug gang or perhaps for Manning's own gang, fearful that he might talk."

The hospital room had been previously occupied by murder

suspect Johnny Longo, the veteran Miami Sharks quarterback. Longo had been moved earlier in the day to another room because police considered Manning a more dangerous threat.

Manning was injured earlier Wednesday after his Mercedes sedan crashed on the Florida Turnpike at the Fort Lauderdale-Pompano city line. He led 12 police units on a 14-mile chase from Boca Raton at speeds of over 120 mph.

Police said he fired numerous rounds at the pursuing vehicles with an Uzi. Police did not return fire for fear of hitting other motorists along the toll highway.

Manning's car slammed into a tractor-trailer. He was airlifted to Fort Lauderdale General in "critical" condition with assorted crash injuries.

The Friday editions of the *Miami Morning Journal* relegated such crime news to its Broward County regional page. The lead story was about Congress' debate on the flat tax, and there were assorted political and Latin American news stories. The bomb story was by now old news, but the badly beaten morning paper did cover the FBI/NTSB press column in a one-column headline and five inches of story that jumped inside to Page 18A. *Journal* columnist Herb Gold, however, had a blockbuster item.

HERB GOLD
Sun Air posts profit
on crash insurance
CRASH CASH: *Here's a frightening thought for the flying public. Sun Airlines, bogged down in a strike with its mechanics, will make money on the crash of its DC-10 that carried the Miami Sharks to their deaths in the Everglades last week. That's because the Miami-based carrier over-insured the aircraft. The exact figures haven't been confirmed; but American Commercial Insurance would not deny it. Industry sources estimated the value of the aircraft at $31 million, and we understand*

that Sun Airlines CEO "Bud" Westinghouse had it insured for $35 million. Robin Martin, the spokesman for Sun Airlines, said that the airline's policy was not to disclose internal financial matters.

In addition, airline insiders tell me, Sun Airlines will also salvage parts of the doomed jet, and these parts will be returned to service in other DC-10s in the carrier's fleet. I don't know about you, but I'd be hesitant to board any plane of a carrier that can make money by crashing.

BUNNY TALE: I hear tell that widow-lady, Bunny Rubin, isn't wasting any time in finding a new hubby. With the late owner of the Miami Sharks, Sol Rubin, still fresh in his grave, the widow and now team owner reportedly has chosen team president Jack Cabot as her main squeeze. If she decides to lure the dashing and handsome Cabot to the altar, will that be her third, fourth, or fifth trip? Frankly, it looks to me like Bunny wants to rob the cradle this time instead of a rest home . . .

#

Westinghouse flew into a rage when he read the lead item in Gold's column. He flung the newspaper to the floor of his office and spat on Gold's column. He called his advertising agency and pulled the schedule for the *Morning Journal*. He called his main attorney to threaten a suit against Gold. He called the publisher of the *Morning Journal*.

The bottom line, however, was that the DC-10 was indeed over-insured, and the carrier would indeed salvage some of the wreckage.

A company spy among the striking workers later informed Westinghouse that the insurance story tip was provided to the columnist by Kelly. The tip was given to Kelly by Tony Tenuto of the Transportation Employees of America Union—the very same Mafia union boss that Sal Gattino had sought for help in blowing up the very same jet.

The company spy did not know about Tenuto's suggestion to

Kelly that the machinists sabotage the jet. Westinghouse believed that Kelly and some of his union thugs were capable of such an atrocity.

The CEO wanted to go public with a charge that the union blew up the jet.

"I wouldn't do that, Captain Westinghouse," Robin Martin advised after listening to him rant and rave. "You have to rise above that level. I know you're feeling hurt by that slap by Gold about the insurance, but that's old news. Reasonable people know that you wouldn't sabotage one of your own DC-10s. The majority of the public will think the same way. Anyhow, think of all the folks who don't read Gold's column, and who don't even read the *Morning Journal*."

Bunny read Gold's column and smiled. She knew her relationship with Cabot couldn't be kept a secret forever. In fact, she didn't want it to be.

So when others in the media called asking for her reaction, she simply replied, "How interesting. You know, it's tough to be a strong woman in a man's world. I think there are many men envious of a woman owning a pro football team. . .Certainly Jack Cabot and I are close friends. He is our club president and a man my late husband hired to lead our team's front office. I have a great deal of respect for him. . ."

Bunny wasn't a feminist. She detested NOW and all liberal politics. But in her hour of need, she was quick to act the victim and embrace these organizations. Soon she was deluged with offers to be on talk shows, and women's magazines wanted to feature her.

It worked, because e-mail and snail mail started pouring into the Sharks' office from understanding women all over the world—including the First Lady in a handwritten note on White House stationery.

Bunny was on a roll now.

Then came a call from her secretary. "Two gentlemen from the FBI are here to see you, Mrs. Rubin."

She gasped for air. *Oh, my God. What do they want? Do they know?*

They introduced themselves as Ronald Gibbs and H.R. Rawson of the Washington office.

"Mrs. Rubin," began Gibbs, who appeared by age to be the senior of the two agents, "please accept our condolences on the death of your husband. We. . .we hate to intrude at a time like this, but. . ."

"I understand," she replied, although she didn't. "But what, Agent Gibbs?" Bunny was scared, but she managed a pleasant smile and a friendly tone in her voice. "Gentlemen, please be seated."

The two agents found chairs. They appeared a bit uncomfortable.

"Thank you, Mrs. Rubin. As I was about to say, do you know a Klaus Müller?"

Bunny was seated in front of her large desk, and the name was like a slap in the face. The muscles tightened in her body, and she felt sweat on her hands. She managed to remain cool, and quickly made a decision not to lie about knowing Müller, since it was obvious that the agents in front of her had evidence of a connection.

"Yes, I know of him," she said after a brief pause. "Actually, he was a friend of S.R.'s. What did he do to get in trouble with the FBI?"

"He's not in any trouble with our agency," Gibbs said. "He's dead."

"Dead?" Bunny was shocked, but fought showing any unusual emotion.

"Yes, ma'am."

"How? When?"

"We aren't at liberty to give you that information," Gibbs said. "You see, he died while working for another Federal agency. We have been assigned to. . .er, contact anybody he knew in the United States."

"Was it an accident? I don't remember Mr. Müller being sick or anything."

"Like I said, Mrs. Rubin, we aren't at liberty to provide that information."

"Okay, gentlemen. How can I help the FBI?"

"Your name, address, and phone number were among his estate items that included a photostat of a check for $25,000 signed by you. Is this your signature?" Gibbs handed Rubin the document.

She took a look at it and nodded her head.

"May I ask what this check was for, Mrs. Rubin?"

"I don't know, gentlemen."

"You don't know what a check for $25,000 was for? I find that a bit hard to believe, Mrs. Rubin."

"Mr. Gibbs, I was a co-owner of the Sharks in name only. My husband conducted all of the business matters. He didn't believe in women's lib. On occasion, he would have me sign or co-sign checks. This was one of those times. I never thought to question S.R. about what this check was for. You know, this is a pro football team, and we issue a lot bigger checks to many players every week—despite what the players' union may say."

Rubin's manner disarmed the two agents. They chuckled about the players' paychecks line.

"It's no big deal, Mrs. Rubin," Gibbs said. "The check was deposited to a Swiss bank." Before she could react or reply, Gibbs and his companion stood. "Well, I guess that's it. We are sorry to have taken up your time."

The agents were on an assignment for the CIA. They knew that Müller had been killed while on a 007-style mission to terminate an Iranian intelligence officer suspected of directing terrorist attacks. The CIA's concern was that the ex-East German Communist might have leaked his illegal mission to someone who could bring it to the attention of Congress.

Satisfied that any business dealings the Rubin family had with Müller were buried with Sol Rubin in the Everglades, the agents' report ended the CIA's interest in the matter.

The news of Müller's death freed Bunny of the guilt trip she had experienced since the crash of the team charter. She no longer had to be concerned with the fear of exposure in the media. She was smart enough to realize that Müller had lost his life in some covert operation. If it was the CIA, that agency wasn't about to leak any information about a connection with one of their agents and the Rubins.

Anyhow, she wisely reasoned, if her cover story was good enough for the FBI, it was good enough for anyone else. Bunny couldn't complain about fate, because she had attained her goals without becoming an accomplice to murder. As her adrenaline rush slowed, she wondered if she could have coped with being responsible for the death of even her husband, not to mention the other 104 souls.

Yes, I could. Owning this team is power. All the fuckin' WASPs and Jews will kiss my Irish ass from now on. Even Jack had better stand tall.

#

Gattino had to leave his house and go for a long walk after he learned of the hospital shootout that had claimed two drug dealers instead of Longo.

Why is this happening to me? With all the money I donate to the Church, why is God doing this to me?

#

Leroy was awakened at his Miami home at 2:15 a.m. by a phone call from the Fort Lauderdale police. It was to assure the major that Longo was unharmed and still in custody. Coming out of a sound sleep, Leroy never questioned that the hit was intended for the drug dealers, not for Longo.

Later, when it was learned that the hit man used an old-fashioned Thompson submachine gun, not an Uzi or a sawed-off shotgun or even a handgun with a silencer, the major's mind started banging away.

"Carlos," he said to Investigator Baptiste later that morning in their police headquarters' office, "what is the weapon of choice of your drug-running, wetback amigos?"

"Uzis."

"What about a tommy gun or a Thompson submachine gun?"

"Major, those are old gringo weapons," the investigator said. "You know, like in the gangster movies of the 1930s."

"Like a Mafia hit man of the 1930s might use. . ."

"Major, you don't mean what I think you mean?"

"Yes I do, Carlos."

"But, sir, such a hit man would be in his 80s or 90s. Even the Mafia has come into the modern world of weapons."

"Carlos, I don't hold that University of Miami degree against you, but think back to one of our most recent gangland hits."

"You mean that Syracusa shooting at the frog restaurant on the Beach?" the investigator replied with the excitement of a contestant on a TV quiz show.

"Bingo! I do see you making sergeant without the need for minority points on the exam."

"That hit man used a Thompson submachine gun, too," Baptiste said. "The Miami Beach cops passed that one off as a drug caper, because the headwaiter described the hit man as a young Hispanic dressed like a Jewish tourist."

Leroy leaned back in his office chair and lit up a fresh Camel. "Carlos, I think you should pay a visit to that French restaurant."

"But, sir, that's out of our jurisdiction."

"Carlos!"

"Yes, sir. I'm on my way. If Internal Affairs puts my ass on the line, I hope you will be a character witness at my hearing."

Baptiste was soon en route to La Stelle Restaurant to have a chat with Miguel Medina. If the Miami Beach cops found out a City of Miami investigator was on their turf and trying to make them look bad. . .well, Carlos didn't want to think about the consequences.

#

Larry Bloom knocked over two cups of coffee that morning when he read the rival morning newspaper. He even yelled at his secretary. The managing editor had been on a roll, and he didn't like being beaten on anything, even if they were tidbits by the rival rag's columnist.

When the phone rang, Bloom gave one of those impersonations of a "What the fuck do you want?" response, except it was a "Y-e-a-h!" That was fortunate, because the caller was Kangaroo News Ltd. CEO Andy Lyon.

"Good day to you, too, Mr. Lyon."

"Larry, you sound as if you need a vacation."

"Sorry, Mr. Lyon. Things have been a bit hectic around here the past week, you know, and. . ."

"I know, lad. You, Casey, and that new skirt. . ."

"Buffy Zei?"

"Ah, yes, Buffy Zei. Well, all of you have made me right proud in the coverage of the plane crash. I knew you were doing some good shit, because my wimpy son-in-law called me. Concerned about lawsuits and stuff. Sorry I have to leave Jack in Miami, but my daughter loves it there. Also, you know, the grandkids are involved in the school stuff."

"Mr. Patterson and I get along."

"Larry, you don't have to bullshit me. Jack can be a pain in the ass. Thank you anyhow for putting up with him as much as you do. Anyway. . .I want to show you my appreciation. That Casey is a pistol! Best hire you ever made, Larry. I'm adding him to our Kangaroo News Syndicate.

"Now, about that vacation. I thought you and the mate might like to pop on down to Sydney for a couple of weeks. You know, like at our expense. I'll give you a tour of corporate, then leave you both plenty of time to do the tourist thing."

"That's mighty generous, Mr. Lyon. My wife and I will look forward to it. Oh. . .er, by the way, Casey is getting married."

"Married?" replied Lyon.

"Yes, sir. He's going to marry a flight attendant. Nice gal."

"Probably looking for free flights as the spouse of an airline employee," Lyon observed in a dry manner. Then he laughed heartily. "Give Casey my best. Buy the couple a generous wedding gift. Charge it to me. Good day."

#

Bob walked into the ME's office just as Larry was hanging up the phone.

"There you are! I just got off the phone from Sydney. The old man was ape shit about Gold's scoop of the romance between Rubin and Cabot."

Bob slumped into a chair in front of the ME's desk and pulled out two Churchill cigars. He tossed one on the desk and prepared to smoke the other one.

"Larry, you're full of shit," he said as he worked a match against the tip of the cigar. "The old man probably promoted you to publisher. . ."

The ME picked up the cigar and unwrapped it. "So this is what you do with the money you make on your inflated expense sheets."

"Blame me on the bimbo and Cabot item," Bob said. "Cunill was sniffing that out even before the crash. Maybe Bunny Rubin planted the bomb so she could rid herself of her hubby."

Larry held up his left hand. "Don't even think that, Bob! And for God's sake don't write it!"

"Relax, Larry. I've got enough to do with the Longo caper. You know Hess is giving it second thoughts."

"You mean Longo might not be the murderer, after all?"

"Not exactly."

"What do you mean, not exactly, Bob? We've already tried and convicted that sucker."

"True, Larry, but if we may have erred a bit, our readers can count on *Miami P.M.* to fight for the truth. If we save an innocent guy from Old Sparky, who'll remember that we nailed him to a cross in the early goings?"

Larry laughed. It was a knowing and appreciative laugh. "You son of a bitch. You truly understand the mission of tabloid journalism. By the way, what are you writing for tomorrow?"

"Look in your computer. It's under bobcolumn."

BLAME BETTORS FOR SHARKS' TRAGEDY

MIAMI—*If the FBI can pin the Miami Sharks charter crash on the Mafia, this should serve as a wakeup call to the evils of illegal sports betting.*

Maybe the Mafia planted the bomb that killed 105 innocent people, but it is those who make illegal bets that are the mob's conspirators to mass murder.

Gambling has become socially acceptable.

The things that were once bulwarks against gambling—the family, the church, and the government—have all been seduced by the lure of false riches.

By most signs, America has decided that gambling is okay. Lotteries are everywhere. In Florida, the state lottery is there to help improve education and make a few lucky players instant multimillionaires.

Point spreads appear in newspapers including this one. Some dailies even carry gambling advice columns.

Only rarely do we read or hear the stories of failure and grief that far outnumber the stories of instant millionaires.

We in the media defend providing such gambling information under the guise of freedom of the press under America's Constitution.

I was challenged by a visitor to write this column. The

visitor was Tom McClellan, a reformed compulsive gambler who now heads the National Council on Compulsive Gambling. You should hear McClellan talk about gambling's effect on sports.

"How about a basketball player who once made $2.5 million a year," says McClellan, "and now can't pay a $50 debt?"

McClellan spoke of the compulsion's power.

"Illegal and legal sports gambling are getting bigger," he said. "It's an explosion. Does anyone remember the recent gambling scandals at Boston College? Both the basketball and football teams were involved.

"How about the owner of a pro football team who gambled away his own millions as well as the ownership of a $215 million franchise that his father had left him debt-free?"

McClellan doesn't have to tell tales of gambling evils from afar. Just look right here in our tropical paradise. The late Sharks owner, Sol Rubin, was a big bettor. God only knows what caused Sharks quarterback Johnny Longo to become so hooked that he stands accused of murdering a Mafia soldier.

McClellan won't let the media off the hook. He shouldn't. Is the media any less guilty than those of you who place even the most modest bet with your neighborhood bookie?

The modest bets add up. And the big ones make Mafia families rich and result in such astronomical numbers that I wouldn't put it past the mob to blow up a commercial jet to protect its interests.

Big Brother is waging campaigns to save our American youth from booze, tobacco, and drugs. What about placing that first bet?

McClellan shocked me by showing me reports and statistics of youth addiction.

"Some 90 percent of teenagers questioned in a survey by our council said that they had gambled within the past year," he said. "While that statistic may be shocking, it should not come

as a surprise. After all, kids tend to emulate their role models and moral protectors."

Our kids grow up in a Florida culture that encourages them to get involved in betting. We live in one of the gamblingest states in the union. We have everything but casinos, from parimutuels to the lottery. But that is just the tip of the iceberg compared to the amount of money bet illegally on sports.

"Most compulsive gamblers start gambling before age 14," said McClellan. "In some of the urban areas, they will start gambling for money at age nine."

You call South Florida law enforcement agencies and school administrators, and they insist there is no problem. These were some of the same people who ignored the drug problem 30 years ago.

Compulsive gambling is a losing proposition. Bookies will tell you that gamblers never win. Gambling is the road to ruin.

The challenge is to protect our kids from becoming the next hooked generation that will make the Mafia richer and more powerful than ever.

Maybe it could start right here on the sports pages of Miami P.M.

Publishers and editors listen to their readers. If you demand that we purge gambling information from our pages, it will happen.

Until then, every one of us will have blood on our hands for the crash of the Sharks charter into the Everglades.

#

Larry's initial reaction was anger that his columnist would rap his own paper's policy. In his heart, however, he knew that Bob was right. One thing was for certain: he would be getting an angry call from the fifth floor as soon as the first edition hit the street.

"I should spike this treacherous piece," Larry asserted after taking a deep breath.

"You have that right, boss. But you won't."

"Why won't I?"

"Because, Larry, you know I'm right. We both know it won't change anything, but sometimes it's good to cleanse our souls."

Larry lit the cigar. "When you're right, you're right!"

CHAPTER 22

"Foul whisperings are abroad."

William Shakespeare
Macbeth

Bob was in the sports department, where he was checking his mail, when he learned that he had a visitor.

"There is a nice little old lady here to see you, Bob," the receptionist said. "So please, no profanity. Her name is Angela Conte. She says she is the late Dom Conte's mother."

"What the hell?" he proclaimed to the empty sports department.

Bob greeted the woman. She had white hair, wore wire-rimmed glasses, and was attired like the typical Miami Beach retiree. She sported a dark blue blouse over white slacks and a cheap pair of white athletic shoes. She struggled with a department store bag, but refused Bob's offer to carry it.

Inside the conference room, she explained slowly that she was all alone now that her son was dead. Her only means of support was a monthly Social Security check and a small pension check from her late husband's job.

"I have here, Mr. Casey, something you might want," she said in a heavy Italian accent.

"What might that be, Mrs. Conte?"

"Information. . .records that my son kept before that horrible person murdered him," she asserted.

Bob was interested. "What kind of records?"

"Dominic was a good boy. He took good care of his mamma, you know."

"Yes, I'm sure he was a good son, Mrs. Conte." He hated being patient, but Bob saw no reason to badger the old lady, even if her son had been a scumbag.

"I have some of Dominic's material here." She pulled two spiral notebooks out of the shopping bag. "They have to do with the business he did with Mr. Gattino. Dominic said if something bad happened to him, this would be an insurance policy for my old age. I think maybe you would be willing to pay me for these books?" The woman passed a steno-style notebook to the columnist.

He flipped through it. Neatly printed inside was a record of bets collected from a clientele that included Johnny Longo. Then she presented a bombshell. A file folder containing photocopies of five years of checks from Gattino to Dom Conte.

"Don't go away, Mrs. Conte," he said, the excitement showing in his voice. "I'll be right back."

Rushing into Bloom's office, Bob interrupted a conversation between the managing editor and the city editor.

"Can't you say 'excuse me' or something like that?" the city editor snapped.

"Boss, I need some money," he said, ignoring the city editor.

It wasn't easy to scrape up $5,000 for a down payment just to examine at length Mrs. Conte's documents. The publisher was out of town, and Bloom had to beg the business manager to cut such a sizable check. In the end, Mrs. Conte had a check while Bloom and Casey had a bag full of records.

After an examination of the contents with attorney Walden, it was decided that the most prudent course of action was for Bob to write a column hinting at the existence of damning evidence. That, they decided, might be enough to panic Gattino.

"Have you gentlemen considered turning this information over to the police?" the attorney asked.

"Not after I spent five Gs for it," asserted Larry. "Bob, be damn careful the way you go after Gattino."

"Thanks, boss, I appreciate your concern for my health. I really don't think Gattino will send a hit man after my ass."

"Not your health, Bob. Our asses are on the line on this one. I don't want us defending a libel suit."

Walden nodded in agreement.

#

Bob Casey's Working Press:
Conte's notes point to mob don

MIAMI—*Slain former Miami rogue cop Dominic Conte left records connecting him with the Mafia's illegal sports gambling stranglehold on Florida.*

I have obtained documents that finger the Mafia's gambling don—records kept by Conte before his death last month in a seedy Miami motel room.

Conte allegedly was the bookmaker who tried to blackmail Miami Sharks quarterback Johnny Longo to collect illegal sports bets totaling an estimated $2.5 million.

Apparently, the bookie handling Longo's big wagers was the slain mobster Augie "Lucky" Syracusa.

Police theorize that Syracusa was gunned down because he strayed from his Mafia speciality in the construction business to freelancing in booking gambling action.

Conte's records connect him with Sal "The Saw" Gattino of nearby Hollywood. Gattino reportedly is the illegal sports gambling don for New York's Lorenzo family.

More shocking is the material from an anonymous source which has been furnished to this columnist. This links

Gattino to the bombing of the Sharks charter jet November 28.

One can only wonder why Special Agent Morris Meeker and his keystone FBI pals haven't pursued this avenue. Probably too busy testing the offerings of South Florida coffee and doughnut shops.

In the calls, faxes, and e-mail I have received from you readers, many of you are wondering why I keep harping on illegal gambling. Some of you think that sports gambling is harmless recreation.

Just ask victims' kin like Martha Longo about how harmless gambling addiction is.

Maybe Meeker should ask some of the families of victims of the Sharks jet bombing how they'll feel if Gattino and the Mafia are responsible for that tragedy in the Everglades.

Gattino and his Black Hand pals can be renamed the Red Hand because of the blood of at least 105 victims aboard the downed Sun Airlines DC-10.

What about our esteemed IFL commissioner, Pete Wilson? The commish and the league act as if there was no team tragedy. Wilson keeps saying, "The games must go on."

Already Las Vegas oddsmakers are posting a morning line for the World Bowl.

Those who bet money with the Mafia on pro football are as much to blame for the death of the Sharks as the bomber himself.

Meanwhile, I have evidence that could put Gattino and his henchmen on Raiford's death row.

#

Casey's column triggered quick reactions.

"What is it with this yellow journalism? If that hot shit columnist is withholding evidence in a capital crime case, he's going to find his sorry anti-FBI ass in jail. This Casey sounds like some mouthpiece for a right-wing militia group."—Morris Meeker.

"Casey's just a plain, old-fashioned muckraker, Morris. His goal in life is to raise hell and sell newspapers. Do you think the Mafia blew up that plane?"—Capt. Dick Norton.

"What's this 'coffee and doughnuts' line? That's for us city cops, not the fucking Feds in shiny shoes."—Maj. Leroy Hess.

"Goddamned, fucking, Mick cocksucker! I'd like to cut off his balls and stuff them in his big mouth!"—Sal Gattino.

"What does he mean, the Mafia blew up my plane? It was the goddamned Machinists Union!"—Bruce "Bud" Westinghouse.

"What shit! Doesn't Casey know it was Westinghouse who blew up that DC-10 to get the insurance money?"—Mike Kelly.

"I'm sick and tired of that yellow journalist taking cheap shots at me and the league. Is there some way we can deny Casey accreditation to IFL events?"—Commissioner Pete Wilson.

"Bless you, my son. You seem determined to stir up a hornets' nest."—Father O'Malley.

"Five thousand dollars? You gave $5,000 to some old bag lady, Larry? For that anti-Italian piece by Casey? People want to gamble. I think Casey is wasting our valuable space with such juvenile tirades. Did Walden approve this column?"—Publisher Jack Patterson.

"That's the way to raise hell and sell newspapers, lads. Too bad that thick son-in-law of mine doesn't understand the newspaper business. I wonder why I keep him on as a publisher."—Kangaroo News Ltd. CEO Andy Lyon.

#

Meeker was upset by the constant cheap shots at the FBI. But the special agent didn't hesitate. He knew he was risking a Fourth Amendment fight, and common sense told him you don't get in a pissing contest with folks who buy ink by the barrel.

Nevertheless, Meeker called Bloom and asked for the materials that Casey had in his possession. As expected, the managing editor refused. Meeker was savvy enough to hold off on any rash action such as raiding the *Miami P.M.* editorial offices and seizing Casey's notes or any material relevant to the bombing. *I'll bide my time and wait for a decision from Washington.*

Meeker told Dick that he really didn't believe that it was a Mafia job. "If don Gattino wanted to rub out Longo," Meeker said, "there are plenty of traditional mob ways to accomplish that. Blowing up a commercial jet isn't one of them, because that's a federal crime. Our field agents cleared Gattino, because Longo's debt had been run up to the renegade Syracusa. Maybe Gattino had Syracusa terminated for his misdeeds, but Longo appeared to be too high a profile for the gangsters to risk a public execution."

Regardless of what he believed, Meeker still wanted to find out what Casey knew. *No sense risking a major incident now.* Maybe the columnist would go public with the facts. Newspapers wanted to be first with the news. Law enforcement preferred to operate with the protection of the "ongoing investigation" clause in Florida's Sunshine Law.

Meanwhile, Meeker prodded a team of agents to keep up on his theory that maybe it was an act of sabotage by Kelly or some disgruntled union strikers.

#

Steve Rubin ignored the advice of his mother and filed a suit challenging his late father's will that gave Bunny ownership of the Sharks. He had flat-out rejected his stepmother's offer to be a club vice president.

"Why should I take scraps?" he argued. "It was my father's intention that I would be the team owner, not that Irish gold-digger he married after dumping my mother. My dad's intention was one thing, but because he was consumed with avoiding the so-called death tax that would have probably cost his family the team, he made his wife co-owner. My dad strongly believed that his wife was a bimbo who would be happy to be a figurehead owner while his son ran the franchise."

Young Rubin hired a flamboyant Miami attorney, Ellis Markowitz, to handle the suit. Markowitz took the case, even though he realized that it was without merit. He liked the media attention. Perhaps Mrs. Rubin would be willing to make a generous out-of-court settlement to avoid airing her dirty Irish laundry in the media. Regardless, he knew that the kid had enough money to pay his legal fees, so it was a win-win situation.

Markowitz had a brilliant mind. He kept telling himself so. He was so obnoxious and fiercely argumentative that he would have terrorized a pit of king cobras.

#

Father O'Malley didn't even have second thoughts about having dinner with Sal and Maria Gattino at their modest Hollywood ranch home. Both had been parishioners long before his assignment at St. Vincent's. They were generous with their financial support of the local parish. Maria was active as a volunteer and very popular at events at which she cooked.

The priest was aware that this was no ordinary Italian family residing in this modest neighborhood. Other parishioners who lived in this neighborhood had told—no *boasted*—that they lived in the safest place in Hollywood. Police statistics would support that there had not been one reported crime there since the Gattinos moved in 12 years before. That didn't surprise the cops. No burglar, car thief, or such would take the risk of striking in the neighborhood of a Mafia don.

In fact, O'Malley noted that the Gattinos didn't have an alarm system for their house, and they even left the keys in their two cars.

A parishioner had told the priest that two years earlier, a teenager had ripped off Mrs. Gattino's Oldsmobile and took it to a Miami chop shop. Word of the theft had circulated through the underground faster than cyberspace. When the unfortunate teen arrived, the chop shop operators recognized Mrs. Gattino's car.

The car was returned that afternoon with a full tank of gas and a complete detail job. The teen was returned to his Hollywood home in a plastic garbage bag. The body had been cut up neatly with a buzzsaw.

Mrs. Gattino didn't even know that her car had been missing.

Father O'Malley didn't believe all those bad stories about the Mafia. He remembered last year when drug dealers were hustling students at St. Vincent's School, and the Miami Shores cops couldn't solve the problem. Oh, it wasn't that they didn't try. They simply lacked the manpower to rid the neighborhood of the drug pushers.

O'Malley knew that Gattino had the power, but he wasn't about to confront Gattino with, "Oh, Don Gattino, could you and your Mafia pals help solve a problem at our church school?"

Instead, the priest described his problem to Maria, and she told her husband, and presto! The drug dealers vanished into thin air—or as Major Hess would observe, "Under thin water in the Everglades."

The meal was Italian.

"The sauce is magnificent, Maria," said O'Malley. "How do you do it?"

Mrs. Gattino blushed slightly. "When my mother taught me and my sister how to cook for the family, she assumed we'd do it as she did—from memory. It works for most of Mama's Old-world delicacies, but there are times when I lose my way and have to pick up the phone and call my sister Josephine in Brooklyn.

"'What if I use tomato puree for the sauce instead of paste?' I ask her. 'Puree works fine,' she says. Turns out she has been using puree for years as the main ingredient in her Sunday pasta sauce."

Gattino sipped from a glass of red Chianti. "Mama, tell Padre O'Malley about my favorite 'banata.' It's a Sicilian specialty."

Again, Maria blushed slightly. She felt a warm glow throughout her body when she received public praise from her husband. "Si, Padre, think of a spinach pizza pie flipped over like a calzone. I sauté each vegetable in olive oil, arrange neatly on the flattened dough, add cheese, cover with dough, and bathe the outside with egg whites and sesame seeds."

Maria explained that she had learned the recipes at her mother's hearth as a young girl in the village of Campobello di Licata in Sicily, an island at the tip of the Italian boot.

It was a pleasant evening of mostly small talk, and the food and wine both warmed and relaxed the parish priest. He had learned the hard way over the years to stay out of political discussions and such while visiting with parishioners.

It was Maria who brought up the subject of Casey bashing her husband. "What sort of Catholic is this Casey, Padre? Sal and I met him last summer in Germany. He and that nice girl, Suzy. But how come this Casey writes so many bad things about my husband? Sal is a good husband, father, and grandfather. He goes to Mass every Sunday. Sal does famiglia business, but he doesn't blow up airplanes. He helps people who want to bet on sports events. Is that such a crime? We have bingo at St. Vincent's. Florida has a state lottery. You can bet on horses, dogs, and jai-ali in this state, but the liberal press makes a big deal about betting on football."

The don wanted to silence his wife, but he felt good that she was at least defending him for doing the family business. He laughed inside to see the priest squirm when she mentioned church bingo.

"Maria, you make several good points," said Father O'Malley after he drained his wineglass, which was quickly refilled by the don. "Mr. Casey is a friend of mine. We do have different views on matters such as gambling. But I would like to say, as a man of the cloth, that the difference is between legal and illegal gambling."

"But that is too, too simplistic. Why is it okay to bet at an off-track horse parlor in New York, but it is a crime to bet with a bookmaker? Would Johnny Longo have been any better if he had lost all of his money betting on legal events? I think not."

The don interrupted. "Padre. . ." he said softly. "First, my famiglia had nothing to do with Longo's problems. We do not seek to hurt the famiglia business with scandal.

"Second, if our famiglia didn't handle certain action, someone else would—including the church or the state. True, gambling is an addiction, but unlike big tobacco, we didn't get them addicted."

Father O'Malley nodded in agreement. He didn't like to think it, but he knew the old don was right. So he diplomatically changed the subject and asked Maria, "Ah, now what kind of wonderful surprise do we have for dessert?"

CHAPTER 23

"Let the greater part of the news thou harvest be the least part of what thou believest."

Quarters

MORRIS MEEKER POURED Dick Norton a fresh paper cup of coffee, handed it to him, and patted him on the back in a gesture of camaraderie. During the investigation, the FBI special agent and the chief pilot/airline investigator had become friends.

Dick had just finished reading an FBI report concerning a German financial group that was seeking to take over Sun Airlines. Under a deal with Sun Airlines, vice president John Strachan was courting the German carrier Lufthansa to buy a 25% interest in Sun Air while the Bavarian National Bank would create a dummy holding company to obtain even more Sun Air stock.

"Hey, Morris, it's against U.S. law for foreign interests to control one of our carriers," Dick said. "You claim that Strachan would replace Westinghouse because Strachan would buy Airbus equipment and Lufthansa would have a computer sharing code. . ."

"Look, Dick, I know those Huns are trying to take over your airline," said Meeker as he returned to his desk chair. "We will pass our intelligence on to the FAA and the Justice Department. But our mission is to get the SOBs who blew up that DC-10. Right now, I want to solve a mass murder case."

"Do you think the Germans could be responsible?" Dick didn't believe that, but it sounded better to him than the striking airline machinists.

"We can't rule anyone out at this point except Bunny Rubin," Meeker said.

#

Larry Bloom had taken only his first sip of coffee when the phone rang. He had to hunt for it. It was underneath a pile of papers. When he found the receiver and answered the call, it was Jack Patterson.

"Larry, Casey's crusade—if that is the right word—about gambling has me concerned."

"How's that, Jack?"

"Our ad director says he is getting heat from the area parimutuel establishments. You know, Larry, they are big advertisers. . ."

"Why should that concern them?" interrupted the ME. "Casey's bitch is against the illegal sports betting. You know, the kind practiced by the Mafia."

"Now, Larry, that M-word is another problem. Several Italian-American organizations are complaining that we are giving them a bad name. They think that Casey, being Irish, is biased against Italians. Can't we tone it down a little? Instead of 'Mafia,' couldn't we refer to it as the mob or organized crime? I even had a call from the director of the United Way, who is concerned about us picking on Mr. Gattino. Seems he's a good supporter of local charities."

Larry listened in polite silence. After checking his watch and allowing the publisher to vent for five minutes, he said, "I get your point, Jack. You'd like us to be politically correct. I had several German-American groups in here the other day, too. They were complaining about us mentioning the Nazis. . ."

Things were back to normal in the *Miami P.M.* editorial offices.

#

Investigator Carlos Baptiste drove to Miami Beach to visit Miguel Medina at the La Stelle restaurant. It was a touchy assignment, since the Miami P.D. lacked authority on the Beach. He knew the Beach cops would be more than pissed if they found that Baptiste had not requested their help.

How could Baptiste get the information?

Both capers took place outside of the Miami P.D. jurisdiction. The Longo case was officially closed. Why was the major so hot to find out if the hit man in both capers was a Mafia employee?

It was not that his unit lacked work. Anyhow, it was kind of fun to be playing this cloak and dagger stuff. *Being a detective is really very boring. Only on TV and in the movies can we shoot wise guys, romance the broads, and break major cases with fantastic police work.*

"I am a clerk with a badge and a gun," Baptiste kept telling his family members. "I'm not a Dirty Harry. I have never fired my gun except on the police range. I check out and follow up on cases that are reported by the uniformed cops on road patrol. The rest of the cases I get from snitches."

The front door to the restaurant was open. Baptiste walked in with a fish market salesman. The investigator could now tell his wife, Carmen, that he had been inside La Stelle.

He waited his turn to see the maitre d', who was giving the fish guy an audience. He glanced at a menu for amusement. *I'd have to take out a second mortgage to take Carmen here for dinner.*

Finally, the fish salesman left.

"Mr. Medina?"

"That's me, señor. How can I be of service to you today?"

"I'm police investigator Baptiste," he said with a quick flick of his gold badge, hoping the man wouldn't recognize it as different from the Miami Beach police badge.

Medina smiled but said nothing.

"I've been assigned to do a follow-up on that shooting incident here. I understand that you gave the Beach. . .er, us a statement with the description of the perpetrator."

"That's right, señor. Have you caught the bad guy?"

"Would you mind giving me his description again?"

"Why, Officer?"

"Oh, our other officers might not have copied everything down. It's just routine." Baptiste pulled out a small spiral notebook. In it, he had a copy of the description that had been released by the Miami Beach police at the time of the shooting.

Medina didn't hesitate. He gave a similar description, but there were some red flags raised that made the investigator suspicious. So he pressed on, not in a threatening, third-degree manner, but in a cordial and low-keyed style like a patron asking what kind of soup was on the menu.

Then he shocked Medina and put him on the defensive.

"Why did you lie to the police? There was no Latin-type druggie. You just made that up. Why? Why are you covering up for a cold-blooded murderer?"

"How dare you!" He uttered a righteous protest. "Who is your superior? I'm going to—"

"You aren't going to do a damned thing, mister. I've already talked to your valet parking guy from that night." Baptiste had not interviewed the valet parkers. It was just a long shot, and the risk was about to pay off. "If you tell the truth now," the detective said as he softened his appeal, "then there won't be any problems. If you force me to continue to interview. . ."

"Okay, okay," Medina conceded. "I was scared he'd come back for me if I talked. He was a well-dressed Italian. He carried a violin case. He had good taste in wine. That's why I went to the wine cellar. Anyhow, the ones he shot were nothing but a bunch of hoods. So what's the big deal?"

"The big deal, Mr. Medina, is that it is still against the law in Florida to murder anyone—even no-good hoods. Have a nice day."

As he reached the sidewalk, he almost ran into a uniformed Miami Beach traffic officer who was about to write a ticket on

Baptiste's unmarked Ford Crown Victoria parked in a 15-minute delivery zone.

"Excuse me, Officer, but that's my car."

"Good. I'm about to write you a ticket for illegal parking."

Baptiste displayed his gold badge.

"What's a Miami dick doing in this neighborhood?"

"I was checking out the menu at La Stelle," he said, feigning a grin. "It's our anniversary, and the wife wanted something special, so. . ."

The traffic officer smiled and put away his ticket book.

"It's a little rich for our blood," the detective said.

"No problem. If you want to take the missus to La Stelle, I can get you a deal. Professional courtesy, you know. I work details at this joint. Since the shooting, the owner loves cops. Know what I mean?"

Baptiste nodded.

When Baptiste reported back to Hess, the major yelled, "Bingo!"

"Okay, so we know the same hit man is responsible for both capers on the Beach and in Lauderdale," said the detective. "They're still not our cases."

"Wrong, amigo," said Leroy. "I lay you 10-1 that the hit on the hospital was not ordered on the drug dealers, but on Longo. It appears to me that the Mafia wanted Longo dead and maybe for more reasons than the small fortune he owed them."

"But who is the hit man?"

"Well, amigo, I don't think there are many hit men with an MO of a submachine gun. That's the kind of guy you'd find in a late-night TV movie. When we find him, I'll wager he leads us straight to Don Gattino's front door."

Baptiste was a bit confused. "Okay, Major. So what's this intelligence going to do for us? The two shootings aren't in our jurisdiction. You gonna pass the intelligence on to the Beach and Lauderdale P.D.s?"

Hess started to laugh uncontrollably.

"What's so funny, sir?"

"If we pass this on through channels, there will be some pissed-off cops in both Miami Beach and Fort Lauderdale."

"Why's that, Major?"

"Amigo, we all have ego problems. How do we explain that you were playing detective in their back yard without a major incident?"

"So we do nothing, Major?"

Leroy shook his head. "Wrong. We get the intelligence to them by a different messenger. Like your snitch. You know, the one the Beach cops are holding on a minor B&E."

"You mean Jesus Ortega?"

"Yes, I mean him. You visit him in jail and provide him with this intelligence. He gives it to the Beach cops as a deal. He beats the rap, but he owes you. Then you're back in business. The Beach cops save face by thinking that good old-fashioned police work led them to the Mafia hit man, justice is served, and everybody's happy."

"What about the Lauderdale cops?" asked Batista. "I haven't got a snitch being held in Broward."

"Don't get greedy, amigo. I'll check with our other units. There's bound to be a deal that'll benefit us and them."

The phone rang. Leroy picked it up.

"Major Hess, I'm Officer Cathy Custer with the Plantation police. Recently I was transferred to undercover work involving narcotics. I was going over some old paperwork, and I came across a request from your department for any information on drug dealers who might be involved in the football team crash."

"Yes, Officer Custer. Go on."

"Right. I made a routine traffic stop a while back, and for some reason I made some intelligence notes. The driver I stopped was named T.J. Lewis. He's a BM with a Miami 10-20. He said he was headed to visit Muhammad Johnson. . .you know, the pro football player."

"So?" The major was losing interest. "You stopped a black man driving a car with Dade County plates. It was night in Plantation, and he fit your department's profile. Right?"

Custer was a bit embarrassed, but she pushed on. "Well, sir, our department does have its profiles. I'm sure yours does, too. Anyway, I remember reading a story about the priest who survived the Sharks' crash being interviewed in a newspaper. He said Johnson gave him the initials of a drug dealer—"

"We know all that, Officer," interrupted the major. "A lot of people are known by their initials. Some happen to be drug dealers."

"He was driving a current model Mercedes roadster. You know, the kind with the $125,000 sticker. He held a title, not a lien."

"So? Do only white folks drive expensive imports in Plantation?"

Custer ignored the major's racial dig. "I ran a check on him. His only source of income is $38,000 annually as a mechanic for Sun Airlines. He has some juvenile arrests, but no convictions. All were drug related."

The major's attitude changed abruptly. "T.J. Lewis, you say?" Leroy quickly jotted down the information on a legal pad at his desk. "I appreciate your call, Officer Custer. It just might be very important."

#

Once again, Buffy Zei came up with a lead story that attracted a lot of attention. Cortez, Lewis, and Youngblood read the column with great interest and concern.

MIAMI GATEWAY FOR HEROIN VIA FLYING "MULES"
by Buffy Zei, Miami P.M. Reporter

MIAMI—Remember heroin? The deadly drug is making a dramatic comeback, thanks to Colombian drug lords who are increasing purity by 15 times and drastically undercutting the prices of Southeast Asian heroin.

The heroin gateway to the United States is Miami International Airport.

To get the drugs into this country, the drug lords employ "mules," the term for airline passengers who smuggle drugs. The mules are often young couples who are struggling to capture the American dream of owning their own home and living in the suburbs.

"The cartels will use a pregnant woman with two kids, no husband, and a mortgage payment," U.S. Drug Enforcement Administration agent Steve Edwards said. "The mules swallow dozens of condoms filled with heroin. They train themselves by swallowing grapes in a condom. They place it in the back of their throat and work it down. They use some chloraseptic to numb the throat." Mules risk death from overdosing if the condoms break, or long prison terms if they're caught as drug smugglers.

The drug lords show no mercy when they find they have been cheated or that someone has become a government informant.

Edwards said it is common practice in Colombia for drug lords to take revenge by "killing someone's entire family, including the pets. They then blow up the house."

Edwards, who is commander of the DEA office in the Colombian capital of Bogotá, reportedly has a $20 million bounty on his head.

"That's literally speaking," said Edwards. "One drug lord wants my head in a basket, and he's willing to pay the executioner $20 million."

Edwards has survived several assassination attempts.

"We are dealing with the scum of the earth," Edwards said. "One of the mules who escaped detection at MIA last month apparently overdosed when a condom broke because he had a bowel movement. They slit him open to get the other condoms out of his stomach. Then they dumped his body in the Everglades."

Dave Stowers, a U.S. Customs supervisor at MIA, tells of mingling with incoming passengers and looking for signs of smugglers.

> Stowers collared a 27-year-old Orlando woman who was traveling with her four-year-old daughter and a man posing as her husband. They were taken to an interview room, where agents found that the couple had seven pounds of heroin sewn into the linings of several jackets. The seven pounds of heroin would bring about $2.3 million on American streets.
>
> "For this risk, a mule is paid between $5,000 and $10,000," Stowers said. "In this case, the mother lost her child to a state agency and faces a long prison term."
>
> Stowers warns, however, that the use of mules is temporary.
>
> "Eventually, they will seek bigger shipments in cargo by using ships and planes, some of them in commercial carriers."
>
> Last year, passengers at MIA were arrested for carrying 1,248 pounds of heroin, up from 96 pounds five years ago, according to DEA records. A kilo of cocaine wholesales for about $18,000, compared with $90,000 to $120,000 for a kilo of heroin. Southeast Asian heroin costs twice that much.

#

The drug dealers were angered by the story, and some of their associates suggested that it might be better to suspend business for a while until the heat was off. Such suggestions prompted Lewis and Cortez to make a plan of action.

"Too bad that asshole Edwards wasn't on that plane," said Youngblood.

"You know, Jose, I have an idea how to solve our publicity problem."

"Get some of my Colombia pals to buy a Miami newspaper?" Cortez replied as if his companion was making a funny.

"Get real, man," snapped Lewis. "Take the whitey who writes the sports column and is trying to fuck the Mafia up the ass. He thinks they bombed the fuckin' plane."

"So?" asked Cortez.

"So, Jose, why do anything to change Casey's opinion of the

fuckin' wops? Why don't we get him so pissed off at those fuckers that he and his newspaper fuckers forget about us?"

"How we gonna do that, T.J.?"

"Find his wife, gal pal, or even his kid, and snatch 'em."

"You mean, then we tell him to lay off us?"

"No, you dumb spick! We kidnap one and pin it on the wops."

"Yeah, I like that, man," replied Cortez. "But when we let her go won't she rat on us?"

"Let her go?" Lewis said incredulously. "You crazy? She's destined to be dinner for the sharks."

"Those poor, dumb wops won't know what hit 'em," said a laughing Lewis.

CHAPTER 24

"Down to Gehenna or up to the throne,
He travels the fastest who travels alone."

Rudyard Kipling
The Winners

CHRISTMAS AND NEW Year's passed. Media attention and public interest in the tragic Sharks' crash had faded. Bob Casey, however, was determined to avenge Jorge Cunill's death. Suzy and Larry Bloom were concerned that Casey was being consumed by the hunt for the bombers.

World Bowl XXXV took place the last Sunday in January. Bob wasn't looking forward to spending a week in Los Angeles. Not with the plane disaster probe continuing. Not with the goods that could bring down Gattino and his Mafia gambling empire. Not with spending a week away from Suzy.

But this was business, and the World Bowl was pro football's biggest Sunday. Plus, Kangaroo News Ltd. had designated Casey as their lead columnist throughout its newspaper empire during the big game and the week leading up to it.

The World Bowl foes were Buffalo and Dallas.

Bob knew that it was a bittersweet World Bowl, considering that in public the IFL was still mourning the Sharks' tragedy. Behind the scenes, however, he knew that the other owners were still fighting to protect their players from being claimed by the Sharks. Many of the good ol' boys had once considered Bunny Rubin a bimbo. Now they had to treat her as an equal.

Some of the fans and the media believed that Miami should be in the championship game instead of Buffalo. Bob had angered many readers by responding, "It would be unfair to the Snowmen if they had to play Miami a second time, since they already beat them once."

The intrigue was lost on most of the crazed pro football fans who were willing to pay scalper prices for the $500 tickets, Bob told Suzy over the phone from the LAX Marriott.

"Unlike Florida, California does not have a scalping law," Bob said. "Would you believe, Sky Princess, that Wilson wanted to hike the game ticket price to an even $1,000? While his league staff realized that most people would pay the grand, they advised the commissioner against such a move. It would have showed just how greedy the IFL is. In truth, the commish probably realized that the IFL Players Association would demand an even bigger share of the pie."

A media horde of 2,000 had been accredited by the IFL for the week. For Casey, his Kangaroo News syndication meant that he was competing against the international media.

It would also be a heavy week for Mafia bookie operations throughout the world. In Miami, Gattino's earlier concern that the lack of a local team in the World Bowl would result in a decrease of action was proving false. Even with Dallas going off an 18-point favorite, bettors in South Florida were overwhelming their neighborhood bookies and jamming the long distance lines to Las Vegas as well as out-of-country betting dens.

#

Bob Casey's Working Press:
World Bowl suckers: They bet on it

LOS ANGELES—The World Bowl always brings out the suckers in mass.

But when you have a morning line mismatch between the Buffalo Snowmen and the Dallas Texans like today, it's a field day for the Mafia bookmakers throughout the land.

When you have a team favored by a big point spread, it can stir all kinds of ideas among the high rollers. These are the Mafia's kind of people. I'm certain that in South Florida, Don Sal "The Saw" Gattino is drooling today.

Remember that report last year that one guy had won a million-dollar bet on the World Bowl?

Before you shed tears for the bookie that handled that action, I have learned from an extremely reliable source that one guy bet a million and won. This meant that the bookie made only $280,000 on the game.

Consider this week that between $60 million and $70 million will be bet legally in Nevada. But when we talk about illegal wagering—from office pools to the mob—we're talking about as much as $10 billion.

There is a rumor making the rounds here in Miami that hints that the odds favoring the Texans could rise to 21 points before the kickoff in Heineken Beer Stadium (formerly known as the Rose Bowl).

I have also learned that there is a group here that is willing to put down $550,000 to win $500,000.

According to gambling sources, the history of the World Bowl proves that money shows 'on' the favorite early in the week, and money shows 'on' the underdog late in the week.

Surprisingly, a growing cash cow for Vegas and the Mafia is the World Bowl intermission.

"People don't realize how much is bet at halftime," says a spokesman for the Nevada Sports Palace. "You're betting on a game that is 0-0, and the new line is based strictly on the score for the third and fourth quarters. It's also based on how the first two quarters went, and it usually reflects the pregame line.

"For example, let's say that the Texans are ahead 28-14 at halftime. The new line for the second half might favor the Texans by six points or thereabouts. The reason you get plenty of halftime action by high rollers is that they've seen enough to have an opinion, and depending on the situation, they either want to get further ahead or get even."

Proposition bets—who wins the toss, who scores the first touchdown, who kicks the first field goal—have proven to be another bonanza for bookmakers.

"The only time bookmakers took a beating on a proposition bet was five years ago when Miami played the Philadelphia Bells in Los Angeles," said the spokesman. "The line on players scoring touchdowns had offensive tackle Norm Amundsen listed at 12 to 1. The late coach Don Sherman had used Amundsen in the backfield several times on short and goal situations, and the six-foot-three, 325-pound lineman had scored twice during the regular season.

"By game time, the odds on Amundsen had dropped to 2 to 1. He scored late in the game. And the bookies lost big on that proposition."

It is rare for the Mafia or Vegas to take a World Bowl betting bath. The biggest took place back in World Bowl XXIII. when New York beat Baltimore 35-31.

The New Yorkers opened a 2 1/2-point favorite, and the line went all the way to 4 1/2. There was a lot of big money on the New Yorkers early in the game, bet by the same guys who bet the Crab Cakes when the line went up to 4 1/2.

They won both ways, and major books took a licking. But that's the only time it's ever happened. For both the Mafia and Vegas those are pretty good odds.

> *Right, Don Sal Gattino? I hope the blood on your hands for the Sharks plane tragedy doesn't soil any of your greenbacks in the counting room.*

\#

Bob wondered if he was becoming jaded about getting paid to spend a week in Southern California just to write a daily column about what he considered the "Bore Bowl" of sports.

Am I getting old, tired, and bored with this job? Maybe I should consider writing a general column. Or is it that I really don't like spending a week away from Suzy? More likely, it's not being back in Miami, riding shotgun on the investigation. I owe it to Jorge to solve that case.

Bob couldn't walk through the hotel lobby without someone asking if he had World Bowl tickets to sell. "Save your money," he'd reply. "Take that $1,500 or $2,000 and buy a giant TV with it. You'll see the game better and in more comfort. And you'll still have that big sucker to entertain you for the rest of the year."

\#

All the team front office types were on hand, including the Sharks' Bunny Rubin, Jack Cabot, and Jim Moses. Bunny and Jack no longer hid their feelings. Bob noted them holding hands and smooching in public.

As much as Bob loathed Bunny, even he was forced to admit that she really wasn't the bimbo he had believed her to be. Glowing reports about B.R., as Sharks employees now referred to her, were escaping the club's front office. Her employees actually liked her. She appeared to be letting Cabot handle all the football business. Besides, he was very talented in scouting and evaluating personnel.

Bob had grown tired of repeating stories about the crash to fellow writers. Many writers were fascinated, and the columnist had become a news item himself.

Sunday proved a success for all associated with the International Football League and its World Bowl. There were 101,232 fans in the stands in Pasadena, and a 73 share for the HOP Network with an estimated 142 million viewers. A TV commercial spot of 30 seconds cost a cool $1 million.

The winning team's players would receive $52,000 each, their opponents $38,500. World Bowl bettors placed $79 million in legal wagers, and a whopping $1 billion illegally.

Gattino and his fellow Mafia gambling associates loved the World Bowl because an estimated $90 million would be bet on the game through their connections.

#

"Despite the Longo scandal, high-profile drug capers, and a rudderless strategy under a gutless commissioner, the International Football League has remained the king of sports," Bob told Suzy over the phone the night of the game.

"Gee, I thought baseball was our national pastime, Bobby. I mean, my Dad lives and dies for his beloved Philadelphia Phillies."

"Baseball was once king, Sky Princess. Not anymore. Television has made football king. Sports is such a draw that the networks will pay outlandish prices to telecast the games."

#

Bob Casey's Working Press:
Just a typical Bore Bowl
PASADENA, Calif.—Coach Lou Berger of the Buffalo Snowmen swallowed hard and tried to put up a brave front after his team's defeat by the Dallas Texans in Sunday's World Bowl XXXVIII. He was noticeably despondent after the 37-20 trashing.

If the Miami Sharks had escaped the tragedy in the Florida Everglades three months ago, they might have had a chance to redeem themselves for their memorable game in Dallas on Thanksgiving Day.

There are no guarantees that if the Sharks had been saved from that evil bomber, they would have beaten the Snowmen in Buffalo in December. But if they had, would they have been a tougher competitor here Sunday afternoon?

The big disappointment, I'm sure, for many Dallas backers was that their team didn't cover the spread which was 18 and ½ points at kickoff. The Snowmen lost only by a mere 17 points.

Pardon me, suckers, for suggesting that the Mafia—there I go again using that bad word—might have found it easier to "move the line" on the Bore Bowl than to fix it.

I have learned from a reliable source that one group used a combination of legal betting in Las Vegas and illegal betting with bookies to influence lines and catch middles. That practice led to a raid last December by Miami vice cops.

The Miami vice cops charge that more than 50 sports bettors in Las Vegas were so linked to betting rooms in Miami that they shared proceeds from bets in a $400 million betting ring, which was allegedly the brainchild of Don Salvatore Gattino of nearby Hollywood, Fla. Nearly $6 million in cash was seized at eight Las Vegas casinos from accounts operated by the bettors.

"Local gambling operations in South Florida are so intertwined with those in Las Vegas that they are part of the same network," says Maj. Leroy Hess of the Miami police. "We don't know how far the network extends."

Two weeks ago, Hess raided nine homes and one wire room in Miami. He arrested 22 suspects, whom he alleges raked in $150 million a year in bets for the Mafia.

"What I want the citizens to realize is that when they bet $100 with these bookies, that $100 will be used to sell drugs in the neighborhood, to purchase weapons that may kill cops, and to fund loan-sharking activities."

> *Don't expect Hess to be getting a fat white envelope with thanks from Don Gattino.*

\#

Back in Hollywood, Gattino was in a rage. He had to go for a walk outside his home. *Fuckin' Mick! Every one of his columns in that toilet paper is ripping me. I've had it! I'm gonna have to teach that motherfucker a lesson.*

The don wanted to spend his energy on a new project: offshore gambling. His sources estimated that last year, Americans bet $65 billion. As much as 95% of that was bet illegally.

That was why he was enterprising offshore books, claiming that they were not subject to U.S. law. Using a toll-free number and accepting credit cards, cyberspace gambling would be the next major enterprise for the Mafia.

The fuckin' Feds have yet to take an official stand on offshore gambling.

Gattino smiled when he thought of how futile it would be for the G-men to enforce such a law. He knew that plenty of action was being phoned from the States to the United Kingdom, where sports gambling was legal.

Gattino had outlined the advantages to the godfather.

"We make every bettor open an account of at least a grand," he said. "We have no credit and no welshers to hunt down. We also get a bigger audience, thanks to computers and telephones."

The godfather knew that the old don was on the right track. "They say you can't teach an old don new tricks," he said with a chuckle. "You prove those suckers wrong, Sal."

Gattino wondered if offshore betting would make the local neighborhood bookie as obsolete as telephone operators. *Frankly, I don't give a fuck about nostalgia.*

"Local books too often take only certain action such as football or basketball, so as not to get burned by the money lines in baseball and hockey," he had informed the godfather. "And they avoid calls, you know, if some sucker wants to make a late big bet. We can offer every sport, including tennis, golf, and auto racing."

The godfather said he would give Gattino the green light as soon as the Casey/Longo matter was resolved.

"You must understand, Sal, that some fuckers believe we bombed that plane. Until it's proven otherwise, our business interests are taking a hit."

#

The Mafia controlled the Transportation Employees of America Union. President Tony Tenuto had handpicked Mike Kelly to lead the TEAU local in Miami, not because Kelly was a crook, but because he was basically honest. Tenuto knew that Kelly's honesty and ignorance of the Mafia's control over the organization was a big plus.

"The Feds can't bag Kelly because he's clean," Tenuto told the godfather. "So we let him do his labor thing. Meanwhile, our inside guys are looting baggage, smuggling, bookmaking, and doing some other profitable stuff. Kelly is blind to all of this, because he has such a big hard-on for what he believes is the real enemy—the airline's management."

The TEAU president and Chicago boss, Abe Goldman, enjoyed their inside joke about the possibility some day of management being a front for the Mafia, too. "How do you think Kelly would feel if he knew he was serving the same master as he was fighting?"

Goldman was also concerned by the drug smuggling operations of some TEAU airlines' members. The Mafia was not involved. And Goldman did not want to get involved, because drug capers attracted too many law enforcement agencies.

"You know, once the Feds start sniffing for drugs, they can come up with leads to our real activities," Goldman told Tenuto. "Let the Colombian spicks do the drug shit. We'll stay with legitimate business."

Tenuto and Goldman, however, shared a common fear that Gattino had masterminded the bombing of the Sharks charter to make a statement about gamblers trying to welsh on their debts. After all, they reasoned, Gattino had sought help from Tenuto on such a project, and Tenuto had even had one of his soldiers explore the possibilities with Kelly.

Goldman wondered, too, "What if Kelly decided that blowing up that plane would put the fear of God into Sun Air management? If he did, and it comes out, our very lucrative operations will be fucked. I think, Tony, as a precaution, we should, you know, back off of supporting a takeover. It's something we can explore later. Now, it's kind of a hot potato."

"Abe, you don't really believe that Kelly would bomb a plane?" Tenuto asked, hoping that his involvement in hinting at sabotage would fade away.

"Fuck yes, Tony. Fuck yes. Those machinist yo-yos of yours would kill their own grandmothers if they thought it would further their cause."

#

In Miami, Bubba Youngblood was starting to sweat his part in the bombing. But his fellow drug dealers, T.J. Lewis and Jose Cortez, were unconcerned.

The trio was what Kelly called his "Rainbow Coalition." He needed them in order to unite other workers with the mechanics. Youngblood appealed to the rednecks, Lewis to the blacks, and Cortez to the Hispanics.

The trio served Kelly's purpose, so he turned a blind eye to their extracurricular activities.

"We appreciate what Kelly has done for us," Lewis said. "But that was then, and this is now. We need some shit to stay in business. And this fuckin' strike, you knows, is killing our business."

The strike was turning nasty, and the drug dealers knew that they needed the planes flying to Colombia again.

It was a trickle, only a trickle, but nevertheless non-machinist union workers were crossing picket lines and returning to work. While the strike was costing Sun Airlines millions of dollars a day in lost revenue, it wasn't as devastating as the cost to workers, who lived paycheck to paycheck. The ranks of striking pilots were thinning, too. Worse, industry solidarity was weakening.

#

"That's because ALPA's fat strike fund was starting to hit the pockets of members with other airlines," Dick explained to Meeker. "Commercial airline captains have a reputation for being very, very conservative with their money."

Veteran aviators, who had initially remained off the job in support of the strikers, started to get antsy about the trickle of new hires coming aboard the fleet.

It was into this complex maze that Meeker's agents entered for facts that might connect Kelly and/or other union machinists to the bombing. Meeker felt strongly that the bombing was an inside job. If so, then why?

"Although your friend, Mr. Casey, would probably disagree," Meeker said, "our agents' methodical probe into the machinists' local and the international TEAU were bearing fruit. It has revealed possible connections with the Mafia and the takeover scheme of Sun Airlines. Proof was still not strong enough to make a case in court, but I feel like a bloodhound who has just smelled the end of the hunt."

Dick gave Meeker a brisk military salute.

"Dick, my friend, it is time to call in the hounds from Justice, DEA, and IRS and turn them loose on our union friends," Meeker told Norton over their morning coffee.

"What about the FAA, Morris?" asked the chief pilot.

Both men laughed.

Dick wasn't convinced that the bombing was a union plot, but he was shocked to learn of the Mafia involvement in the union, as well as the takeover scheme. As a pilot, he had always trusted the ground crews, even though there was a certain animosity between them and cockpit crews.

"You know, Morris, during the war. . ."

"The Second World War?" interrupted the FBI chief.

"No, goddang it! The Vietnam War," said Dick. "We trusted our ground crews with our lives. We had a special camaraderie in the Air Force that wasn't the case in the Army and Marines.

"There wasn't that stiff formality between the ranks. In commercial aviation, too often the cockpit crews have placed themselves on the throne and look down on the ground crews."

Meeker tried not to laugh, but he couldn't help himself. It was good, he thought, to work with a man like Norton who had a good sense of humor. *God only knows, there isn't much to smile about in this bombing case.*

"In reconstructing the aircraft from its wreckage, our lab people hope to give us a connection to the bombers," Meeker said. "It would take people with aviation knowledge as well as access to the aircraft. The connection to your DC-10 cargo door mishap back in Detroit raises a red flag."

"Why, Morris?"

"Because we have found out that one of the mechanics that serviced your DC-10 in Detroit was Mike Kelly," said Meeker.

"Oh, my God! Now I remember. He was the one that forced the cargo door shut back in Detroit."

#

Tuesday morning at 7:30, Leroy paid Bob a surprise call at his condo.

"What the hell do you want at this ungodly hour?" Bob greeted the major. "I am recovering from my World Bowl adventure."

"Is that any way to greet a buddy?" A glance at the columnist, who had only a robe over his bare body, revealed a man in need of a shave and a lot of black coffee. "You awake this morning, Bob?"

"Hardly. I didn't get much sleep last night."

"I can see that. You look like shit. I can understand why. You flew the damn red-eye home."

Bob nodded.

"This isn't exactly a social call, but I thought you'd like to know right away," Leroy said. "And I didn't want to leave it downtown for some smart *Journal* reporter to find." Leroy set down the shopping bag full of documents that Mrs. Conte had given Bob that had triggered his editorial campaign against Gattino. "I had our experts go over this shit. Gattino is right. It's bogus. There isn't one, not one print, belonging to Conte on any of the material. The bank records, well, nothing checks out. Our experts claim that even the older records were printed fresh recently."

"What about Mrs. Conte, Leroy? Why would she give us this stuff?"

"Oh, her?" The major pulled out a mug shot and passed it to Casey. "Is this Mrs. Conte?"

"That's the woman."

"Elizabeth T. Mastroni. Age 52. Lives at 1708 Surfway, Miami Beach. Married. Husband, John R., is the CEO of Southern Trust Bank. Occupation: homemaker/aspiring actress."

"Huh? Actress?"

"Yep. Bobby, old boy, your Mrs. Conte was really Mrs. Mastroni. Seems Mrs. Mastroni had a distinguished career on Broadway. Even did some Shakespeare."

"Oh shit!"

"Yep. You can say that again. That was before she met John boy. But she remained active in local theater groups."

Bob was both angry and fascinated about how he had been duped. "Go on, Leroy."

"She answered a classified ad for an actress to play an elderly Italian mother. It was run by a downtown employment agency. She was told that it was an audition for a small role in a new TV crime series. And they told her that if she could convince you—a friend of the producer—that she was Mrs. Conte, she'd get the gig."

"She did that, all right, Leroy. So how did you find her?"

"I didn't. She came to us. When she found out there was no TV crime series, she became suspicious. She didn't know if it was a practical joke or some kind of scam. We checked out the agency. The manager got the job order by phone with the promise of a fat commission. He was so awed by the promise of future assignments from a TV production company, he failed to check out the caller."

"Wonderful," moaned Bob. "Who would want me to look like such an asshole in print? Was it Gattino pulling a sting? Or was it someone else trying to make Gattino the fall guy?"

"Bob, when we find out who hired the actress, we'll find the aircraft bomber." The major smiled briefly. "We do have some good news."

"Good news?"

"I guess our SIS boys have a hot lead. It came from the Plantation P.D. Their intelligence is leading to drugs, not gambling, as a motive for the bombing. A Plantation officer has given us the ID of a subject, and SIS is checking him out. It may not be anything, but you never can tell."

"Well, you're doing better than the Feds," Bob said.

"If they're in our jurisdiction, we'll get the bastards, I promise you, Bob."

"I pray we do," Bob replied after regaining his composure. "We owe it to Cunill and those other 104. I think daily about Jorge, and I'd want to personally torture those SOBs to death."

"Something will break," Leroy said. "I'm betting it's going to be an inside job."

#

The mayor of Palm Beach was used to special and discreet requests from the rich and famous. So he was happy to handle the paperwork for a marriage license and to perform the ceremony in city hall that made Veronica "Bunny" Rubin the new Mrs. F. John Cabot.

Jack had wanted to wait. It was, after all, less than three months after Sol Rubin had been killed in the plane crash, but Bunny wouldn't wait. He was pleasantly surprised that Bunny didn't want a big, formal wedding. She insisted that she wanted to marry him and get on with the rest of their lives.

Mrs. Jack Cabot. Won't all those Boston WASPs be impressed now? I can't wait to stick my new title up their pompous, old-money asses. No more being mistaken for a JAP or a shanty Irish.

Since he really did love her, he had given in, and here they were in posh Palm Beach. It was a brief ceremony on a sunny morning that was made pleasant by the ocean breeze. Attorney Jim Walden and his wife were the witnesses.

Bunny had earlier received good news from Walden. "Your late husband's kin haven't a prayer of overturning his will." The lawyer explained that there were no loopholes in the will. "Steve Rubin and Markowitz can waste their time and money, but they haven't a prayer. So enjoy your honeymoon."

#

What a week! Thank God for that plane crash. I just love my position as the Sharks' owner. When I get back from my honeymoon, my first act will be to fire that SOB Paul Dungan. Let him shoot off his big mouth. He will be seen as just another disgruntled employee. Also, I've got to get rid of Jack's secretary. She's much too young and foxy for his own good.

Looking in the bedroom mirror, Bunny smiled. She liked what she saw: a woman of wealth and power. The owner of a pro football team worth more than $700 million. She knew she owed it all to the crash.

Jack was attired in a three-button navy blue business suit, and Bunny was awesome in a simple but expensive white dress that fell two inches below her knees. She wore a simple white orchid pinned to her dress. The diamond wedding ring was part of a set that included an engagement ring that had belonged to Jack's late grandmother and had come from the Cabot family treasure chest.

The newlyweds treated the mayor and the Waldens to lunch at the Breakers' Hotel before adjourning to the presidential suite for a week-long honeymoon before next week's IFL owners meeting. To show their sense of humor, they had registered under the names of Jack and Veronica Lodge.

Fuck you, Sol Rubin, wherever you are! May you rot in hell!

"What are you thinking, Bunny?" Jack asked as he looked out on the beach from their honeymoon suite.

"How nice it is to be Mrs. Jack Cabot instead of Mrs. Sol Rubin," she replied. "Now let's make love. I want to wash out the memory of that fat slob."

CHAPTER 25

*"The drama's laws, the drama's patrons give.
For we that live to please, must please to live."*

Samuel Johnson
Prologue

THE FOLLOWING MORNING, Bob met Leroy for breakfast at a pancake house near Miami police headquarters. He wanted to find out if any progress had been made on the follow-up of the black airline worker driving the Mercedes roadster.

"Look, Scoop, I've got two of my best guys working on that," Leroy said. "If Mr. Lewis is dirty, they'll find him. You know, I'm getting more convinced that it was an inside job and not a Mafia hit."

"Come on, Leroy, you don't believe some unhappy airline mechanics would bomb one of their. . ."

Ring! Ring! The sharp, piercing noise resulted in both men reaching for the cell phones on their belts.

"It's mine," said the major, who turned on his portable police radio with a cell phone built in. "Yeah, Carlos. . .You don't say. Maybe this will solve our Q-31. . .right. . .Yes. I'll be right in."

"What's a Q-31?" Bob asked.

"It's our radio signal code for a homicide. Shit, Bob, you should know our codes by now."

"Why doesn't the Miami P.D. join the 21st Century and use a 10-code system? You know, like most law enforcement agencies. Leroy, you know, you work for an electronically challenged police department."

Leroy laughed and tossed him the check for the meal. "Pay it, and you can come to my office for your big story of the day."

"This better be worth the $13.49," Bob said as he glanced at the check en route to the cashier.

"Oh, Scoop. Leave a big tip. I eat breakfast here all the time."

Bob tossed a $20 bill on the table and followed the major out of the restaurant.

The brisk walk to the Miami P.D. and the quick ride up the elevator to the CIS office on the fifth floor took less than 10 minutes. Leroy nodded a couple of times to uniformed officers in the lobby. Bob tried to find out what was happening, but the major just repeated, "You'll see."

Baptiste greeted the major and columnist at the CIS entrance. The investigator was in shirtsleeves that exposed the shoulder holster and the gold investigator's badge clipped on his belt.

"I put her in your office, Major," said the investigator. "Her mouthpiece is with her."

Bob was astonished. It was Martha Longo with Milton Stein, the noted national criminal defense attorney based in Miami.

"Good morning, Mr. Casey," Stein said. "Meaning no disrespect, since I read your column on a regular basis, but I don't think you should be in here. . ."

Martha waved her hand. "Let him stay, Mr. Stein. I think it's important that he hear what I have to say."

"Well, I. . .er," said the attorney, who was caught off guard by his client's wish. "I guess I have no further objections. . .unless, of course, Major Hess has."

Leroy didn't.

"Mrs. Longo has a statement to make, and she is well aware of her rights," Stein said.

Baptiste activated a tape recorder on Hess's desk and signaled for her to begin.

Her manner was composed. She talked in a soft voice and in short sentences. At times, she made gestures with her hands, as if she were making a speech. She impressed the two cops and the newspaperman with her calm demeanor. If she was nervous, she did not display it outwardly. The experienced trio was taken by her presentation of what they would find to be a horror story.

"Gentlemen," she began and looked straight at Hess and then at Casey. "My husband did not kill Conte. I did."

There was a pause as the statement hit Hess, Baptiste, and Casey.

"Please continue, Mrs. Longo," Hess said with a reassuring smile. The major saw no need to ask questions at this time, since the woman was talking freely and with her lawyer present. Baptiste would have probably jumped in here, but he followed his commander's lead and remained silent.

"This is something that has been on my conscience for a long time. I should have come forward at the time, but I. . .I was in a state of shock. No, make that panic. Where should I start?"

"From the beginning, Martha," Stein suggested.

She did.

"I don't remember exactly. I was scared. I felt helpless."

She slowly told the whole story of the incident.

"Then he took the gym bag and flung it at me. I don't know why. Maybe it was the only object nearby. I saw him coming. He was staggering and trying to get a gun out of a holster on his ankle.

"Somehow I got the gun from the bag first. He laughed. He said I didn't have the guts to use the gun. I. . .I started pulling the trigger." Martha Longo's eyes were moist. She had lost some of her composure. "I d-didn't mean to kill him," she stammered softly. "I was afraid. I must have sat on that bed for an hour or more looking at his body and my empty pistol. It was a nightmare. I thought about calling the police, but I remembered my children. Would you believe me? Would the state take my kids? How would it look to hear about their mother in a cheap motel with that. . .that horrible gangster?

"It has been weeks of hell for me, gentlemen. As a Catholic, I have suffered for my sin. My priest urged me to come to you, but. . .when you arrested my husband, I had no choice but to confess."

"Can you tell us, Mrs. Longo, what you did with your gun?" the major asked in a soft, non-threatening voice.

"I flung it into a dumpster at a strip mall. I'm not certain where."

"Thank you, Mrs. Longo." Leroy asked Stein and his client to retire to the waiting room. That was a signal to Bob that the major wasn't about to throw her in a holding cell or book her.

"Do you buy that sob story, Leroy?" Bob asked.

Leroy gave the columnist a dirty look. "I do. Most of the evidence is consistent with her story. Our eyewitness saw a car registered to Johnny Longo leave the scene. The medical examiner's report showed that Conte was legally drunk, had been involved in sex, and did indeed have a wounded penis.

"Most importantly, however, the black panties we found at the scene belong to Mrs. Longo. Tell me, Bob, where would we find a juror in Dade County who would believe she was having an affair with that scumbag?"

Stein furnished the investigators with a statement from the Miami Hospital Emergency Room the night of the incident. She had used a phony name of Mary Klimkiewitz, sure that the hospital would misspell it, and paid cash. The E.R. doctor had noted on the record that it had appeared to be a brutal date rape case, and that the police should be notified. It had been a busy night in the E.R., and the paperwork had fallen through the cracks of the hospital system.

The attorney also provided a copy of the stock sale for $50,000, which included the IRS withholding forms.

"What about the gun?" Bob asked.

"With her statement, we don't need it," Leroy replied.

"Okay, gentlemen, then why did you collar Johnny Longo?" asked Bob.

"None of the evidence ruled Johnny Longo out," Leroy explained. "I figured Conte must have just entertained a gal pal, or more likely a hooker, before Mr. Longo dropped by."

"Shit, this turn of events makes me look like a shmuck," Bob said. "What the fuck will my readers think?"

The two cops laughed.

"Hey, pal," the major said. "We just pulled your balls out of the fire. You will have an exclusive column, and you can credit the Miami P.D. for its great detective work in breaking this case."

"Right," Bob snapped. "She walked in of her own accord after being pushed here by Father O'Malley and the guilt trip of being a good Catholic. . ."

"Hey, Scoop, you tell it like it isn't, and we both look good to the public," the major said. "I'll even buy lunch next time."

Bob knew that Leroy was right. "You guys going to charge Mrs. Longo?"

"We could charge her. . ."

Before Baptiste could finish his sentence, the major cut him off. "With what, Carlos? Leaving her panties at the scene of a brutal rape? Come on, amigo. Conte was a dirty cop. He was a Mafia soldier, and he was blackmailing the woman."

Baptiste started to protest, but changed his mind, knowing that the major was right.

"That lawyer of hers would eat us alive in court," Leroy continued. "I don't believe that even the state's attorney would be dumb enough to let it go that far. I think we should give her a medal for wasting that scumbag. You have to have respect for a wife who was willing to sleep with a creep to protect her husband."

"The sad part, Leroy, is that her asshole hubby doesn't appreciate her," Bob said.

"Oh, he will after reading your tear-jerker of a column, Mr. Casey," Baptiste advised. "It isn't easy to have to eat humble pie, is it? We cops get plenty of that shit for a diet."

Leroy went to the waiting room. "Officially, Mrs. Longo, I cannot condone what you did," the major said. "Unofficially, I think you are one helluva brave lady. We have to turn our investigation over to the state attorney, but we are classifying this as a justifiable homicide. Self-defense."

"And my husband?"

"I'm sending Investigator Baptiste to Fort Lauderdale with the paperwork that will release him from police custody."

Stein glared at the columnist. "And you, Mr. Casey, we'll be seeing you in civil court—"

Mrs. Longo stood up. "Stop it, Mr. Stein," she said in a calm and self-assured voice. "Mr. Casey was wrong in thinking that Johnny was a murderer, but that was my fault. Mr. Casey is right about Johnny's gambling addiction. I hope, Mr. Casey, that you will keep up your crusade against illegal sports gambling to prevent people like my Johnny from getting hooked on. . ." Martha Longo started to sob. "Excuse me, gentlemen, but it's. . .it's been quite an ordeal."

Bob didn't reply to Mrs. Longo at the time. He did it in his column, which accompanied *Miami P.M.*'s lead story about the Conte slaying. The scoop angered editors of the *Miami Morning Journal*, who wanted the Miami police chief to explain why Casey was privy to Mrs. Longo's confession.

"Chief, it was just a matter of Casey being in the right place at the right time," Hess explained.

"Leroy, you're full of shit," replied the chief. "Unofficially I was pleased to see those liberals at the *Journal* get scooped. The bottom line, however, is that we cleared a nasty case involving that embarrassing fuck Conte."

#

Bob Casey's Working Press:
Martha Longo: True love

MIAMI—I was wrong. Johnny Longo, the Miami Sharks' quarterback, is not a murderer.

This is not a murder story. No, this is a love story.

Martha Longo, his brave wife and mother of their three children, was forced to kill a drunken and drug crazed blackmailer, Dom Conte, in order to protect her husband from his Mafia gambling debts.

I listened Thursday morning to Mrs. Longo tell Miami cops of her night of terror in the motel room of disgraced former Miami police lieutenant, Dominic Conte.

It was Conte, a soldier of the Mafia, who was trying to collect on Longo's $2.5 million gambling debt.

This shows how low the Mafia can be, when one of its henchmen blackmails and sexually assaults an innocent mother.

Martha Longo was willing to risk her life to pay off Don Sal Gattino's evil gambling empire, which has trapped her husband in an addiction just as deadly as drugs.

The Mafia, of course, is only part of the problem. You—any one of you who bet even a dollar on a sports event—are partners in crime with the mob.

Every time you bet, think of Martha Longo. Think of her family and what it has endured because of her husband's gambling addiction.

The veteran quarterback remains hospitalized but free of criminal charges in the Conte death. However, he has been sick for a very, very long time. The sickness is compulsive illegal sports gambling.

Thanks to basic, old-fashioned detective work by Maj. Leroy Hess and investigator Carlos Baptiste of Miami's finest, the Conte case is closed.

Now it's time for all those in law enforcement to get serious about cracking down on the Mafia gambling empire before Longo stories become commonplace.

I suggest, too, that Special Agent Morris Meeker and his FBI lackeys get cracking and solve the Sharks' air disaster. I think the trail of death will lead to the Mafia, and the trail starts with gambling victim Longo.

Also, what is the International Football League's policy on players, coaches, and yes, even officials, who get hooked on gambling?

Commissioner Pete Wilson has a policy on drug use, but he still doesn't believe that illegal gambling is a far greater threat to pro football than pothead players are.

Does Wilson really believe that his millionaire gladiators don't shave points or even throw a game or two?

Wilson will probably continue to keep his fat head buried in the sand and take action only against Longo.

The old quarterback isn't a criminal. He's a sick man, and he needs professional help from organizations such as Gamblers Anonymous.

You can expect Wilson and his league of toady owners to hang Longo out to dry. The exception could be Sharks president, Jack Cabot, who has shown himself to be a champion of players with addictions such as the late Muhammad Johnson, who battled back from cocaine dependence.

Meanwhile, Johnny Longo is blessed to have a loving wife who has gone more than the distance for him.

Now it is time for Longo to leave the hospital, throw away his crutches, and join the crusade against illegal sports gambling.

The Rev. Francis J. O'Malley, pastor of St. Vincent's Church and the Sharks' chaplain, believes that God spared Longo from death in that terrible crash for a reason. That reason may be only to create a public awareness of the evils of illegal sports gambling.

#

Gattino's hands actually trembled with rage as he read Casey's column Tuesday afternoon in his Hollywood home. *That fucking Mick!*

But as the gangster cooled down, he realized that Martha Longo had done him a big favor in wasting that wise guy traitor Conte. *That cocksucker was actually trying to shake down Longo's wife for that $2.5 million! Well, now Longo won't talk to the cops, so there is no sense in another contract on him. After a while, the people will get tired of Casey's anti-gambling, anti-Mafia crusade. People always do.*

CHAPTER 26

"I only ask to be free. The butterflies are free."
Charles Dickens
Black House

Suzy was exhausted. She checked her watch. It was 9:05 p.m., and the Friday flight to Miami, scheduled for a 4:00 p.m. takeoff, had been delayed by a mechanical problem at New York's La Guardia.

Suzy was unhappy because she had wanted to get back to Miami in time to have dinner with Bob. She hadn't seen him since his return from the World Bowl, and she had scheduled this flight to give herself a long weekend with him.

"Ah, I see you're being the good management type, Suzy," said the captain of the Boeing 727-200. "Back to the ranks of coffee, tea, and me."

Ann Parker butted in. "We need a management woman to protect us from you sexists in the cockpit."

She was kidding, and the captain and Suzy laughed.

The captain was right. She had jumped back into service to help plug a hole in the cabin crew dike. She was at the end of a four-leg Miami-New York day that had started with a 6:00 a.m. show at MIA.

It was nearly midnight when the captain began his initial descent into the Miami area.

Suzy had cross-trained in the 727s to become more valuable during the strike. She was pleased with some of the new hires like Bonnie Moran, who had finally earned gold wings. Still, she had enjoyed working this flight with Ann Parker.

"Ann, I'm bushed. I don't know how you do it."

Parker laughed at the compliment. "See, Suzy, it pays to hire us senior citizens. Gosh, I love this job. I love to fly. Don't you? I mean, don't you miss flying, now that you've become a management desk jockey?"

"I miss old friends like you, Mary, and Chris," Suzy said. "I still haven't gotten over Chris's death. If I had been on board. . ."

Parker touched Suzy with affection. "I know, Suzy."

Suzy rebounded quickly. "I surely don't miss working holidays, though, and bidding for a schedule based on seniority. Or that horrible airport motel in Detroit."

The two women giggled.

"Do we still stay at that dump on our DTW layovers?" Parker asked.

"Yes, we get a good crew rate there," Suzy replied while fighting off a yawn.

"Well, don't ever let them put you in room 222."

"Why's that, Ann?"

"That's next to 220. For years, a pilot or first officer was assigned to 220, while a stewardess got room 222. Doesn't that strike you as a strange coincidence?"

"Nope."

"Well, Suzy, you all know there was a peephole the men had discovered. . ."

"No!"

"Yes, ma'am. They got me when I was a silver winger. I was ready for my bath when I started to dance to an old disco song on the radio."

"You were naked, Ann?"

"Sure was. Guess who was in the room next door?"

"I don't know. Who?"

"Captain Westinghouse."

Suzy gasped. "No, not our boss! How did you find out? What did you do?" Suzy was really into Ann's story, as she fired off questions like a machine gun.

"Well, Captain Westinghouse is a heavy smoker. I got suspicious when I saw the smoke coming into my room from the wall. I thought the room was on fire.

"Dumb little ol' me called the desk to report the fire, jumped into my trench coat, and ran down to the lobby. There was no fire, of course. The crew at breakfast gave me this shit-eating look. They were in on it, too."

Suzy was a little confused. "What was Captain Westinghouse doing there?"

"He was getting some hours in to keep his pilot's certificate. Apparently the cockpit crews had discovered that peephole a long time ago, and it became an inaugural event for new-hire stewardesses. Sort of an initiation rite, or something."

"And you just went along with it! That's terrible. You should have had those bastards arrested. That couldn't happen today."

Parker smiled. It was a gentle but knowing look. "Suzy, pardon me for asking, but. . .what room did you stay in your first year on a DTW layover?"

Suzy reflected. "Did I? You know,. . .oh, those SOBs!" Even though it was history, Suzy was angry and upset.

"Well, Suzy, at least you didn't dance to a disco number," Parker said in an attempt to console the younger woman.

"No, I didn't, Ann. It. . .it was an exercise routine on TV."

The two women looked at each other and laughed.

"I could have called the cops or gone to the union or a lot of things," said Ann. "But we both know that I would have been history in the airline business. So I made the most of it. I went to bed with Captain Westinghouse."

Suzy was shocked. "You didn't!"

"He really isn't a bad guy, you know. It was fun for a couple of months. He has the pick of all our young flight attendant crop. I got some nice tokens and shopping sprees. More important, a few years ago, when my brother lost his job as a gate agent when Eastern folded, I asked Captain Westinghouse if he could help Robert. And he did. That's why Robert didn't strike, and he's working at RDU. That's why I'm working, too."

"Didn't you feel used by Westinghouse when he dumped you?"

"Not really, Suzy. I knew it wasn't a long-term relationship. I had just been divorced. I guess I was just horny and lonely. Here was the boss making a fuss over little ol' me. At 44, I was flattered that I could beat out all the kids."

Suzy couldn't help her curiosity. "How was he in bed?"

"He wasn't quite a slam, bang, thank you lover. He wasn't any worse than my ex. Anyhow, at least Captain Westinghouse doesn't snore."

The bounce and the reversal of the engines as the 727's tires touched down on the runway ended their visit. Suzy liked Ann, and she was glad she had learned about room 220.

I'll never tell Bob. I don't think he'd understand. Golly, I can't wait to be with Bob. But not tonight. I just want a hot bath and my beddie.

#

On the ground Friday night, Lewis was growing impatient as he monitored the progress of the Sun Airlines flight from New York. At 12:05 a.m., the monitor lit up *Arrived*, and Lewis used his cell phone. "It's on the ground," he said. "Come and get me."

Lewis met the white minivan outside. Inside were Cortez and Youngblood.

"I hope the fuck you got it right, Jose, and the bitch is on this flight," he said as the van circled the terminal.

"Cool it, amigo," said Cortez. "I know where she parked."

"Okay, guys, you knows what has to be done," Lewis continued. "No fuck-ups. Understood? Good."

#

At the airport, Suzy took her navy blue trench coat and folded it over her rolling black crew bag. She walked slowly through the nearly empty terminal and into the parking garage. Even on this first Saturday of February, the day's tropical heat was still present in the concrete garage. She started to sweat. A parking ticket reminded her that her car was on level five.

She smiled when she spotted the green Mustang GT convertible parked all alone on the fifth deck. She always grinned at her Florida tag: SUN STEW. Mary Rich ragged her about the abbreviation of stewardess. Suzy always countered, "Now, Mary, you tell me how I can get FLIGHT ATTENDANT in seven letters on that tag."

"You miss me, baby?" she cooed as she wheeled her bag to the parked car. She didn't pay attention to the white van that approached from out of the shadows. It pulled to a stop, and the driver rolled down his window.

"Excuse me?" asked Cortez. "Are you Ms. Peters?"

"Why yes, I am Suzy Peters."

The question didn't sound threatening. She was really too tired to think about it. Before she could react, two men in ski masks exited the rear of the van.

As Youngblood grabbed her from behind and put her in a bear hug, Lewis placed a strong-smelling cloth over her face before she could scream. She struggled briefly before fading into unconsciousness.

It was over in an instant. The two men carried her into the van, along with her coat and luggage. There was a brief stop to pay the parking fee before the van headed out of the airport.

Cortez handed the cashier a $20 bill.

"Excuse me, sir, I need your parking ticket," said the woman cashier.

"Oh, Bubba, give me the ticket," Cortez said.

Youngblood fumbled through his pockets. "Damn, I had it," he said. "I can't find the sucker."

Cortez smiled sheepishly. "Sorry, señorita, we no have it."

"Well, sir, you'll have to pay the whole day's rate. I'm giving you a break, because I could charge you for a month."

"Gracias, señorita."

#

It was after 3:00 a.m. when Bob fell asleep in his recliner. He was still bushed from his World Bowl trip, and he was excited about Suzy coming over for the weekend. He had even purchased two bottles of Dom Perignon for the occasion, and he was dreaming of making love to her.

The cordless phone woke him with a jolt. It was the condo's security officer.

"Pardon me, Mr. Casey, but this is security. You have a FedEx package here, and the driver said it was important that you get it right away."

"Can you bring it up?" His watch showed it was only 8:00 a.m. "I'm not fit to be seen in public."

Five minutes later, the security officer handed him the package, and Bob palmed him a five spot.

Wondering what had happened to Suzy, Bob struggled to find his reading glasses on the den desk. He ripped open the standard FedEx envelope and found a handprinted letter in bold black ink, and a pair of women's black panties. The black ink declared:

Casey:
We have your girlfriend, Suzy Peters.
    These are her panties.
    If you want to see her alive again, you will not call the cops or tell anyone.
    You will stop writing shit about our family business. We will be in touch.
    Remember. We are watching you. Don't do anything dumb.

He felt as if someone had punched him hard in the gut. He couldn't suppress a scream of "N-o-o-o-o!" His knees felt weak. He went to the bar and poured himself a tall glass of Chivas Regal.

Bob was trying to stay cool and not panic.

This is something you see on TV. It doesn't happen in real life. Maybe it's a gag. Is Suzy playing a prank? Maybe she decided to go home instead of coming here. Yes, that's it!

He hustled into the den and grabbed the phone. His heart was pounding as he dialed Suzy's apartment.

"Hi. This is Suzy. I'm not here right now, but I want to hear from you. Please leave a message. Thank you for flying Sun Airlines." *Beep!*

That bastard Gattino!

#

"I'm too angry to be scared, but I need your help, Leroy." Bob nervously paced Hess's office later Saturday morning.

"Sit down, for God's sake, and have some hot coffee," Leroy said. "Or damn it, I'll make you sit down. You're making me nervous."

Bob didn't argue. He slumped into a chair and took the paper cup of coffee and doughnut that the major thrust into his left hand.

"Listen, my friend, you did the right thing in coming to me," Leroy said softly. "First, I have to warn you, we won't have jurisdiction if she was grabbed at the airport. It really should go to the FBI as soon as possible."

"I trust you, Leroy. That's why I came to you and not some other police agency."

Taking a drag on a Camel, the major said, "Bobby, I have to really question if even the Mafia would be this blatant. I mean, kidnapping the fiancée of a high-profile newspaper columnist isn't exactly their MO. If Gattino wanted you silenced, he would have hired a gun to whack you."

What Leroy said made sense, Bob had to concede, but he still knew he had to first explore the Mafia connection.

The major nodded and proposed a game plan. "If you really believe Gattino snatched Suzy, and he hasn't contacted you yet, then you call him."

"How do I do that, Leroy? Look under 'Mafia' in the yellow pages?"

The major handed Bob a slip of notepaper. "Here's his home number in Hollywood. Don't ask how we have it, just use it. Remember to be cool. Don't piss him off, or he might not agree to meet with you. Let him set the meeting place. He'll feel more comfortable that way, if he agrees at all. And call him from your cell phone."

"Why would he talk to me?" Bob asked. "Wouldn't that be admitting that he kidnapped Suzy?"

"If it is a kidnapping," explained Leroy, "he wants something in return for Suzy. He certainly knows he can't keep Suzy a prisoner forever. Frankly, if his goal is to stop the bad press, you'd think he would know that a kidnapping caper would have the opposite affect. That's what bothers me."

Hess's cop instincts told him that this kind of kidnapping was much too campy, much too Hollywood-style. If Gattino wanted to silence Casey, the old don would have whacked him a long time ago. As a rule, the Mafia did not mess with honest cops or honest members of the media.

"Look, Bob, Gattino should know by now that the public isn't going to get worked up over one newspaper columnist's anti-gambling crusade. He's a bit pissed, perhaps. If the don is clean, maybe he knows the real fuckers. Remember, he lives in Broward County, not Dade. I can't help you much there."

#

Maria Gattino answered the phone. She didn't even ask who was calling. Mafia wives learned that before their wedding day.

She believed that it was family business. Who else would have the unlisted number that changed every month for obvious reasons?

"It's for you, Sal."

Gattino was more than surprised to hear Casey's voice.

"How the fuck did you get my home number?"

"Look, Gattino, let's dispense with the small talk. We need to talk."

"Talk? Why the fuck would I wanna talk with you?"

"Because you have something that I want back," Casey said, masking his emotion. "Maybe I have something you want."

"A trade? What the hell are you talking about, Mick?"

"Listen, you wop bastard, if you don't meet with me tomorrow, I'm going to come to Hollywood, kick down your front door, and use your face for a punching bag."

Gattino laughed at the threat. He begrudgingly admired Casey's courage in threatening him, a Mafia don. He was almost ready to terminate the call, but his curiosity got the best of him.

What kind of trade was the Mick talking about? *Maybe it's a scam or a cop sting.*

"Gulfstream Park," Bob announced after ending the call.

"Gulfstream Park?" Hess repeated. The location didn't please the major. "Why did you agree to Gulfstream Park? It's not even in Dade County."

CHAPTER 27

"Is there any point to which you would wish to draw my attention?" remarked Sherlock Holmes.

A. *Conan Doyle*
Silver Blaze

"THIS ISN'T A fucking TV show now," the major cautioned. "The old don is a murdering cocksucker, but he hasn't lasted all these years because he's dumb. Don't expect him to admit anything. Keep your cool. That's why you aren't wearing a wire. Frankly, I'm surprised he wants to meet with you like this. But if he wants something in exchange for Suzy, he'll be playing word games with you."

The gates opened at 11:00 a.m., and Bob was among the first to enter the grandstand entrance. It seemed strange to have to buy a two-dollar ticket, but he didn't want to call attention to himself by entering through the press gate.

A warm tropical sun bathed the racetrack as early-bird spectators arrived. People were milling around the rail at the finish line watching the toteboard's flashing lights give the early odds for the first race.

He spotted Gattino reading a track program near the finish

line rail. He was attired in a Panama straw hat and a flowered sport shirt which hung outside his navy blue slacks. He was chewing on an unlit cigar. The don recognized Bob, and waited.

"So what is this shit you want to discuss, Mr. Newspaperman?"

Bob carried a shopping bag. It was full of the documents given to him by the actress. He remembered Hess's coaching to remain cool. He talked slowly and in a soft voice.

"I have some interesting documents in this bag. I thought we might make a deal, you know, for my merchandise. . .that you have in, er, your possession."

Gattino recognized that the columnist was upset about something. "What? What kind of deal?"

"Well, I got your note and—"

"What fucking note? I never sent you no fucking note."

Bob was a bit shaken by Gattino's aggressive approach to the conversation. Why was the don stonewalling him? Did he think the conversation was being taped?

"Er. . .I thought you wanted to trade, you know, for something."

Gattino leaned against the rail and turned to face Casey. "Trade? Trade for what?"

"My fiancée, Suzy Peters."

The mobster laughed. "I don't know what the fuck you're talking about." The don was a step ahead of the newspaperman. "Someone kidnapped your girl? And you think it was me?"

Bob nodded.

"Why would I do such a stupid thing?"

"Because you're afraid we'll expose you for blowing up the Sharks charter."

The don betrayed no emotion except to throw up his arms in a sign of disbelief. "I thought you had to have some brains to work for a newspaper. You. . .you a college boy. You have shit for brains. What would I profit from blowing up an airplane?"

"To even the score for Longo's big-time gambling debts. You

had 2.5 million reasons."

So this is what this is all about. The Mick thinks I want to shut him up by snatching his girl. "I don't know nothing about no gambling debts," the don replied slowly choosing his words. "I hear tell those debts had been canceled by the unfortunate death of a Mr. Syracusa."

"Well, what about Conte?" Bob demanded.

"I've heard a rumor that he made the same fatal error that the late Mr. Syracusa made," said Gattino as he lit his cigar.

"What was that?"

"They both let greed get them into trouble."

Becoming frustrated, Bob pulled out a notebook from the shopping bag and stuck it under the don's face. "What about this shit? It connects you with Longo."

"Let me see that book," demanded Gattino.

Bob handed it to him and waited for a reaction. Gattino flipped through some pages, laughed, and handed the book back.

"This document is about as genuine as dead Conte's mother. I would have thought you would have checked it out, Mr. Newspaperman. I haven't laughed so hard as I did when you wrote that stupid column."

"I agree, Gattino, and I hate to say it, but I think someone is trying to screw you."

"Who would be that fucked up to mess with me?"

"Obviously, someone seeking to nail you for blowing up the team plane. Now who would do such a thing?"

Gattino started to think. *Maybe the fuckin' Mick is making sense. Could it be some wise guy? Maybe a fuckin' Fed trick? I don't think the Feds would kidnap an innocent girl.*

"Then who has Suzy?" asked Bob. "That is, if you really don't have her." There was a trace of panic in Bob's voice.

"Why would I want your girl?"

"To stop me from hassling you in the press."

"Mr. Newspaperman, you have a vivid imagination, or you've seen too many movies. I hear that those wise guys don't whack no newspaper people or their families. Bad business, they say. Or so I've heard. Sure, you piss me off. Sort of like a fuckin' mosquito. I squash a fuckin' mosquito."

Bob felt foolish. If Gattino didn't have her, then damn it, maybe he would help find her. *Ask this Mafia bastard for help? God no.*

However, he couldn't help himself.

"Then who. . .who has Suzy? And. . .and why would they suggest it was your people who did it?"

Gattino really didn't care about Casey's problems or about the fate of the girl. He was, however, intrigued and angered by the possibility that someone or some group was trying to frame him.

"If I were you, I'd call the FBI at once," the don said. "This is something you can't do with your computer or your newspaper."

"Well, Gattino, if it isn't you or your wise guys, who did it?" Bob returned to his aggressive posture.

"How the fuck should I know? Furthermore, why the fuck should I care?"

Bob couldn't debate that. "You're right. But. . ."

"But what?" snapped the don.

"You could help me find Suzy," Bob asserted.

"You're crazy! Why would I do that, even if I could?"

"Because, Gattino, it would be good for your family business," said Bob. "Find Suzy, and you find the bombers. Then you'll only have to put up with my column hassles, not the Feds. Or worse yet, the wrath of the public toward mass murderers. Sure, you can squash me, but not public opinion."

Gattino's nasty mood subsided. He knew someone was trying to frame him with a kidnapping, not to mention the plane bombing. *When I find the fuckers, I'm gonna cut off their balls.*

Gattino was convinced that he had to consider finding the kidnappers. He didn't want the Feds and the media whacking him with a bogus rap. That would be bad for family business, and it would upset the godfather.

"Tell you what, Mr. Newspaperman," he said, softening his tone. "I'm gonna find out who did this thing. The sons of bitches that are trying to slander my good name won't get away with it. You have my promise on that!"

Bob was jolted by Gattino's offer. "Far be it from me to tell you how to conduct your business," he said in a cordial manner, "but. . ."

"But?" prompted the don, now more intrigued about Bob's thoughts than trying to intimidate him.

"But, Gattino, look at it this way. If you find the fuckers, the world has to know that it was them that blew up the plane. If the cops make the collar, that will happen. And the public will hate the bombers, not you. You can therefore keep that Robin Hood image with your fans."

Gattino's smile was genuine. "Maybe, Mick, you ain't so dumb after all. Who knows, maybe I'll find Suzy. Then maybe you'll owe me."

"Why do you think I'd do you any favors?" Bob asked.

"Who do you love more, Casey? Your girl or your yellow sheet?" Having made his point, Gattino smiled and changed the subject. "You know, that Suzy is a nice girl," he said without a trace of sarcasm. "She has been a stewardess on some of my flights. My wife thinks she's a nice Catholic girl, too."

"So you will help?" Bob asked, trying to contain his eagerness.

"Maybe. I'll think about it. It has become a matter of family honor. As they say, 'Don't call me. I'll call you.'"

Bob was encouraged.

"Oh, if you and your flat-footed pals are gonna be here for the first race, put some green stuff on Rome Pizza. He's a long shot, but his family blood line is exceptional."

Bob started to say thanks, but instead asked, "Don't you need my cell phone number?"

"I have it," Gattino replied as he joined two burly young men in business suits. "Who do you think we are?"

"That figures," Bob said in a whisper.

"Oh, say hello to Major Hess," the don said as he departed to the ringing of the bell for the start of the first race.

#

Bob found Leroy in the grandstand, where the major was putting his field glasses back in their case.

"Gattino knew I was with you," he told Leroy. "How did he know? Who leaked it to him?"

Leroy touched him on the arm. "That fucker has informants everywhere, including inside our department. I'd hate to side with that fucking gangster, Bob, but I believe he's telling the truth. You gotta let us handle this case now. As far as I'm concerned, the snatch took place at Suzy's apartment. That's in Miami, so it's our case. Time is running out."

Reluctantly, Bob nodded his agreement. He knew that the major was right. Now he was scared of the unknown. *If it wasn't Gattino, who was it, and why?*

"Look, Leroy, level with me," Bob said. "Is there any chance Gattino will get involved?"

Pausing to light a Camel, Leroy pondered a reply.

"I don't want to kill any hope, Bob, but I haven't a clue what the SOB will or won't do," the major said. "Frankly, I'm surprised he was willing to meet you. He knew that column about Mrs. Conte was full of shit. Maybe he just wanted to find out what you knew or didn't know."

As the two men headed for the Gulfstream parking lot, the first race was finished and posted on the toteboard. The track announcer boomed the results over the PA system. "The winner of the first race is Rome Pizza."

Bob glanced at the paddock area toteboard. It posted Rome Pizza at $134.50, $89.20, and $52.

"You should have had a few bucks on Rome Pizza," Leroy said with grin.

"Well, that fucker Gattino was right about one thing today," Bob said. "He knows how to pick horses."

#

Leroy felt an obligation to Casey. He was bending department regulations and the law a bit by claiming that the kidnapping had taken place within the city limits of Miami.

"Have you checked out the airport?" Bob asked on the drive back to Miami.

"Hey, Bob, you know damn well I have no jurisdiction there. That's Dade County. If I ask for Metro's help, they'll grab the investigation. If I send one of our guys, I risk getting my ass in a sling, because this is such a high profile case."

Bob, of course, didn't like Leroy's position, but he understood it. "Okay, Leroy, drop me off at my car. I've got work to do."

"Where are you going?"

"The airport."

"What can you do there?"

"More than you guys, Leroy."

"That's no fair," protested the major.

"Yep, Leroy, you're right. But there's no law against letting me see if my old military police training has faded away yet."

Stopping at Bob's Corvette in the visitor's parking lot at the Miami P.D., Leroy said, "If you find something, *anything*, don't play the hero. Call me. Understand?"

Bob nodded as he started the Corvette. "Sure, Leroy."

At the airport, he remembered that Suzy usually parked in Building One, near the Sun Airlines terminal. He drove slowly up four floors of the garage, but no luck.

"Bingo!" he exclaimed out loud. His heart beat faster as he recognized the forest green Mustang convertible. He checked the doors, the trunk. They were locked. Then he spotted Suzy's key ring against the right rear tire. Picking it up gently, he pressed the keys against his heart.

Oh dear God in heaven, please help me.

Bob combed the area near the Mustang. *It's amazing the junk that's on this floor. Cigarette butts, candy wrappers, parking tickets. Hello? What's this?*

He picked up an airport parking ticket.

Could it be Suzy's?

He was about to drop the ticket in his shirt pocket with the key ring, but a second look revealed that the ticket was clocked in at 7:09 p.m. Friday. *This isn't Suzy's. Could it be. . .no. Maybe . . .*

An excited Bob remembered that it could contain prints. He secured it in an envelope he found in his computer case.

Now how can I talk to the parking garage cashiers that were on duty Friday night? One of them should remember something about a person paying, because they lost their ticket. Maybe it's a lead. Or maybe just a coincidence.

#

Bob burned rubber to return to the Miami P.D. He didn't even lock his car doors as he raced into the lobby. "Buzz Major Hess," he told the uniformed officer behind the reception cage.

"Calm down, Bobby," Leroy said. "Slow down. You have an airport parking ticket. Okay, okay, I'm sending it to our crime lab. But anything more sophisticated will have to go to the FBI."

"Can you do more?"

"No promises, Bobby, but let me see if I can call in some chips from the Metro commander at the airport. Now go home and get some sleep, and let me see what we can come up with."

#

Hess had to notify the FBI about the kidnapping. He left out, however, the part about Casey's possible evidence and that the snatch probably took place at the airport where the victim's car was parked and her key ring found. Instead, he just notified Metro Dade that Casey had received the ransom note in the city. The FBI and Miami police would handle the investigation.

#

It was Monday morning when Bob was summoned to the FBI's Miami Office. Although he feared that the Feds would fuck up the kidnapping, he had no other option. He was rooting for the Mafia to come through, and for the cops to get lucky with the ticket.

Agent James Duckworth appeared to be only a couple of years out of the FBI Academy. His hair was short, and he dressed in an Ivy League business suit with button-down collar shirt and a conservative tie. Duckworth asked Casey to check the statement that he had given the Miami police. This was exchanged for a copy of the ransom note.

"Would you mind making a copy of this for us?" The agent handed him a black marking pen and some white letter paper.

Bob dutifully started to copy the note until after the third one, he realized, *those fuckers think I wrote this fucking note!* He was steamed. *The FBI is breaking my chops with this foolish writing exercise.*

He took the papers and pen, walked to Duckworth's desk, and tossed them on it. "You asshole! You think I wrote this goddamned note? Next thing you'll want me to take a polygraph to see if I made up the whole thing. Well, my fiancée is being held hostage by someone somewhere, and you bunch of keystone cops are treating this case with as much enthusiasm as if someone had pissed on one of your unmarked cars."

Duckworth stood up. "You're talking to a federal agent, sir. . ."

"No, I'm talking to a rookie who hasn't got a clue on this investigation. You can take those writing samples and use them for toilet paper." Bob turned to leave.

"I didn't tell you that you were dismissed!"

Bob laughed. "I'm not in the Army, sonny. If you want me to stay, then book my ass."

Two shirt-sleeved agents seized Bob by the arms and cuffed his hands behind him. The agents hustled him to a holding cell while Duckworth proclaimed, "You, asshole, are under arrest. You have the right. . ."

Bob demanded the phone call promised with the reading of the Miranda, but Duckworth said that would come later.

Bob wasn't mad; he just wanted to get even. He was also panicking about Suzy's safety. What if the kidnappers knew he had been in contact with law enforcement? He had never felt so absolutely helpless.

Four hours later, two agents escorted the columnist from the cell to an interview room. There, Duckworth and agent Constance Burns presented him with copies of everything from his bank statement to a list of his phone calls. They had a pile of photographs, including the visit to Gulfstream Park. There was a series of shots of him talking to Gattino.

"Okay, Scoop, explain your clandestine meeting with a known Mafia don. . .a don you claim kidnapped Ms. Peters," said Burns, a young woman with a New York accent.

"It's not 'Scoop,' Ms. Agent. It's Mr. Casey." He fought for self-control. "I'd like to call my attorney, James Walden. I believe I have that right."

"If you didn't make this kidnapping up to try to embarrass this agency, why would you need a lawyer?" Duckworth asserted. "Only guilty people want lawyers."

The relentless questioning continued for almost three hours. He refused to make any comments. He just kept asking to call Walden. Finally, the two agents started the good cop, bad cop routine. While Duckworth took a hike for coffee, Burns turned on the charm.

"Now, Mr. Casey, I know Agent Duckworth can be a bit unreasonable," she said softly.

For the first time, Bob had the chance to size up one of his interrogators. She appeared to be in her late 20s, with short blonde hair. *Probably about five-foot-six with long legs. She is probably packaged into a size ten, but she's really a size eight.* Her white blouse was open down to three buttons, and he couldn't help but notice a black bra that was just plump enough.

She must think I'm a real shmuck if she thinks I'll fall for this charade.

"Me? I'd like to believe you," she continued. "Perhaps I can offer you some coffee? A soft drink?"

"Cut the crap," Bob said. "Just let me call my attorney."

Burns acted as if she hadn't heard his demand. "Look, Mr. Casey, you can be out of here in time for dinner. We just need your help in resolving this matter. Did you and Ms. Peters have any problems? She is a flight attendant, and we know what a life that can be for a woman traveling all the time. Do you think she might have sent you the note? You know, maybe she needed some attention."

Bob responded with a cynical laugh. "You people are incredible. No, you're just stupid. If you're stupid enough to treat a syndicated newspaper columnist like this, I damn well have to believe you aren't capable of solving a kidnapping, much less finding out who blew up the Sharks charter."

"Now, Mr. Casey, that kind of attitude won't get you home for dinner."

"Fuck you!"

The muscles in the female agent's face tightened. He could see that she was fighting to control her emotions. Before she could make another move, the door opened.

"Agent Burns," Duckworth said in a surprisingly formal manner, "this is Federal Judge Glickstein, Major Hess of the Miami police, and Attorney Walden. Mr. Walden is representing Mr. Casey."

Bob enjoyed the pained expression on the female agent's face.

"And, Agent Burns, I think you know me?"

Burns swallowed hard and acknowledged a "Yes, sir" to Morris Meeker, who entered the room followed by Dick Norton.

"Good," Meeker said. "I'll expect to see you and Agent

Duckworth in my office just as soon as we've finished issuing our most sincere apologies to Mr. Casey."

Duckworth spluttered, "But, sir, we have. . .you know, charged Mr. Casey. . ."

"Then uncharge him, Duckworth. Then both you and Burns join me in extending our sincerest apologies to Mr. Casey."

Bob's experience with the FBI had taken a different turn when Duckworth had called the Miami police to get dirt on the columnist. He had been directed to Hess.

"Bob, it is true that you can't un-arrest anyone," explained Leroy. "But as far as Meeker is concerned, his agency never officially arrested you. You don't have a problem with that, do you?"

"No, Leroy, I don't."

"Good. Now let's get back to finding Suzy. I think Baptiste may have come up with something."

#

Understandably, Meeker was embarrassed by his agents' actions, even though it was his action to initiate the investigation of Casey.

"How many times do I have to tell you, we do not get in a pissing contest with people who buy ink by the barrel!" he scolded the agents.

He was ever so right. The first salvo was fired in Tuesday's editions with this Page 1 headline that keyed to the lead story about Peters' kidnapping, as well as to Casey's column in the sports section.

WOMAN HELD BY HOODS
TO MUZZLE BOMBING?

Bob Casey's Working Press:
Please, don't harm my fiancée

MIAMI—I don't know who you are, but I know why you did it.

That's why I share this information with the good people

who read this column.

Yes, I know why you kidnapped Suzy Peters, my fiancée and a Sun Airlines in-flight manager, near her Miami apartment last Friday night.

You want to stop me from revealing you as the cowards who bombed the Sharks charter DC-10 last November 27. You think I know who you are. By holding the love of my life captive, you believe you will muzzle me. Wrong!

Suzy, if you can somehow read this, know that I love you. Know, too, that dedicated law enforcement agencies are working hard to find you. They will. I promise you that. My love, understand, too, that criminals cannot be permitted to muzzle Miami P.M. or any other daily newspaper.

If we permit this, then terrorists and other criminals will be encouraged to become bolder, and more innocent, young women will face kidnapping or worse.

Those who are really responsible for Suzy's kidnapping are basically good people. You are reading this column right now. You who like to place illegal bets on sports, or maybe you who are a recreational user of pot or coke.

You are the people who support the Mafia and their criminal allies. They are the leeches of mankind. That 110 bucks bet on a Sharks game goes into the coffers of hoods such as Don Sal "The Saw" Gattino, who is the underboss for the Lorenzo family of New York.

It is you, the good people, who support loan sharking, strongarmed union tactics, prostitution, protection, and drugs, just to mention a few Mafia businesses.

I will not appeal to you bastards who have Suzy to return her unharmed. How can anyone talk reason to cowards who would bomb a commercial airliner?

My faith in God sustains me during this time of terror.

I have met face to face with Gattino. He denies that his

hoods have anything to do with the bombing and or kidnapping.

I don't know if I believe him. Who else would have reason to do such dastardly deeds? Maybe drug dealers?

#

Maria Gattino cried when she read Casey's column Wednesday afternoon. The old woman's eyes were red and still damp when she confronted her husband when he returned to their Hollywood home for dinner.

"Sal, how could you do such a thing? This Suzy is such a nice girl, a good Catholic girl. How could you do such a thing?"

The hard-boiled Mafia don was transformed into a repentant husband by the old woman's admonishment. "Maria, my love. What you talking about?"

She picked up the tabloid and thrust it at him. The don already knew the contents.

"Hey, we don't have anything to do with this, Maria. Honest. I swear on the altar of God. In fact, I'm gonna see what we can do about finding the suckers who have that girl."

"Oh. . .you mean that, Sal?" Maria started to cry again.

"Now, whatsa matter?"

"Oh, Sal, I'm so happy you're going to save that Suzy. You know, she's a good Catholic girl who never misses a Mass at St. Vincent's. . ."

"Yeah, yeah. We'll take care of it. I promise. Now what is that wonderful smell coming from the kitchen?"

"Your favorite shells and sausage, with extra salsa. I almost tossed it in the garbage after reading that article."

"Ah, extra salsa. You know, Maria, I love you."

The don's stomach was anxious for the coming meal, but his mind was working fast on the kidnapping. He excused himself briefly to make a phone call to one of his lieutenants.

Suzy Peters lay on a metal military cot. Her left hand was secured to the cot with a set of handcuffs. It was dark, and the air was stale. Feeling dirty and uncomfortable in her flight attendant uniform, she wanted to take a hot bath.

She was more concerned about her personal hygiene than fearful for her life. She felt raped, but she hadn't been sexually molested. She was groggy and sick to her stomach, which made her sleep most of the time. She had no sense of time, and she figured she must be drugged. The smell of urine bothered her as she remembered the pail next to the cot. She shivered and pulled the thin blanket around her, noting for the first time that it was a blue passenger blanket used on board Sun Airlines flights.

God, what time is it? They must have taken my watch. What day is it? Bob, where are you? I miss you so much. Who the hell are these creeps who kidnapped me?

Alone and cut off from the world, she remembered from reading a magazine article on the subject of hostages that being isolated could challenge the mind of any person. Suzy tried not to dwell on the negative. After all, she was still alive. She believed strongly that God had not spared her from the Sharks charter crash to let her die at the hands of some crazy terrorists. So she worked hard to only think about the good things in her life and make plans for her wedding.

Suzy had no way of knowing that she was in a room in an abandoned discount store in Liberty City. It had been looted and partially burned during a ghetto riot over a case of alleged police brutality. To the outside, it looked as if it was still a rotting edifice.

Inside, however, part of the back of the building had been restored and even air-conditioned. The building was used as a garage. The white van that had been used in the kidnapping, and eight other vehicles including a new blue Mercedes roadster, were parked inside the building.

#

The phone rang in Gattino's den. It was his private line for family business.

The don hurried, because he thought it might be good news from the soldiers. But it wasn't his boys; it was the godfather.

"Salvatore, old friend, I am a bit concerned about some articles in the Miami newspaper. This Mick sports columnist now appears even in a New York paper. He says bad things about you and about us. You know, we do not like such notoriety."

"Godfather, we are taking action as we speak. I have the boys combing the city for the creeps who did the kidnapping."

"Then it wasn't you, Sal?"

"Hell no, Godfather. I wouldn't do such a thing without asking permission. I know the girl. She's a good Catholic. Maria likes her, too. She thought I had something to do with it. She was mad. I thought she might hit me over the head with a frying pan."

Lorenzo laughed softly. The young Godfather could picture the old don, who could kill without flinching, cowering in front of his old wife.

"Your people did very well on the World Bowl," said the godfather. "I see you have hiked our college and pro basketball action, too. This makes me very happy. Now if you can get us out of the newspapers. . ."

"Godfather, you know, it's a bum rap. We didn't blow up no airplane, and we didn't snatch no girlie. That Casey is a fuckin' pain in the ass. I should have put him in concrete shoes last year after he started all this shit about the evils of gambling."

"Sal, listen to me," implored Lorenzo. "When the bombing is solved and the girl is back giving blow jobs to that yellow journalist, people will get tired of his shit about the evil of sports betting. When the readers get bored, the publisher will do our job for us and make Casey write about sports, not gambling. Capisce? Now when we get free from such bad publicity, we need to meet with the Chicago and Detroit families about casino gambling."

"The Florida voters have said they don't want casinos here. It's those fuckin' Baptists, you know," Gattino said.

"I know that, Sal, but what about the gambling ships?" The godfather answered his own question. "We know there are more than 30 commercial boats sailing out of Florida ports that offer blackjack, slot machines, roulette, and other games of chance. These 'cruises to nowhere' pick up a boatload of passengers and head out to sea. Once they are three miles out into the Atlantic, or nine miles offshore in the Gulf of Mexico, they're in international waters."

"I know this, Godfather, but. . .but these boats aren't run by our family. They're run by the cruise ship lines."

Gattino paused and exhaled.

"Godfather, does this mean we are going into the cruise ship business, too?"

"Not so quick, Sal," Lorenzo said with an amused chuckle. "You'll get to take Maria and the grandkids on plenty of cruises, I promise you. Our first order of business is to buy some state lawmakers so Florida won't ban gambling ships. Our family won't be officially involved until after the law is passed. The press and the Baptists won't find any direct link at that time. Later, we make the cruise line people an offer they can't refuse."

Lorenzo said he was doing business with Jerry Pritzi in Detroit and Abe Goldman in Chicago.

"They aren't interested in our sports betting operation. However, we need Goldman's expertise from Vegas, and we're paying off some old debts to Pritzi."

"Pritzi has most of the Broward and Palm Beach counties' lawmakers and judges in his pocket. Many helped in bending the laws so Pritzi could build all those nice skyscraper condos along the beaches."

Now Gattino's only problem was finding the kidnappers.

If I let it be known through the community that finding the fuckin' kidnappers is worth a hundred Gs, we'll get some snitches in no time.

CHAPTER 28

"The good ended happily, and the bad unhappily. This is what fiction means."

Oscar Wilde
The Importance of Being Earnest

Casey:
This is your last warning.
If you ever want to make love to your girlfriend again, stop knocking the Mafia. We have already killed 105 people. Another one will be no big deal.

THE MESSAGE CAME to Bob's apartment via FedEx on Tuesday. He immediately called Leroy.

"I've got a tap on your phones, but not your cell phone," Leroy said. "I'm surprised they haven't called yet."

Leroy knew that the odds were low that a kidnapping victim would ever be rescued. Since it had been nearly a week since Suzy had been snatched, he knew that wasn't good news. But he didn't want to say anything that might depress his friend.

"Leroy, I'm starting to panic," Bob said. "I know you guys are doing your best, but. . ."

"Keep your cool, Bob," replied the major in a soft voice. "We're going to get your Suzy back safe and sound. You have my guarantee."

#

It was almost midnight, and it was quiet inside the abandoned store in Liberty City. Suzy Peters' kidnappers were not in a high state of alert. Only one cocaine kid, a 15-year-old boy, stood guard while five others were sleeping. The two ringleaders, T.J. Lewis and Jose Cortez, couldn't sleep. With two one-way tickets to Colombia in their possession, they were making plans to leave Friday night.

Lewis finished snorting a line of cocaine. He felt better. For a while his problems were suspended, but he was sober enough to know that he would have to take action soon. He was running out of patience almost as fast as he was running out of money.

"Where the fuck is Bubba?" asked Lewis. "He should've been back hours ago."

"He went home to get some of his personal shit," replied Cortez. "He thinks he's going with us."

"I'm worried about that redneck, man," Lewis said. "I think he's yellow. He's already pissing in his pants. He has become expendable."

"This damn strike has cost us, and we have to skip town tomorrow for Central America," Cortez said. "I don't think no redneck will fit in in any neighborhood in Colombia."

"That's why you'll waste whitey when he returns," Lewis said. "Along with the bitch."

The Sun Airlines strike had reduced to a trickle the number of flights to Colombia, and had dried up their pipeline of drugs. Lewis and Cortez' pushers had deserted them, including all but six of their cocaine kids.

"You know, Jose," said Lewis, "that fuckin' Kelly promised us the strike would be a quick one and that Westinghouse would fold the tent early. It seems Kelly misjudged Westinghouse big-time."

"Yeah, man, it appears that management is winning the strike," agreed Cortez. "But the end won't come in time to save our business."

Lewis condemned his bad luck.

The bombing of the Sharks charter had been a mistake. Cortez had rigged the explosive device for the cargo door of the DC-10 that was scheduled to leave Dallas/Fort Worth for Colombia, not the team charter.

He kept replaying in his mind the sequence of events up to the bombing. He had conceived the idea during innocent talks with Kelly about the most vulnerable part of the DC-10. Kelly had recalled the near crash of Norton's flight out of Detroit nine years ago.

Cortez, who had spent three years after high school in the Army in an engineering outfit, used his demolition training to construct a basic small, plastic time bomb. The device was attached inside the rear cargo door by Cortez, who had impersonated a Sun Airlines non-striking gate agent. Gate agents and other non-union employees had been drafted to serve as baggage handlers at DFW. With his company ID card and the confusion of unfamiliar faces, he'd had no problems moving freely around the aircraft just before dawn on Thanksgiving.

To prevent anyone from using the rear cargo hold, Cortez had filled out a maintenance report that the rear cargo door's locking device was jammed. It stated that the cargo should be stored in the forward and central compartments until the rear door problem could be attended to after the DC-10 returned from Colombia. Under normal circumstances, the scheme would have been doomed by the checks of mechanical supervisors. But the strike conditions made it easy for the sabotage.

"You know, Jose, if it wasn't for that fucking management-type serving the Sharks charter, we wouldn't have this shit," Lewis said.

The mechanical problem suffered by the Sharks charter had resulted in management's decision to scrub the Colombia flight and assign the sabotaged DC-10 to the football team.

"The failure to lock the Sharks' aircraft's pin that locks the nose landing gear was a blunder that really cost us," Lewis continued. "If they hadn't switched planes, we'd have gotten the scum of a task force of U.S. federal agents, including Meeker, who were closing in on us. Damn ground crews! If only they had locked the nose gear pin while on the ground. When they tried to move it, the fuckin' gear collapsed."

"Yeah," said Cortez. "That asshole station manager! Under orders from Miami that the Sharks charter was priority, he ordered the Colombia flight canceled. Then he gave the goddamned other 10 to the fuckin' football team."

Lewis felt sorry for himself. Oh, not for the 105 people his bomb had killed in the Everglades, but for the bad luck that had spared the federal agents.

Why is God punishing me? Why am I so unlucky?

Cocaine served Lewis as a therapeutic device, an antidote to stress, disappointment, and the problems of everyday life. Lewis' main problem had become a lack of cocaine.

Before the airline strike, Lewis could boast, "I have coke 365 days a year. It is bad business to be without coke." Now the phones rang in the old building, and they went unanswered. "If they think you're out, they'll go to somebody else," Lewis told Cortez. "If they know you can get coke, and you have a rep for good coke, they'll wait."

Lewis was pondering snorting another line, but he was interrupted by Cortez, who held two bottles of Budweiser. "Breakfast."

Lewis took the bottle, popped it open, and took a long swig. "Yeah, man, breakfast."

The two men were alone in what had once been the manager's office in the abandoned discount department store. Six other members of the gang, mostly street-smart teenagers who distributed drugs to the sellers, were in the main room.

Lewis had run part of his operation in a loosely organized way, hiring workers as needed to sell cocaine and crack in a variety of locations in Dade, Broward, and Palm Beach counties. He had drawn from a sizable labor pool of teenagers who had dropped out of high school and were unemployed. Like workers in a legitimate industry, the kids had a chance to be promoted and make more money.

Cocaine selling required mobility, careful planning, and swift action. Lewis, a product of the Liberty City ghetto, had such talents. He knew that to keep his kids loyal, they had to snort cocaine regularly. Lewis preached to his kids that those who snorted would have more control and discipline than those who did crack or freebase.

"How come you up so early, my main man?" Lewis asked.

"Couldn't sleep, amigo."

"Yeah, me too. Hey, T.J., where the fuck is Bubba?"

"That's a good question."

"What are we going to do with the little lady, T.J.?"

"Waste her," replied Lewis without hesitation. "She ain't any good to us now that we is gonna skip town for Colombia."

"You mean kill her, T.J.?"

"Listen, man, kidnapping is a fucking capital crime. You want her around to testify against us? Hey, man, what's another casualty?"

"Right. But hey, man, can't we have some fun first? I mean, T.J., she's built like a brick shithouse."

Lewis laughed. "Maybe we should both give her a thrill. She ain't lived until she's had a big, black cock up her tight ass."

"Think she would be willing to give me a blow job, T.J.?" Cortez was getting hot just thinking about Suzy Peters.

Lewis paced the small room. "I'm really more concerned about saving our asses, Jose, than fucking some stewardess bitch. We have to skip the country. I've been in contact with my friends in Colombia. They said we would be welcome to join the Cali cartel."

"What about the rest of the bros?"

"Fuck 'em. They don't need children down there any more than they need Bubba."

"Right, amigo."

Lewis decided he needed another line of coke.

As T.J. prepared to get higher, Cortez felt his penis getting hard, and he left for Peters' office cell.

Both men had been guzzling Budweiser throughout the night and into the morning. Cortez was smashed, but not enough, so he grabbed two fresh bottles out of an ice chest.

Suzy heard the door open, and the light flooding through it bothered her eyes. She had been awake most of the night, and was preparing for the worst.

"Hello, señorita flight attendant," Cortez said as he approached the bunk bed. "You thirsty, hey? I've got a cold beer for you."

Peters was parched. She was uncomfortable in her soiled clothing, and her body ached from being handcuffed to the cot. She had only a plastic bucket for a toilet, and it was very difficult to maneuver while drugged and having one hand handcuffed to the military-style cot. She was hoping for water, but a beer would do for now. She could smell the foul beer breath of her captor before he seated himself on a chair next to the cot. He carried two bottles of beer. He handed one to her.

"Thanks," she said humbly as she grasped the cold bottle. Suzy took two long swigs from the bottle. In her haste, some beer slopped on her blouse. Cortez watched in silence as she consumed half of the bottle.

He had been drinking all night and was drunk. He saw her breasts heave, and he could see that she had a really hard and firm body. He would hate to kill her, but that would be later, after Youngblood.

"You know, señorita, I can be your friend," he said slowly, his speech slurred.

Suzy remembered reading a magazine article that advised hostages or kidnap victims to try to become friends with their captors. Such a strategy, the author claimed, would make the captors hesitate to do violence.

"If you wanted us to be friends, you'd let me out of here," she said. "I haven't done anything to you. You seem like a nice guy.

I'm sure we could be friends." Her voice was calm, displaying none of the panic she felt at the moment.

Cortez laughed softly. "Señorita, I cannot let you go now. Maybe later. Maybe if you prove to me you really want to be my friend."

"How's that?" she asked as she took another long swig of beer.

"By playing with this snake in my pants," he said recklessly as he placed his hand on her left leg and moved it slowly up inside her skirt.

Suzy shivered. *My God, the bastard is going to rape me!*

#

While Meeker's FBI agents were grilling Mike Kelly as a bombing suspect, the Miami cops had come up with a positive ID on the tommy gun hit man, and the lab had lifted a print off the parking ticket found by Casey.

"Notify both our contacts in the Fort Lauderdale and Miami Beach P.D.s about our find," Leroy Hess said over the phone. "Let them fight over charging Jimmy 'The Trigger' Scalise for murder in their jurisdictions. His last known address was in LA, but let Lauderdale and the Beach boys worry about that."

"Looks like you can bag Gattino when Scalise is charged," Bob said.

The major laughed. "I'll bet you a good dinner, Bobby, that Scalise won't have a clue who hired him. Scalise is a freelancer, not family."

"So, Leroy, what do you get in return for catching Scalise?"

"Other than the satisfaction that a hit man is out of service, two departments owe us a few blue chips," the major said with a smile.

"How did Baptiste do it?"

"He hunted down the parking lot kid at the restaurant on the Beach," explained Leroy. "The kid remembered that the suspect was driving a National rental car. Would you believe that Scalise rented it with his own credit card?"

"Unbelievable!" said Bob. "Not very bright."

"Hey, Bobby, most of the stiffs we grab aren't brain surgeons, you know. In addition to Baptiste acting like a bulldog, he needed some luck, too. With Scalise's ID made, the parking lot kid was also able to pick him out of a rogue's gallery."

Leroy picked up a report sheet.

"Speaking of luck, you may have struck oil at the airport. The parking ticket print belongs to a Wilbur Youngblood, AKA 'Bubba,' of 1010 SW 115th Terrace, Miami. He was in the Air Force for four years, and we traced his last known job as a mechanic at Sun Airlines. At Sun, he is a union rep and flunky for Mike Kelly."

"What are you waiting for, Leroy?" Bob asked excitedly.

"Hold your horses, Bobby. This Youngblood has no criminal record. There is always a chance that even if this is his parking ticket, it's only a coincidence."

"Leroy, for God's sake. . ."

#

Youngblood had planned only to get some fresh clothes on his visit home, but his gal pal, Diana, had dropped by. They both got drunk on cheap gin and ended up in bed.

The hulking Youngblood was in the missionary position on top of Diana when he felt a metal object against his head just as his penis exploded inside the naked woman.

"Okay, loverboy, get up slowly so I don't have to blow your head off," said a husky male voice in the darkness. "I have an Uzi pointed at your redneck head."

"Who the hell are you?" asked Youngblood as he climbed off Diana. "You the cops?"

Diana was terrified.

"Hey, bimbo, get your clothes, and get your ass outta here," the gunman said to the woman. "Our business is only with the big fella here."

Thinking it was the police, Diana was happy to scoop up her clothing and stumble out of harm's way.

There were two white males, and they handcuffed Youngblood to a chair. He remained naked, his penis dripping. Suddenly he felt cold.

"Who the fuck are you guys?" Youngblood asked. "I have my rights. You guys need a search warrant. . ."

The gunman pointed the tip of his Uzi at Youngblood's penis. "This is our warrant, asshole," the gunman replied. "It was issued by Don Gattino. He don't take kindly to fucks like you impersonating our family."

The bedroom door opened, and in stepped Gattino with another man who was carrying a large bag. The don wasted no time and said nothing. The man reached into the bag and handed Gattino a power chainsaw.

Gattino fired up the motor, and the saw was guided to within a few inches of Youngblood's penis.

The naked man felt a chill. This wasn't the cops. It was the Mafia. There would be no trial with clever lawyers. *Oh, fuck!*

"As I see it, shit-for-brains, you got no time to decide if you still want your cock and balls, or if you wanna rat on your pals," Gattino said as he came closer with the chainsaw.

#

Meanwhile, at Miami Police headquarters, as Bob was pleading with Leroy to take action, the columnist's cell phone rang.

"Mr. Newspaperman. You might want to check out a big story at 4185 SW 83rd Avenue. And this time, get the fuckin' facts right!"

Click.

"Leroy! That was Gattino!"

Hess's unmarked Ford Crown Victoria, with flashing blue lights, arrived with four other marked Miami P.D. units at the upscale, two-story townhouse at 115th Terrace. The front door was ajar.

"You stay in back of me," Leroy ordered Bob, who felt uncomfortable in body armor as they entered with caution.

The major had his Walther PPK .380 out, but when he reached the second floor master bedroom, he returned the weapon to his shoulder holster.

"What have we here?" he said as he spotted a naked Youngblood handcuffed to a chair.

The big hulk was shaking, and just mumbled, "Thank you, thank you for saving me."

On the dresser was a tape recorder with a large note: *For Bob Casey*.

As he reached for it, Leroy said, "Hold it, Bobby. That's evidence."

"Fuck you, Leroy," the columnist snapped as he grabbed the recorder and turned it on.

"This is Bubba Youngblood. I want to confess to being part of the gang who sabotaged the Sharks charter. . ."

"What's that buzzing sound in the background, Bob?" Leroy asked.

"Quiet!" shouted Bob. "The fuckers are holding Suzy in Liberty City. . ."

The major ordered a uniformed sergeant to read Youngblood his rights and book him. Then he called dispatch for more backup units to meet him at 1234 Martin Luther King Avenue.

Bob's heart was pounding. "I don't believe the fucking Mafia found Youngblood and made this dirtbag confess," he said to the major as they drove rapidly to Liberty City. "But will a forced confession hold up in court?"

"Let's save Suzy and get his fellow dirtbags first, Bobby," said Leroy as he hit the gas pedal and the Ford's 315-horsepower V-8 engine roared. "Just be happy we didn't waste our time on Youngblood's original 10-20. He had moved, and it took a fuckin' don to find him."

That point hit Bob hard. "Yeah, Leroy, I see what you mean about luck. It would have been a real hassle to locate this stiff. Oh man, that's scary."

#

It was 3:12 a.m. by the major's watch as he led a caravan of marked and unmarked Miami police units to the abandoned discount department store in Liberty City. They raced silently to the scene with neither sirens nor blue flashing lights.

At that early hour, it was a trip of about 15 minutes through nearly deserted city streets. To Bob, however, it seemed like an eternity. He felt a rush of adrenaline in the racing police car as Leroy barked out instructions over the car radio.

"Is Air One ready?" he asked.

Bob heard the whirling overhead of the police helicopter. It was in place over the old building and ready to mark its prey in a bright searchlight.

Leroy's car screeched to a halt as a busload of SWAT policemen were climbing out of their vehicle. The black-clad cops in battle armor looked more like combat troops than cops.

The SWAT cops waited for the major as he briefed the unit's commander.

If not for the fact that Suzy's life was involved, it would have been a very exciting adventure for the newspaperman. *Instead, I'm scared shitless. Oh please, God, please let us find Suzy alive and in good health.*

A quick check by the major showed that his men were in position. He spoke into his hand-held radio. "Go."

A Paul Brunan look-alike SWAT team member wielded a sledgehammer. In three swings, he knocked open the door. At the same time, the police chopper sprayed the scene in light as a dozen SWAT members swarmed inside.

The SWAT cops caught the cocaine kids by complete surprise. It was like a commando raid. One teenager managed to fire off several rounds on his Uzi, wounding one officer in the arm. But the kid was cut down in a hail of fire, and the five other kids meekly surrendered without raising their weapons.

"My God, we got a bunch of juveniles here!" shouted a SWAT officer as he looked at the youthful face of the mortally wounded 15-year-old on the concrete floor.

"The kid with the Uzi in his hands wasn't playing with a toy," the major replied. "He was ready and capable of blowing our asses away."

The SWAT team collared Lewis before he could reach for his Uzi. The cops wrestled him to the floor and cuffed his hands behind his back.

"Read the scumbag his rights," shouted Leroy.

"Hey, you pigs need a search warrant," Lewis screamed. "We have our rights. You can't do this to us. It ain't legal."

Leroy and Bob raced frantically throughout the first floor of the 80,000-square foot building. The major's flashlight moved up and down doors that once were offices for the store.

Then he spotted a door with *Manager* on it. It was closed. He motioned Bob to be quiet as he approached the door and tried the handle. "Damn!" he mumbled. "The fucker's locked."

It wasn't. It was only stuck.

#

Inside the manager's office, oblivious to the noise at the rear of the building, Cortez unbuttoned his fly and out popped his hard-on.

"See, señorita, this is how we become friends," he said to Suzy.

In his passion and intoxication, Cortez had forgotten he had given Suzy a beer bottle. As he closed in on his prey, she swung the bottle hard, and it smashed across his nose, knocking him to the floor. He felt the pain and the blood, and knew his nose was broken.

"You fucking gringo bitch!" he screamed. "I'm going to cut your cunt out!"

Suzy was scared. She had acted by sheer reflex. *Maybe I'd have been better off if I'd given in to him. Now the sucker is hell-bent on raping me. And. . .maybe worse.*

Cortez was still shaken and on the floor. He found the switchblade he carried in his right sock. He snapped open the blade. He struggled to get to his feet, slowed by his drunken stupor and the pain. He was oblivious to the commotion in the other part of the building. His mind was occupied with revenge and rape.

"You gonna pay for this," he said as he righted himself.

Cortez hadn't bothered to lock the door to what once had been the automotive department's manager's office. In the major's effort to kick the door in, he slipped on an old oil slick and landed hard on the floor. The impact knocked his Walther PPK .380 into the room.

"Damn door wasn't locked, after all," Hess moaned.

This left an unarmed Casey to face the knife wielder.

"Oh, Bobby!" Suzy screamed hysterically. "Look out! He's got a knife."

Bob never hesitated. He surprised Cortez with a flying tackle that left both men groping on the floor. Although his opponent was high on something, Bob found that the younger man was a very strong street fighter.

Cortez kicked Bob savagely in the groin and followed it with another potent kick to the ribs. Cortez picked up his knife and hit Bob in chest, but the body armor deflected the knife. In a second try, he was momentarily distracted when Suzy's beer bottle flew by his head.

"Oh, fuck! Wide right," Bob muttered in despair. He struggled to fend off his attacker. Cortez caught his left arm, and he felt the sting from the blade as it sliced his skin.

Cortez raised the knife again as Suzy screamed, "Oh, no! Help! Help!"

Pop. Pop. Pop.

Cortez moaned. His knife dropped and made a clanging sound as it hit the concrete floor. Bob could see bloodied holes in Cortez' chest as the man doubled over like a sack of potatoes.

The major was seated on the floor, and in his hand was a smoking snub-nosed Smith & Wesson .38 he had pulled from an ankle holster.

"My throw-away weapon," Leroy said. "Sorry it took so long. You okay, Bobby? Miss Peters?"

Before Bob could respond, four SWAT officers burst into the room. "You guys okay?" barked a sergeant.

The major shook his head. "You know, Bobby, there's never a cop around when you need one."

Bob laughed in relief at his gallows' humor.

"This sucker is still alive, Major," said the sergeant after checking on the downed and wounded Cortez.

"Get an ambulance for him and EMS for me and Mr. Casey," said Leroy. "I think I fucked up my back. How's the arm, Bobby?"

Bob and Suzy held each other while a policeman used metal cutters to remove her handcuffs. An EMS technician tended the columnist's wound.

"You learn that action in the Army MPs?" asked Leroy.

"No, from college football, Leroy. But I'm thankful you made me wear that body armor."

"Yeah, if you hadn't, that SOB would've killed you, you know," the major continued. "But I think Miss Peters is glad your football skills paid off."

"Yes, oh yes," asserted Suzy. "But if it wasn't for you, Major Hess. . .well, you know. . ."

Leroy smiled. *Sometimes being a cop is good shit.*

Two officers led Lewis into the room to face the major, who was still seated on the floor.

"Looks like you're headed for Raiford and Old Sparky, dirtbags," said Leroy. "So why don't you help yourself and start signing."

"I know my rights, and I ain't saying nothing," replied Lewis.

The major held up the tape recorder. "Hey, scumbag, you recognize this voice?" He clicked the player on.

Lewis' expression paled. "That fuckin' white rat!"

"Sergeant, book this lowlife and his wounded pal on kidnapping and drug dealing charges," Leroy said as a pair of EMS technicians checked his back. "Notify the Feds. They'll add the murder and other assorted raps."

Bob Casey's Working Press:
Now the healing can begin

MIAMI—Newspapermen aren't supposed to make news. We are expected to report news in a fair and impartial manner as observers, not as participants.

Trying to be an observer, I became a participant, and perhaps even a major player, in the tragic drama that began last Thanksgiving in Dallas and ended yesterday in a dingy, abandoned store in Liberty City.

It was here that the cops nailed the yellow bastards—pardon my choice of words—who had planted an explosive device aboard a Sun Airlines' DC-10 charter that killed 105 innocent people.

It is now up to the courts to deal with these criminals.

I became a participant in this sordid tale because the love of my life, Suzy Peters, was saved on two occasions during this ordeal. I truly believe that it was Divine intervention both times.

First, she broke her right hand in an accident, which resulted in her missing that ill-fated flight last Thanksgiving on which she would have been a flight attendant. Second, she survived the terror of being kidnapped and held captive by the drug dealers, who had become mass murderers in order to protect their criminal activity.

As a born-again Catholic, I give thanks to God for answering my prayers regarding my fiancée. At the same time, I pray for a healing of the heartbreak suffered by the loved ones of those aboard that doomed flight.

Now that the criminals responsible are under lock and key, please pardon my lack of objectivity in rooting for a jury to dispatch them to "Old Sparky."

The irony of this tragedy is that those who were killed in the crash were not the intended victims of these criminals. They had planned their evil deed on another Sun Airlines flight that had been scheduled for Colombia, because it was carrying among its passengers a group of United States law enforcement officers hot on the trail of these cowardly drug dealers.

We should remember that the horrors of the ordeal were the results of the evils of drugs.

At the same time, we should not forget what the tragedies of sports betting did to the family of former Sharks quarterback Johnny Longo. Next time you place a bet with a bookie think about this.

Drugs have destroyed many individual athletes over the years, but never in our history has this evil destroyed so many innocent lives as last Thanksgiving night in the muck of the Everglades.

Years from now, people will forget that a pro football team died that night. They will forget the individual names of the dead and maimed. The Miami Sharks have survived to play another season. This is probably the true memorial to those souls who perished Thanksgiving night.

Considering the many athletic teams who fly throughout the year, it must be a tribute to the commercial airline industry that this was the first time since 1970 that a major disaster has befallen an American team.

Like the lesson of the R.M.S. Titanic's tragedy in 1912, this is another lesson that nothing is invincible. Even the high and the mighty are vulnerable.

CHAPTER 29

"There is no such thing as justice—in or out of court."
Clarence Darrow
New York Times Interview

FEDERAL AGENTS, OPERATING on the information volunteered by Youngblood, who was promised the Federal Witness Protection Program, quickly rounded up the remaining six Sun Airlines mechanics involved in the drug smuggling ring, but not participants in the bombing. FBI Special Agent Morris Meeker, along with Drug Enforcement and U.S. Customs officials, used their collective public relations clout to convince the mainstream media that the Feds had been onto the mechanics all the time.

"Now you know why we city cops dislike the Feds so much," Leroy told Bob over lunch at El Rick's. "We do all the grunt work, and they take all the glory. It sucks. It really sucks."

After the initial but fleeting glory for the Miami cops, the Feds quickly put on a spin that they had infiltrated the drug smuggling ring. The feds created a tale that Youngblood was actually working for them, not merely a snitch.

The two friends laughed knowingly.

For going along with this spin, Youngblood not only was spared prison, but he could enjoy the good life with a new identity in the federal witness protection program.

"I wonder what kind of American Express card the feds are giving that cocksucker Youngblood," said Bob.

Faced with multiple murder charges, along with assorted raps including drug dealing, Youngblood would have considered himself a fortunate felon to escape Florida's electric chair, Old Sparky. The best Don Gattino could have provided was Mafia protection and comforts inside prison.

Youngblood couldn't believe his good fortune when Meeker explained his role in the coming federal and state trials, which could last a couple of years.

#

"In a perfect world, we wouldn't have to make deals with scumbags like Youngblood," Meeker told Dick Norton. "Youngblood is our key witness. I suppose we can console ourselves that he was merely a conspirator, because Lewis and Cortez actually rigged the bomb. He knew, of course, and did nothing."

Dick shook his head in disbelief. "I can't believe our mechanics could sabotage an aircraft."

"Greed, Dick. Greed. The money is so overpowering in the drug business that it corrupts even the high and mighty. Murder is part of the drug business. These drug lords make Mafia dons look like bush leaguers."

"Why can't we stop the drug trade?" Dick wanted to know. "We spend a lot of effort cracking down on tobacco use, but we can't stop the drug trade."

Meeker shook his head in frustration. "It's the same story with drugs as it was with booze during Prohibition. There aren't enough resources or law enforcement to win this war. We aren't a police state, and the drug dealers take advantage of our laws. The same was true of the bootleggers during Prohibition."

"I've heard some suggest that we legalize drugs," Dick said. He certainly wasn't in favor of that, but he remembered that the gangsters had profited during Prohibition.

"You won't hear me say that, Dick. Trouble is that there's a market for drugs in this country. And those using drugs are not just those poor souls trapped in the ghetto. They're the rich and famous. The entertainers, the athletes, and some of our country's bigshots. Hell, we have people in the White House using drugs."

Dick began to understand the problem better. "Well, Morris, you did put a big ring out of business. The good guys win some of the time."

Meeker, of course, knew that the drug gang had been served up to the Miami cops on a silver platter. He didn't know how or why. Maybe the Cali Cartel hadn't liked the bad publicity from the bombing of the wrong DC-10. *Why would Youngblood give a detailed confession on a tape recorder to a bunch of city cops?*

#

Bob wondered what good telling the truth would do in this case.

The truth was that the Mafia had done the job that law enforcement couldn't. The bastards who had bombed the Sharks charter and murdered 105 people had been brought to justice.

In doing so, Gattino's thugs had also saved Suzy's life. As much as he disliked Gattino and the Mafia, he owed them that. He had unfairly blamed them for the bombing, just as he had blamed Longo for the murder of Syracusa.

Yes, it bothered him. He was a newspaperman who believed in truth and justice. This wasn't a black and white issue, but one clouded in shades of gray.

Leroy Hess had his silver leaves on his blue uniform, the raiding cops had citations, and Bob had the big story, including a generous $10,000 bonus from Andy Lyon. Jorge Cunill's murder had been avenged. And most importantly, he had Suzy back safe and sound.

Perhaps those were the only two things that mattered. He knew he would still campaign hard against illegal sports gambling, even though Gattino was right about that, too. *No one really gives a damn about the evils of gambling.*

A bright midmorning sun bathed Casey's condo. Suzy, attired in a short white terry bathrobe, prepared breakfast in the kitchen as Bob read the lead story in *Miami P.M.*

FEDS: SUN AIRLINES SMUGGLING RING BUSTED
by Buffy Zei, P.M. Staff Reporter

MIAMI—Federal agents, using hidden video cameras on Sun Airlines planes, penetrated a ring of aircraft mechanics suspected of helping smuggle millions of dollars worth of drugs into Miami. The ring was also responsible for the bombing of the Sharks charter last Thanksgiving, the FBI said yesterday.

Six more Sun Airlines mechanics were arrested last night at Miami International Airport, FBI Special Agent Morris Meeker said.

The arrests come after three members of the mechanics union—Jose Cortez, "Bubba" Youngblood, and T.J. Lewis—were arrested by Miami police in a Liberty City raid last month.

Lewis and Cortez are being held in lieu of bond. Seriously wounded in a shoot-out with Miami police, Cortez remains hospitalized in critical condition. Meeker said that Youngblood was working for the FBI and will testify in court against the gang members with ties to the Cali drug cartel in Colombia.

Meeker said in regards to the case, called Operation Whitebird, that heroin and cocaine from Colombia were stashed in fishnet type material behind panels in the aircraft's ceilings, lavatories, kitchens, and cockpits.

The federal agents relied on an informant, apparently Youngblood, to discover drugs, which were also hidden in cock-

pits in areas of "sophisticated avionics and electronics equipment," Meeker said.

The federal agents said that there was no danger to the flying public because of drugs being stored in these areas.

The six mechanics, charged with conspiracy and possession with purpose to distribute cocaine and heroin, were not implicated in the bombing of the Sharks' jet.

"The six were caught on videotape and taped on phone conversations and bugging devices as they took part in the smuggling," Meeker said. "The routine for smuggling the drugs was for planes to arrive from Colombia and continue to another Sun Airlines city with the drugs still aboard. The cocaine and heroin would be taken off the plane after it returned to Miami on a domestic flight in order to allow a 'cooling off period' to determine whether federal agents might try to confiscate the drugs."

The six arrested in Miami were Jose Martinez, Roberto Grande, Carlos Rubio, Mario Lopez, Miguel DeJesus, and Felipe Arnez. They appeared in U.S. District Court, where they were denied bail.

#

Suzy, of course, would be a witness in the coming federal and state trials. Her kidnapping was such a minor event in the coming prosecution, though, that neither prosecutors nor defense lawyers would spend much time questioning her.

Defense lawyers wouldn't even put Lewis and Cortez on the stand. The defense would spend its time trying to discredit Youngblood as a witness.

Suzy strongly believed that her prayers had led to her rescue.

"Life can be so complicated at times, Bobby," she said while serving a soft-boiled egg in a holder on the dinette table.

"Sky Princess, how did you know I liked my eggs like that?"

She patted him on the head. "Your buddy, Dick Norton, said

soft-boiled eggs were more important to you than sex. . ."

"He did not!"

"Did too. Would Sky Princess ever lie to you?"

"No."

"Good. Then eat your first egg before it gets cold. I have two others in reserve."

Bob and Suzy would on occasion discuss her kidnapping and rescue. The columnist marveled at her inner strength during and after the ordeal.

"It was my faith in God and my love for you, Bobby, that sustained me," she said.

"Well, Sky Princess, I admit that I prayed and prayed. Twice my prayers were answered. I'm not about to question my success. I admit I have some problems with the Church and its teachings, but you and I will be regulars at Father O'Malley's Sunday Masses from now on."

It was difficult for Bob, but he bared his soul to Suzy about his moral dilemma about not reporting what really happened in Youngblood's confession.

"Bobby, I guess I have to appreciate that Mr. Gattino saved me from being raped and murdered. I owe him my life. If it was Hitler that had saved me, I'd feel the same way. That doesn't mean I support the Mafia any more than I'd have supported the Nazis. If you went public, you would make the Mafia folk heroes. Ask yourself in this case, 'How important is the truth of the Mafia's involvement?' Would anyone believe you? Would anyone care?"

Bob appreciated Suzy's analytical mind. She was right. The bottom line was that Suzy was safe, and the bombers would pay for their crimes.

"Hell, Bob, you can still crusade against illegal sports gambling. You don't owe that to Mr. Gattino, and I'm sure he doesn't expect it. I think he knows, as you do, that the public couldn't care less about the evils of gambling. As long as people want to gamble, the Mafia will flourish."

He hugged Suzy. "Why am I so lucky to have a beauty with brains in my arms?"

"Because God put us in the same place at the right time," she replied.

He couldn't disagree with that, either. So he kissed her softly on the lips and snuggled with her.

"Let go, you brute! I have to fetch my master's other two soft-boiled eggs."

#

Although Don Gattino's gambling enterprises continued to grow and flourish after terminating the drug dealers, the media attention doomed the planned Mafia takeover of Sun Airlines and forced the striking machinists to agree to a basic contract settlement to save face.

Mike Kelly was livid with rage about the embarrassment his once-trusted henchmen had caused the TEAU local's cause. The local union leader, however, had little choice but to try and save some face with a basic settlement with Westinghouse.

"There'll be another day," he told Tony Tenuto in Chicago. "We lost a battle, but not the long labor war. When our new contract expires in three years, we'll be back."

Tenuto, president of the TEAU, really didn't give a damn about the Sun Airlines settlement. That was because now that the Miami-based carrier would resume its full schedule, there would be more baggage and freight to be plundered by his Mafia soldiers working with union members.

With federal agencies crawling all over investors trying to take over Sun Airlines, Tenuto had ordered the Mafia front investors to seek business elsewhere. Kelly was squeaky clean, and therefore the Miami local would survive any federal probe.

Westinghouse had followed Dick Norton's suggestion about beefing up the pilots' salaries and benefits. "It will work, Captain

Westinghouse, because pilots are the key to keeping planes in the sky."

It worked.

#

Bunny Cabot wasted no time in shedding her late husband's name. She even erased his name from Sol Rubin Stadium. For $30 million, the football stadium became Sun Airlines Stadium.

At the same time, she played the "build me a new stadium or we skip town" game, pitting South Florida against Los Angeles.

Steve Rubin didn't get a first down in his court challenge of his stepmother's sole ownership of the Sharks. As soon as the judge made that clear, Bunny made Jack Cabot co-owner for as long as they were married.

Bob hated to admit it, but the truth was that Bunny Cabot was a shrewd businesswoman. Her husband was a natural in player personnel, and with draftees and free agents he was aiding Moses in rebuilding the Sharks to a World Bowl contender for coming seasons. As for her attempts to kill Sol Rubin and even blow up the team plane, Bunny believed her conscience was clean, because she had not been directly responsible.

Other IFL owners were grumbling among themselves that the league's Disaster Plan was too generous. Some had approached Commissioner Wilson to change the plan. Not wanting any bad publicity yet, Wilson convinced the owners that they needed a cooling off period.

Then he left them with a sobering thought: "What if this season, *your* team jet suffers an accident?"

#

Jack Cabot told the owners' tale to Bob over lunch at the Miami Downtown Athletic Club. While Cabot nibbled on a chef's salad, his guest unashamedly gobbled down a shrimp cocktail and lobster bisque soup, and was halfway done with his 16-ounce T-bone steak.

"I have a favor to ask, Bob."

"Looks like I'm going to order dessert, too, Jack."

Jack was in no hurry. There was coffee and Hennessy's XO at $30 a snifter. Even a box of real Cuban cigars.

"I'm not trying to run up your bill, Jack," Bob said with a grin. "But I was blackballed for membership here a few years ago. The only way I can get in is as a guest."

"I can think of several members who would have cast black balls," Jack said with a slight grin. "I believe the late Sol Rubin and your publisher, Jack Patterson, were among them."

"Okay, Jack, what do I owe you for my feast?"

Jack's tone became serious as he toyed with his cognac snifter. "Remember Rufus Thompson?"

"Sure. He's upstate doing time for selling drugs. Shame. He was one helluva running back. So?"

"He's up for parole next month. I need your help."

"I'm flattered Jack, but I'm not on the Parole Board."

Cabot explained that he needed some editorial support. He told about Johnson's program to scare the shit out of potential criminals. He told him that Thompson's program had even worked with Muhammad Johnson.

"If Thompson is paroled, he has a job with the Sharks," Jack said. "With the temptation of drugs and gambling to our young players, especially the African-Americans, I think he could prove a real-life model of the consequences. In addition, I think he got a stiffer sentence because he was a big-name football player. I talked with Colonel Hess of the Miami police. He busted Thompson, you know. The colonel supports my idea."

Bob sensed a story. He was touched by Cabot's compassion for the long-forgotten felon. *How the hell could a decent guy like this end up married to such a bitch as Bunny?*

"Tell you what, Jack. I'll pay a visit to him at Tomoka next week. If I agree with your assessment, I'll do a column or two."

"Thanks, Bob."

"I'll have another Hennessy's XO, Jack. I don't sell my column cheap."

#

As for Johnny Longo, he was finished as a player. If the injuries in the plane crash hadn't done him in, the investigation by Commissioner Wilson would have.

The evidence was overwhelming that Longo had been a big-time bettor, but the league investigators couldn't prove that he had shaved points or dumped any games. The commissioner took the easy way out. He suspended Longo for one year for betting on IFL games.

Cabot tried to help Longo. He and Moses promised him a quarterback coaching job with the Sharks as soon as his suspension ended.

"Like many high-salaried players, the thought of a low-paying assistant coaching position wasn't very appealing to the former star quarterback," Cabot told Bob. "He had enjoyed a very high standard of living. Unfortunately in his case, he had not invested or saved anything. If he had, he would be a multi-millionaire. Instead, he gambled his and his family's future away."

In May, the roof fell in on Longo. All of the businesses he had been associated with during his football career discovered that the quarterback had been stealing hundreds of thousands of dollars from them in a complex scheme to feed his gambling habit.

"It's ironic that on the very same day that former Sharks running back Rufus Thompson was released on parole from prison, he was replaced in the penal system by former quarterback Johnny Longo," Bob told Suzy.

#

Bob Casey's Working Press:
Longo shows gambling's evil

MIAMI—There he stood in Miami Federal Court. He looked pale and gaunt in his bright orange jail jumpsuit.

Once the quarterback hero of Notre Dame and the Miami Sharks, both an All-America and an All-Pro, Johnny Longo had fallen from grace because of a compulsive gambling problem.

Longo was here before Federal Judge Hugh Glickstein because he had swindled nearly a million bucks from people who had befriended him during his days with the Sharks. Most had stood by him despite suspicion of murder last autumn and his suspension from pro football.

Months ago, he was one of the highest-paid players in pro football. In court yesterday, he was so broke that he was represented by a public defender.

The only person who truly fought for Longo at the trial, however, was Tom McClellan, the director of Gamblers Anonymous.

A reformed gambler himself, McClellan knows about the pain of addiction. He asked Glickstein to try to understand that compulsive gambling is a sickness that won't be cured in prison.

His wife Martha, who once killed for him, and the couple's three children have left the Miami area.

"I'm terribly sorry for what I've done," Longo told Glickstein. "I'm ashamed. I hope I can someday prove that I can be an honest person and get my life back in order. I miss my wife and kids."

The judge denied McClellan's appeal on behalf of the former quarterback. He had asked that the sentence be served in a halfway house so that Longo could get daily treatment for his addiction.

"There is no treatment in the federal prison system for compulsive gambling," McClellan said.

"You're not before me today, Mr. Longo, because you are a compulsive gambler," said Glickstein. "I don't question for a minute that you suffer from that. But people have been hurt by your criminal conduct."

I agree with the judge.

Even the heroic, loving traumas of his wife were not enough to make him want to give up betting on sporting events.

The judge then sentenced him to two to five years in a federal prison.

"When he is released from prison, he will still be hooked on gambling," McClellan said. "Compulsive gambling is as addictive as drugs or booze. The results are the same on family and friends."

It is easy to write off one has-been pro football player.

You can take with a grain of salt IFL commissioner Pete Wilson's get-tough stance on players betting on league games.

There are more Johnny Longos out there. The league needs to recognize that gambling is a serious problem and try to help their players before they get in trouble.

As marshals led Longo away in shackles, society was punishing him, but it didn't give a damn about trying to cure his addiction.

As I left the court building, I noticed the long snake line outside a nearby newsstand. Curious, I asked one of the guys standing in line what was happening.

"It's the state lottery, man," he replied with passion. "It's up to $73 million, and I have my paycheck here to buy $400 worth of tickets."

Managing Editor Larry Bloom liked the column so much he FedExed Casey a box of 25 $10 Cubans with a thank you note.

#

Sal and Maria Gattino didn't know if the godfather would be pleased to dine at Cella's on his visit to South Florida. They were pleasantly surprised when he called to pick them up at their Hollywood home in a black Lincoln Town Car. A Mafia soldier was the chauffeur.

The godfather seemed out of uniform in his navy blue blazer, a green polo shirt, and khaki trousers. He presented Maria with a dozen red roses, and Gattino with a bottle of Dom Perignon.

"You celebrate alone later," he said with a warm smile. "Tonight, I honor your 50th wedding anniversary by dining with you at Cella's. We have a little party, hey. Like back in Bensonhurst."

The godfather had reserved the entire dining room of Cella's. Edmund Cella wasn't impressed. Neither was waitress Rose. It was business, however, and the Gattinos were regular customers. While Cella didn't love the Mafia, he wasn't about to risk his health and business by refusing them service.

"Edmund, you have all those Black Hand bums here tonight," Rose said. "I'm working the lounge. The Caseys will dine there tonight, too."

"Hey, Rose, if Father O'Malley is coming to the party, who am I to judge the guests?"

The dining room was filled shortly before 7:00 p.m. when the godfather arrived with the guests of honor. Sal and Maria noted with awe the number of expensive cars parked outside the restaurant, many with chauffeurs milling around.

"Every family is represented tonight," the godfather told the Gattinos. "They have the utmost respect for your marriage, as well as Don Gattino's loyalty to the Lorenzo family."

It was a joyous celebration. Couples introduced themselves and passed white envelopes with anniversary cash inside. A five-piece band played traditional Italian music. Father O'Malley blessed the marriage and was seated in a place of honor next to the godfather.

"You know, Father, for a non-Italian priest, you have honored Maria Gattino very much," said the godfather. "I have learned of St. Vincent's need of a gymnasium."

"Why yes, Mr. Lorenzo, we have started a gym building fund."

"How is the drive going, Father?"

"It could be better, Mr. Lorenzo."

"So I hear, Father, so I hear. How about I give you a deal you cannot refuse. . ."

The priest's face turned ashen.

"Only kidding, Father," he said, placing his left arm affectionately around O'Malley's shoulders.

O'Malley managed a faint smile.

"A lawyer will meet with you Monday at the school. You tell him how much the project will cost, and he will deposit a cashier's check in St. Vincent's bank. It is a gift from Sal and Maria. It is hoped that you might honor them by naming the new building the Maria Gattino Gym."

O'Malley was speechless, because it was a $2,000,000 project.

"Have some good Barbaresco red wine, Father. Salute! Cin-cin!"

"Oh, yes, Mr. Lorenzo, "Salute! Cin-cin!"

O'Malley knew that he was accepting Mafia money. It would benefit the youth of the parish with the badly needed gym. What purpose would be served in rejecting such a gift? *Cardinal Murphy would probably exile me to a retirement home.* Mrs. Gattino most certainly was a dedicated Catholic parishioner who supported many church projects. *God sometimes works in mysterious ways.*

#

Bob and Suzy settled into a booth and spotted Rose.

"What's the celebration in the dining room?" Suzy asked.

"It's a Black Hand party," Rose replied in a sarcastic tone. "Sal and Maria Gattino are celebrating their 50th anniversary. I was given my choice of working there or serving you guys. Not much of a choice, even if the dons are better tippers."

"We need a couple of Chivas and water to start," Bob said.

"I figured." Rose headed for the bar.

She returned early, toting a bottle of Dom Perignon and an ice bucket.

"It's from the gangsters' moll," Rose said as she set up the ice bucket stand. "Mrs. Gattino heard you were here. She thanks you for the flowers. She wishes both you and Mr. Casey a warm and happy marriage."

Bob looked at Suzy. "You didn't?"

"Yes, I did."

Bob shook his head. "I won't ask why. I suppose she deserved your token of appreciation. Sort of a thank you for the old don's help."

Suzy nodded.

If the champagne had come from the don, I would have sent it back. But why insult the old lady on her anniversary? And perhaps I do owe that fucker.

"Oh, and some more news, Bobby."

"What's that?"

"Mary Rich and Vince Lombard eloped and were married in Vegas," she said. "I'm happy for both of 'em."

"Next you'll tell me that Bud Westinghouse and Ann Parker tied the knot," he said.

"You're impossible!" she replied. "Of course not!"

Heck, we're ahead of the game with this bottle of bubbly. Now, on to another subject. "I was thinking about our honeymoon, Sky Princess, and. . ."

Suzy held up her right hand and gently pressed her left hand on Bob's lips to silence him. "I've already booked the Adlon in Berlin and the Marriott in Munich," she said. "I have positive space, first-class buddy passes for us on Sun Air coming and going. Captain Westinghouse even gave us a priority code, which means we can't get bumped."

Bob smiled warmly as he reached across the table to hold hands with Suzy. "I guess this means we'll have to invite Captain Westinghouse to our wedding."

"We'd better. I've been notified that I, your very own Sky Princess, have been promoted to in-flight services manager," she said, lifting her drink in a toast.

He lifted his glass and clicked it against hers. "I'm impressed, Sky Princess."

"You ought to be," she said. "I got a healthy pay hike."

"I would hope so. Someone in this family has to be able to support us." He feigned a frown. "Does this mean you'll no longer prepare my soft-boiled eggs for breakfast?"

Suzy started laughing, then crying. "Oh, silly, I love you so much."

The emotion engulfed Bob, too. He felt tears of happiness welling up in his eyes. They continued to hold hands while looking into each other's eyes.

"I love you, too, Sky Princess," Bob said. "Now, about my eggs. . ."

Printed in the United States
2705